S0-AHI-748

Tegné

Soul Warrior

By Richard La Plante from Tom Doherty Associates

Mantis
Leopard
Steroid Blues
Hog Fever
Tegné: Soul Warrior

Tegné

Soul Warrior

Richard La Plante

A Tom Doherty Associates Book
New York

This is a work of fiction. All the characters and events portrayed in this novel are either fictitious or are used fictitiously.

TEGNÉ: SOUL WARRIOR

This book is printed on acid-free paper.

A Tor Book
Published by Tom Doherty Associates, Inc.
175 Fifth Avenue
New York, N.Y. 10010

Tor Books on the World-Wide Web:
http://www.tor.com

Tor® is a registered trademark of Tom Doherty Associates, Inc.

Design by Lynn Newmark

Library of Congress

Cataloging-in-Publication Data

La Plante, Richard.
Tegné : soul warrior / Richard La Plante.
p. cm.
"A Tom Doherty Associates book."
ISBN 0-312-85977-5
I. Title.
PR6062.A66T44 1995
823′.914—dc20 95-34765
CIP

First Tor edition: November 1995

Printed in the United States of America

0 9 8 7 6 5 4 3 2 1

For Richard Girling Sears, my grandfather

ACKNOWLEDGMENTS

I wish to acknowledge and thank the Gower Publishing Group for their kind permission to use selected pieces of the *Tao Te Ching*, written by Lao Tsu in the sixth century B.C. and translated into English by Gia-Fu-Feng and Jane English.

I would also like to thank my friend Professor Roger T. Ames for his kind permission to use selected pieces of Lao Tsu, *Tao Te Ching* as adapted and translated by himself and Rhett Y. W. Young and published by the Chinese Material Centre.

Special thanks are also due to Senseis Terry O'Neill and Dave Hazard for their friendship, encouragement, and ability to provide accurate technical advice on the many forms of combat relevant to *Tegné*.

Lao Tsu

Lao Tsu, an older contemporary of Confucius, was keeper of the royal archives at Loyang in the province of Honan in the sixth century B.C. According to ancient legend, as he was riding off into the desert to die—sick at heart at the ways of men—he was persuaded by a Chinese gatekeeper to write down his spiritual teachings in order to preserve them for posterity.

AUTHOR'S PREFACE

Although *Tegné* is a work of fantasy and fiction, I have grounded my text on actual personal experience. Most events and conditions which are described, both physical and psychological, are based upon similar occurrences which I have participated in, witnessed or have seen documented. Having had a long and avid interest in Eastern philosophy, including the internal, spiritual practices of meditation as well as the more external forms of Japanese armed and unarmed combat, I have used both Indian and Japanese terms throughout the book.

However, as I have stated, the book is fantasy and fiction, and no historical foundation or factual chronology exists within its chapters. Yet I do hope there is a certain truth in *Tegné*, for truth, by nature, transcends the confines of time and space.

CONTENTS

I

THE VISION

Under Heaven
All can see beauty as beauty
Only because there is ugliness
All can know good as good
Only because there is evil

(Lao Tsu, Honan Province,
sixth century B.C.*)*

Yeon 966

Temple of the Moon

Lunan Province

The Elder entered the nine-foot-square stone meditation chamber. He placed his hand against the heavy iron shutters of the single window and pushed outwards. The rusted metal, grown thick and porous during the ninety days of the monsoon, held firm against the small, almost effeminate, hand. Yet there was an uncanny strength to this diminutive man, a strength that had little to do with sinew and bone, and gradually the shutters gave way, allowing the first cascading rays of the rising sun to penetrate the gray cell.

The Elder squared his shoulders, inhaling the chill air. Daylight played upon the braided strands of silver hair which began in a knot on the crown of his otherwise smoothly shaven head and fell down the back of his silken robes. From the open window he could just make out the hazy outline of the high mountain peaks which formed the eastern perimeter of Lunan province. His views to the north and south were blocked by the jutting Tiyuku face, for the Temple of the Moon was built into this enormous mountain and its inner recesses, including the fifty meditation chambers, were carved from the rock itself.

He stood perfectly still, and, for a moment, reflected upon the sheer strength of purpose which had enabled his predecessors to create this impenetrable place of peace. Then he knelt upon the small Mandarin rug, sitting back to rest his hips upon the heels of his feet in the traditional sei-za position. His slow exhalations formed a fine, white mist in the morning air, and the faded gold threads of the carpet merged with the yellowed silk of his heavy robes. He inhaled deeply, filling his lower abdomen, retaining the breath for an interval of sixty heartbeats, then exhaled to the same count. He remained focused directly ahead, concentrating on the small copper disc which was attached to the gray stone wall in front of him. Mounted upon the disc was the insignia of his Brotherhood, a polished golden quarter moon with a single silver star positioned below its southern tip. At first the moon and star simply reflected in the Elder's close-set brown eyes. Then, as the meditation deepened, his eyelids closed and the reflected sign internalized, penetrating his surrendered consciousness. Finally, the Elder increased his breathing rate, creating a rapid, chugging respiration. His body temperature soared in response, taking him into the Dragon Zone.

The kundalini energy was awakening, uncoiling with tingling, electric pulses in the base of his spine, climbing up the central nerve, entering, opening, energizing each of the seven chakras en route to its final destination.

The Elder had been "open" for six yeons, yet still hovering on the surface of his consciousness was the memory of the original procedure. The excruciating pain which had accompanied the slow twisting of the diamond drill. The concentration required to bore into the frontal bone, an exact finger's breadth above his nasal bridge, dead center between his eyes. The memory of the infinite strength which held both his arms and legs, allowing not the slightest movement, while the Exalted Priest performed the operation. Twenty minutes which became eternity. The high-pitched, metallic whine, the perspiration and blood dripping down his cheeks, the superhuman effort to control his breathing, to maintain silence, not to scream out. And finally, the searing blue light, brighter than any light on earth, exploding in his brain.

And now, as then, the Elder was in Vakos, the State of Inner Vision. Viewing through ajna, the third eye. There were shadows moving in the void, silhouettes; then his cerekinetic focus, activated by his hyper-slow respiration, began to make the "vision" crystallize. His last, fading threads of consciousness beheld a vast desert landscape.

* * *

Desolate, barren, burnt chalk-white by the four suns which rose in the north, south, east and west, converging at center-point to form one, enormous, burning white nebula.

There was no wind, no life amidst the jagged rock formations and wide, uneven craters, only the thick, vaporous heat rising from the sun-bleached earth.

In the distance, a thin humming began—like the beating of fine, silken wings. Gradually, the sound took a physical form, rising through the vapor. The form moved closer, finally materializing into a horse and rider.

The rider wore billowing, flowing robes, his hair shimmered gold, yellow and blue. An aura was formed by the colors, encircling his ivory-white face; his deep, wide turquoise eyes were fixed firmly ahead. The horse was gleaming silver, its hooves flying across the earth, but not touching. No sound accompanied the horse and rider. They were perfect beauty; the swirling colors so exquisite that they totally captivated the Elder. There was such joy, such great vitality to the rhythm of the movement . . .

Then, from the vapor, rose the black, shadowy shape. The shape became firm, forming into a long, sinewy, catlike body. The eyes burned red and the snarling mouth was pulled back to reveal long, white fangs. The fore-claws were extended, fully unsheathed, as the Cat leapt, tearing the rider from his silver mount.

Rider and Cat fell to the ground, forming a grotesque union. The man did not struggle as the frenzied animal ripped the limbs from his body, finally biting through his neck, severing his head.

Only then did the Cat look up, and then see Him standing above her. He was the Father Protector, tall, exceedingly broad-shouldered. His long, golden hair hung midway down the back of his fine, white, silken robes. His skin was the same ivory as the skin of the rider. The Cat knew him; she snarled as she backed away. He raised his right hand, his long, graceful fingers extended. From the fingers a blue stream of light emanated, forming an arc between the hand and the savaged rider. The Cat backed farther away, her image growing faint, as the blue light encircled the fallen man, wrapping round him, strand by luminous strand, finally encasing him completely.

The Cat disappeared within the vapor as the Father Protector turned and faced the Elder. His face was beautiful in a way which exceeded the confines of male or female. His cheekbones were high and defined, his ivory skin flawless, his lips pale, and his huge, turquoise eyes like watery pools of prana, Earth energy, forever vibrating, forever in flux. His face was close now. Nothing else was important. A single tear formed in his right eye; the tear built and fell, rolled down his cheek, forward, forward, until there was only this single tear, rolling through time and space. The tear became defined . . . it was a Golden Fetus, flying forward from infinity. The embryo was nearly formed; the Elder could almost see the child's Earth body. And from some primordial recess of his soul, the meaning of his vision began to surface:

IT WAS THE TIME OF THE BEAST. IT WAS ALSO THE HOUR OF CONCEPTION. THE GOLDEN SON WOULD RISE. THE EARTH WARRIOR WAS COMING.

The energy was intense, near breaking-point . . . Then, the cry of birth shattered the vision.

Tabata stood above the Elder. "Are you not well, Elder, I heard your scream?"

The Elder rose from the prayer rug. He cupped his head in both hands. The point between his eyes throbbed. Looking up, he searched Tabata's eyes.

"We can wait no longer. I have spoken to you of a mission . . . far from here, beyond the Valley, deep into Vokane."

Tabata revealed no weakness, no hesitation. He was Shihan of the Temple, Grand Master of Empty Hand, and he had been chosen by the Elder nearly two yeons ago. He was prepared to turn his back upon the Order, to walk forth from the cloisters of the Brothers of the Moon. It was a mission from which he would never return. Tabata remained still, as he entered zanshin, the state of calm, complete awareness.

"I am ready," he stated.

Tears welled in the Elder's eyes, as he extended his arms toward Tabata in a final embrace.

II

THE BIRTH

Evil is born from good
Good from Evil
The two spring from the same source
But differ in name
Light from darkness
Day from night

(Lao Tsu)

Yeon 966

Zendow

Vokane Province

Midday in Lunan; daybreak in Vokane. Three thousand vul, a time difference of six hours and a desert as wide as the Great Sea itself separated the Temple of the Moon from the mighty Zendow, which stood like some dark, conquering giant in the far corner of the eastern province.

This fortresslike city stretched nine vul from east to west, and was five leagues from north to south. Throughout the seven hundred yeons of its existence it had been the home of two religious orders and three powerful, warring clans.

It was a religious sect, the Kundani, who constructed the city; the building taking the better part of two hundred yeons. And although most of their records were destroyed in the Great Fire of 400, remnants showed that the Kundani were a sect of sun-worshippers. Peaceful and productive, they occupied the city for most of its original three hundred yeons.

Then came the Manons, a fierce, nomadic tribe from the great northern steppe region. They descended with their steel-tipped arrows and heavy wooden clubs, thousands of them, traveling from the arid, treeless steppes and through the lush Forest of Shuree.

The Kundanis' sole means of defense was a mass prayer to D'Oro, their sun god. Consequently, they were slaughtered to a man, and their city taken.

However, it was legend that D'Oro finally did respond to the Kundani prayer. For, one hundred yeons later, a solar explosion caused the Great Fire, destroying the Manons in a single spontaneous combustion, leaving the walled city vacant and cindered with the exception of the huge, circular configuration of slablike stones, some ninety feet in height, which formed the Kundanis' timeless tribute to the god they had worshipped. The walled city stood, burnt and empty, for nearly two hundred yeons.

It was in Yeon 700 that a small cluster of traveling monks rediscovered it. There were no more than three or four hundred of them. They had survived the arduous eastern journey from the upper Lunan Province, traveling across the Valley of Sand, and making their way deep into Shuree. They hailed the walled city as their promised land, named it Lunalle, and began the enormous task of renovation.

Twenty-five yeons they labored, day and night, rebuilding the northern wall and carrying fresh timber from the surrounding forest to replace the charred floors and fallen beams. No sooner had they completed the bulk of their restoration than the wandering Yusun Clan invaded from the west. The Yusuns scaled the high walls and drove the monks from their holy grounds; not without resistance, for these Brothers were from the Temple of the Moon, a martial order, and many Yusuns were amazed at the ferocity and practiced skill with which these empty-handed monks fought. Sheer numbers decided the outcome and the surviving Brothers fled, driven back through the forest and into the Valley, where the burning sun scorched their unprotected skin, finishing the slaughter that the Yusuns had started. Thus the Valley of Sand became known as the Valley of Death.

The Yusun rule was brief; they were a cattle- and horse-breeding clan and were unable to settle properly within the confines of the city. They needed the prairie and the grazing land at the base of the Western Mountains. Most of the clan had, in fact, moved on by the time the first party of Zendai descended upon them.

The initial Zendai war party was barely one thousand strong, yet their impenetrable, shining black body-armor, distinguished by the Sign of the Claw, and their precise discipline in the military arts made them invulnerable. It was the first time any Yusun had gazed upon the fine, single-edged, curved blade of the katana. A perfect killing weapon, and wielded with such skill and grace that more than once its victim was so mesmerized by the flashing steel that his limbs were severed before he thought of defense.

The Yusun Clan either fled or surrendered in the face of these huge-boned, bronzed, godlike Warmen. For the Zendai were a pure race, finely bred, and would tolerate no less than perfection in their offspring. Zendai bred with Zendai; it was more than law, it was religion.

They had come from the deep sun of the south, beyond Miramar, and beyond the High-Peaked Mountains, from a land bordered by the Great Sea. Yet this master race had grown, multiplied beyond that dry land's ability to support them. And, like the Manons, the Zendai traveled away from the sun and toward the moist, fertile soil of Shuree.

It was the Zendai who named the province Vokane, which in their ancient tongue meant "Mother of Life," and the Zendai who called the walled city after their own clan, the City of Zendow. It was this conquering clan who were first led by the great Warlord, Volkar, the invincible giant, the purest of pure. Volkar, of whom each succeeding warlord for six generations was of direct descent. Volkar, the forefather of Renagi . . .

The sun was just beginning its climb above the sky-scraping, spiked ramparts, casting long, dancing shadows onto the paved streets below. The morning was tranquil, its quiet, still energy like a newly born babe waiting to be slapped into life. Voices, small yet distinct against the high stone walls, echoed in the interconnecting courtyards surrounding the palace. Slowly, Zendow was awakening . . .

A single knock on the thick carved oak door and Zena entered Renagi's chamber, carrying the large wooden bowl, steam rising from the water. Close behind, Hiro shuffled, two clean, thick, white cotton towels folded over his right arm.

"Good morning, Master," Zena said, and the two servants bowed.

The sunlight streamed through the arched window as the Warlord slid from beneath the blue, embroidered blanket. Still partially erect from a night of dreams and a bladder full of red wine, he strode, uninhibited, in front of his attending servants.

At thirty-five, he was nearing his peak; that time when mind and body become one, the mind sharp, seasoned by experience, the body supple, strong and quick. Watching him move to the bath-chamber, Zena marveled at how the lean, muscular frame seemed rooted to the floor, the Warlord's feet able to grasp the bare wooden boards as assuredly as his hands were able to grasp the katana.

Renagi watched the deep yellow stream arc toward the porcelain bowl.

"Today is the first day of Celebre—the show of strength, the ride through the Province," he spoke aloud to himself. "Once a yeon they must see me, see their Warlord . . . they must bow down to the Red and Black . . . yes, I will ride Kano."

His voice trailed off as he shook the last drops from his now flaccid penis. Still thinking of the day ahead, Renagi turned and gracefully took the step down from the bath chamber.

This Celebre I must put the fear of God into them. Six Celebres since I've been there, and each yeon their grain production has diminished. It is time for a visit . . .

Zena and Hiro waited, motionless, the water steaming in the bowl. Renagi moved to the center of the floor and stood, feet together, facing the sun-filled window. Arms to his sides, he bowed to Sol-Ra, God of Light. Eyes concentrated, Renagi eased his clenched right fist to the point slightly above his chin, a hand's breadth away. His open left hand, equally slowly, came up to cup over his right clenched fist. He inhaled deeply, the breath filling his lower abdomen, then, eyes never wavering, he began the Morning Form.

Renagi had performed the Form every morning for twenty-five yeons, and now as he neared "The Peak," its powers were opening to him. With each lower breath he was able to take energy from Sol-Ra and, with each exhalation, transfer that energy to his fist, or his knife-foot.

The Form took twenty minutes, not a second more, not a second less. By the last thrust his energy force had built to explosion; and with the final expulsion of breath from his diaphragm, his war cry cut the morning air, echoing in the lower courtyard.

Then, assuming the first position, Renagi bowed again to Sol-Ra, crossed his arms in front of his body and returned to normal stance. Only now did he acknowledge Zena and Hiro. In unison, the wizened, white-haired Zena and the younger, dark Hiro, bowed to their master. The water was now the proper temperature, the thick, white cotton towels ready. They were honored to bathe Renagi—particularly on this first day of Celebre.

Yeon 966

Slave State of Ashkelan

Vokane Province

One hundred vul to the west of Zendow, Asha-1 baked beneath the sun. It was the first of six such village communities which lay within the Green Triangle, a particularly fertile zone which ran five hundred vul from north to south. The entire area was designated Ashkelan, the "state of slaves."

The practice of "culling" this group of people, of specifically disposing of their strongest, most dominant males, thus interbreeding only their weaker genes, had begun two hundred yeons previously, with the Yusun Clan. The practice was instigated by a need for a controllable labor force to produce the grain required within the walled city. The procedure had resulted in a working tribe of albinos. A cruel tradition which the Zendai had carried on.

The sun was just reaching danger level as Maliseet looked up to the clear, azure sky. She placed the last of the carotene into the round straw basket. *Mother will be pleased,* she thought, *there is enough carotene to last until High Solstice. Strange that without this long, pointed, orange vegetable we could tolerate no sunlight at all. How awful it would be, never to feel the warmth.*

Maliseet looked at her forearm. Her white Ashkelite skin was nearly translucent, and a circuitry of delicate blue veins ran beneath the fine epidermis. She had no natural pigmentation, like the rest of her people, only the temporary protection which the regular ingestion of carotene provided. She glanced again at the brimming basket. Yes, Mother would be very pleased.

A single bead of moisture formed on her brow—a warning. Maliseet reached into her apron, found the blankers; thick, black-lensed spectacles that protected the retinas of her eyes from the ultra rays. She fixed the blankers in place, bent down, took hold of the leather strap and hoisted the basket to her shoulder.

Raine's eyes searched the horizon. Behind her, the tiny, windowless, thatched cottages of Asha-1 formed uniform rows on each side of the dirt road. Maliseet had been gone since daybreak; why was she always the last home? Every other family would be indoors by now, asleep or spending the heat of the day huddled, conserving energy, around the underground ventilation shaft. But no, not Maliseet, she loved the sun, even though it could kill her.

This time I will teach her, thought Raine, *this time she will stay indoors for three days . . . this time.*

Raine's plans for punishment melted as she saw Maliseet round the bend. Her daughter was exquisite; tall for an Ashkelite, nearly five feet, six fingers, and remarkably full-bosomed. The fine, silken white hair hung well below her slim, strong hips. And the legs—they were the best feature of her body—long legs, feminine yet muscular, and sure. The face was her father's; proud, high cheekbones, full sensuous lips, and large eyes set wide apart. They were warm, glowing eyes, nearly amber in color, unusual in comparison to the vapid pink eyes of the other Ashkelites.

Maliseet's father had been a fine-looking man, until the Clan singled him out—made him responsible for the entire grain production of Asha-1. They demanded quotas that were impossible to fill—impossible, unless he worked the danger levels. They threatened his family with death. Every day, Akid worked from sunrise to sunset, and into the night, for one full harvest he worked. One full harvest and his single, thin layer of skin was burnt to the bone.

"Mother!" Maliseet called, holding out the full basket of carotene. Raine ran to her daughter and took the heavy wicker basket from her.

"Come, girl, we must get inside," she said, putting one arm around Maliseet and urging her toward the village and the shelter of their hut.

Five days into the ride. Two more to travel, Renagi noted as Kano surged forward. This stallion had a rhythm unlike any other horse he had ever ridden. A full eighteen hands of white, throbbing muscle and a wild spirit which merged with Renagi's own. Only the

Warlord could mount Kano; it had been that way since the Yusun breeders had presented the stallion as an offering of peace. Renagi and Kano, the perfect wakan, that mysterious merging of souls.

Today was no different. Renagi, mounted on the white giant, was invincible. Kano bucked and pranced, aware of the power he surrendered to his master.

The Procession of Celebre wound its way through town and village. Renagi's jet black hair was oiled, pulled tightly back and plaited, his brown, slant Mongol eyes alive with fire, his broad shoulders made even broader by the black Zendai war armor; its blood-red "Sign of the Claw" cut deep into the shining leather and alloy. Renagi held his back straight—perfect posture, his square jaw set; he spurred Kano onward.

Behind him, riding in exact formation, was the Procession. They were the Twelve Chosen Warmen. From village to village they galloped, and in each village Renagi's minions kissed the earth as he passed. Failure to pay homage resulted in death.

It was sunset, and the Procession galloped on. Tomorrow, they would begin the homeward journey, and the midnight feast of Celebre. But, for now, there was one more village to visit, and that village was Asha-1.

The ultra rays were at safety level. The blankers could be removed, the fieldwork continued. One by one, the doors of the small cottages opened. Groups of Ashkelites walked out into the dirt road. There was the usual conversation, a minimum of anxiety—each knew it was the time of Celebre, yet the general feeling was that the Procession would not enter Asha-1. The Zendai had not bothered with the village for six harvests. What interest could Renagi have in the Ashkelites? As long as they produced, and kept their place, Renagi did not need to view his slaves.

Maliseet joined a work party, two boys her own age, and a woman slightly older than she, perhaps twenty. The four walked slowly toward the Easterly Fields. They were just nearing the point where the road narrowed to a small path when the ground began to tremble, as if the earth had come alive with thunder. Maliseet looked in the direction of the sound, straining her eyes against the sun. In the distance, she could see the dust billowing from beneath Kano's hooves; she could distinguish a black-suited figure in the horse's saddle. The Procession galloped toward them.

Those Ashkelites already in the fields were, by now, running back toward the village. Maliseet fell into step as she ran toward Raine, who stood waiting nervously at the door of their cottage.

"Do not be frightened," Raine spoke as much to herself as to her daughter. "No harm will come—show them respect. Remember, show respect."

On each side of the road, the Ashkelites formed straight lines. The women who had been in the fields were brushing the dust and earth from their heavy cotton dresses, and the men were straightening their tunics and trousers. The Procession entered Asha-1 through the east gate. The Warmen broke gallop, tightened ranks, as the panting, snorting horses moved slowly forward, between the two lines of Ashkelites.

Maliseet had been twelve yeons when the Procession last came. The fear had been contagious, yet she also remembered the fascination. This time was no different. Now, she could see the giant white stallion, the silver and turquoise amulets hanging from its great leather saddle. She could distinguish the indestructible, black shining armor, and the red claw. She could clearly see him, the Warlord. In spite of her fear, she found it impossible not to stare . . .

"Get down, child!" Raine's desperate voice cut through Maliseet's thoughts. Instantly, she knelt, joining the others, kissing the earth, paying homage to the Warlord.

The Procession stopped. Renagi and his twelve Warmen sat still. The Ashkelites remained prostrate, the black cloud of death hanging above them, and for a long, tortured moment every rustle of clothing, every uneven breath, even the beating of a single heart, foretold doom.

The body-hugging chest protectors and the wide, tubular armguards gave each of the Warmen a pronounced muscularity, a malevolent power. They remained poised, their blackness in contrast to the tranquil blue of the sky, as if together they formed the barrier which prohibited access to all that was sure and certain.

"All of you. Up. Stand up," Renagi's voice rang out, deep and resonant.

Some visibly trembling, others were controlling themselves as the Ashkelites stood at attention. The Warmen studied the faces, searched the eyes. If even a flicker of defiance shone, the katana would be drawn and life taken.

Stillness, deathly quiet, that time when each Ashkelite fought to control the nervous energy. No sudden cries, no whimpering, no rapid movement . . . nothing . . .

Then, the deep voice: "It has been brought to my attention . . ." Renagi scanned the faces, as if he spoke to each of them separately, "that the quotas for Asha-1 are below any other village in Ashkelan . . ."

Silence. A long pause . . . "That grain production has fallen by half . . ." looking, questioning . . . "Did you not think that I would know this?"

The pitch of his voice began to build; "Did you not think I would care?" Renagi's voice was louder, deeper, "Did you not expect me to come here?"

The voice was a weapon, filling the air, inescapable.

"Did you not think that you would answer to me," now a deafening, punishing roar, "Answer to ME!"

The black silence again fell upon the village. The Warmen, eyes darting from face to face, itchily fingered the hilts of their katanas. Finally, Nakos, the production leader, stepped from line, prostrated himself, kissing the earth. Renagi, with a gesture of his gloved hand, signaled the frail man to rise.

"Master, Warlord, I beg your forgiveness." The voice was thin and reedlike, yet it bore a certain resigned strength.

Renagi nodded, indicating that Nakos should continue.

"Within the last six solstices our male population has decreased by four score. Our work-teams are primarily composed of women and children."

The voice droned on with excuses: the lack of rain, the rampant carcina amongst the male population, the shortage of carotene, the increase in ultra rays.

Renagi was now only half-listening. His attention had shifted. She stood half a head taller than any of the women around her. Even in the heavy cotton work-dress the breasts seemed swollen, ripe. The parts of the legs that were visible, the calves and the bare feet, were unusually muscular for an Ashkelite. And her face, not the usual thin lips and sunken eyes, the face was superb.

"We have now trained our younger, mixed work teams to an efficiency level comparable to the level achieved by the male teams of the Fifth Solstice . . ." Nakos felt he was getting through, convincing the Warlord.

Renagi held up his huge, black-gloved right hand, stopping Nakos in midsentence.

"What is your name?"

"I am Nakos."

"Nakos, I have heard enough. I do not want excuses, I want grain. Nakos—from this Celebre you are solely responsible for the grain production of Asha-1. That production will equal the production of the Sixth Solstice. If it does not, I will be able to find no reason for the existence of Asha-1—do you understand?"

Nakos knelt, kissed the earth, and accepted the certain sentence of death. The matter closed, Renagi turned his full attention toward Maliseet.

She knew he had been watching her. She could feel the sharp, burning energy from his snake-lidded eyes. She was frightened, yet the fear was counterbalanced by sheer fascination.

Renagi felt no need for discretion. He turned in his saddle, facing her completely.

"What do they call you?"

The voice had regained its velvety richness, no longer threatening, but still commanding.

"I am speaking to you."

He gazed upon her fully. There could be no question, no doubt as to the object of Renagi's attention. As she stepped forward, she felt Raine's hand grip her left shoulder, then fall away. She felt naked, alone and, finally, fully frightened.

She knelt and kissed the earth.

"Maliseet. Maliseet is my name."

Her high, quavering voice hung on the still air . . .

"Maliseet . . ." His pronunciation, the emphasis on the last syllable, the slowness in the delivery, all gave the name a gravity, a fated quality.

The Warmen sat alert; they waited. Any resistance would be instantly stopped. They waited . . . waited. Renagi's hand rested dangerously on the hilt of his katana.

Menra sensed the process of decision. Why was Renagi not

drawing his sword? Why was he not now holding up the head of this Ashkelite bitch? Surely, he had singled her out for slaughter; and now the Warlord would demonstrate how little one Ashkelite life meant . . . He would gain great face with the Warmen. He would remind these slaves of his omnipotence . . .

"Maliseet . . . a fine name."

Renagi smiled generously, straightened in his saddle, turned, heeled Kano, and galloped up the dirt road toward the east gate.

The dangerous moment past, the relief was instant. The Ashkelites fell to their knees. The Kiss of Earth never held such meaning, never were they in greater awe of their Warlord.

God of the Sun, he is a master . . . The thought flashed through Menra's mind as he waved the Procession on, following Renagi to the east gate and out of Asha-1.

To let those poor idiots feel his power of life and death, and then to give life, what a stroke!

The Procession, now in perfect formation, galloped as one, Menra in the lead position, a perfect twelve paces behind Renagi. Twelve paces, a long enough distance to show respect, a short enough space to close quickly if trouble threatened.

Suddenly, Renagi pulled heavily on Kano's reins. The giant stallion came to a snorting halt. As quickly, the Procession halted behind. They were barely two miles east of Asha-1.

Renagi turned, "Menra, come here. I want a private word."

The Warmen sat, stony-faced. Menra edged forward, toward Renagi. What could be the meaning of this, had something been overlooked, had something displeased him . . . ?

Menra's mount was now side by side with Kano, ahead of the halted Procession. Still, Renagi's voice was hushed.

"The girl, the one called Maliseet. Go back, bring her to me. I am trusting you. Not one Warman must be aware of what you do . . . no one must see her enter the castle."

Menra's mind whirled. What reason? To bring an untouchable, a slave, into Zendow . . .

"Do you understand?" Renagi's voice jogged Menra's attention.

"Yes, Master, I understand."

"Go then, and remember, no one must see the girl."

* * *

Perhaps it was premonition, perhaps mother's instinct. Raine felt a foreboding . . . she had refused to allow Maliseet to join the evening work-teams. The others had turned on her—how could she refuse? She, of all Ashkelites, should know the impossible demand placed on Nakos, how could she withhold her full efforts? Surely, she must remember her own husband, staying in the fields alone, long after the others had taken shelter. Still Raine held firm—no, the girl would not return to full labor till dawn.

Once inside their tiny hut, Raine ordered Maliseet into the far bed chamber. Why was her mother acting this way? It wasn't at all like Raine, yet there was no arguing with her, her command was final, giving no room for disagreement.

Maliseet drew the curtain to the bedchamber. A cot and a small oak chair filled most of the space. Maliseet lay on the cot, closed her eyes, and her thoughts drifted. *Maliseet* . . . His soft, rich, velvety voice said her name over and over again . . .

Raine sat on the bench next to the central ventilation shaft. She stared at the door . . . what was it? The feeling was so strong. Was it the memory of Akid, her husband? Yes, that was it; the Procession had triggered the association with death. They had killed her husband, just as they would kill Nakos.

It had begun the same way. Everyone had joined in, worked to their limits to help Akid maintain production. Worked into the danger levels. Then . . . with the first symptoms of carcina, with the first tiny, white water blisters on their backs, the panic took hold. Soon, it was Akid who labored alone, just as it would be Nakos. Give them three moons, at most six. God, they were a weak race, a pathetic race. Yes, that was it; that was the reason for this irrational fear.

It will be over by morning, the Procession long gone. Yes, it will be over by morning.

At first it sounded like someone running, far in the distance. Then, as the sound drew closer, it became more distinct. It was the steady rhythm of a single horse.

Raine sat upright, every ounce of her attention directed to the clatter of the hooves. No one in Asha-1 had a horse, they were forbidden. Could it be a messenger, someone lost?

The horse was close now, slowed to a walk, directly outside the door . . . now moving past . . . silence. Raine tried to control her short, gasping breaths. She tried not to panic.

The knock was hard and sharp. Raine stood, and stared at the door. Three more knocks, more insistent, the old door shaking in its frame. Raine inhaled deeply, then slowly exhaled. Steeling herself, she walked to the door.

"I have been told by those in the field that I will find the girl called Maliseet here," Menra said.

Raine remembered this one. He was the closest to the Warlord, the senior rider in the Procession. Now, alone, his huge body filled the entire space of the door. His deep brown eyes searched the room behind Raine, his bearded face concealing any intent or emotion.

"I am her mother." Raine's voice betrayed her; it was a frightened, pleading voice.

"Then you will be honored to know that the great Warlord Renagi requests your daughter be brought to him."

"Why? For what purpose? What need does he have of my daughter?"

Quickly, with complete economy of movement, Menra was inside the hut.

"Where is the girl?"

Maliseet stepped from behind the curtain, walked from the bedchamber. Menra's eyes focused on her. She was inexplicably calm. A feeling exuded from her, an aura. Perhaps she would not be hurt. The feeling extended, took hold of Raine, wrapped her in its safeness, calmed her.

"I am Maliseet."

Raine stood transfixed. Menra walked to the girl, gently extending his hand. Maliseet allowed him to lead her from the door.

It was as in a dream, Raine watched, unable to speak, to protest, to fight. As if it had all happened before—she was merely watching for the second time . . .

Menra mounted the rippling black stallion. Once securely in the saddle, he bent down and, with a single motion, lifted Maliseet behind him.

He looked once at Raine, a deep, searching look, a look that was almost an apology. Raine stared, captive in the vacuum of what was taking place. How delicate Maliseet seemed, her pure, nearly translucent skin, her fine, white hair, her cotton dress; all so vulnerable in comparison with the blackness of the Warman.

Finally she made contact and held Maliseet's eyes. And in that moment, the mysterious calm which prevented the pleading tears and screams held Raine's instincts at bay. One long moment of contact and the Warman's heels dug lightly into the black, muscular flanks. They were gone.

Raine watched them ride through the east gate, watched as the horse became a tiny speck in the distance, finally disappearing. Still, she looked after them, as the hollow inside her began to fill. Now it was coming, the aching, the throbbing, growing with every breath. Slowly, she turned to face the desolate, empty room.

One step, two steps, and the feelings began to rise up from the depths of her; deep, primordial feelings, engulfing her, overcoming her. It seemed her life energy had been, in one instant, sucked from her loins. Raine collapsed, tasting the earthen floor; finally, crawling on her hands and knees, she began to sob. A sob that became a howl, a howl that became a shrieking, desperate scream; a scream that became blackness.

"Yip!" The ki-ai was short, sharp. A quick expulsion of breath from the diaphragm. The squat, bare-footed Warman back-shifted slightly. The lunging kick fell short of its target, the solar plexus.

No hips, you cannot make distance with a kick without pushing from the hips.

The observation passed quickly through Renagi's mind as he studied the two Warmen. This was Renagi's favorite event, the freestyle kumite. Any man from any province could participate. All techniques were permitted, including joint breaks and strangulation. A contest was decided on submission only, one contestant either unable to continue, or unwilling. No one was ever unwilling, the loss of face would be too great. Better to die.

The taller man readjusted his stance. In spite of his long legs he had been unable to connect.

The other contestant shifted forward, then back, in a steady, mesmerizing rhythm. He felt no need to commit; it was better to unsettle him first, make him anxious. It was obvious that the taller man did not want to enter punching distance, and certainly not grappling range. No, his opponent was much too well-rooted to risk close-in fighting. The two stood face on. They were nearly still, motionless, studying each other, waiting for the break in breath.

Renagi sat in the Velchar, a carved stone seat, lined in black and red velvet cloth, three body-lengths above the fighting square. Zena and Hiro knelt in sei-za position on each side of their master. On the next level, one pace below, the select Warmen of the Procession sat, their silver goblets brimming with heavy red wine.

In each of the four corners of the Great Hall, a member of the Council of Zendai occupied a carved stone seat. One hundred more Warmen took kneeling positions at ground level, surrounding the square. No civilians entered the Great Hall while the kumite took place, and certainly no women. Today there had been eighteen combatants; there had been six deaths, four men crippled permanently from joint displacement, one blinded, three dehydration blackouts and two concussed. Two combatants remained in the competition: the finalists.

Renagi scrutinized the two in the square. The taller man had the physical advantage, yet the short one was distinctly more centered. Even from this distance Renagi could feel the dark, deep-set eyes bore into the tall man. There was nothing more intimidating than stillness, and the little man had certainly mastered the slow, deep, lower breathing that enabled a warrior to be calm in the midst of battle. Renagi watched the short but thick feet as the toes curled, pulling the floor, allowing the energy to flow upward.

Renagi saw the movement before it began. The low, lunging slide from sochin to an extended zenkutzu stance, the right hand drawn back in nihon-nukite, the two-fingered spear. This would be it, the little man flying toward the tall man, the spear-hand shooting toward the eyes, the force great enough to penetrate the soft tissue and go up into the brain.

"Hissss" . . . the ki-ai sizzled through the Great Hall. And then, the unexpected, the waza. As the fully committed nukite attack crossed the halfway mark of the square, the tall man spun and performed a fine back-thrusting kick pulled round at impact. The full force of the small man's charge was met with this perfectly balanced technique.

The snap of the seventh cervical vertebra was marginally louder than the "yip" ki-ai. For a moment, the small man froze, his head bent back, paralyzed, gazing in agony . . . the tall man used the moment to spin forward, the kicking leg now a pivot as he drove his elbow up into the tip of his opponent's mandible. The smaller man's head was now held only by skin, the vertebrae and spinal cord severed as he fell dead to the stone floor.

Everything—the breathing, the anxious eye contact, the short mae-geri—had been a ploy, a feint, a method of making the small man confident, of making him commit.

The tall man turned, and amidst the loud, staccato hand-claps which constituted the Zendai sign of acceptance, he bowed deeply to the Warlord.

Renagi stood, turned slightly to his left. Zena was there, the fine, shining katana held forward, its etched silver hilt glowing through the silk braiding. Renagi took the katana, cradled it, and slowly walked down toward the square. By the time he arrived the combat zone had been cleansed of blood, the dead man removed, and the tall man bowed in rei position before his master.

The katana was two hundred yeons old, the fine steel of the blade had been pounded flat, folded over, pounded again, folded and tempered one hundred times. Never used in battle, never held as a possession, never given life, never given soul. A katana could belong to one man only, carried always by his side, and finally buried with its master.

Tanak wept openly as Renagi bade him to rise and accept the fine, long sword, thus welcoming him to the honored and select Clan of Warmen.

The ride had been comparatively easy; the beautiful, white-skinned child seemed weightless behind him. Menra had, on two occasions, been conscious of the warm, round breasts pressing against his back. Yet only once, when they had stopped to rest and she lay quiet, asleep beside him, did he contemplate the heat of her body, the sweetness of her loins. And even then he had controlled his thoughts, halting them. After all, it was an act punishable by death to fornicate with an untouchable, an Ashkelite. So the journey had continued and now they were entering the outskirts of Zendow. Menra remembered the Warlord's command: "No one must see the girl." He would use the secret tunnel, enter the castle by its bowels, then take her to a holding cell before he summoned his master.

As Menra left the fifteen-foot-square cell, lit by a single torch, he could not help but again notice her eyes. If she was frightened it was not evident, not in those wide, amber, open eyes. Menra would have known—after all, he was the senior Warman, trusted above all others. His life, his death, rested on his ability to read men, to read what was written in their eyes. This Maliseet was indeed a strange one; he looked once more at her, sitting alone on the solitary wooden bench. She was not frightened.

By the time Menra entered the Great Hall, the Feast of Celebre had begun. The same vast space that hours before had hosted the freestyle kumite, the same vast space that had seen seven deaths, and one great victory, the same Great Hall that had, for twenty yeons, hosted this event, was now a place of laughter, of boisterous camaraderie, of warm red wine, of drummers, acrobats, women and children. In the hall's center was the Warlord's table, the Twelve Warmen of the Procession seated in lines to either side of Renagi. Beyond them sat the Military Council, the chief advisers and one hundred of the most honored Warmen.

As Menra walked toward the table, he was quick to notice the glowing young face of the newcomer. He sat at the end of the table facing Renagi. Tanak looked up, caught Menra's eyes and bowed his head, humbly acknowledging the older man's entrance. Menra bowed quickly to Renagi, and took his place in a heavily carved oak chair, on the right-hand side of his Warlord.

"And it was a successful trip?" Renagi lifted the silver goblet, knowing full well that Menra would not have returned otherwise.

The serving-girl had just finished filling the large goblet when Menra grasped it and lifted it in a toast. He wanted to say, "A prize worth waiting for," but thought better at the last; perhaps it would show impertinence, or a presupposition of his master's purpose.

"A successful trip," was all Menra said.

Renagi smiled broadly, his great white teeth brightening his face, as his slanted, hooded eyes became tightly closed slits in the wide, olive-skinned brow.

"Then drink, drink!" Renagi bent closer, hushed, conspiratorial in tone. "Madame Wang has two new ones for you tonight—a gift from me . . . virgins, true virgins, not Wang's usual restitched impersonators."

Renagi bellowed with laughter. Yes, Wang was known to use the needle and thread. But then, a continual supply of clean, fresh girls below the age of twenty was not always easy to produce, even with the standard fifty golden kons paid to the parents.

Menra relaxed, the heavy red wine soothed him, taking hold and giving him a warm confidence. The toasting began, the traditional raising of glasses. First to each of the Warmen, then to the members of the Military Council. Now the goblets had been refilled at least one dozen times, for it was the custom to gulp, not sip, the wine. Drunkenness was desired on this night of Celebre. All actions were condoned, even verbal insult to the Warlord—as long as it remained in jest—no one was accountable. The drunken Zendai was clearly a different man to the same Zendai in a sober state. All was forgiven.

The new Warman, Tanak, stood for his toast. Barely stood, as he raised his glass and fell backward to the cheers and applause of the now roaring Zendai and Warmen. Tanak picked himself up, knowing that even through the haze of his drunkenness he must maintain face this evening. He hoisted his body back to the impossibly long table. All eyes were upon him, the table had quieted, he could feel them urge him, will him.

Taking control, Tanak stood, lifted the once-again brimming goblet.

"To my Warlord, whom I am, from this night onward, honored to serve."

The Great Hall shook with the shouts of "Hei! Hei!" as clenched right fists punched into the air. Finally, Renagi stood, firm, secure.

"I declare the Feast of Celebre."

On cue, the bare-chested drummers began the beat. Deliberate, then slowly building, as the finest serving-girls carried in the gigantic boar, sitting atop a silver tray, an apple in its huge, tusked mouth.

Four hours later, the table began to quiet as one man, sometimes two at a time, stood, bowed to Renagi, and wound his way to the

Willow World. Wang would have a good night, the Feast of Celebre could see her to a fortune in golden kons. Each girl fetched five kons for an hour, and in this state many of the men required a fraction of that time before they gave up, impotent from the wine.

Menra had conserved himself, had drunk just enough to fuel his fire, to promise a long, hard ride to the heavenly plane. His thoughts traveled more and more to Renagi's "gift" . . . virgins? Yes, it was time to make the move. He stood.

Renagi's hand shot out, caught him by the sleeve of his red battle tunic. Menra looked down, into the hard, dark eyes. He knew the question.

"She is in the holding cell, beneath the escape tunnel," he said.

"Did anyone see you enter?" Renagi's voice was insistent.

"No one."

The hand released its iron grip. Renagi grinned his white-toothed grin. Menra walked toward the door.

"Maliseet."

The voice was the same rich velvet, but the timbre was somehow changed, there was a gravelly, slurred quality. The girl looked up; she had been sitting as Menra had left her, on the wooden bench. She had been expecting the Warlord; ever since she had seen him that afternoon it had been impossible for her to think of anything else. Somehow, this handsome, fierce man had captivated her thoughts. Now, here in front of her, he stood. For a moment she panicked . . . what was the correct response, what should she do . . . ?

Quickly, she knelt before him and kissed the hard, cold stone floor.

The hand was warm against her neck.

"Get up. Let me look at you."

Maliseet raised her head, her gaze riveted on the reddish blue, clawlike mark that extended from the right wrist to the midpoint on the top of the wide hand. He noticed her gaze.

"The Royal birthmark," he said proudly.

She was standing now, close to him. The smell of wine from his mouth was not unpleasant, but there was a wildness to the man that made her uneasy.

"Like my eyes, it is a sign of purity. Like my eyes," he repeated the words slowly as if they were a command.

Maliseet looked into the slanted, deep brown eyes. She was, at once, lost. For the first time since the Warman had come for her, she felt the protective shell of her fantasy broken. A quiver began deep within her as she stared into the Warlord's face; she felt his uncompromising dominance. Her body began to tremble.

"You are cold?" Again the warm hand touched her. "Come with me, this is no place for a . . ." he hesitated, then, bordering on sarcasm, ". . . princess. An Ashkelite princess."

Menra had been twice to the heavenly plane with the first offering. Twice before the screams of pleasure had given way to screams of pain; she had, indeed, been a virgin, yet schooled brilliantly in the art of arousal and inner contraction; probably by Wang herself. Now Menra relaxed, drew slowly on the long-stemmed pipe, filling his lungs with the smoke of the elixir. Somehow the smell always reminded him of violets. As to whether the elixir actually prolonged life Menra was uncertain, but surely the state of total ease which the drug induced was reward in itself. Forty minutes longer and he would be ready for the second "gift."

His thoughts drifted with the white smoke as the small, tight rings floated lazily toward the top of the canopied bed. What was his Warlord doing right now? Was he questioning the young girl—about what? Surely, Renagi could not find the Ashkelite attractive?

Then Menra recalled the full, warm breasts pressing against his back. What would those breasts look like? With such a delicate skin, the nipples would have to be pale and pink. Would the aureolas be large, would they cover the entire curve of the breast? And the sacred triangle; the hair must be fine, silky and white. He had never seen a woman with a pure white mound.

Menra was now fully erect; he reached to the top of the round, ebony bedside table, picked up the tiny brass bell, and summoned Madame Wang.

Maliseet allowed Renagi to guide her through the stone passages, the torches providing a flickering light. They were alone, and their footsteps echoed in the high ceilinged corridors. Finally they came to a solid, stone wall. Renagi had kept his hand upon her shoulder as they walked, and now, turning to him, she felt the hardness beneath his robes. She stepped backward, away from him.

"Be still, I will show you something," he said brusquely, his face half-covered in shadow. Then, turning, he shoved the heel of his palm firmly into the wall, to the right of her head. Involuntarily, she jumped forward as the concrete moved behind her. Renagi caught her, laughing.

"Go ahead, go up," he said, indicating the narrow, winding steps behind her.

Up she walked, feeling his hot breath on her neck as he followed. Her upper thigh muscles were strong, well-developed from the continual squatting and standing motions of the harvest, yet the winding stairs tired her; they seemed to have no end. She moved on and on through the blackness . . . Thump! Straight into another solid wall. Maliseet fell backward, momentarily stunned.

"We have arrived." Renagi's voice was teasing, almost playful.

Another palm-heel. The concrete rose, revealing a domed room—the shape of the quarter moon and a myriad of six-pointed stars cut through the ceiling, allowing the full natural moon to illuminate the canopied bed and thick Miramese carpet.

"Come into my temple," Renagi urged. "Would you care for wine?" There was a mocking tone in his voice. "There are ten of these chambers, used by the former occupants as meditation rooms. We have a more worldly purpose for them."

Renagi's voice was hardening, becoming insistent. He began unfastening the sash, loosening his red-and-black embroidered robes.

"Maliseet, shall I entertain you?"

In one dramatic moment, Renagi discarded the robe and stood naked in front of her, his throbbing, erect penis jutting out, appearing enormous in comparison to his tight, sinewy body. She stood, frozen in fear, unable to stop staring at this man whom she had fantasized as some fine prince or king. He walked forward and gripped her.

Her body recoiled. "No! No! Leave me . . . Leave me! You cannot do this! Leave me!"

With a single sweep of his arm he ripped the thick cotton dress from her; she wore nothing underneath. Her breasts were larger than he had imagined, beautiful pink pendulums, the aureolas huge, covering the entire front of each orb, the nipples delicate but thick.

Maliseet broke his grasp. There was no escape, but still she ran. She got as far as the bed before he was upon her.

She screamed, "Please, please, dear God, don't do this to me. Please, my lord . . . Please."

By now Renagi had her pressed backward on to the silk bedcover, holding her down, his hands against her shoulders while he spread her legs with his thighs. He lowered his head to her, licking her skin, working downward, below the navel. His tongue felt the fine, silken hairs growing in a thin line, leading him toward the place of magic.

"Please, stop, please, please!" Maliseet screamed.

Her screams echoed over and over, becoming meaningless, animal noises. Then she felt the iron grip upon her hair, pulling her head back as his mouth lowered upon hers, cutting off her voice, his hot, thick tongue pushing inside her mouth.

His other hand was upon her vagina, his fingers prying, opening the contracted lips. Then he released her, raised up and away from her, and quickly brought his clenched fist round in a vicious swipe to the side of her head.

"Be still!" he commanded. It was then that he entered her, using the spittle from his mouth as lubrication. The pain was somehow detached, dull, yet ripping.

Three days later a work party, harvesting far on the outskirts of the Easterly Fields, found Maliseet wandering toward Asha-1, her white cotton dress in shreds, her body red and swollen from overexposure to the ultra rays, her face, legs and arms blue with bruises. The amber eyes were vacant, staring; she seemed incapable of speech.

Carefully, touching her only enough to guide her, they led her to the village.

Raine heard the knock on her door. She didn't move; some had been more persistent than others, but eventually they had all gone, leaving her to her anguish. This one would not stop. Knock! Knock! It continued. Finally she stood, rubbed her tired, sunken eyes, ran a hand through the hair she had twisted into knots, and walked to the door. Knock! Knock!

She pulled it open, and was at once blinded by the sun. Slowly, as her eyes focused, she thought she was dreaming. In the center of the two men and one woman stood her beloved Maliseet.

"We found her in the fields."

The woman's words were empty, unnecessary to the mother whose deepest prayers had been answered. Her eyes full of tears, Raine looked from face to face in grateful reply, then gently took her daughter by the shoulder and led her inside to the cot in the back sleeping chamber.

Day and night she attended Maliseet, laying cool, vinegar-lemon compresses on the swollen forehead, encouraging her to sip the warm broth of carotene and crushed almonds which would, she prayed, restore a balance to her damaged skin. And all the time she prayed, prayed for her daughter's soul.

On the seventh day, Raine noticed a subtle change in Maliseet's expression, a new light in the child's eyes.

"Are you feeling better?" she asked.

"Stronger, much stronger," Maliseet replied, the first words she had uttered in more than a week.

Odd, Raine thought, *she seems so void of emotion, empty of gladness. She must know she is safe, she is home.*

The next morning, Raine found her standing naked by the side of the cot, examining her body with her hands, rubbing hard over her abdomen, squeezing her breasts. It was a personal, intimate moment, and Raine turned quickly to leave, hoping the girl had not seen her.

Maliseet looked up, and Raine halted.

"Do you think I can return to the fields?" Maliseet asked. The words were more statement than question. The bruising was much fainter, the redness less raw, the compresses and carotene were working. Raine moved toward the girl, to help her back to the cot.

"You still need rest, the skin is not completely healed," Raine said.

Maliseet stepped back. A look crossed her face, a look Raine had never seen before, a hard look. "I am fine, Mother. Please, don't touch me," she said.

Raine backed away, wounded. She told herself that all this would pass, as soon as she could talk to her child, find out what had happened, comfort her.

But it did not pass; not for days, then weeks, finally one month. Any attempt to rekindle Maliseet's memory of the missing days was met with a hard, stone stare. She was now fully recovered, physically, and she had resumed full work shifts, yet there could be no real contact with her. Raine's feelings of sympathy for the girl, and of her own inadequacy in the face of Maliseet's ordeal, were now giving way to anger. Anger at her daughter for shutting her off; the one person in the world that Raine would die for, and Maliseet was refusing to share her feelings, her thoughts, her warmth.

Five months passed. The interaction within the close walls of their tiny cottage was cold, basic. Raine had cooked, cleaned, washed, worked the early harvest shift; Maliseet had worked with the dawn, dusk and alternate night teams. The pattern was always the same; the girl would return from the field, sit briefly while her mother served food, answer only with "yes" or "no," refuse conversation. Then she would go to her chamber, pull the curtain, and not re-emerge until it was time for her next work-team.

Five months of living with a total stranger, thought Raine, as she watched Maliseet enter the bedchamber and pull the curtain across the door behind her.

Raine sat on the wooden bench, looking at the heavy, drawn curtain. Five months with no human warmth, hardly any contact. Her anger was sharp and focused. Five months was too long; her daughter's behavior was inexcusable. Raine stood and walked purposefully toward the drawn curtain.

In eighteen summers, she had never laid a punishing hand on Maliseet, but if now that was what was needed, then so be it. Raine drew in a breath, felt the bottled anger ready to explode, and tore back the curtain.

Maliseet stood naked, her eyes bulging with fear and shame, her hands cupped over her swollen stomach.

"I am carrying his child." She cried. "I am carrying the Warlord's child."

* * *

By the seventh month the outward signs of the pregnancy were impossible to hide. The morning sickness had continued and, in fact, grown more severe with the passage of time. Finally, Raine had forbidden Maliseet to work in the fields. The last four weeks had been an exhausting and silent exercise in the repression of fear, fear for what was to come.

The contractions began on the eve of the last day of summer; the child came with the rising sun, the head first, and as Raine pulled the bloody infant from the spreading pelvis she was astounded at the thick golden hair.

Not the white hair of an Ashkelite, she thought as she tugged in synchronous rhythm to Maliseet's strained efforts to force the child from her body.

Maliseet did not cry out. Not once. Instead, her face was set in a grim, determined mask.

"A boy! It is a boy!" Raine shouted aloud, overcome with the miracle of birth and forgetting, for an instant, the circumstance.

"Shut your mouth!" Maliseet spat the words.

Raine stepped back, stung, holding the quietly breathing baby in her arms. Then she took the heavy shears from the table and cut the umbilical cord, separating the baby from its mother.

The cord! The cord is like spun silver, she noted, shocked, then turned quickly as the baby screamed in her arms. *And the eyes! The eyes are blue!*

III

THE MISSION

Know the strength of man
But keep a woman's core

(Lao Tsu)

Yeon 967

Zendow

Vokane Province

Tabata sat cross-legged on the outer edge of the clearing. Concealed by the late spring leaves of the tall oak tree, he sat in the shadow of Zendow. The stronghold was breathtaking—thick, bonded stone walls standing half an octavoll in height, an intricate complex of sentry-boxes, open guard-posts and iron spikes designed to discourage even the most ambitious of climbers. And, hanging from every rampart, the great billowing banners of the Clan, the red claw painted boldly onto the black silk cloth.

How many Earth lives have led me to this moment, mused Tabata as he rubbed more dirt into his already filthy begging robes. *How much training, how many months of fasting? How many days of solitude?*

He recalled the last nine months; the long trip west from the Temple, the thirty solitary days in the burning, desolate Valley which separated Lunan Province from Vokane. He remembered the dreams which began in the Valley. Strange, recurring dreams of ivory-skinned men with infinite, turquoise eyes. Men of the spirit, who would guide him, protect him. Men he could nearly recognize, as if he had known them but forgotten or, perhaps, was about to know them.

These spirit-men often remained in his conscious mind as he began his daily meditation. Their image helped him to achieve the transcendental state. A state so free, so void of constraint, that on many occasions he had felt vast sorrow in returning to conscious function. Yes, the last nine months had opened new doors, given him new self-awareness.

Yet, many nights he had lain looking at the stars, listening to the sounds of the forest, and imagining himself once again in the warmth of the Brotherhood, at the Temple. In the early mornings he would find himself listening for the clatter of donkey-drawn carts across the cobbled courtyard, or the laughter of the apprentice brothers as they assembled for morning kata. He had learned that in these ways he was still a man of sentiment, a man who yearned for human companionship, for deep spiritual conversation. At first, he had thought of this as weakness; now, in the last months, he had come to accept the longings, to recognize them as no more or less than a facet of his earth nature, the outer layer of his Earth soul. He recognized in them the very basis of what he was: an artist, whose form of self-expression was his own body. The forest had taught him, expanded him. He had studied the ways of its life, the insects, the animals, the birds. He spent hours observing their survival, the techniques with which they hunted, defended their territory, raised their young.

Tabata continued his daily practice of the classical Temple Forms of Empty Hand. He held the fine linear movements of the Jion-ji katas in deepest respect. Yet now he had begun to expand them, incorporate into them the stances and motions of the forest life he studied; the upright, darting strike of the praying mantis, the low, slinking stalk of the margay, the patience and quick ferocity of the coyote, and the visual concentration of the hawk. Taking the classical form Jiin as his foundation, Tabata elaborated upon the kata by adding the "forest" movements. He practiced the new kata each evening at sunset and, through its practice, he grew in tune with his surroundings. The forest became his teacher.

His body had also changed. Gone was the superfluous weight. He had carefully followed the Elder's instruction regarding his intake of food. He had learned to prepare the young leaves of the oak and beech trees, to boil their bark, creating a broth that both nourished and cleansed his system. Cutting back on the traditional Temple diet of rice and grain, thus limiting the soft yin thoughts and righteous attitudes that the diet produced and increasing his harder, more aggressive yang self.

"You must become aware of the ambitions and desires of the men outside this Temple," were the Elder's exact words as he explained the new regime. Tabata had adhered to every detail, and now, finally, on this thirtieth day of the lunar month, Mayo, he was in Zendow, as instructed, dressed in the guise of a beggar.

The birth had been visible in the astrological charts for many yeons; the Senior Astrologers had been able to pinpoint the precise time and date. With the signs imminent, a select unit of beggar-monks was despatched from the Temple, trained to be unobtrusive yet totally observant. Renagi's secret liaison was discovered, the subsequent pregnancy monitored. The Elder's vision of "The Birth" was the last sign, the final link in the complex pattern of events that led Tabata here, now, as he watched and waited for fate to unfold.

Hours passed, the sun burnt to an ember, night fell. Tabata maintained his cross-legged vigil, allowing himself only periodic phases of light sleep. He had fasted for three days in preparation—not enough time for his body to grow weak, but time enough to clear his physical system and ensure the sharp function of his mind.

He breathed in deeply; the smell of morning was on the light, southerly breeze. His eyes were closed, resting. He could feel the faint footsteps, perhaps one hundred paces to his right. In spite of his immense self-control, Tabata was aware of his own excitement, the increase in his heartbeat. He opened his eyes.

She was just entering his field of vision. A young woman, perhaps sixteen or seventeen yeons, with the long white hair and distinctive pale skin of an Ashkelite. The young woman carried the bundle close to her chest, carried it carefully, as if it were alive. Yes, this was *it*, it was actually going to happen.

Tabata performed slow breath retention as he brought his heartbeat back to calm-focus level. The woman walked ahead, proud, her face set firm, the eyes aimed forward. Her gait was nearly a march as she entered beneath the first sentry position.

The voice came from a mechanical voice enhancer, the words echoed.

"Halt! Do not step beyond the designated threshold. Halt."

The woman ignored the command.

"Halt," again the word echoed.

Tabata watched as two fully armored guards walked from the main gate, barring her way. There was a brief exchange of words, one guard looking to the other, then back at the young woman. She extended the bundle; Tabata could now make out the outline of the infant.

One guard bent down, looked closely, backed away in what appeared to be amazement. He said something to the other guard, then turned and ran toward the main building. Once, the young woman attempted to push past the guard but was easily repelled and held in check.

Perhaps fifteen minutes had passed since her arrival. She stood sullen, silent, looking down at the infant. Finally he came. Tabata instantly recognized the shining, oiled black hair, the slant-hooded eyes. How often had this fierce Warlord been described to him?

Accompanying the Warlord was an older man, of perhaps fifty yeons. Tabata backed farther into the shadow of the huge, gnarled tree.

Renagi bent close, looked at the infant. He seemed relaxed as he turned to the older man and spoke. The young woman reacted by pulling away, her body movements conveying anger.

Sharp and fast, Renagi's attendant snatched the infant from her grasp. She flung herself upon him, was lifted off and held in the air by one of the guards. Renagi snapped an order. The man looked at him once, a long, questioning look; Renagi repeated his order.

Carrying the infant, the attendant turned and moved quickly away, taking a dirt path which branched off from the main road.

Tabata could just hear the young woman's screams as the guard carried her into a dark recess below the main wall, out of view of the sentries. Renagi and the second guard followed.

Tabata stood up, straining to see. He saw the gleaming steel blade as it flashed through the air, severing the young woman's head—continuing on its path, cutting through the neck of the armored guard; woman and Warman fell as one, their blood mixing and soaking the earth.

The second guard stood in horror, his eyes wide, his mouth half-open in question. Renagi spun, and with an overhead motion, the blade arcing high, pulled from the hip—brought the katana downward, splitting the man's skull into perfect halves, cutting down through his neck and into his torso. At first there was no blood. The man stood, frozen. Renagi pulled the blade from the man's sternum, resheathed it as quickly as it was drawn, and took one step back. The man began a twitching, spasmodic dance, the blood shooting, gushing from the long incision.

Renagi turned, and started for the main gate, leaving the young woman and the two guards dead.

Tabata closed his eyes; he could feel Maliseet's sad young spirit travel through him, then up, and into the void. He bent his head forward, touched the thumb of his right hand to his right temple, the middle finger to the left.

"May your transition from earth body to spirit be gentle. May your next birth be at one with the light." He whispered the ritualized words from the Temple's Book of Passage. Then Tabata turned and followed the trail of the attendant and the infant.

Tabata used hengetsu, the swift, silent, half-moon sweeping run, as he moved through the brush. The attendant was in his eyeline, only a hundred paces ahead. It was essential that Tabata be neither seen nor heard.

Menra veered to his left, ran up on to the grassy knoll overlooking the fast-moving, blue-white water. He stood completely still, calming himself. He had served Renagi for thirty-five yeons; had been assigned as his personal attendant from the day of the Royal birth. How honored he had been to be selected as guardian to the Royal heir. He had watched Renagi grow, mature, assume the position of Warlord. He had loved and obeyed his master, never doubted him, never questioned his commands—until now, at this moment.

He looked at the infant cradled in his arms. The baby did not cry; in fact, it seemed perfectly content. Could it be so? Menra knew he must never ask. Yet she was the same young woman he had brought to Zendow just under a yeon ago. Yes, it was Maliseet who had brought this child to Zendow, who claimed him to be the Warlord's son. It was Maliseet who had the courage to confront Renagi.

The infant had light hair, similar to that of the Ashkelites, and the skin was pale, but the eyes? They were not pink, they were blue. No Ashkelite had blue eyes. God, could it be true? Could his Warlord have broken the most sacred of laws, could he have mixed his Royal blood with an untouchable? The infant was bundled, its body hidden by the old woollen blankets. Should he dare to look? With his right hand, Menra pulled the blanket aside, reaching into the cotton-cloth, grasping the infant's right arm, freeing it from the wraps.

"A male child, a boy!" he gasped. And there in front of him, on the infant's right wrist, was the Sign of the Claw, the royal birthmark. Menra stared, on the edge of shock.

"God of Light, I pray that I am forgiven for what I have done. May I be forgiven for the knowledge I must bear, for what I must do," he intoned.

Then, he rewrapped the infant, steeled himself and threw the child into the swift currents of the river below. The small body hit the water with a dull thud, landing on its back, its face placid, eyes open. The woollen blanket and cotton padding broke most of the six-foot drop.

Quickly, the water engulfed the child, taking him under. Menra watched, transfixed. Up the child bobbed, moving quickly downstream. Under again, then resurfacing.

Is he dead? Surely he has drowned. What should I do? Menra's mind raced. *I must make sure he does not live.*

Ahead was the waterfall, certainly he would not survive the fall. *But I must be sure . . .* Menra pushed back his human feelings, buried his heart. *Now, of all times, I must not fail my master.*

He was about to start after the boy when he heard the growl. A low, guttural growl. A sound so menacing that the hairs on his neck stood rigid. Menra looked up.

There, standing on the opposite shore, was the Cat. Menra stared, blinked, then stared again. Surely he was dreaming. No panther could be this large, nearly the size of a stallion; shining black, eyes burning with a red glow, the glistening white fangs extended.

"A sign of the Devil," Menra uttered as he turned and ran. Behind him, the howling came.

* * *

Tabata listened, heard the howl, recognized this final omen, and dived headlong into the swirling water. The pounding river beneath the waterfall dragged him under. He allowed himself to be taken, to sink down into the dark, churning froth. Finally he touched bottom, his bare feet could feel the cold, large stones beneath the mud. He pushed hard against them.

His thrust coincided with the baby's fall. As Tabata broke the surface, his arms extended, the infant crashed roughly into his chest. Tabata folded himself around the screaming baby boy and kicked hard for shore . . .

IV

THE FIRST TEACHING

What others teach, I also teach; that is:
"A violent man will die a violent death!"
That will be the essence of my teaching.

(Lao Tsu)

Yeon 983

Shuree Forest

Vokane Province

The clearing was man-made, the ground free of stones and shrubs and the entire area twenty paces in diameter.

Yesterday's wood burned as embers in the deep, square fire-pit and a simple earthenware pot hung suspended by a single chain above the pit. A thick stew of herbs and forest vegetables simmered slowly.

Several feet to the side and behind the fire stood a thatched hut. The hut was large enough for two men, its reed and grass thatch pinned tight against the latticework of the timber frame.

The forest surrounding the clearing was dominated by the silver gray bark of the ash, the jagged foliage of the oak and the sheathed clusters of needle-sharp leaves on the high evergreens. The trees provided a natural tent above this forest home of Shihan Tabata and his student, Tegné. Only during the most severe winters were the master and his pupil forced to vacate these premises and take up short-term residence in the caves to the west, near the lip of the Valley.

Three hundred vul to the east, farther than Tegné had ever traveled, was the southern tip of Ashkelan, and, beyond that, lay Zendow.

"Ich." Tabata's voice rang out, cutting the chill of the early November morning.

Tegné's fist shot toward the flame of the candle. Tabata scrutinized the hip movement, the rotation on the central axis as the fist stopped half-a-hand before the flame.

"No kime. Without kime there is no technique. Again, focus your energy," Tabata demanded.

"Ni." Again the punch. The flame quivered slightly. "San, chi. Ich, ni, san, chi"; over and over Tabata shouted the command to strike. Over and over Tegné responded, the sweat building on his brow, frustration causing his forehead to furrow.

"Ich!" Tabata yelled. Tegné was angry; angry at himself for his failure to succeed at this lesson, angry with Tabata-Sensei for pushing him onward. He readjusted his loose, low, sochin-dachi stance, brought his right fist back, close to the fully twisted hip. "Yeii!" Tegné ki-aied as his hip snapped forward, throwing the fist toward the flame. The flame blew backward, almost extinguishing. Tegné willed it out. On the verge of his wishes the flame flickered, then burst back into life.

Tegné stared at the flame, looked once at his teacher, then turned away in disgust.

The Sensei studied the boy. For sixteen summers he had nurtured him, taught him, trained him, loved him as a father. Tegné had been a spirited infant, waking at all hours with fits of violent screaming. More than once, Tabata felt cursed with this "mission." Never had he dreamed, as he swore the sacred vows of his Order, that his greatest contribution would be the parenting of an outcast son.

Tegné stood before him, the sweat causing his pale skin to glisten as the blood surged through his veins, defining his newly muscled upper torso. Tabata looked into the deep-set blue eyes. *Tegné—born of the angry water*, he reflected, as he raised his hand, preventing the next punch. His voice was gentle, "I believe you are missing the meaning of this lesson."

Tegné avoided his Sensei's gaze.

Tabata continued, insistent. "The flame will extinguish only if the punch is perfect. Perfect kime, perfect timing, and perfect attitude. To be perfect you must relax, be natural."

"Perfect?" Tegné repeated the word. There was the hint of challenge in the breaking adolescent voice.

"Yes." The strong tone of Tabata's answer restored his student's manner to one of respect. Tabata used the moment, contorting his face, imitating the frustrated, angry boy; he flexed his biceps and performed a stiff, comical punch in the air.

"Perfect," Tabata said, flatly.

Tegné exhaled; his shoulders relaxed, and his lips parted in an easy, engaging grin as he saw the flicker in his Sensei's eyes.

"Now, come with me," Tabata continued, placing the lighted candle on the ground. Bending, he picked up the cotton top of Tegné's training gi and placed it around the boy's shoulders. Then he guided him to a spot on the outer perimeter of the clearing.

"Sit down," Tabata said. "Perhaps it is time for a new Sensei," he added, as he urged the boy into a comfortable half-lotus position. "Keep your eyes straight ahead, regulate your breathing," he instructed as he moved behind the boy toward the underground food stores.

Tegné stared into the dry, dense underbrush. The thick evergreen trees overhead blocked the sunlight.

What is he doing? Tegné wondered. He turned toward the hurried sounds behind him.

"Do not look at me. Look straight ahead. Raise your ki from your seika-tanden. Focus through your eyes. Become aware," Tabata snapped.

Tegné turned back abruptly. Tabata appeared at his side, their evening meal in hand. The filleted trout was attached to a ball of cotton twine, secured on the carved wooden fishing hook.

"Straight ahead," Tabata reaffirmed. He moved quickly, quietly into the underbrush. He looked toward the east, toward the west, then turned his eyes north. Satisfied, he pivoted and stared enigmatically at Tegné. The boy's curiosity was consuming his discipline. Tabata anticipated the question and put a finger to his lips. Tegné remained silent, but watched, intrigued, as Tabata carefully placed the trout underneath a pile of crisp, golden leaves. Then the Sensei stepped backward toward the clearing, unraveling the twine as he moved.

"Watch the bait carefully," said Tabata, as he laid the remainder of the ball of twine on the ground. Then he began to howl, "Whoo-oop! Whoo-oop! Whoo-oo-oo-oop!"

Tegné turned and looked up at his Sensei. Tabata had removed the top of his gi. Bare-chested and moving his arms in a counter-rhythm to his legs, he was alternately bringing each knee up tight to his chest and stamping his bare-soled foot solidly against the hard ground. His fingers were extended and bent clawlike, causing the total effect to be that of a stationary running movement with the legs while the hands and arms seemed to assist by pulling at the air in front of him. The entire sequence was performed in unison with the howl. Tegné stared, genuinely moved by the sheer physical grace of the strange movement.

Is this a kata, some form I have never before seen? he wondered, in awe of his Sensei's ability to inject such controlled spontaneity to virtually any physical act.

It was then that the breeze caught the leaves above them and eclipsed Tabata's body in a fluttering half-shadow. Perhaps it was the sudden movement against his Sensei's bare flesh, perhaps even the deepening twilight, but for a moment Tegné was certain that he saw a four-legged animal before him, running against the wind, its eyes caught fierce and bright, staring from the shadows.

"Not at me . . . concentrate on the bait." Tabata commanded.

"I have not done this for a long time," he said, smiling. "Ah, yes . . . yes . . ." he motioned again for Tegné to turn toward the forest, ". . . different rhythm, that's it, a different rhythm."

"Whoop. Whoop, Whoo-oo-oo. Whoop!" Tabata howled, with renewed vigor.

Tegné studied the clearing. He focused his eyes on the pile of leaves, straightened his back and centered his breathing. The steady, low "Whoop. Whoop. Whoo-oo-oo. Whoop!" became mesmeric. His heart seemed in perfect synchronization with the "dance."

It was dusk when he awakened. He could feel Tabata's presence to his right side. He dared not turn and look, realizing he had dozed off, perhaps missing his Sensei's lesson. He focused his gaze on the forest directly ahead. Thirty paces away, the glowing, black eyes stared back at him. The prairie wolf sat motionless.

"Pay attention to your teacher," Tabata whispered as he pulled the twine, moving the mound of leaves forward. The wolf did not budge; wonderfully alert, alive, yet completely still. Again, Tabata tugged on the twine; no response.

"Concentrate your eyes, release your mind," Tabata whispered. Tegné allowed his mind to drift, focusing his eyes on the animal. He brought his breathing to a slow, steady rate.

The wolf was silhouetted in the moonlight. Tegné studied the expansion and contraction of its chest, becoming gradually aware that the rhythm of the wolf's breathing was exactly in time with his own.

Tabata tugged again at the twine. The hungry animal eyes followed the movement of the bait. Again, Tabata pulled, and this time Tegné felt the tug deep within his own solar plexus, as if Tabata's action had actually touched a point in his own abdomen. His eyes moved involuntarily; he watched the bait jerking through the underbrush. Now he could feel the hunger, the control, the earth beneath him.

Snap! The movement was lightning quick. Tegné jerked forward, his stomach in mild spasm. As he recovered, regaining his seated position, he glimpsed the wolf, the trout in its mouth, springing through the underbrush, disappearing into the moonlight. The connection was broken.

"Did you see that!" Tegné's excitement was a near shout.

"See what?" Tabata's voice was quiet, calm.

"The wolf! The wolf!"

"The wolf?" inquired Tabata, his voice remaining low.

Tegné calmed slightly. "The wolf took the bait," he answered, feeling slightly foolish.

"And?" Tabata pressed.

"And we do not eat tonight . . ."

The answer was flippant, yet Tegné felt strangely defensive. Tabata smiled, nodding his head, looking at the boy. Then he bent forward and lifted the burning meditation candle.

"To begin. You saw patience, relaxation and perfect timing. That is what your eyes saw. I believe, however, that you also *felt* the wolf," said Tabata.

Tegné's feeling of discomfort heightened as he shrugged his shoulders, cocking his right arm back, the fist tight to his side.

"Feel the wolf," Tabata urged.

For some reason, the insistence on the words "Feel the wolf" angered Tegné, as if they were somehow a violation of his privacy, an unwarranted intrusion into his inner self. His body tensed as he threw the punch. The fist contracted sharply in front of the candle flame. The flame did not waver. He looked up and believed he saw Tabata about to laugh.

"That's enough! I will not do any more," Tegné growled. "I want to learn to fight. This," he said, looking at the candle, "has nothing to do with fighting."

Tabata's voice was stern, commanding. "Fighting? This has everything to do with fighting. You *are* fighting. Yourself, the candle, your teacher. Because you are impatient, angry." Tabata looked down at the boy; Tegné's fists had suddenly relaxed.

"Did you *feel* anger in the wolf?" Tabata asked. He did not wait for an answer. "No, you did not . . . the anger is in yourself. You are full of anger," he said, handing Tegné the burning candle.

"Stand back." Tabata's voice was sharp.

Tegné held the flame a half-pace from Tabata's extended fist.

"Go back more," said Tabata.

Tegné obeyed, moving the full pace backward. Slowly, fluidly, Tabata pulled his striking arm back.

"If the wolf was like you, he would starve. Your mind and body do not work as one. You know this, the wolf told you—you felt it. And now, for some reason, you wish to ignore it. You must learn to listen, to see, to feel . . . concentrate, make this single act perfection . . . One punch . . . relax, flow like water, then *become iron.*"

With that, Tabata unleashed a fast, flowing punch—his hips pivoting toward the flame, as though the hips themselves were enough to extinguish the light. A *whoosh!* of air accompanied the technique . . . Tegné and Tabata stood in darkness as Tegné felt the last, stubborn, defensive wall of anger give way to trust.

"Forgive me, Sensei. May I try again?" he said, simply.

Tabata bowed, extending his hand and accepting the candle. "Be patient. Wait for the energy in you to rise. One time. One chance," he said quietly.

The boy's punch was fluid. Throughout the movement, Tegné remained aware of the earth beneath his bare feet. Whoosh! The flame extinguished, and sensei and pupil shared the quiet darkness.

Yeon 983
Zendow
Vokane Province

The straight-stepping punch was basic, too basic. Zato's body was stiff, awkward, the tension constant as his right fist drove toward Renagi's throat. Easily, and with no waste in movement, Renagi caught the fist in his own mittlike hand and simultaneously performed ashi-bari, sweeping Zato's leading foot from under him, sending the young man sprawling on the ground; then, without disrupting his flow, Renagi executed the "axe" kick, heel extended. Down, down, the "axe" descended toward the head of the young man. An instant before contact the foot snapped to a halt, hovering perilously close to the bridge of Zato's nose. A moment later, Renagi withdrew the technique, backed away and looked down at his son. Zato managed a tight-lipped smile.

His father bent forward, extended his hand and helped the boy to his feet. Renagi flushed with pride as they gripped, right hand to right hand, the Sign of the Claw on his own wrist seemed to wrap round and intertwine with the identical mark on the wrist of his son.

Zato was fifteen yeons, a strong, fine-looking boy. The Zendai woman chosen to produce the Warlord's heir had been superb; tall, large-boned, with glowing bronze skin and deep almond eyes. Her bloodline could be traced through ten generations of Zendai—she was pure, and now, although Renagi desired her less and less frequently, Natiro would occupy a place of power within the order of the Clan.

Zato brushed the dirt and gravel from his loose cotton combat uniform, faced his father squarely, and bowed. He knew that Renagi scrutinized him thoroughly, so he made sure the bow was executed properly from the hip, eyes looking up, maintaining a continual awareness of his opponent. He felt relieved as Renagi returned his courtesy and acknowledged the end of their kumite. Zato turned to leave.

"No! It is not over . . . Now you must watch. Use your eyes and your mind—continue to learn . . ."

Renagi's words stopped Zato in midstep. "Now you." Renagi's

voice hardened as he motioned for the three trainee Warmen to face him.

Without hesitation, the men sprang to their feet, bowed, and faced Renagi in fighting stance.

At fifty-two years old, the Warlord had tapped the very source of the fighting form. He seemed to ingest the vital energy of the movements, becoming more powerful and deeply grounded with the passing years. His body weight had increased marginally, which added to the muscularity of his frame. He required minimal movement in his kumite, concentrating on subtle body-shifting and the use of his powerful stance. An aura surrounded him, an impenetrable field that required the young Warmen to call upon every ounce of their courage.

Menra stood close by, always attentive to his master. He noted the caution with which the three trainees edged forward, and he moved farther to the right, allowing them ample room to shift and maneuver.

Although this sparring was performed as exercise, meant to build fighting spirit and technique, it carried with it a powerful element of fear. The Warlord was notoriously rough with his new men, and today the atmosphere was charged with danger.

Menra kept his eyes on the Warlord as he heard the heavy footsteps behind him. Finally Menra turned as the gate guard approached from the far end of the courtyard. He waved the man to a halt, chastising him with a stern look. The guard stood nervously on the outer boundary of the combat square.

What does he want? He knows he is interrupting . . . The thoughts passed with mild anger through Menra's mind.

The trainee in the center position was clearly the most aggressive. He edged forward, preparing an attack. Menra studied closely as the young man tensed slightly, took in a deep breath and lunged, right leg extended, the ball of his lead foot aimed toward Renagi's solar plexus. The Warlord waited until the fraction of a second before impact, then shifted to the left, stifling the kick with a downward palm-heel block.

Simultaneously, Renagi struck the attacker's jaw with a short, right, jabbing punch. The blow was deceptive, launched with less than one foot to travel, the power generated completely from the counter-clockwise rotation of Renagi's hips. The attacker dropped heavily to the ground.

Menra shook his head, marveling at the Warlord's ability to generate such enormous power with an absolute economy of movement.

The two standing Warmen moved in unison, quickly closing on Renagi from opposing sides. The Warlord did not evade their charge, instead he sank low into an open-toed sumo-style grappling stance, concentrating his eyes to the front, exercising his zanshin to gauge their distance.

Menra watched intently. Still he missed the subtle body shift as Renagi forced his hip into the right-side attacker, securing a strong grip on the man's thrusting arm and heaving him upward and across, timing the throw to coincide with the forward lunge of the remaining Warman. For an instant, Renagi and the Warman seemed a struggling mountain of muscle and flesh. Then, in a masterful backward slide, Renagi disengaged himself, pushing hard as he moved away from the two tangled bodies. The men struggled, trying to maintain balance, then collapsed in a heap on the ground.

Renagi remained motionless, eyeing the three prone Warmen. Then, slowly, he turned, caught Zato's eye and exploded with a full, deep laugh. His white teeth flashed in the afternoon sun. Menra smiled and nodded his head. The Warlord was unquestionably a master.

From the corner, the gate guard noisily cleared his throat. Menra turned and grudgingly waved the man forward.

"Master," the guard's voice was anxious.

Renagi's "Yes?" was clipped, impatient.

"There is a beggar in the Great Hall, he demands to see you."

"A beggar?" Renagi repeated. "A beggar who *demands* to see the Warlord?" His voice rose with indignation.

"He came this morning. We put him out, but he has come back. Four times he has come back," the guard apologized. "He is a very strange man; he claims to hold vital information, for your ears alone."

Renagi's face grew dark. He studied the gate guard. The Warlord seemed on the verge of explosion. Then, in a complete and premeditated reversal, Renagi bellowed with laughter.

"A beggar! A beggar! Well, why do you delay? Show him in."

The guard exhaled audibly, relieved by Renagi's good humor, and, as he turned and exited the courtyard, Renagi looked toward Zato, then eyed the trainees.

"Sit down, sit down. We will have a bit of amusement."

Sore from their encounter but enormously glad that the "sparring session" had ended, the trainees bowed to Renagi, then moved into the cool of the courtyard. They were just sitting down when the gate guard reappeared, a haggard, bent, gray-bearded man in tow.

Zato and the Warmen suppressed their laughter as the beggar, a determined glint in his eyes, walked straight toward Renagi, his stiff, shuffling steps giving him an unintended air of pomp.

Amused, Renagi watched the old man approach. Less than two paces away he stopped, met Renagi's gaze, and bowed low before the Warlord. Renagi caught the flicker of light in the old gray eyes. *Probably insane*, he thought, as he performed an exaggerated, low bow before the beggar. Renagi could hear the muffled laughter from Zato and the Warmen.

"Well?" spoke Renagi, in his most dignified voice.

The beggar, undisturbed by the histrionics, maintained an air of gravity. "I have seen him," he said, his voice low and clear. "I have seen your son."

Renagi felt suddenly and without reason disquieted by this man. "My son? My son is here," he answered.

"The Ashkelite," said the beggar, simply.

Renagi's sudden shift of mood seemed a complete contradiction to the still-laughing and cajoling Warmen.

"Ashkelite?" Renagi's pronunciation indicated the offense the word caused him.

"I have seen him. White skin, golden hair . . ." Before he finished the last word, Renagi caught the grizzled old neck in a vicelike grip, his fingers digging deep into the throat.

"Old man, do you know who I am?" he growled. Then, without waiting for an answer, "I am Renagi, Warlord of Zendow. A Warlord *cannot have an Ashkelite son.*"

The words were final. Renagi's fingers encircled the man's windpipe.

Zato and the Warmen no longer laughed. Instead, they stared, stone-faced. Although too far away to hear the precise exchange of words, they realized the "game" had become deadly serious. The old man was beginning to choke, his eyes bulging as he stared down at Renagi's right, grasping wrist.

"He bears your mark," he gasped.

Slowly Renagi released his grip. "Stand still," he commanded, then turned and scowled in the direction of the Warmen, "Out . . . leave me alone with him."

For an instant the group stayed still, too frightened to move.

"Now!" bellowed Renagi.

In unison, they leapt to their feet and ran from the courtyard. Zato stopped, turned once to look at his father, then followed the Warmen through the gate.

Renagi walked four steps and halted, eye-to-eye with Menra. "Many yeons past. The baby you took to the river. What happened?" he demanded.

"I did as you told me, Master," responded Menra, his mind screaming the impossibility of the infant's survival.

"Did you watch the baby drown?" Renagi pressed, his eyes piercing. Menra lowered his head.

"I will not ask you again." Renagi's voice was taut, insistent.

Menra grew calm as he looked up, full into Renagi's face. "Master, I could not watch your son drown." At last at peace within himself, he was free of the burden.

Menra saw the movement begin, the back-fist swinging up from Renagi's left side. He made no effort to defend against the strike, no effort to evade it. He had disobeyed his Warlord, harbored a secret, defiled a sacred trust. He accepted this retribution.

Renagi's rage erupted in a screaming ki-ai. The back-fist caught Menra flush on the right temple, driving the bone inward, compressing his brain.

Menra collapsed to his knees. He wanted to speak, to say "forgive me," but his mouth would not be controlled. Now the blackness was coming, he could feel the dark, numbing grip. He let go.

Renagi stood above the fallen man. A sadness rushed through him, then the sadness turned to anger, the anger to a steely resolve. Renagi turned and walked back to the beggar. The old man was petrified.

"Where is he?" Renagi's tone was icy-cold.

The beggar used every reserve of willpower to control his trembling. This was his chance, his only chance, his last. He pitched his voice low to conceal his complete panic.

"My name is Kenuke-Oyama." He forced the words. Renagi remained stone-faced, showing no sign of recognition. "When you came to this province, you drove me from my land," the man pushed on. "I was feudal lord of Western Shuree."

Renagi nodded, coldly.

"You enslaved my only son."

Now Renagi began to understand. This old fool had the audacity to believe he could strike a bargain.

"Yes?" said the Warlord.

"I am an old man. I have no need of land. But my son . . . my son . . ." The beggar's fear gave way to sorrow as his voice quivered.

Renagi anticipated the flood of emotion and stepped back. "You wish me to reunite you with your son?" he said simply, sparing himself the old fool's tears.

The beggar's face seemed to light from within. "That is my wish, Warlord."

"You have my word," Renagi stated sincerely, solemnly.

The beggar began a low, thankful bow. Renagi's question halted him in midmotion.

"Where is this Ashkelite?" His voice was businesslike, firm.

"In Western Shuree, in the forest. This side of the Valley of Death. He lives in the lower cave region with a hermit monk . . ."

Renagi's eyes registered satisfaction. Keeping visual contact with the beggar, the Warlord walked to Menra's lifeless body and drew the katana from the dead man's belt. The midday sun sent reflections of light from the finely folded steel of the blade.

The beggar began to back away. Renagi held his eyes firm as he walked slowly, purposefully toward the cowering man. Finally, with less than one pace between them, Renagi extended the katana to the beggar, hilt-first.

"Show me exactly where he is," he said, urging the old man to grasp the extended hilt.

With an involuntary sigh of relief, Kenuke-Oyama accepted the sword. Hurriedly, he began to cut a rough map in the earthen courtyard. He indicated the Valley, the surrounding mountains, and then scratched a series of crosses to show the caves at the base of the mountains. He finished his crude map with a large, deep circle. Pointing toward the circle he said, "I have seen them here, an encampment. They live in the open, perhaps take shelter in the caves during the winter."

Satisfied, Renagi took the katana. His thick, calloused fingers wiped the dirt and gravel from the blade. He looked silently into the old man's eyes. It was a burning, raging look.

"Your word, Master, you gave your word," the beggar pleaded, backing away, his arms held up in defense. He hardly detected Renagi's sliding motion, in fact the initial entrance of the razor-sharp katana was absolutely without pain; only shock as he saw the blade buried nearly to the hilt, through his rib cage beneath his heart.

"I will keep my word," Renagi snarled, "Your son died many yeons ago."

Now the blade began its deep, intense burning. Kenuke-Oyama exhaled in spurts, the blood beginning to gush from his mouth. In a final, instinctive effort, he gripped the exposed steel near the hilt and tried to push the blade from his body. He felt his hands grow slippery with blood as the katana cut the grasping fingers to the bone. He heard Renagi's growl, like a mad, rabid animal. "Now you join him." Renagi ripped the katana downward, pulling to the left, disemboweling the old man. Then, slowly, he withdrew the blade, and dropped it beside the dead man before walking briskly from the courtyard. His mind raced. *How much did they glean from what the old bastard said?* he wondered, desperately recalling the episode word by word. *Did they notice I was shaken, or would they think I was merely offended at the affront? Yes, naturally I would be mortally offended. An impostor, an Ashkelite impostor. An Ashkelite claiming to be my son. An imposter, that is what I will tell them . . .*

He pulled the thick hemp rope, sounding the assembly gong. Within seconds the Warmen began to gather in the Great Hall. Renagi scanned the faces, making sure the gate guard and the three trainees were in attendance. What he had to say must be heard by them, must be clear. He could leave no doubt, no room for rumors to begin, to undermine his absolute authority.

By now, nearly four hundred of the Warmen had gathered. Zato entered the hall from the left side, and Renagi noticed the three trainees grouped near his son. Finally, Renagi spoke. His voice was resounding.

"I have been informed this afternoon that a grave breach of conduct has occurred." The room quietened, allowing the words to ricochet off the thick marble walls and vaulted ceiling.

"An Ashkelite, an untouchable, a slave, has risen to call himself . . ." Renagi paused dramatically, ". . . to call himself Zendai."

A murmur rose in the crowd. Renagi continued, "Not only Zendai, but this bastard claims to be . . . my son."

The men erupted in outrage. Renagi met Zato's gaze, saw the stunned bewilderment on the boy's face. Raising his arms, he quieted the Warmen.

"Naturally, it would serve their purpose to kindle such a lie, to cause insurrection amongst us. As I speak, this impostor is in hiding." Renagi paused, scanning the faces. "I will take six of you with me. We will rout him out, destroy him." There was no doubt in any of their eyes; they accepted his statement as truth.

"Now line up in order of rank." He was in control, matter-of-fact.

The gathering legion of Warmen formed tight lines, structured according to seniority, shoulders squared, eyes forward. If Menra's absence was noted, it was not apparent. It had been many yeons since Menra had ridden in a war party, and Renagi was fully aware that within this pecking order no tears would be shed on account of his attendant's "sparring accident."

Renagi pulled Tanak, the senior Warman, aside. "Pick out five of the strongest," he instructed, then waited as Tanak made the selection. The Warlord dismissed the remaining men, leaving only the six.

Daybreak, and the six Warmen sat astride their horses in the outer courtyard. Frost lay on the ground and thick, white breath billowed from the snorting stallions. The Warmen were dressed in their winter gear, the thick lacquered leather body armor clinging tight to them.

With a clatter of hooves, Renagi rode through the far gate and trotted toward them, his huge, white horse almost identical in appearance to Kano, his sire.

Tanak looked up as Renagi pulled firmly on the reins. "All prepared and ready, Warlord," the senior Warman said confidently.

At that moment another, unexpected, rider appeared from the adjacent courtyard. The Warmen turned to see Zato, fully suited, riding toward them.

"What are you doing here?" There was nothing friendly in Renagi's voice.

Zato was caught unprepared for his father's severity. "I am coming with you," he answered meekly.

The Warmen remained quiet as Renagi allowed a long, angry silence. "You are *not* coming with us," he said, then added scathingly, "You are going back to your *mother.*"

The words held a belittling connotation, and Zato was desperate to save face in front of the Warmen. He eyed his father, his lips tight, face seething.

"I said *go back!*" Renagi bellowed, nearly shaking the boy from his horse. With this final command the Warlord turned, heeled his stallion and galloped toward the main gates. The six Warmen followed.

Zato sat motionless, watching the seven men vanish into the thick woods and heavy mist.

Yeon 983
Shuree Forest
Vokane Province

Tegné retained his half-lotus posture, not more than a single pace from Tabata. Their light, upper-level breathing was synchronized in the slight chest movement. Tegné had not reached the transcendental state, yet through this daily practice he had begun to feel traces of the freedom it held. Tabata had begun teaching the boy the classical asanas, stretching postures accompanied by breath retention and control. When Tegné's body reached a level of flexibility, enabling him to sit comfortably in full lotus for two or more hours, Tabata introduced the practice of contemplation. At first, objective contemplation; the quiet, focused study of nature. The study of a single oak leaf, the reason for its structure, the method by which the organism sustained life, drawing water and nourishment from the earth, transmitting the digested food throughout its intricate system of veins and capillaries.

Tabata used the objective contemplation to develop Tegné's powers of concentration. Then, when the boy had naturally begun to link the external world with his own body, when he had begun to understand intuitively his own part within the whole, Tabata had directed the contemplation inward. He urged Tegné to feel the beating of his own heart as it sent blood, carrying nourishment, through his own veins. In time, Tegné realized he was also connected to the forest, and the forest to the Earth, a small part of this gigantic living organism. He recognized the nature of his human condition, the smallness of his self, and the greatness of the Earth's spirit. Tegné had begun to attain that most essential quality, humility.

Tabata had given the boy a simple mantra, a phrase which, when repeated continuously during the deeper contemplative state, led to the brink of true meditation. The mantra began with the boy's name, "Tegné," repeated over and over until the name became merely a word without connotation, a single star in a galaxy of stars. As soon as this state was achieved the mantra was altered. "I am a wave, make me the sea," repeated until his mind was without thought or emotion. Tegné hovered here, on this plane, feeling the beginnings of the transcendence.

They are the sacred circle,
The Seven Holy Spirits,
They are the Primal Virtue.

Tabata was in Vakos, deep within the vision. He had come to know his dream men as the Protectors. Now he was able to commune with them, breaking the ties of Earth, to soar through the void and find them. Guardian spirits. They waited, guided, made him understand. Gave him the strength to witness the black, satanic body as it rose from the vapor. To gaze into the eyes of the Beast. Swirling chasms of darkness, windows which looked into the heart of evil; mirrors which reflected the hidden horror of every mortal soul.

One moment without form, the next a compelling fantasy. A

woman, a feline. Exquisite in grace and movement. Captivating. Enticing. Drawing one closer. Encompassing. Deadly. And just as he could stand no more, just as he was willing to be drawn toward this dark power, to surrender, the Protectors were there. Encircling, shielding, helping him to accept the gravity of his own role in their ancient struggle. Making certain he realized the truth of the prophecy. For the millennium was near an end, and the Seventh Incarnation was imminent; the seed of the Beast was to be manifest on Earth. Manifest in the form of a female, a daughter.

Without sorrow, without attachment, Tabata felt his own frail mortality, realized his time was short, and understood more clearly than ever the importance of the young man who sat before him.

"I pray that I have taught him well, prepared him for what is to come," Tabata whispered.

"I thought you had stopped breathing," Tegné cajoled, as his Sensei's eyes opened.

"One day, perhaps, but not today," Tabata answered, a fine warmth in his voice.

Tegné looked with love toward his teacher, feeling the deep calm produced by the two-hour meditation.

"Are you beginning to find the way?" inquired Tabata. Tegné looked puzzled. "Through your meditation and your practice of the Empty Hand," Tabata said, becoming more specific.

"Yes," Tegné answered simply.

"And can you tell me the way?" Tabata asked, using this quiet, internalized state to build a firm intellectual understanding of his lessons.

"It is freedom from emotion. No anger, no passion, no violence. It is clarity; the same clarity in meditation as in Empty Hand," Tegné explained, sure in himself.

Tabata smiled, urging the boy to continue.

"The punch, the strike, the kick, each of the movements is an exercise in perfection, awareness. Each; when performed with an unclouded mind, leads directly to our center, finding strength in our source," Tegné continued.

Tabata listened, allowing the words of his pupil to fulfil him. "And in Empty Hand, what is the meaning of victory, of defeat?" he asked softly.

"There is no meaning, Sensei, both are illusions, clouds before the eyes. The meaning of Empty Hand lies only in the perfection of self," Tegné answered.

"Do you experience fear during your training, during your meditation? Are you frightened of death?" Tabata centered on the word.

Tegné sat still, quiet. Finally he replied, "Yes, Sensei, I am . . . Yet, I will not allow my fear to prevent me from pursuing my path. I will move on in spite of it, until fear, too, vanishes like the clouds of thought and emotion. The way is to rise above, both during meditation and Empty Hand."

Satisfied, Tabata stood, motioning for the boy to join him. Together they walked to the center of the clearing, and stopped in front of the unlit meditation candle.

"And do you understand, Tegné, that the same power, the same source which takes life, is also able to give life?"

The Sensei drew his right knife-hand back far behind his right shoulder. He hesitated, allowing Tegné to ponder. Then, as understanding dawned in the young, blue eyes, Tabata brought the knife-hand smoothly, sharply across the wick of the candle. As quickly, he withdrew his hand and relaxed, smiling.

Tegné gasped, nearly disbelieving what he saw. The unlit meditation candle flickered into life, the flame burning full and bright.

They had been riding for eight hours. The horses were tired and the Warmen wondered if Renagi would ever call a halt to this journey. Since leaving the gates of Zendow, the Warlord had not spoken, had broken gallop only when the forest was too thick or the terrain too rough to push his stallion onward.

Tanak had never seen his master in such a state. He observed the tension in Renagi's neck and shoulders . . . *Surely, one pathetic slave claiming to be a Royal heir is more deserving of scorn than fury*, he reasoned, maintaining the appropriate twelve paces behind the Warlord. *The man seems possessed . . . God help the Ashkelite when he finds him . . .*

Tanak's thoughts were disrupted by Renagi's sudden slowing of pace. He brought his mount to a trot, the five Warmen behind him doing the same. Renagi sat still, then turned in his saddle and signaled them to approach.

"Tonight we will camp here," he said. "In the morning," he

pointed to the Warmen outside of his circle, "you three follow the narrower, less traveled route. If you should come upon him, bring me the head, the right wrist and hand. I understand this bastard may be tattooed." He extended his own wrist, displaying the Sign of the Claw. "Do not fail."

Morning. Arton, Herok and Zanar were making little progress. They had departed at dawn, determined to find the Ashkelite. Each knew their success would guarantee seniority amongst the Warmen. Yet, within two hours of beginning their ride west along the narrow dirt trail, barely wide enough to trot single file, the underbrush had become dangerously thick, the trees full and the stony ground impossibly uneven.

Zanar, the archer, Herok, the swordsman, and Arton, the grappling master, rode forward in silence. The trees were gnarled, thick; they stood proudly, as though the passing years had made them wise, and now they mocked these impudent human creatures who possessed the audacity to penetrate their darkness. The remaining leaves completely blocked the sun, creating an unnatural coldness to the air, and the trail was now little more than a narrow furrow created by the recent autumn rains, treacherous with sharp rocks and crumbling earth.

Finally, the three Warmen dismounted, and each led his horse forward.

An hour later, Arton spoke, breaking the long, tense silence. "I say we turn back, catch up with the others, this is leading nowhere."

"And how do we explain that to Renagi?" answered Herok. "We were lost, the trail was too difficult?" he asked sarcastically.

"There will be *no* turning back." Zanar's words settled the discussion; he was the senior Warman of the three and the responsibility rested with him.

Dusk came, and they were tired, hungry and cold. Herok had taken the lead, point position. The ground was soft and wet, still he increased his pace, sighting the small area of flattened scrub less than twenty paces ahead. He pushed himself forward, tugging at the reins, dragging his horse with him in spite of its neighing protests. Herok had just touched the outer edge of the small clearing when he stopped, bent down and picked up a small piece of timber.

"Someone has been here!" he said, excited, urging the others forward. He held the small, burnt log under his nose, sniffing the freshly charred wood. "This fire was recent."

Suddenly, all feelings of hunger and fatigue vanished. The hunters, having scented the prey, felt vigor return to their bodies.

"Tonight we stay here, no fire, no noise; in the morning we find them," Zanar said.

Quietly, the three Warmen unsaddled their horses, then used the thick woollen saddle blankets to wrap around their shoulders as they unpacked their field rations and prepared for a long, cold night.

Less than five leagues to the west, Tabata sat in sei-za, tuned to the unsettled movement of the forest. Tegné lay close by, curled asleep near the rising warmth of the evening wood. Tabata looked at the fine young face. Tegné's waist-length golden hair lay across his upturned shoulder and then fell back, cascading on to the pine needles which lay upon the forest floor.

Still, he is so vulnerable . . . thought Tabata as he watched the boy's calm, even breathing, . . . *and to know what is expected of him* . . . Tabata allowed this moment of sentiment for the young man who had been his adopted son. Then he refocused his energy, entered the state of zanshin, and resumed his mental preparation for what lay ahead. He had sensed danger in the air for the past three days. It was not the instant, quick danger of a hungry wolf or prowling bear. This was danger of another kind, a dark foreboding, heavy with the finality of fate.

There will come a time; you will know in your heart and your soul that your work is complete. Prepare for this time, do not let circumstances catch you unawares, or all you have done will be lost. They had been the Elder's words. Again, Tabata looked at the sleeping boy. *So much I would like to tell him, so much I can never tell him.*

As if he could sense Tabata's thoughts, Tegné stirred, nearly waking, then lapsed back into sleep. *Yes,* thought Tabata, *fate is the hunter.* Again Tegné stirred. This time, Tabata shifted his mind position, entering the peaceful void and allowing the young man to sleep.

Sunrise . . . not one Warman had slept more than three hours. The noises of the forest and the knowledge of human life so near kept their defense mechanisms high. They had waited silently and impatiently for the first break of day. The ground was cold, a frost had formed, and the thick horse blankets had been a poor substitute for a roaring fire.

Zanar was the first to speak. "Not another night like that . . . we find him today and we get out of here, then it is finished."

Midday. The autumn sun was exceptionally warm, the frost had evaporated and the earlier, morning mist was gone. A light, westerly breeze drove the small, scattered nimbus clouds through the blue sky. Tabata had not slept, the feeling of danger was strong.

Tegné was an arm's length from him, leaning over, picking the bitter marjoram leaves from the tall, pink-flowered plant. Tabata reached out, intending to adjust the small sack slung across Tegné's shoulder. His hand stopped dead as it entered the icy void surrounding the boy.

"Caw, caw . . ." Instinctively Tabata withdrew his hand and looked to the sky. The huge black hawk, its wings spread, hung motionless, its body obscuring the sun. Tabata watched the giant bird circle once, twice, three times, then silently disappear, vanishing into the light.

A time when your work will be complete. Pay heed to the signs . . .

"Tegné, come here," Tabata said gently.

Placing the last leaves into the sack, Tegné straightened up and walked toward his Sensei. He had noticed a subtle change in his teacher these last few days. The change was difficult to explain; Tabata's manner had grown more serious, the twinkle in the old man's eye had been replaced with perhaps a touch of sadness. Tegné had wanted to ask if there was something troubling him, but he did not. If his Sensei wished to confide in him he would.

Tegné stood facing his teacher. He was nearly as tall as Tabata, and he looked searchingly into the deep brown eyes. For a long moment there was silence between them, then Tabata took the "Sign of the Brothers" from his own neck and placed the leather thong, which held the circular disc, with its silver quarter moon and single gold star, around the neck of his pupil.

Why is he doing this? I have never seen him without the Sign of the Brothers. The medallion is part of him . . . Why? Tegné questioned, without voicing his thoughts.

At last, Tabata spoke. "Many yeons ago I left the temple of my brothers. I came to this forest alone. I had a mission."

Something in Tabata's manner, in the weight of his words, made Tegné pray his Sensei would stop, take back the medallion, wipe this moment from his memory.

"To save you from the river, to train you, to be a father to you . . . Tegné, you were my mission . . . now our path together is near an end."

Tegné could hold back no longer. Sorrow burst within his heart, and the questions began to form again on his lips. The questions that had long burned inside him, the questions he could never ask.

"Why, Sensei? Why have you never told me of my parents or where I came from, why you have trained me? Why was I your 'mission'?"

The words hung clear and motionless in the space separating the Sensei and the boy. Tabata stood still, his eyes locked on those of his student. An impenetrable wall surrounded him. Tegné turned his head down and away, ashamed.

Finally, Tabata spoke. "I have not because it has been forbidden me to do so. You have been unable to ask because I have hardened my heart to you before the question could so much as leave your mind. Now, for this moment, my heart is open to you. And still I cannot reply. Yet I will tell you, there will come a time when you will know. And I command you, ask no one these questions. Trust. Wait. For time holds the answers."

Tegné raised his head, saw the compassion in the eyes of his teacher. He recognized the love, yet there was more, much more inside those dark eyes. There was an acceptance, a final acceptance. *Is it death?* Tegné wondered.

"Our spirits will never part," Tabata said simply. Then, as if in afterthought, he looked again at the medallion. "Follow the Light of the Moon . . . remember, the Light of the Moon."

The trail had widened, allowing Arton, Zanar and Herok to mount and ride their horses. Still, they had moved slowly, cautiously, not wanting to give warning of their presence.

Arton was first to notice the trampled path branching off from the main trail and leading into the dense forest. With a shrill whistling signal he drew the attention of the other Warmen. Then, dismounting, he pointed at the flattened grass and underbrush.

Now the strict military training of the Warmen took hold. Zanar, immediately in command, signaled for the horses to be tied, and the men to proceed armed and on foot, no voice communication between them. He crouched low to the ground and examined the footpath. It was well worn and about one pace wide, no clear marks of heel or shoe prints. Zanar used his hands and fingers to explain in sign language; the path had been used frequently and by two people. The grass was bent, yet not broken, indicating the bare feet and trained, sure movement. The most recent indentations showed the length of stride to be about one pace from toe to heel, probably two men of between five-foot-five and five-foot-nine in height and ten to eleven stone in weight.

Two men—exactly what we have come for . . . he thought as he motioned for Arton and Herok to follow him. Silently, in a state of alertness, the Warmen tracked their prey. The sun set, and the full moon began its rise.

Tegné sat cross-legged, staring at the placid, closed eyes of the Sensei.

Time holds the answers . . . The words danced and played on the still surface of his mind. The incident of the medallion had come and passed, and now Tabata insisted again on the usual ordered routine of meditation, Empty Hand training, rest, food, more training and meditation. *As if nothing of any importance has happened,* thought Tegné. Yet, the medallion hung around his neck, its fine metal alive in the light of the moon. And his teacher sat in front of him, close enough to touch, yet present in physical form only, for Tabata's mind and spirit had gone beyond. Finally, Tegné closed his own eyes and tried to control his drifting thoughts.

Tabata was in Vakos. The seven ethereal, white-robed and hooded men beckoned him, guided him and, as his finer astral form floated close to them, they urged him to gaze into the turquoise flux of their eyes, to gaze into infinity, allowing Tabata this final, calming preparation for what was to come. Only the thin, glowing, silver thread extending from the crown of his head prevented Tabata from forever leaving his coarse, restricted Earth body. Only this fine thread and the latent knowledge that his Earth karma was not yet complete.

Tabata's first awareness as he returned to conscious function was the unnatural stillness of the forest. He brought himself rapidly to zanshin. His eyes remained closed as he concentrated his energy on the sporadic warning cries of the owl. Then silence. Tabata opened his eyes and spoke in a low whisper, "Tegné, Tegné."

Tegné looked up. What was his Sensei doing now? He *never* interrupted a meditation.

Tabata anticipated the boy's reaction. "Be still, don't speak," he whispered.

Tegné kept his body motionless, allowing his eyes to search the perimeter of the clearing, looking into the dark, forest.

"Very quiet, like death," Tabata's words were barely audible.

Tegné recoiled. In response, Tabata reached toward him, firmly and reassuringly gripping the boy's right forearm and wrist, the wrist which bore the mark of Renagi.

Tabata breathed in, a long, deep breath, as he moved his eyeballs high in their sockets, employing his night peripheral vision to scan the perimeter and surrounding trees. He made out the black silhouette of a man climbing upward into the thick-branched beech tree about thirty paces to his left. He did not allow himself to linger on the man, but quickly shifted his focus to the rustling sound in the underbrush directly ahead.

The thought, *Keep the left covered, defend to the front* . . . flashed through Tabata's mind as Herok, his katana high above his head, exploded from the forest. In one sweeping movement, Tabata rose from sei-za, at the same time pressing down with his right hand, forcing Tegné lower to the safety of the ground.

There was a look of surprise, even shock, on Herok's face as he watched the old man flow like liquid before him. Then he felt the paralyzing pain as Tabata's thrusting heel pushed deep into his groin.

Herok collapsed screaming, the katana still gripped in his left hand. Struggling, the Warman rose to his hands and knees, and just managed to shout, "The boy! Take the boy!" when Tabata's instep crashed into the upper ribs near his heart. His last image before losing consciousness was of Arton's lumbering charge, as the wrestler caught the old man and hoisted him into the air.

Drop him, drop him . . . give me room to shoot, willed Zanar, poised on the thick branch, his wide, steel-tipped hunting arrow loaded and drawn.

Arton could feel no movement. The old man was apparently dead. He was about to squeeze once more, to be sure, when he felt the heat, so hot that he could not bear Tabata's body near him.

Arton released his grip, and Tabata slid to the ground, continuing the Dragon Breath as he rebounded, bringing his head up under the wrestler's jaw, driving hard, forcing Arton's head backward, momentarily exposing the vulnerable wind pipe. With his right spear-hand, Tabata struck a percussive blow, breaking his larynx. Arton collapsed, choking for air. Tabata pivoted, his eyes searching for Tegné.

The boy stood four paces behind him to his left. Tabata recognized the glazed look in Tegné's eyes; fear, paralyzing fear. He was about to call out when Zanar released his arrow. The spring-loaded war-tip opened upon entry, fanning out against the flesh and gristle of Tabata's chest, thudding through his rib cage below his heart. The Sensei's final command of "Go! Run!", intended for the boy, was caught, blocked in his throat. Tabata sank to his knees, the unspoken plea trapped in his eyes.

Tegné's legs carried him toward his Sensei while his mind screamed for him to run, to leave this nightmare behind.

On the other side of the clearing, Herok had recovered enough to go for the boy. He lurched forward unsteadily, his arms raised high, the katana between his hands.

Tegné had just reached Tabata's body. He gripped his Sensei's shoulders, trying desperately to lift him. With a supreme effort, Tabata turned his head upward, his eyes meeting the eyes of his student. Suddenly the Sensei's face was old and drained of color.

"Please, no, don't die. No . . ." Tegné's tears had just begun when Herok began his lunge, the katana held before him, the curved blade aimed straight at the center of Tegné's back, between his shoulders. *Straight through and into the heart.*

As if in answer to his spoken prayer, Tegné felt Tabata's body tense, as if he was about to stand. Then, with an unexpected jolt, the Sensei swung his right arm in a cutting motion, slamming the forearm against Tegné's thigh. Tegné was flung to the left, in time to see Herok's sword sever the extended right arm and shoulder of his teacher. Blood spurted in a fountain of red, and Tabata groaned as he fell face forward.

Tegné turned on Herok, raging against him. The Warman released his grip on the katana, leaving the blade buried deep in Tabata's flesh.

"I'll tear the head from your shoulders!" He vowed, enraged that the boy was still alive.

Behind the Warman, Tegné was certain he saw Tabata move, attempting to crawl toward the Warman's foot. Tegné prepared for the inevitable charge, sinking into a low stance. Yet as Herok fully faced him, his eyes wild with the intent to kill, Tegné felt his spirit give way. He stared at the Warman as a condemned man might stare at his executioner, accepting the inevitable outcome of their clash—death.

It was then that Tabata reached out and grabbed Herok's ankle. Herok spun around on him. "Yaaa!" the Warman shouted, kicking savagely at Tabata's face, shattering the old man's nose. Tegné's fear broke inside him.

He sprinted for the thick of the forest and into the night, his screams continuing inside his mind.

Zanar fumbled with the arrow, cursing out loud as he watched the boy disappear. Quickly, he climbed down from the branch and walked into the clearing.

The swordsman could hardly meet Zanar's gaze, so great was his humiliation at allowing the boy to escape. Together, the Warmen examined Arton's body. Blood ran from his mouth, down his chin and across the black leather of his tunic; his windpipe had been crushed. Zanar looked once more at Herok, shook his head and turned toward the old man.

Tabata lay on his back, the arrow embedded in his chest. Herok's katana lay on the ground beside him, next to Tabata's right arm. Herok stepped scornfully on the outstretched hand of the severed limb, bending to retrieve his sword. Carefully he drew the blade between his thumb and forefinger, to clean it as he reinserted the steel into the wooden lining of his scabbard.

Strange . . . There is no blood on the blade, he mused.

"We get the horses, find the boy," Zanar said, interrupting Herok's thoughts. "There is no going back!"

They had reached the edge of the clearing when some strange, inexplicable feeling made Zanar turn and look back. His hand shot out, gripping Herok. Both men froze.

How can this be? Herok's mind reeled.

"It is impossible," Zanar answered aloud.

The decomposition of Tabata's body was already in its advanced stages, the skull and rib cage fully exposed. Dumbstruck, the Warmen watched as the robes and skin flaked off, blew upward, funneling into a shimmering spiral, rising into the night sky. Within seconds, the spot where Tabata had lain dead was empty. No blood, no clothes, no trace of the Sensei. Herok stared, glassy-eyed. "God of Light, deliver me from Satan," he prayed.

Tabata's ki-ai broke the spell, rolling from the heavens like thunder, causing the ground to vibrate where the Warmen stood.

"Come on! Move! Now!" Zanar's command snapped both Warmen to their senses. They turned and ran from the clearing.

Tegné covered the first two vul easily. The running had dispersed the adrenaline inside his body and numbed his fear. He maintained a rhythmic pace, following the trail west. He knew the Warmen would pursue him, yet he still clung to the dirt path, not wanting to enter the forest and lose the guiding light of the moon. He remembered the fallen man screaming, "The boy! Take the boy!" His mind searched for a reason; why, why did they want him? Enough to kill and to die. Yet on top of this another thought plagued him. *I have been a coward. A coward in the face of battle. I abandoned my Sensei.*

Mind like water. Mind like water. Tabata's words overrode his anxieties. Now, of all times, he must be clear, calm. *No negative thoughts. They will drain you, make you weak.* Again he heard Tabata's voice as he quickened his pace, keeping to the trail, following it down, toward the low, treeless plain. He hesitated, looking ahead. He knew if he continued forward he would be completely exposed, an easy target.

Follow the Light of the Moon . . . The words seemed to float next to him. He was running full-out by the time he hit the bottom of the trail. Now the ground began to rise gradually and the fleshy bulk of muscles covering the front of his thighs started to burn.

Too fast, I am moving too fast, he told himself. Still, he knew they were coming. Closing. Mounted, riding . . . he could sense the heartless beat of the hooves against the earth. He could not slow down; he would push on until he found that place inside himself where no limits existed, no pain . . .

Run . . . run . . .

Zanar checked the trail; he was relieved to find the footprints running in a consistent direction west, not varying in stride, giving no indication of intent to alter course. Herok rose in the saddle, trying to keep his bruised testicles from the uncomfortable contact with the hard leather.

Zanar remounted, looked once at Herok and spurred his horse. The stallion leapt forward. Herok followed.

This was a chase, the road was wide, the ground dry, and the moon full and bright. Zanar and Herok raced along the western path. Minutes later they arrived at the wide, open plain. Zanar raised his open hand, signaling a halt.

Both men stretched high in their saddles, scanning the clear ground ahead. Zanar's lips parted in a satisfied smile, his heart began to pound. For, directly in front of them, not more than six hundred paces, he saw the small, running figure; the golden hair glowing like some incandescent halo in the light of the moon.

Now we have him, Zanar thought.

It was then that Tegné looked back and saw the dark, mounted silhouettes. Watched the horses spring to life, surging toward him. Ahead, perhaps a hundred paces, a sharp rise led into a thick patch of woods. He willed his leaden legs to move faster, to climb the last hill. He was near the top, gasping for breath, pulling the grass and roots with his hands, slipping, struggling.

"There! There!" Herok shouted above the thudding of hooves, pointing toward Tegné as the boy crawled into the thick underbrush. "There's no way out, just the valley behind!"

"Circle right, I'll go left, then we close on him," Zanar commanded.

Tegné lay face down on the earth, grateful for this moment of rest. Slowly he pulled himself to his hands and knees, breathed in, aware of the aroma of the dry, autumn leaves. He felt them shroud him, protect him.

The Plane Beyond

Time: Synchronous

The Protectors sat in a circle, legs folded beneath them, spines erect, hands joined. Father began the chant, a low hum originating in his diaphragm. Filling the space before him with a dense, textured joining of molecules which grew visible to his eyes.

"Aoum, aoum, aoum," the six joined in, concentrating on the center point, causing the vortex to form. Father felt the dangerous drain of vital energy as the seven continued the "aoum," forcing the vortex to harden, to take the coarse form of the first vibration, the Earth plane. Finally, as their shimmering, etheric bodies grew faint from this combined loss of prana, they saw the young, finely chiselled face materialize; tired, frightened blue eyes, long golden hair. The Protectors would watch Tegné closely now, as they prepared for their descent on to the Earth plane. Tabata had done his work; theirs was just beginning.

The patch of forest was thick, causing the Warmen to dismount, moving on foot from opposite directions, toward each other across the moist, uneven ground.

Herok's eyes adjusted rapidly to the limited light as the moon filtered through the skeletal branches of the tall trees. *Like hunting a rabbit*, he thought. It was then that the idea formed in Herok's mind . . . *Concealment . . . patience. Let him come to us . . .*

Tegné moved quietly, hugging close to the trees. He breathed long, even breaths, calming himself, turning all senses inward, listening. The forest was still, no birds, no animals. *Very quiet, like death*, Tabata's words warned him as he searched the trees and underbrush with his eyes. Nothing, no movement . . . then he noticed the flicker of light from beneath a bush ten paces away. The light flashed, then was gone, the bush flapping downward. A fox? A rabbit? Tegné was uncertain but for one thing; the lair would give him protection, a place to hide until nightfall. He crept cautiously across the small clearing and bent over the bush. Gripping it below its barbed leaves, he pulled it toward him.

Herok sprang from his crouch, driving his heavy fist into the boy's frontal bone, below the forehead.

Tegné was unguarded, completely unprepared, and the punch caught him flush, sending him reeling backward. He collapsed onto the ground as Herok jumped from the shallow hole, drawing his katana and rushing toward him.

"Wait! Wait!" Zanar shouted, leaping from the thick limb of the elm and running to the fallen boy. The archer squatted down, rolled Tegné over and pulled back one of the closed eyelids. A sarcastic smile parted his lips, "You did not kill him . . . A perfect shot, and you did not kill him."

Herok saw no humor in the observation. "Then perhaps he will feel his right wrist as I cut it slowly from his arm," he retorted.

Zanar backed away as Herok bent over the boy's body and pulled the arm out to the side, laying it straight on the ground.

Yes, he will feel it, thought Herok, aware of the dull, thudding pain in his own swollen testicles. He raised the cold, steel katana, allowing the blade to hover above Tegné's wrist. He turned toward Zanar.

Zanar nodded "yes," and Herok brought the blade down, cutting slowly, lightly through the first layer of epidermis. Tegné groaned. Again, Herok drew the katana across the wrist, slowly, making sure the second incision was slightly deeper than the first.

The growl came from the rear, low and menacing. Herok looked quickly at Zanar.

"Finish, let's go," Zanar said.

Quickly, Herok raised the blade high, preparing to sever the wrist in one final cut. This time the growl was loud and close. Both Warmen spun round.

She was directly behind them. Each saw his own death in her red, burning eyes. Black, magnificent, she glared at them; her white fangs, long and pointed, shining wet with drool.

Herok knew what was coming, yet he was unable to move, mesmerized by this evil incarnate. He felt a sickly hollow in the pit of his stomach, mixed, somehow, with an extraordinary sexual excitement as she moved purposefully toward him, singling him out of the two.

She paused an instant, her hot, sulfurous breath bathing his face. Then, in one simple motion, she drew back her unsheathed foreclaw and swiped his head from his shoulders.

Zanar stood frozen, watching, motionless with horror. His mind screamed, *Use the katana, die as a Warman, use the katana!* Awkwardly and without purpose, he drew his blade. She waited, her eyes devouring him, then her huge, fanged jaws opened and closed, engulfing his head, shaking him, moving downward and crunching through the bone of his sternum and ribs, tearing his body in half. For a brief flash Zanar knew he had entered the bowels of hell; then it was over, and his dismembered torso fell to the earth.

Now she concentrated on Tegné, gliding toward the boy, gazing down into his vulnerable, unconscious face. At last she lowered herself to the ground, pushing close to him. She felt the desire build within her as she nuzzled him, licking him lovingly, her great, dry tongue massaging his soft, white neck. She heard him moan, felt him shudder as she took him gently in her jaws and carried him from the woods, down into the Valley.

It was in the Valley that the Protectors waited, using the last of their drained resources to take Earthly form. They stood, hands joined, as she carried the boy toward them.

She laid the body on the dry, sunburnt earth. Snarling, she held her ground, willing, at this level, to test their strength. Father stepped forward from the line; behind him, the six closed ranks, joined hands and chanted the "aoum." Father extended his right arm, the long, ivory fingers stretching toward Tegné. The thin blue arc began to form.

The Cat snarled, exposing her fangs. The beam inched forward, the chant grew in intensity, as slowly the blue arc encircled the boy's body, weaving Tegné in the warm, luminous cocoon. She watched as the healing shell formed. She could attack, rip savagely at the fibers, tear the shell, take the boy. She knew that on this plane her power was superior. Yet she watched and waited, permitting these fading guardians a last, hollow victory. After all, it was not the boy but the man she wanted, the warrior—the fulfilment of this golden-haired child.

She looked once more as the last blue fiber wrapped around the pale skin. Then, howling in defiance, she turned and leapt upward. The Protectors watched as the enormous black body vanished into the night sky.

Father walked forward and knelt beside the cocoon. Tegné lay, eyes closed, breathing slow, deep breaths. Father smiled, imagining the beautiful, multi-colored visions that flooded the boy's dream mind as the protective fibers vibrated gently.

"He is the one?" Kusan's mind transferred the question.

"She has chosen him," Father relayed.

"But he is a child," Kusan protested, his face and mouth motionless.

Father concentrated on the gold and silver medallion, the symbol of the Brothers of the Moon. "He will be trained. Then he will return. Yes, he is certainly the chosen one."

Renagi, Tanak and the two Warmen followed the trail west; they found no sign of human life. Finally it narrowed, leading them to the high, western precipice overlooking the desolate Valley. Nothing.

At this point, Renagi decided it was best to retrace their route, pick up the tracks of the secondary party and join them in hope that their search had been more fruitful. The deep hoofmarks were easy to locate. They led through the dense forest and into the encampment.

Arton's body remained where he had fallen. A thick cluster of flies and black forest ants were at work inside his open mouth and hollowed eye sockets.

"Bury him, quickly!" Renagi ordered the two younger Warmen, then turned toward Tanak. Their eyes met; no words were necessary.

"Tanak and I will ride on. You can catch up with us when you have finished," the Warlord said.

The tracks led out of the forest and onto a hard dirt path. Due east. It was nearing sunset when Renagi and Tanak arrived on the outer ridge overlooking the wide, open plain. They sat a moment, surveying the land ahead.

"Use the magniscope," Renagi said.

Tanak pulled the long metal tube from his saddlebag; he sat high, pushing with his boot heels into the stirrups of the shining leather saddle, his back and neck straight as he snapped the scope open. Lifting the instrument, he adjusted the calibrated handle to level four, and aimed the viewfinder at the horses' prints directly ahead. The locking device anchored and the thin, silver mercury in the lens below pointed toward the rise.

Tanak snapped the magniscope shut and turned toward the Warlord. He was about to speak when the thunder of hooves caused both men to start.

The two younger Warmen galloped up the hard path toward them. Tanak waited until they reined in their horses, then he turned, raising his hand, pointing. "There on the rise," he said as he indicated the high mound of earth leading into the patch of wood. "The boy must have tried to lose them in the bush."

No sooner had he finished than Renagi spurred his stallion, galloping ahead. Tanak and the others rode close behind.

An uneasy, indefinable feeling gripped them as, cautiously, they dismounted and made their way through the giant elms and along the uneven forest floor. The red, setting sun was hidden amongst the dense branches, and a cold chill penetrated their body armor. They formed a semicircle, keeping visual contact as they spread out, moving forward.

"Master . . ." It was Nicon, the youngest Warman, whose voice broke the quiet. He stared at Herok's severed head; it lay facedown in the dirt. The skin where the head had been ripped from the neck was lacerated, the jugular vein hanging shrunken and white.

"Light a torch . . . Now!" commanded the Warlord.

Tanak struck the firestone, and ignited the thick sulfur stick. The foul, pungent smell filled the air as the group converged on the clearing.

The rest of Herok's body was six feet from the head, the visible skin a bluish gray, drained of blood. The remains of Zanar were close beside it. He had been cut cleanly in half, and only the lower body could be found. Renagi sensed panic. "Look for the boy . . . Look for the boy," he repeated, stern, not allowing his own anxiety to surface.

"What could have done this, Warlord?" Tanak whispered as

the group, keeping close together, scoured the ground.

"A bear, a tiger maybe . . . Do not dwell on it, find him," the Warlord answered, equally unnerved by the unnatural ferocity of the attack.

Five hours later, they had searched every inch of woods, pushing on until they reached the jagged rock edge, the sheer drop below them. It was nearing midnight. The full, yellow moon hung heavily in the sky, and the warm, dry wind blew up from the Valley.

Finally, reluctantly, Renagi turned to Tanak. "Nothing, nowhere . . . he is gone. Gone."

The senior Warman saw the terrible anguish etched deep into the Warlord's face. Renagi's eyes were vacant, his skin waxen in the moonlight. Then, something new and uncertain shone in the dark, slanted eyes.

Is it madness? wondered Tanak as Renagi spoke again, low and guarded, "But, by God, I will find him. He cannot hide from me forever. I will find him . . ."

V

THE TEMPLE

The ancient masters were subtle, mysterious, profound,
responsive.
The depth of their knowledge is unfathomable.
Because it is unfathomable, all we can do is to describe their
appearance.
Watchful, like men crossing a winter stream
Alert, like men aware of danger
Courteous, like visiting guests
Yielding, like ice about to melt
Simple, like uncarved blocks of wood
Hollow, like caves
Opaque, like muddy pools.
Who can wait quietly while the mud settles?
Who can remain still at the moment of action?

(Lao Tsu)

Brothers Yon and Unsu found the young man lying unconscious at the edge of the Valley, below the twin-peaked mountains. The Elder had provided them with the directions, exacting and precise. Their instructions were to find the boy and to ensure that he arrived safely at the Temple.

Now, as they knelt beside the body, both were fascinated by the long golden hair and the pale, smooth skin. For the province of Lunan was populated by a dark-haired, swarthy people, and the Temple was the frequent recipient of their unwanted children, placed outside the gates in hope that they would be accepted, adopted and raised within the Brotherhood.

"Blue. His eyes are blue," Unsu whispered as he gently lifted the lid of one of Tegné's closed eyes.

"I can find no wounds, no serious injuries," Yon concluded, discontinuing his superficial inspection and turning toward Unsu.

"What is this?" Unsu questioned, pointing toward the thin, pink scar which ran across the top of Tegné's right wrist, directly above the birthmark.

"An old incision?" Yon mused, then added, "The scar is faded, the cut healed," as he ran his thumb lightly across the line.

"And he is breathing quite normally, I just do not understand why he is unconscious," Unsu continued, bending close to Tegné's left ear. "Wake up, wake up. Can you hear me?" Unsu spoke quietly, so that if the words did take effect they would not frighten. "Wake up, wake up."

Tegné's face remained placid, without expression.

"It is no use. I will prepare the litter," Yon said, already beginning to unfurl the coarse hemp-cloth body sling. He inserted the twin wooden carrying poles and, together, they lifted Tegné on to the cloth.

"He is heavy," Unsu noted.

"Well developed for one so young," Yon agreed, looking down on to the hard flesh visible through the separation of the robe covering Tegné's chest. "Perhaps the leather thong around his neck is causing him discomfort," he added, as he bent and lifted the single braid of leather. "How could we not have seen this?" he exclaimed disentangling the medallion from where it had fallen to the side of Tegné's neck.

Unsu knelt beside Yon and both men stared at the shining disc, identical to those discs worn only by the three senior Brothers of their Order.

"I do not understand," Yon said.

"Nor do I," Unsu answered.

Then they lifted the carrier from the ground and began the long trek down from the mountain rise and to the plain below.

The ride from the Valley was slow, and Unsu and Yon stopped regularly to gauge the condition of the young man, still unconscious, whom they dragged behind on the low flat-bedded cart.

"The Elder must have known of his condition, that is why he insisted we brought the litter," Yon reasoned as he rolled easily in the saddle, over the bumps and ridges of the dirt road. "Surely, when we reach the Temple, he will tell us what is behind this mystery," he concluded.

Yeon 983

Temple of the Moon

Lunan Province

The Elder did nothing to lift the shroud of secrecy. Instead, Yon and Unsu were thanked sincerely and deeply for their arduous trip to the ridge of the Valley. Then the unconscious body was briskly lifted from the cart, covered with a warm cotton shawl, and transported to the far reaches of the remedial quarters inside the Temple complex.

"What is your name? Your name? Your name?" The voice was soft, lilting, washing over him.

"Tegné," he answered, as gradually his eyes focused on the unfamiliar face before him.

"Tegné, Tegné . . . From the raging water," the voice replied, satisfied.

The face was a perfect oval, with small, deep-set brown eyes shining from smooth, bronzed skin. The head was without a trace of hair except for the single, thick, silver braid which hung down below the narrow shoulders. The nose was not protrusive, but rather flat, its width only marginally less than the full, pink-lipped mouth beneath it.

Not a single wrinkle in the skin, Tegné observed fleetingly. Yet it was not a young face, in fact the gentle eyes seemed ancient wells of wisdom. Somehow they reminded Tegné of his Sensei, Tabata, and in that instant the recollection of the Warmen and the death of his Sensei caused him to recoil; he pulled the white cotton sheet closer to him.

"Good! Good!" exclaimed the Elder, placing a dry, cool hand against Tegné's forehead. "Release the cerecortex," he instructed the attending physician.

The physician, a tiny man, his body swathed in a linen gown and his face masked in similar material, bent and removed the thin silver needle from the point on Tegné's forehead directly between his eyes.

Tegné felt something give way, something heavy but at the same time intangible. He was aware of the wetness of his eyes before he realized he was crying.

"Release the meridians," the Elder ordered.

Through his tears, Tegné could see the thirty-six needles which outlined the periphery of his body and extended all the way to a point in the center of each foot. The physician whisked the needles from his flesh, dropping them into a flat wooden box beside the mat.

"Acupuncture. Clearing the system. Allowing the ki to flow," the Elder explained as he sat beside Tegné on the mat and cradled him in his arms. "It is quite natural to have this emotional release. You have been through a great trauma. But you are safe now," he continued.

Tegné felt foolish, small and humiliated at his display of emotion. Still, he could not stop. Images of his Sensei, the love, the lessons, the patience, the compassion, flowed through his mind. He knew somehow where he was; this was the Temple, the original home of Tabata, and in that realization he knew at once that his childhood was past, over and gone. Gone with the Forest of Shuree. And now he was alone.

An hour later the tears subsided and Tegné sat up on the cot, the Elder, cross-legged, beside him. The physician had departed shortly after the onset of the tears, realizing his work had been successful and that privacy was the next requirement.

"Welcome to the Temple of the Brothers of the Moon. I am the Elder Brother."

"Tabata, Sensei, is—" Tegné began.

The Elder raised his hand, halting the final word. "I know, I know—no longer of this Earth."

"How can you know?" Tegné asked, awed by the serenity of this tiny man and by the grace with which he spoke.

"I know because you are here, because it is all in the correct order of events," the Elder answered.

"Correct order of events?" Tegné repeated. *Does he also know that I abandoned him? That I am a coward?*

"Yes," the Elder answered, as if reading his mind, his tone suddenly clipped, his eyes narrowing and his lips tight. His entire demeanor changed in that single moment, and again Tegné was reminded of Tabata, the stern teacher and disciplinarian. And Tegné understood immediately that this diminutive man was not a man to be questioned, that there was tempered steel behind the glowing eyes. Tegné nodded, silently.

"As soon as you are able, I want you to begin training in the Dojo," the Elder said, again warm and friendly. "You will be an uchi-deshi," he added.

Tegné had never heard the term "uchi-deshi," and the puzzlement showed on his face.

The Elder smiled. "Uchi-deshi means 'special student.' An inside student. You will live and breathe only to train in Empty Hand. You will eat and sleep within the confines of the Dojo and you will study with Yano Sensei. No distractions. One thousand days," he explained.

"Thank you, Elder." Tegné accepted the gift, feeling uncertain as to its implications but aware of one thing: now was not the time to question or resist, now was a time to adapt, and move with the natural flow of circumstance.

Yano Sensei was a big, gruff man, perhaps ten years younger than Tabata; he had, in fact, been one of Tabata's assistant instructors when Tabata was Grand Master of the Temple.

Tegné felt truly dwarfed as he bowed for the first time to his new Sensei. Yano nodded in return and extended his hand, indicating that Tegné should present him with the hand-written note of introduction from the Elder. Tegné stood just under five-foot-eight, and Yano was easily half a head taller, six-foot-two or three and seventeen stone in weight. His head was large, even for his enormous body, and as near a perfect square as was possible for a man's head to be. It reminded Tegné of an iron-worker's anvil, dark, hard and unforgiving.

The eyes were mere slits in the flat face, and Tegné could barely discern their brown-black color as Yano scrutinized the brief letter of introduction.

"Uchi-deshi, uchi-deshi." Yano rolled the words off his tongue as if he found them particularly distasteful. "You?" He looked up, giving a single, sweeping glance over Tegné's body. "A gajiin, an outsider?"

Yano was making no secret of his aversion to the blonde-haired, blue-eyed stranger whom he had just been ordered to guide in the Way of the Empty Hand. "Tegné." Yano pronounced the name as though it were a fatal disease he had recently contracted. "I will tell you now what you may expect in this Dojo, and what I will demand from you. You will report to me each morning at the sixth hour. You will be attired in a training gi, a white sash and bare feet. From here we will leave the monastery by the eastern side gate and run along the dirt road away from the Temple. We will run for one hour. You must never run ahead of me, but stay within a single body-length behind. If I set a fast pace, you follow. If I run slowly, you run slowly. Do you understand?"

"I do, Sensei," replied Tegné, bowing.

"We will return to the Dojo where you will perform three hundred pressing-up exercises, three hundred sitting-up exercises and three hundred squatting movements. When I am satisfied with your progress in these simple forms, I will instruct you in the use of the power stones, the chikaraisha. Then we will begin basic blocking, striking and kicking. And each day we will practice sparring exercise." Yano went on, the words coming in staccato bursts from his thin, stretched lips. "There are three classes each day for students of the Dojo. Each class is two hours in length. You will attend every class. I will also expect you to train alone for a portion of each day. In all, at least ten hours every day. You will be personally responsible for the cleaning of this Dojo, the floor, the toilets, and you will be at my call for any other duties I wish performed."

Yano took in another breath in order that he could continue. *He will never stop, never*, Tegné thought as he turned his head from Yano's piercing eyes.

"Face me, face me!" Yano barked, his voice sharp and coming from deep in his belly. Quickly, Tegné snapped his head up and met the burning gaze.

"Never move your eyes away from me when I am speaking," Yano said. Then, without waiting for Tegné's acknowledgment, he continued, "On the third, fifth and seventh day of each week you will, between the second and third training session, be tutored in speaking and writing skills. On the evening of the sixth day you will dine with the Elder in his private chamber. There you may discuss your training and your progress. One thousand days." Yano searched his new student for the first sign of doubt.

One thousand days, Tegné repeated in his mind. The knowledge that he would be twenty yeons when he emerged from this apprenticeship began to overwhelm him.

"One thousand days." Again Yano said the three words, observing that their weight hung visibly on his student's shoulders, "and when you have completed your training, you will have accomplished what an ordinary student accomplishes in twenty-five yeons," he finished. Then, strangely, he bowed to Tegné.

Tegné instantly returned the courtesy as a thin, tight smile formed on Yano's lips.

"Now I am going to kill you," Yano said quietly.

And as the sharp, unexpected front kick crashed sickeningly into his abdomen, Tegné was certain that Yano meant it.

Renagi waited alone beneath the cluster of stars cut into the domed stone ceiling of his pleasure room. It was the twelfth full cycle of the moon since his return from the ill-fated search party.

He listened closely for the footsteps along the long wooden corridor which separated the main living quarters of Zendow from these private chambers. Finally, he heard the sharp clicking of the cleated heels which accompanied the soft, padded steps of slippered feet.

Renagi stood up from the bed. He could hear the muffled male voice outside the door; he could not make out the words but he heard the gentle female voice answer, then the cleated heels walked back up the passageway and their sound disappeared. Slowly, the brass handle turned and the door opened.

She stood a moment, framed by the light of the torches in the corridor, then her eyes adjusted and she focused on the Warlord. He remained motionless in the center of the room.

She steeled herself, quieting the doubt and nerves which threatened to make her turn and run back up the passage and away from him. Then, in a movement that required all of her theatricality, she let the shawl slip down, away from her shoulders, and at the same time removed the dark veil from her face.

She is good, very, very good, Renagi thought. He felt the first warmth in his testicles as the blood began to concentrate in his groin. "Take off the dress."

She maintained her position in the far corner of the room, except now, confident of his acceptance, she closed the door of the chamber. Then, turning to face him, she unfastened the crude ties of the heavy muslin dress and let the yellowed material hang open on her body. She wore nothing beneath.

She could see him clearly now in the center of the room, his wide leather belt loose and his hands working to unbutton the front of his trousers. He was already naked from the waist up, and his torso appeared solid and powerful.

She knew by instinct not to approach him; instead, timing her movements with his own, she removed the muslin dress, tossing it beside her, then kicked the red velveteen slippers from her feet. She looked directly at him, her excitement having little to do with his aroused nakedness. No, her excitement was caused by her sheer ability to manipulate this great and feared Warlord, by her own inner strength and her capacity to overcome the initial terror of entering this pleasure chamber. She stood still, statuelike. She knew what would come next; she had performed this rituallike routine ten times previously and always it was the same. Now was the critical time; she must not move.

Yes, look at her . . . the whiteness of the hair, the pink of the skin, the full, rose-petal nipples . . . Renagi thought as he moved his hand down along the line of his abdomen and into the thick hair beneath his navel. 'Turn, turn to the side,' he whispered, his voice deep with sensuality.

She turned, drawing her shoulders back slightly, raising her full, hanging breasts, giving them a jutting appearance. Her nipples were just beginning to rise.

"Good," said Renagi, his hand now gripping his penis, rubbing slowly up and down the shaft. "Now walk to the bed."

Walk to the bed, she repeated the command to herself. He had never asked her to walk to the bed before, she knew the body paint and false hair would not bear up to close scrutiny.

"Come, Maliseet, come to the bed," Renagi insisted.

Maliseet? That was not her name. Who was Maliseet? What was happening?

Guarded, carefully, she walked to the bed, standing as far away from him as possible.

"Lie down," he said, staring at her. She did as she was ordered, knowing that the thin layer of oil-based paint would stain the quilt. She knew enough not to speak, not to voice the questions that had begun to fill her mind.

She tried to relax her tightening muscles as he crawled toward her, hovering above her spread legs. She affected a low moan of pleasure as he lowered his head between them and began the tentative licking of the now-dry orifice below the trimmed, bleached line of pubic hair. She pushed her hips up, forcing herself into his mouth as every fiber of her begged to pull away, to escape. It was as if he was tasting her, nibbling to see if he found the taste inviting, preparing to consume her.

She wondered if the crudely fitted hair-piece had slipped or become dislodged from her head against the hard pillow, but dared not raise her hands to find out. She had begun to perspire from nervousness, and she could taste the grease from her face-paint as it rolled in tiny beads from her upper lip. She kept her eyes locked tight, willing her body to respond to his probing tongue.

"Maliseet," he whispered.

She heard the name again as she felt his hot breath against her face and smelled the stale, heavy scent of red wine. Still she kept her eyes closed.

Now he was directly on top of her, his bare chest pressing into her breasts while his right hand fumbled between her legs, trying in vain to guide his suddenly flaccid penis into her dry opening. She reached down, finding him with her own hand, hoping to revive him.

"No! Maliseet would not do that!" he shouted, and the spittle from his mouth landed on her painted cheeks.

She opened her eyes. Even by the light of the moon she could see that the Warlord was crying. She withdrew her hand. She was trapped in this terrible moment and uncertain as to whether comfort or ignorance was the correct response. She remained quiet, still.

Awkwardly, Renagi disengaged himself from her and got to his feet. "That will be all. Tell Wang I will not require your further visits," he said, his voice filled with a sad defeat.

Relieved, she rose from the bed, rushed to the door and picked up her dress.

He did not watch as, quickly, she put the costume back on, wrapped the shawl around her body and up over her head, turned, and left the room. The door remained open, and the torchlight cast flickering shadows across the floor and onto the stained quilt.

Renagi left the palace by a little-used passage. He walked purposefully from the secluded grounds and toward the sector of private dwellings. For it was in this sector that Natiro lived, and it was this strong Zendai woman whom he sought.

The time was nearing the third hour when he climbed the low, wide stone steps which led to the leaded glass door of her elegant, two-storeyed dwelling. There were no guards in this private sector; there was no real necessity even to lock one's door. For there was no crime in the private sector of Zendow.

Renagi closed the door behind him as he entered the hallway. A single torch remained lit, and he used its light to find his way to the servants' quarters on the lower level.

The servant woman was awake, lying on her back upon the low, narrow cot. Her eyes reflected the light of the wall torch, and they reminded Renagi of a forest doe, caught in the beam of the flame; frightened, aware, yet protective of her young. It took only an instant for the old woman to recognize the Warlord, and when she did she leapt from the bed and onto her knees, kissing the bare boards of the floor.

Rehind her, Renagi saw the glint of steel from the short-pointed dagger, left undisturbed beneath the bedcovers.

"Wake your mistress. Tell her I am here and wish to see her," Renagi said.

The old woman rose from the floor. She was clad in a coarse cotton nightdress, and the material dragged against the wide oak boards as she shuffled from the room.

Renagi followed her as far as the staircase, then veered off into the large, paneled reception room. He sat down on the padded, high-backed seat with its two raised armrests. The seat was covered in soft, black leather, and was ornamented with shining brass studs, each embossed with the Royal sign. It was a totally masculine piece of furniture and it reminded Renagi of the first evening he had come to be entertained in the new house. All the surrounding furniture in the forty-by-thirty-foot rectangular room was of a soft, feminine design. Exquisitely carved, hard black lacquered tables and chairs, the work of the carver so intricately joined that it was impossible to imagine that each of the pieces was not cut from a single block of wood. Only in the far eastern province of Miramar could one find this craftsmanship, and the hard, shining wood from which it was created. The seats of the high-backed chairs were padded and covered in the palest of blue silk. The beautifully matched furniture surrounded a large, square, gold-and-blue silk-threaded carpet. It was instantly apparent that the black leather and brass-studded seat, although flawless in design and workmanship, stood out conspicuously. Yet Renagi had known at once that the seat was his own, placed in the house by Natiro, in honor of her Warlord.

He placed his right arm on the armrest and pressed his back into the soft leather.

Natiro was soundly asleep when the quiet voice called her name.

"Natiro-Mis, Natiro-Mis." Natiro opened her eyes.

"The Master, Mis, the Master. He waits for you," Darya continued.

"Now? The Master? Where, Darya, where is he?"

"He waits in the room below us," Darya answered.

"Light the torch. Prepare my bath. Use the lemon oil, and leave my mauve robe on the bed. Do it quickly, Darya, then tell the Master I shall join him shortly," Natiro replied. "Thank you, Darya," she called after the small, white-haired woman as Darya scurried to prepare the bath.

Natiro rose from the bed and slipped the sheer nightgown from her shoulders. The gown fell behind her as she walked across the room, to face herself in the full-length mirror. Her bedchamber was south-facing, and the light of the moon shone through three large, leaded windows.

Natiro was thirty-five yeons. She had been twenty when she had given Renagi his heir, Zato. A single child was the custom of Zendai women; it was known that after one child the body would return to its former state. Three children, four children; that was for the lower caste of women, the breeders, who reproduced until their sagging, distended stomachs resembled the flesh of cattle.

Yes, Natiro was Zendai, dark and pure of blood. Her father, Rakeen, had been chief military advisor to Renagi's father. It would have filled Rakeen with pride to know that his daughter had given the new Warlord his heir, and that his grandson would one day be Warlord of Zendow. But Rakeen was gone, passed into memory.

Hard to imagine that I, too, will grow old and sleep away, Natiro mused as she viewed her naked body in the reflection of the mirror. In the soft light she could see no difference between the tight, bronzed flesh of the reflection and her recollection of herself as the twenty-yeon virgin who waited nervously, alone, in the chambers of the Warlord. Her breasts were not large, and that had proved advantageous as she matured, for they still sat high and firm on top of the delicately muscled rib cage beneath the wide-boned, sculpted shoulders. The nipples were full and brown, and Natiro smiled as she remembered the Warlord's delight in their responsiveness to his warm, rough-skinned fingers.

She could hear the water running into the porcelain bath as she turned side-on to the mirror. Her belly was smooth, and ran flat down, protruding only slightly just above the pubis. The slight protrusion was, in fact, very much desired, as it displayed just the hint of opulence and again maintained the distinction between the Zendai women and the poorly fed working caste of female. The black hair of her pubis stood out long and thick. She ran her hand through it, drawing it farther out and upward. Zendai men loved their women to have a full thatch; it was the ultimate sign of fertility, and was known to cushion the ride to the heavenly plane. She had certainly not disappointed Renagi in that respect, for his ride was accompanied by deep groans of pleasure and, upon the release of his seed, she also had felt rapid, unexpected contractions. She was certain then that she had conceived. And, true to her intuition, Zato was born nine months later, the Royal heir.

The bath water had ceased to run, and Darya was just emerging from the chamber, a towel in her hand.

"Will you require your back sponged, Natiro-Mis?" Darya questioned.

"No. No, Darya. I am going to be very brief. Our Warlord has been forced to wait long enough. Just place the robe on the bed, then go to the reception room and attend the Warlord until I arrive."

Renagi had been an infrequent visitor to the private sector of Zendow since installing Natiro in this strong, stone-built house nearly fifteen yeons ago. Perhaps eighteen or twenty times he had appeared, usually in the depths of night. Yet, Natiro was always available to him, that was tradition. On his initial visits she had presumed as much as to insert the thin protective membrane into her vagina, offering a discreet protection from an unwanted pregnancy. Yet, with one exception, it had not been her sexual favors that Renagi sought; it was, instead, her considerate conversation and unpatronizing opinions as to matters of state and the general governing of Zendow. Natiro felt deeply honored to be privy to this confidence.

The idea of the protective membrane did not cross her mind as she wrapped the robe around her body, glanced long into the mirror, then turned and walked from the room.

Renagi rose to his feet as she entered through the arched door. He held a goblet of Miramese red wine in his left hand. Darya was quick to appear behind her mistress.

"May I bring Mis a glass of wine?" she asked.

"No, Darya, I will not be taking any wine. You may go back to your quarters. If we should require anything further, I will ring for you."

Darya smiled and bowed, then departed, leaving the Warlord and Natiro alone in the large room.

"How very thoughtful of you to honor me with your visit." Natiro spoke the words sincerely.

"It has been a long time," Renagi said, avoiding her gaze.

She sensed his vulnerability; perhaps it was in his posture, somehow wounded, pleading. She moved closer to him, softly touching his arm and guiding him to his leather seat. He permitted himself the indulgence of her attention, yet instead of soothing him she seemed only to confirm his weakness.

"I am sick. Sick inside," he confessed.

Natiro sat beside him, gently touching his thigh. "Sick? I do not understand. My master appears perfectly well."

"It is a sickness of mind," Renagi answered.

Natiro controlled her urge to move back, to pull her hand from the Warlord's thigh. Instead she sat still, morbidly fascinated by the sunken black of his eyes. The eyes seemed to her, suddenly, to resemble the hollow, lifeless holes in the rough, elasticated masks she had known as a child; the masks that had once been used to cover the face of someone recently dead. Their purpose was to frighten and dispel any evil spirit which might attempt to take possession of the Earth soul during its transition to the other side.

But the masks were of the past, and Natiro swore inwardly at herself for falling prey to this childish fantasy. The Warlord was here, now, because he needed her; she would certainly not deny him comfort. Yet the look of death still showed in his hollow eyes as she lowered her head and moved closer to him.

Renagi sighed as she nestled under his extended arm. The arm folded around her and his hand rested gently on her right bosom. She felt his lips nibble the scented skin of her neck.

"Shall we go to my chamber?" she whispered.

"Yes," he answered.

There was no urgency to the Warlord as he removed his clothing and laid it on the chair beside her bed. Naked and unaroused he stood as Natiro removed the robes from her body. She did not excite him physically, yet at the same time he knew that she was the epitome of Zendai womanhood, and for this he admired her; for the breadth of shoulder, the long, almost muscular legs, the hirsute pubis, the high firm breasts, the cascading black hair, the strong, wide face and large brown eyes. His observation was becoming clinical when Natiro broke the mood by performing a perfect dancer's pirouette, spinning round in the moonlight and landing to face him with a wide, playful smile on her lips.

"Very good! You would have made a fortune in Wang's," Renagi said, suddenly joking. Already he was beginning to feel refreshed, and the memory of the tainted scene, earlier in the evening, began to fade.

Yes, this is how it should be. A Zendai man and a Zendai woman, he concluded, brushing against her naked flesh. *This is proper, the natural order*, he confirmed as he felt the surge in his penis.

There will be no time to insert the membrane, Natiro realized as his hardness grew against her inner thigh. *I must not break the moment. Perhaps it is not my time of the month anyway . . .*

He entered her caringly and the ride to the heavenly plane became a slow, steady joining of souls.

Tegné had integrated well into the formal classes of the Dojo. At first the other young men had stared blatantly at his golden hair, blue eyes and light skin, but within a few weeks of the exhaustive training no one so much as gave him a second glance.

Even Yano had come to like his gajiin uchi-deshi, particularly admiring the quiet, accepting fashion in which Tegné had endured his initial beating. The Dojo Sensei was equally impressed with the depth of knowledge and the level of technique that the young man already possessed.

Yes, Tegné is certainly a tribute to the former Grand Master, Tabata, thought Yano as he watched his uchi-deshi duck and shift below a face-level thrust during the closing moments of a kumite session. He smiled. Tai-sabaki, body evasion technique. That was his contribution to Tegné's mastery of Empty Hand. How often in their private sessions had he charged his student like an enraged bull? And once Yano started, he would not stop. It was speed, and speed alone, that saved Tegné. Until, finally, the young man had learnt the special methods of avoidance, to duck and weave, to spin and to slide.

As for Tegné, it was at first a matter of pride. Many times he felt like crying out with the anger and frustration of one who must confront an insurmountable objective day after day. At times he felt his spirit weaken, almost giving in to the spirit of this relentless teacher. Yet, he did not break, and eventually he realized that through his absolute and determined resistance he was growing, both as a disciple of Empty Hand and as a man. He realized that Yano Sensei was carefully and patiently ordering these changes within him.

That realization was the turning point, the point at which he halted his negative thoughts, heretofore directed at Yano, and began to work positively with his new Sensei. He began to love and respect this tough Dojo master, and through this changed attitude his Empty Hand took on a deeper level of meaning.

Achieve results
But never glory in them
Achieve results
But never boast
Achieve results
But never be proud
Achieve results
Because this is the natural way
Achieve results
But not through violence
Force is followed by loss of strength
This is not the Way

That which is against the Way
Comes to an early end.
(Lao Tsu)

Tegné had finally begun to overcome the anger within him; and accordingly his Empty Hand was fluid, without violence.

"The gonads play an extraordinary role in extracting and concentrating vital elements from the whole body. They produce the replica of the man himself, and they instigate the sexual urge through which the creative hunger of man is satisfied," Master Goswami began amidst the muffled sounds of laughter coming from the back of the large, mat-floored lecture hall.

"The testicular hormone plays an important part in influencing muscular development and strength. It helps to maintain the heart and stimulates the blood-making organs," Goswami continued, turning a sharp eye to the cluster of young men at the back of the room. Tegné was conspicuous on the far left of the line. Goswami temporarily halted his lecture.

"Excuse me," he said, pointing a long, bony finger toward the general area of the disturbance. The thirty or so younger, preadolescent Brothers who occupied the mats toward the front of the hall sat stone-still, averting their eyes and praying that Goswami would spare them this humiliation. For Goswami hated to be interrupted during one of his lectures.

"You. Tegné," Goswami continued, homing in on his target.

Tegné felt the first red flush of embarrassment as he cleared his throat. "Yes, Master Goswami," he replied, suppressing a perverse desire to laugh caused by a combination of pure discomfort and the secret nudge he was being given by a fellow Dojo disciple.

"Perhaps you would be so kind as to step forward," Goswami commanded.

There was another choked outburst of laughter from the back as Tegné rose from his cross-legged position.

"Now," Goswami continued as Tegné slowly made his way through the quiet, seated students toward the front of the class, "we shall continue our discussion on the topic of gonadal control." Goswami hesitated, clearing his throat. "The first stage of control is the process of ejaculation," he stated, eyeing the class for any fresh signs of unrest.

By now, Tegné, still flushed, stood beside the tall, angular instructor and in front of the fifty apprentice Brothers. He was careful not to meet the eyes of his peers in the back line, knowing that a further show of misconduct would only increase his punishment.

"One of the first measures we must take in the control of both nocturnal ejaculation and our desire . . ." he hesitated again, scanning the guilty faces, ". . . for manual relief is to release pelvic congestion. There are no better exercises for this than the inverse act and head posture. Today, Brother Tegné will demonstrate the correct procedure for maintaining the head posture. In fact, he will maintain the posture for the duration of this one-hour lecture."

Then, turning to Tegné, Goswami nodded toward the hard, straw-matted floor.

"Please assume the position," he said, kindly.

Tegné knelt down, both heels raised, his body bent forward, fingers interlocked. Then, supporting his body on his forearms and head, he raised his trunk and hips until they were almost perpendicular to the floor. Finally, he lifted his legs until they were in a straight line with the raised trunk and hips.

"Fine, fine," said Goswami, admiring the posture for a moment before turning back to address the attentive group before him.

"The main questions are these. Do the sperm cells retained in a living state within our bodies produce any substance which has a specific influence on the revitalization of our minds and of our bodies? And, after their death, are these sperm cells reabsorbed, thus supplying us with precious materials which may be utilized in the construction and reconstruction of the body? The answer, in both circumstances, is 'yes.' "

Goswami carried on, looking from face to face, "Sexual control is the key to vigor. The spirit of continued struggle, the power to concentrate not only physical, but mental and emotional energy and the ability to awaken dormant powers; all these are directly associated with sexual control."

With this, Goswami turned his attention to Tegné. "It is not an easy matter to prevent the waste of the fluid. The fluid supplies certain chemicals to the blood. These chemicals provide a proportion of the sexual urge and desire, the other proportion being incited by imagination and association. And when imagination is strengthened by experience, it becomes extremely difficult to harness this creative force. Control can only be achieved through the combination of specific exercises and blood-purification regimes."

Goswami knelt so he could look into Tegné's face. "The exercises include the abdominal posture exercise, the spinal posture exercise, the pelvic posture exercise and the abdominal and pelvic control exercises. But first, as I mentioned earlier, pelvic tension must be relieved, and that is what brings us back to the head posture." Goswami smiled, "Do you feel a relief of tension, Brother Tegné?" he asked, noting the reddening in the pale skin of Tegné's cheeks due to the inverse flow of blood.

"Yes, Goswami Sensei," Tegné answered effortfully, his head feeling crushed against the straw mat. The head posture was not new to him, but he rarely held the position for more than one hundred slow breaths. Today, he had already lost count of his breathing and was now just grimly maintaining balance in the uncomfortable posture. Goswami's face loomed above him and Tegné could detect, through eyes nearly forced shut by gravity, a faint smile on the kundalini Master's thin lips.

Goswami was not native to the Province of Lunan. He was, in fact, discovered by the Elder living in a tiny monastery nearly two thousand vul to the north of the temple, high in the Himilak Mountain region where the air was reputedly so fine and thin that travelers, unused to the altitude, would often succumb to seizures of the heart before their respiratory systems could adjust to the lack of oxygen. The Elder had visited this Himilak temple during a sojourn from his own monastery, and was so impressed by Goswami's display of absolute physical control that he beseeched the Yoga Master to bring his teachings to the Temple of the Moon. Goswami accepted the invitation, and shortly after his arrival in Lunan he provided the Brothers with a demonstration that had since become legend.

In the main courtyard of the Temple, before all its occupants, Goswami had assumed the position of the perfect lotus, his spine erect, his right knee bent and the foot in position against his groin, the left knee and foot in an identical corresponding position, both heels close to the abdomen. Both his arms were extended, his hands placed on his knees.

At this point the Elder had stepped forward and instructed two monks to assist him in blocking Goswami's nostrils with hardening wax. His mouth was similarly sealed, after those close enough to him had witnessed the retroversion of his tongue, thus completely blocking any possible breathing channels. The Elder and his assistants then wrapped Goswami in linen and placed him in a wooden box. The box was closed and locked for all to see. Finally, to the horror of the onlookers, the box was lowered into a six-foot hole, which had been dug into the soft ground of the courtyard. The space above the box was then refilled with earth, barley sown upon it, and the area enclosed by a wall of stone. The Elder ordered round-the-clock surveillance of the enclosure, two Brothers at a time, in six-hour shifts. No one disturbed the box.

There was a certain sardonic humor concerning this strange monk who had appeared after such a long and lonely trek from the Himilaks, lived amongst them for only seven days and then had himself buried in the courtyard.

On the fortieth day the Elder had sounded the giant brass gong, summoning all the Brothers into the courtyard. The box was unearthed and everyone present was encouraged to examine the lock and investigate for any signs of tampering. Satisfied, they opened the box.

Goswami, still clad in the linen wrappings, was found undisturbed in the lotus posture. Once the wrappings were removed, the temple physicians examined the body—there was no pulse, no breath, no external sign of life. Even Goswami's shaven face remained clean, no new hair had grown.

The Brothers were nodding sadly at the futile death of this peculiar man when the Elder walked from the crowd. Bending over the seated body he smacked Goswami soundly in the chest, below the heart. Again he thumped the patch of bare skin with the cushioned palm of his hand. Simultaneous with the second impact, Goswami's eyes snapped open and, like a newly delivered child, he gasped the breath of life.

The Brothers stood silent, believing they had witnessed a miracle as the Elder massaged Goswami's limbs, enabling him to unfold from the lotus position. Finally, the Himilak monk stood before them.

"You have not seen a miracle," Goswami said. "You have witnessed an example of the extreme endurance which my method of exercise and control has enabled me to perform." He then added, "My teacher lived to be two hundred and eighty yeons."

"Goswami's Miracle," as it came to be known despite his insistence to the contrary, had taken place nearly thirty yeons ago. Since that time he had remained at the Temple, teaching the Brothers methods by which they could awaken that vital energy, the kundalini, which, he promised, lay dormant within each of them.

The hour finally ended, and for the closing twenty minutes the entire class had maintained the strict head posture. At last, on the signal of Goswami's ringing prayer chime, the students had been permitted to return to a bent-knee position, and finally to rise and leave the lecture hall.

Tegné had remained on his hands and knees, resting, acutely aware of the dizzying rush of blood as it dispersed from his head and redistributed throughout his trunk and arms. Finally he stood up. He was alone in the Great Hall, except for Goswami.

"Tegné," Goswami called.

Tegné approached, sheepishly.

"Sensei?" he said, stopping and bowing.

Goswami smiled. "Almost all young men your age find amusement in this facet of my instruction," he said.

"I am sorry, Goswami Sensei," Tegné apologized.

"There is no need for indulgence in sorrow or guilt. As I said, it is quite a normal reaction. But that is not the reason for my talk with you now," Goswami continued.

Tegné looked up.

"These exercises in self-control, in awakening your inner vitality, will be of particular importance to you," he said. "You were, at one time, a pupil of Shihan Tabata, is that not true?"

He must know the background of all his disciples, the Elder must keep records, Tegné thought before he answered. "Yes, it is true."

"To have a teacher such as Tabata is a great gift. A fated gift."

"Yes," Tegné agreed.

"There is no need for Tabata's teaching and guidance to be discontinued," Goswami went on. "There are many planes of reality. Many finer, less coarse, vibrational states. Upon the demise of our Earth shell, our bodies, our spirit consciousness passes beyond into one of these finer states. Do you believe this, Tegné?"

"I do," Tegné answered without hesitation.

"If we harness our more basic and primitive desires, if we channel them internally, then we may, through deep meditation, form direct links in communication with those who have gone before us," Goswami said.

For a moment Tegné stared silently at the Master. "How long until I am able to achieve such a state?"

"Sometimes this heightened level of awareness directly follows a trauma of the mind and spirit. That can occur at any time. Enlightenment is spontaneous . . ." Goswami said, hesitating, studying Tegné, ". . . but rare. Practice diligently and you may reach this state in fifteen yeons."

"Fifteen yeons?" Tegné repeated, incredulously.

"Practice diligently," Goswami said, then turned and walked from the hall.

The Warlord now visited Natiro regularly. Perhaps once, even twice each month he would arrive at the elegant house and share food and wine with her. Renagi felt strong and centered when he was in Natiro's presence, and the recurrent attacks of anxiety that had plagued him until his renewal of their relationship had all but vanished.

It was during the fifth month of his visits that she told him she was carrying his child. She had been frightened to divulge this until now, fearful that it would make her less desirable or that somehow the Warlord would consider her pregnancy a device with which to draw him closer or control his feelings.

She was relieved, as if a great, oppressive weight had been lifted from her heart, when Renagi expressed his happiness at the coming of the child.

"A boy, a brother to Zato, that is what I want!"

As for Natiro, the idea of a second child had never so much as entered her mind until that night, nearly six months ago, when Renagi had taken her to bed. At the height of their ride to the heavenly plane she experienced the same strange contractions that she had known at the time of Zato's conception. It was then that she knew. Yet, she had pushed the premonition from her mind, denying its possibility, until her time of the month came and there was no blood. At first she had panicked, considering numerous methods of aborting the pregnancy. But finally she had accepted her condition. And now that Renagi had accepted it, she felt thoroughly justified. What did it matter if her body was no longer that of an inexperienced virgin? If only the coming baby would be male, her life would be fulfilled.

Renagi, also, had changed during the term of Natiro's pregnancy. There was a growing warmth to his manner, a tangible care and concern for this woman who would bear him a second child. His visits to the private sector became more frequent. And, in the back of his mind, the question burned, should he not insist that, after the birth, Natiro join him to live in the palace proper. After all, were love and acceptance not one and the same?

The labor began at midday. As soon as Natiro was certain that the spasms were not going to abate and that the delivery was imminent, she summoned Darya and Anyo, the younger of her servants. Darya had, in fact, delivered Zato, and knew the exact procedures to follow in preparation for the birth. She could also foretell, by the length between the spasms, that the delivery would not take place until well into the night. Thoroughly and methodically she stripped Natiro's bed of its fine sheets and replaced them with several layers of thick, absorbent cotton towelling. Then she saw that Natiro was properly attired in a loose, comfortable nightdress and her body supported by three firm pillows.

"A pot of camomile tea," she instructed Anyo, watching as the short, thick-legged girl ran from the room, anxious to perform admirably on this auspicious occasion.

"Are you in any pain, Mis?" Darya asked, turning again to Natiro.

"No, Darya, but I know he is coming. I can feel him moving inside me," Natiro replied, already sure of the gender as if the gods above would not fail her in this gift to the Warlord. "Darya," she continued, adjusting herself on the bed, rising up so that one of the pillows would slip further down and support her lower back.

"Mis?" Darya was already beginning the gentle, kneading massage to the muscles of the swollen, exposed abdomen.

"I want the Warlord to know that his child is coming," Natiro whispered.

"Of course, Mis. As soon as Anyo arrives with the tea, I will send her to inform the Warlord."

"How long will it be until the baby is here?"

"Ten, maybe twelve hours," Darya replied. "Now it is best if you relax completely, speak as little as possible and conserve your strength. I will take care of everything," she added, her voice becoming dreamy soft as Natiro began to breath in rhythm with the fine, caring massage.

Yeon 984

Asha 1

Slave State of Ashkelan
Vokane Province

Raine struck the two rough pieces of firestone, once, twice and again until the spark caught, igniting the tightly bunched ball of hay. The sharp yellow flames rose from the earthenware heat dish. Now she lifted the tapering yellow wax candle from the wooden work-top and held the new greased wick above the flames. The fire took hold and the single flame burnt bright, dancing wildly at first and finally settling into a strong, steady pulse of light. The hay in the heat dish burned to a crisp red, then extinguished, leaving the candle as the sole source of light in the tiny front room of the hut.

Raine sat quiet and still before the flame, her eyes picking out each of the subtle spectrum of colors from the rising heat, her mind drifting on waves, beyond the sadness, beyond the pain.

Eighteen summers. Eighteen summers since she had awakened to that deathlike emptiness. She remembered that morning as though it were her last; how she lay still on the hard, narrow cot, somehow certain that she was alone in the hut, yet too frightened of that reality to move. So she just lay and listened, hoping she would hear the sound of Maliseet's footsteps or the muffled whimpers of the hungry infant from the other side of the thin partition.

Finally, hearing nothing, Raine had risen and walked toward the dividing curtain.

Maliseet and her baby were gone. The cot where they had slept for the four weeks following the birth was clean and orderly, the space around it swept, tidy. A single cotton dress hung on the last of the metal hooks which were mounted in the wall above the cot. The dress was unwrinkled, yet the eggshell white of its material had yellowed with age. It had been Maliseet's favorite dress, her special dress, and Raine recalled the delight in her daughter's eyes as she had folded and stitched the coarse fabric while Maliseet had slipped in and out of the garment to ensure its perfect fit. Raine had fashioned the dress for her daughter on the eve of Maliseet's fourteenth birthday.

The candle flame flickered, and with its flicker Raine's mind was pulled back from this past memory and into the present. She stood up from the table and walked into the vacant bedchamber. The dress was still hanging on the hook above the cot. She had never touched, never disturbed the tiny room. Yet each yeon, on this eve of her daughter's birthday, she lit a single candle and kept vigil until the rise of the morning sun. Eighteen summers; Maliseet would have been thirty-four yeons.

Morning. A knock on the battered wooden door. Raine rose up from the table and walked across the room. It would be Rawlin, checking on her, seeing that she had food and water. Rawlin was the same age as her daughter, she remembered them both playing as children in the dirt road, and later going to work in the fields together. At one time Raine had hoped a relationship would develop between Maliseet and this tall, kind man. A relationship which could have resulted in marriage, but it was not to be. And now Rawlin, as a token of his respect for the past, had taken it upon himself to look after Raine. She was no longer strong enough to work in the labor parties, and her tight, stretched skin, which had grown even more sensitive with the passing yeons, would tolerate only the minimum of exposure to the sun.

As Raine unbolted the door, she shielded her eyes with her free hand.

"Are you well?" asked Rawlin, stepping inside the hut and closing the door, blocking out the light behind him. He carried a large wooden bucket of fresh well-water and a small sack of new potatoes.

Raine nodded and smiled. Rawlin thought he saw a strange, animal shyness in her red, tired eyes. He placed the bucket and sack on top of the wooden work table. It was then that he noticed the still-flickering candle, the stem melted and spreading in a wide, thick oval while the wick, nearly spent, balanced in the last of the hot, clear wax. He turned and met Raine's gaze. He had forgotten the day, and now he understood why she had seemed particularly guarded. He had interrupted the last minutes of a very private ceremony.

"I am sorry, Raine, truly sorry. I just did not remember," Rawlin apologized.

She smiled and nodded her reassurance.

"Stay. Eat," she said, enunciating the two words very clearly, yet speaking in the spare, tentative style of one unused to conversation.

"I cannot, Raine. Perhaps later I will stop back. I have promised to work the double shift today. There has been a great deal of sickness amongst the men recently."

Raine understood. "A great deal of sickness" was a gentle way of describing the carcinogenic blisters that ate through and ruined the unprotected skin of the field workers.

Yes, I certainly know all about that, she thought as she glanced quickly at the soft, pink skin directly beneath Rawlin's eyes. *Nothing. He is still clean*, she noted, seeing none of the first signs of rawness and chafing.

She stepped away from him, turning, looking at the water and the cloth sack of potatoes. "Thank you," she said, smiling again, releasing him with the two words, allowing him to leave her.

Rawlin fixed the blankers in place as he walked from the hut and up the narrow road toward the eastern fields. As he walked, he recalled the day those many yeons ago that he had stood in the door of the same hut, inquiring as to the condition of his friend, Maliseet. It had been common knowledge that Raine's child was unwell; in fact, she had been unable to work in the fields for over eight weeks. Most in Asha-1 were familiar with the story; she had been found wandering, delirious and badly overexposed to the ultra rays. There were others, just a few, who spoke of a single Warman, one of the men from the Procession, who returned to the village asking specific directions to the hut of the girl, Maliseet.

On that day, Rawlin still only sixteen yeons and strong with the certainty of youth, had vowed to discover the truth. After all, Maliseet was a member of his work party, a friend, and, in his heart, much more. For Rawlin had hoped to couple with her, to build and share a hut, to parent children. And he knew that Raine would not oppose him. So it was with this resolve that he knocked loudly on the door of their hut. He still remembered the protective glare in Raine's eyes as she denied him admittance, saying that her daughter was recovering, resting, and could see no one.

"But it is me, Rawlin. And I love your daughter," he had blurted out.

Even then Raine had closed the door on him, but not before he saw the spill of tears from her eyes. He had remained in front of the closed door, thinking that somehow it would reopen, that Raine would reconsider. But the door did not open again and, finally, belittled and saddened, Rawlin turned to leave.

It was then that he heard the distinct cry of a baby from within the hut. He spun round and, for an instant, intended to break through the thin door. Again, the cry of a hungry babe. This time Rawlin revolted, running from the sound, back toward the fields, confused and betrayed. And in his mind the voices began; the hushed gossip which he had ignored, the voices that claimed the girl had been raped, that the Warman who had sought her out was the attendant of the Warlord. Rumors. Maliseet was pregnant with the Warlord's child, an unpardonable transgression. The very rumors which, in their blasphemy of the pure state of Zendow, threatened every Ashkelite. And now Rawlin was recalling this deadly gossip, wondering, considering.

Two weeks later Maliseet had vanished, and the secret with her. For Raine would not speak of her daughter, never a word, until in time the conjectures grew faint and then, with Raine's continued introversion, all but disappeared.

But that was eighteen yeons ago, I was not much more than a child, Rawlin reminded himself as he neared the end of the dirt road. The path widened and grew less distinct as it merged with the sparse green of the low, rolling hills leading into the work fields.

"What is happening? I demand to know what is happening?" Renagi's voice was a gruff whisper.

He stood in the far corner of the bedroom. He had been there for nine hours, and now he watched the sweat bead and fall from Darya's forehead on to the padded white towelling, which was soaked and stained with blood. And still nothing. No child.

Natiro's eyes were closed and her head moved from side to side amidst her low, anguished moans. Darya worked frantically above the swollen stomach which was rapidly becoming bruised from the constant, no longer gentle, plying.

"The baby will not turn, Master, he remains sideways," Darya answered, controlling the panic in her voice.

"And Natiro? How long can she withstand?"

"I do not know, Master. It is already near daybreak," Darya replied.

The low, unconscious moans continued from the bed, yet the spasms from Natiro's lower abdomen were weakening, and the time between the contractions was beginning to lengthen. Darya had delivered countless children in the forty yeons she had lived in Zendow; she was the most experienced midwife amongst a host of such women. These women occupied an important place in a culture where midwifery was revered, for no physician could perform the birthing skills with such calm and dexterity. It was, in fact, these skills which won Darya her position as Natiro's personal servant, for Darya had delivered Zato.

Yet now, as she hovered over her unconscious mistress, a strange sense of ineptness swept over her. Her fingers could feel the child, the form outlined beneath the mother's flesh, yet there was something wrong, something unnatural in the shape and the position of the moving infant. And try as she might to manipulate its position, to turn the head downward in an effort to guide it through the passage from the mother's womb, the baby resisted, still lying transversely.

"Give her more liquid, more tea," Darya commanded the servant girl. The girl obliged by gently lifting Natiro's head from the pillow and pouring a tiny amount of the honeyed camomile and primrose mixture into her mouth.

Natiro's eyes opened for a moment and it seemed she was trying to form her lips into a smile. Then the muscles which had worked so hard in their efforts to free the unborn child began to relax.

And in that moment of relaxation the baby began its own desperate struggle. Tiny fists and feet pushed out against the strained flesh, causing undulating ripples in the abdomen. Darya tried with all her strength to turn the thrashing mass downward as Renagi dashed forward to the bed.

"Tell me what to do, I will help!" he shouted.

"Hold her legs! Firm!" Darya responded, and for a moment she forgot that it was the Warlord who obeyed her commands.

Midnight, eighteen hours later. They had failed. Natiro lay still before them, her dry, exhausted body breathing its last aching breaths. And, in watching her final struggle, Renagi came as close as ever he could to loving her.

Darya raised her face toward him, tears glistening in her old, tired eyes. She nodded. "It is over."

Then, with a heart as heavy as the stone walls of Zendow, Renagi drew his katana and sliced cleanly through the flesh of Natiro's stomach.

The unborn child lay still, on its side, next to the broken placenta. Darya bent down close to the tiny, motionless body, feeling with her fingers for the faintest beat of the child's heart.

"I am sorry, Master. The child, also, is dead," her voice breaking with sorrow.

The room was illuminated by two candles and Renagi's view of the child, lying amongst the blood and fluid of the open abdomen, was obscured by dark shadows.

"Is the child male or female?" he asked in a lifeless monotone.

Darya bent again over the gaping wound, her intention to free the baby from its mother. Her trained fingers cradled the tiny body as she lifted upward. It was then that she saw the reason for the transverse lie, the cause of death. For the long, hardened umbilical cord had wrapped like a suffocating serpent around the struggling child's throat, strangling it as it tried to turn in the womb. She lifted no farther, instead lowering the tangled infant back into the warmth of Natiro's flesh.

"Female, master, it is female," she said, but Renagi was no longer there to hear her. He had seen the child lifted in the candlelight; he had seen the broken neck, the smothered face. He had seen that the child was female. He walked alone from the house, into the blackness of the winding alleyways and toward the palace, its high walls outlined against the full October moon. And Renagi felt his final chance for salvation as strangled and dead within his own soul as the infant had been within the womb of the woman who had reached out to him.

Knowing others is wisdom
Knowing the self is enlightenment
Mastering others requires force
Mastering the self needs strength.
He who knows he has enough is rich.
Perseverance is a sign of will-power
He who stays where he is endures
To die but not to perish is to be eternally present.

Tegné moved the one thousandth wooden bead from the left to join the nine hundred and ninety-nine others on the long wire frame that formed the abacus. He stood up from the rectangular straw mat, six feet long and two feet wide, folded the single woolen blanket and placed it neatly on the upper end of the tatami. The mat had been his place of meditation as well as his place of rest for the duration of his "one thousand days." And today, like every day preceding it for the better part of three yeons, Tegné pulled the rough cotton trousers of his training gi up over his waist, tying the twin cords tightly before he pulled on the matching jacket and secured it with the heavy white sash. Then he walked from the small, cold stone room and on to the shining, polished, pinewood floor of the main Dojo. He stood alone in the empty space beneath the oil portrait of Grand Master Tabata.

How much this old wood has taught me, he thought, feeling the dry, smooth hardness beneath his bare feet. *How many times have I picked myself up from this floor, how many punches, how many kicks, how many press-ups, sit-ups? All absorbed into its mirrored surface.* And as he remained still, he could again feel the power of the wood seep into him, sending its strength through his flesh and into his heart. Finally, he walked to the far corner of the training hall. In front of him were more than one dozen wooden buckets, each half-full with well-water. Next to the buckets stood a fresh pile of cotton rags, cut large and square, of leftover material from the Temple workshop. He took two of the rags from the top of the pile, placing one in the bucket nearest to him. Then, wringing the rag until it was merely damp, he turned and knelt upon the wooden floor. He had performed this cleaning only nine hours ago, following the last of the three daily classes, and, of course, the floor had remained spotless. But that was neither the point nor the lesson of this morning exercise. For the solo cleaning was also the practice of humility and a chance for contemplation.

Tegné began the slow, circular, clockwise rub with the damp cloth in his right hand while his left hand dried and polished in a faster, counterclockwise rhythm. His forearms were thick and muscular where they emerged from the three-quarter-length sleeves of his gi: they seemed sure and strong, almost as if they belonged to someone other than himself, someone older and more powerful. Yet his whole body had developed in the same proportion, from the fine, smaller muscles which caused his feet to arch, able to grip the bare boards of the Dojo floor, to the more obvious pectoral muscles of his chest which added the breaking power to his hard-knuckled fists.

His body had matured and at the same time been educated. Even his natural way of movement had altered, his relaxed walk had lowered, his center more in line with his natural axis, causing a sure, steady gait with no raising or lowering of the head. And with the continued help of Goswami, Tegné had grown in tune with the original teachings of Tabata, lessons whose meaning was only now beginning to blossom and bear fruit. Yano was his teacher, but Tabata was his source.

In the beginning, during his first months as a "special student," he had resented being singled out, had even felt dishonored and blatantly persecuted, as if he was being punished for the color of his skin, his hair, his eyes. It was only after a dozen or more private meetings with the Elder that he realized this was not the case, and he had accepted the merits of his situation. He recalled the first time the Elder had requested that he talk about the ambush, and the murder of his Sensei, Tabata. It was a subject his mind had buried, his subconscious hidden beneath layer upon layer of protective shield. At first it was as if he was retelling a story he had read in a nearly forgotten book, the characters fictitious and vague in his memory. But the Elder had gone deeper, pushed, prodded and finally revealed the raw and open wound which festered deep within the young man.

The first tears were unlike those of the original awakening following the acupuncture treatment. For these were not the tears of release; these were the tears of terrible pain, suffering and terror. It was as if he had been forced back through the tunnel of time to what now seemed a distant life, and he was compelled to relive that single scene of his utmost anguish; the image of Tabata, the one person closest to his heart, standing alone in the clearing, his body suddenly bent, old, dying. And Tegné, unable to help, powerless, impotent, and yet somehow knowing that the death was intended for him. *A coward.*

"Continue, please. You are observing, you cannot be harmed," the Elder had said, his voice soothing behind the steady click of the metronome.

And Tegné had continued, his mind recalling details which even he, at the time, had been unaware of observing. Gradually, over a period of many of these painful analytical sessions, Tegné was able to work the pain from his mind until, finally, the most relevant and lasting image was of an etheric body of his Sensei, rising from the earth.

"There is no death," Tegné had said to the Elder at the start of a recent session.

"Good. Then you are free from the shock of the experience and there is no need to continue with our catharsis," the Elder replied, turning off the metronome.

"But, Elder, I am still troubled as to the cause of the attack," Tegné objected. "You see, the men who attacked us, they shouted, 'Take the boy, take the boy.' "

"And you remember clearly how these men were dressed?"

"No, Elder. It was at night and I could not describe their exact costume. It seemed a type of war armor, all black, with an insignia, a red insignia," Tegné answered. The Elder nodded knowingly.

Tegné observed the Elder's acknowledgment. "Who were they?"

"Members of one of the warring clans," the Elder answered, refusing to be precise. "Perhaps they mistook you for a runaway slave. You see, the slave class bears a similar coloring to your own."

"A slave? Are you suggesting I am the child of slaves?"

"At one time, Tegné, before the influx of the clans into the east, the slaves you speak of were a fine, pure race of people. It was only when the aggressive, conquering hordes invaded the territories surrounding Shuree that these people were bonded into slavery."

"Without a fight?" Tegné persisted.

"Of course they opposed their oppressors," the Elder answered, "but they were not a militant group. They had never needed to be. And the first thing the clans did was to murder their strongest males, leaving the weaker ones to continue the line. Finally, through a continual process of separating and destroying their dominant offspring, the clan created a state of slaves."

"And I am one of them?" Tegné asked, barely concealing his revulsion.

The Elder smiled, nodding his head. "Your eyes are blue, Tegné, your body is strong, and your skin can tolerate the sun. No, you are not a slave." Yet there was something vague, inconclusive, in the Elder's tone.

"Then who am I?" Tegné asked, and as he did so he unconsciously formed his right hand into a loose fist.

The Elder glanced at the fist, noticing how the thick surface veins, inflamed even by this mild gesture, carried a surge of blood through the bellied muscle of the forearm and through the vivid, reddish blue birthmark. Tegné, noticing the Elder's eyes upon his fist, quickly relaxed the hand.

"You are a disciple of the Temple of the Moon," the Elder concluded.

Still the dissatisfaction in Tegné's eyes could not be hidden.

"Your awakening will take place in stages," the Elder added. "Do not rush, for nothing is gained by violent movement, whether it be of the mind or of the body."

* * *

Your awakening will take place in stages . . . Tegné was beginning to understand just what those seven words meant. For it was a statement that many times passed from the lips of Goswami following his private tuition in the more advanced body postures or the higher levels of meditation.

And at last, through the use of mantra and the concentrated release of his mind, Tegné had reached the transcendental state; that state in which he hovered in the peaceful freedom of the void, behind the attachments of his Earth life, far from the intricate and complex circuit of characteristics that formed his personality, making him individual.

It was in this transcendental state that his true renewal took place, for it was there that Tegné tasted the sweet nectar of the Mother Spirit, and it was there that he breathed in the vital prana, the energy of the source.

And it was there, in transcendence, that the seven Protectors monitored his progress, guiding him toward their light. Waiting for him, just beyond the final veil, that last, thin shell of his understanding.

Goswami had been a powerful influence, and Tegné felt a deep sense of loss on the morning the Master told him of his intention to leave the Temple.

"But your place is here, with the Brothers," Tegné had reasoned, looking deep into the strange eyes whose pupils seemed in a never-ending flux of rapid contraction followed by dilation.

"No, no, Brother Tegné," Goswami answered gently, "I was born in the high Himilak Mountains, and it's there I wish to be when I depart this Earth form."

Tegné stood before the Meditation Master, his mouth wide with surprise, for in physical appearance Goswami seemed young and vital, his eyes clear and his skin smooth.

"Surely you cannot be speaking of death?" he asked.

"I have occupied this physical shell for one hundred and fifty yeons," Goswami stated calmly, simply, as if there was nothing strange in the figure, "And I feel it time to pass on to the next plane, to enlarge my knowledge before I choose my next incarnation."

* * *

True to his word, Goswami departed on a clear morning, one month later. He was bidden farewell by only the handful of Brothers who had been made privy to his journey. Tegné watched, saddened but none the less amused, as Goswami, barefoot and carrying the lightest of bedrolls, smiled jubilantly, waved like a happy child and began the treacherous trip of two thousand vul as though he were taking a mere walk to the well.

"Are you ready?" The words came as a stark surprise, pulling Tegné from his reminiscence. He looked up from his kneeling position, both rags still held in his hands.

Yano towered above him. The sensei was attired in the ceremonial hakama, the black divided skirt. His bare feet were a shoulder's width apart and his fists were clenched tight, hanging like mallets.

As Tegné dropped the rags and rose, his eyes again caught on the thickly calloused first and second knuckles of Yano's clenched fists. And just for a moment the recollection of Yano, standing side-on, urinating on the same bleeding knuckles flashed through Tegné's mind. It had happened after a two-hour session of continuous punching on the straw-padded striking-post, the makiwara. Two hours of repetitious striking. "Seventy percent impact on index knuckle, thirty percent on second. Then the result will equalize on contact," Yano had instructed. "The urine disinfects the skin, then hardens the surface."

Tegné brought his head up, his eyes linking with the thin, hooded slits below Yano's flat forehead. The whites of Yano's eyes barely showed.

"Oss, Sensei," Tegné said, bowing low before his teacher, aware of the taut, dangerous atmosphere in the Dojo.

"Today, last day in special training," Yano snarled. "Most important lesson," the sinister voice continued in its clipped, broken sentences. "Today I kill you," Yano finished, repeating his promise of that first day, one thousand days before.

Tegné looked into the wide, square face, drawn to the darkness of the eyes. There was death inside Yano's eyes, pulling him like gravity.

The first blow was a spinning back-fist strike, performed slowly and purposefully, as if to defy retaliation. Tegné should have evaded the attack. Instead, rigid with fear, he watched the back-fist smash into his shoulder. Followed by a foot sweep that lifted him nearly parallel to the floor, before dropping him to his back.

"Coward! You have no spirit!" Yano bellowed, grinding the knife edge of his foot into Tegné's throat. "You are frightened of death. Death is the ally of a warrior. Do you understand?"

"Yes, Sensei," Tegné struggled to speak.

"With fear there is inhibition. No flow, No spontaneity. You must die. You must accept death."

Yano removed his foot.

"Get up."

Tegné stood, certain that Yano intended to kill him. He glanced toward the door leading from the Dojo. *Escape* flashed through his mind.

Yano, detecting Tegné's lapse in concentration, slid forward and slapped his face. There was a sharp, clicking sound. Stunned, Tegné lifted his hand, fingers probing the gap left by his missing front tooth. He stared at Yano. There was no compassion in the Sensei's eyes, and, suddenly, Tegné felt anger. Yano moved forward and Tegné settled, controlling his breath. *I will not run from this man. If it is my fate to die this day, then I will die.*

Yano's next move was an example of perfection in distance and timing. Covering the gap between them with an apparent side-sliding thrust kick, Yano watched as Tegné moved backward, his joined open palms held before him in an augmented blocking technique. Yano pulled the kick short of contact with the block, then quickly the bulllike Sensei changed both the rhythm and the speed of his attack, performing a shorter, sharper version of the same kick. The knife-edge of his foot connected squarely with Tegné's chest, pushing inward against his ribcage. Tegné was propelled upward and backward, crashing hard against the wall of the Dojo.

Through glazed eyes, Tegné could see Yano line up for the final waza. The Sensei was being purposely slow, obviously setting up his blows in sheer defiance of his student's inability to block or counter.

"Oi-zuki, jodan!" Yano shouted at Tegné, announcing not only the intended front-lunging punch but the face-level target. Yano flew forward, a raging ki-ai spilling from his drawn lips.

Yet this was not Yano, Tegné's Sensei, who screamed toward

him across the glasslike surface of wood; this was death itself, fast and sleek and without conscience.

And Tegné met death with death. Shifting sideways, low and fluid, he barely needed to make contact with his left open-handed block. Yano's head was beside him now, still looking forward, in line with his failed punch. Tegné saw the naked, vulnerable flesh on the left side of Yano's neck, the area protected by the mastoid.

"Heeii!" Tegné ki-aied, and drove a foreknuckle punch into the exposed target. The flesh was soft, nonresistant, and the punch sank deep.

Slowly, Yano straightened, stepping back from striking range. Slower still, he turned toward his student. Yano's eyes were no longer the tight, hooded slits, those hateful windows of only seconds before. Now they were soft, brown and gentle.

A terrible feeling gripped Tegné as he dropped his guarding hands. He stepped toward his Sensei, and as he did so Yano changed before his eyes, flowing and shaping like a crescendoing wave of water.

"Zanshin. You must retain mental alertness until your opponent is dead, or, if it is a sparring exercise, until the final bow. Then it is finished, not before," Yano's voice castigated him through a cloudy haze as Tegné struggled to his feet. The Sensei's double palm-heel strike had sent him sprawling onto the floor, his head smashing again into the hard wood, knocking him senseless.

Yano stood smiling. "Now it is over," he proclaimed, bowing to his student.

Yano rubbed the left side of his neck. "It was a good blow. You released your mind, and your spirit rushed forward," he said as they walked across the floor. "It was an important blow also, for it transcended our relationship of student and teacher. You came out from behind my shadow. You have shed a burden, a weight which has hung like a dark cloud around you since the day we met. Perhaps a grave self-doubt . . . Now, you are a warrior. Yano declared, stopping and looking directly at Tegné.

Tegné was still struggling with the meaning of his lesson, caught in a myriad of confused emotions, for he also knew it was a turning point. Finally, he said quietly, "Sensei, I was frightened I had injured you."

Yano laughed, removing his rubbing hand from his neck, and displayed the unblemished skin.

"Not even a bruise," Tegné observed.

"There is still much for you to learn," Yano stated, maintaining a hint of a smile. Then the Sensei bent forward and picked the long-rooted incisor from the floor. "Take this," he instructed, handing Tegné the tooth. "Go immediately to the remedial quarters. If you are quick, the physician will be able to reset it into your jaw. You are lucky, very lucky. The tooth came out with the root intact!"

Tegné closed his hand around the tooth; he could not recall Yano Sensei ever appearing so jubilant.

Yeon 994

Zendow

Vokane Province

The knock on his door came at sunrise, as Renagi had requested. He had been awake for the latter half of the night anyway, and now he stood dressed and waiting as the daylight from his open window brightened the room behind him.

"Come in," he called, adjusting the front buttons of his black, square-shouldered tunic.

The door opened and Zato stood before his father. There was an undisguised expression of surprise on the young man's face.

"But are you not ready? Your war armor, your katana?" Zato questioned, closing the door behind him.

"I am not going," Renagi said flatly. "I will join you later at the kumite and then, together, we will attend the feast."

"But—" Zato began.

"No." Renagi cut his son off, raising his hand as he stepped closer. "You are old enough to lead the Procession. It is important that you begin to assert your presence," Renagi insisted. "Now sit down. There are things I must say to you."

Zato walked toward the open window, turned and sat finally in the ornate, high-backed wooden chair. The long, carved dragon wrapped around the right arm and extended until its open, fanged mouth spat fire and flame on to the headrest. The dragon was carved into the actual wood of the chair, which was itself made from only three pieces of panouki, expertly and artistically joined together. It had been one of the few remaining treasures from the occupancy of the original monks, and Renagi had overseen its faithful restoration.

Zato settled onto its thinly padded seat, the base of his spine pressed firmly into the curvature of the wood and his arms supported comfortably on the carved rests.

"Built for contemplation," Renagi said, noticing Zato's unspoken appreciation of the fine piece of furniture. Zato lifted his head to meet his father's eyes. "Purity, that is what I want you to understand," Renagi began.

"Purity?" Zato repeated.

"Correct thinking. Correct purpose. Proper speech. Proper conduct. Great effort, constant awareness. Concentration," Renagi stated in an unusual, prepared tone.

"Have I displeased you in some way?" Zato asked.

"Zendai," Renagi continued, completely ignoring Zato's question, "One who leads. One who lives by the strictest of codes, one who conducts himself impeccably in battle as well as in peacetime . . . A Zendai is the personification of purity. Do you understand me?" Renagi moved across the room, his eyes far away yet intense.

"Yes," Zato answered, "I am Zendai and I live by the Code of the Warrior."

"Good, good," Renagi said, his eyes refocusing on his son. "Since your mother died, I have lain with no woman. I will produce no other sons. That has been decreed by the Gods of Light." Renagi's voice grew hushed as he stood directly above Zato, bending down, touching both hands to his son's shoulders. "We . . . you and I, are chosen; the purest of Zendai. We are marked; we bear the Sign of the Claw. We must go forth and never stumble. Do you understand?"

Zato had begun to feel uneasy, a strange, physical revulsion. What was his father doing? What point was he trying so desperately to drive into him? Why, now, had he decided that Zato should lead the Procession? Zato began to rise from the chair but Renagi held him firmly.

"Say to me that we are pure," Renagi pressed.

"We are pure. Pure Zendai," Zato stated, studying the deep-furrowed, masklike face above him.

"And in your thoughts, do you ever lose the way of pureness?" Renagi asked.

"Father, I do not understand," Zato begged.

"Women!" Renagi nearly shouted. "Have you ever found desire for a woman who was not Zendai?"

"Only for sport," Zato retorted.

"Yes! Good!" Renagi snapped, releasing Zato and backing away as his son rose from the chair. "Then let them see you today— Ride tall and proud . . ."—he hesitated, again casting his eyes on Zato—". . . ride through Ashkelan, let them learn to fear you, for they are the weakest, most loathsome of people."

Zato held the Warlord's gaze as he walked across the floor, breaking eye contact only as he reached the door. "Thank you for this honor, father. I will lead the Procession with dignity, I will uphold our family name," he pledged, then turned quickly, opened the door and walked from the room.

Renagi stared after him, then he closed and carefully slid the metal bolt into position, locking the door. The Warlord had already informed the selected Twelve that Zato would lead the Procession; there had been no hint of opposition. In this respect, Renagi was satisfied, as, pensively, he walked toward the fine, high-backed dragon chair. He settled easily into the familiar wooden seat. "No, he could not face another Procession. He could not endure the stares of those limpid pink eyes or the expressions on the white, translucent faces." It was as if they knew, as if they were quietly mocking him. So he had made sure they were terrified. It was only last yeon that he had given the nod to one of his Warmen, and on that signal the Warman had drawn his sword and sliced an old, tottering field worker cleanly in two. *Only one yeon ago, in Asha-IV. Surely, they have not forgotten. One cut, clean . . .*

Renagi breathed in, smiling, feeling momentarily secure in the power of the katana. "Purity," he whispered the word softly. "Unmixed, untainted, innocent," he mused as he became aware of the familiar deadness within his groin. He placed his right hand against the cloth covering his crotch, his index finger unconsciously pressing on the head of his penis. *Yes, it is true that I have not been with a woman since the death of Natiro, yet I have not been without desire . . .* A desire that at once inflamed and disgusted him, a desire that he had at first tried to analyze on a physical level, only then realizing that the desire stemmed from his heart. For it was a particular purity he yearned for, a particular reflection of himself that he had seen only once, and that once was in the eyes of the Ashkelite girl.

The clatter of hooves shook him from his thoughts. He rose sharply from the dragon chair and went to the window. He could see the Twelve clearly as they rode out from the last of the winding roads which led from the stables and into the courtyard. *How clean, how precise,* Renagi thought, admiring the tightness of the formation as the group cantered from the main gates, spreading out as they crossed the demarcation line yet never once losing the cohesion of the unit. *One yeon past, twelve months, and I was holding that lead position,* the Warlord observed, watching as Zato widened his distance in front of the Twelve. As Renagi saw them disappear up the western road and into the Forest of Shuree he recognized the finality of his gesture. For, gradually, he had begun to relinquish his control of Zendow. Today Zato would lead the Procession, and soon his son would stand as Warlord. It was not the way Renagi had planned or foreseen it, but that was the way it would be. For the Warlord felt himself dying, day by day, night by night. His heart. His soul.

Yeon 994
Temple of the Moon
Lunan Province

The class was small in comparison to the other groups of students practicing Empty Hand, but it was his class—Tegné's. He was the Sensei.

He stood at the far end of the small Dojo which adjoined the larger, main training hall of the Temple, and watched as the twenty young Brothers, aged between ten and fifteen yeons, assembled. Their white gis were so new that the starch in the heavy cotton material caused the fabric to rub with the rough sound of wood against wood as they performed their warming-up exercises.

"First, learn to teach children. They will never lie to you; they are always an honest reflection of yourself," the Elder had promised.

The assignment meant that Tegné would be responsible for the introduction of Empty Hand to all the novice Brothers who chose the Martial Way as their path to enlightenment. Of course, his own tuition would continue; he was required to attend two of Yano's main Dojo classes per day in addition to spending one hour in the morning and one hour at the close of each day in the single meditation cells which lay in the massive vault below the Temple.

Tegné had been teaching this particular group for a little longer than three months, and already he could foretell which boys amongst the twenty would succeed in entering the higher ranks. For attitude, much more than natural physical ability, enabled the subtle learning process to continue. As soon as one of the young boys developed feelings of superiority, his individual learning would be slowed or completely halted. It was Tegné's task to sense these shifts in disposition and nip them in the bud. And in fulfilling his role as a teacher, in breaking down the simplest movements and postures so they could be understood and assimilated by this group of youngsters, his own understanding deepened.

He had already graduated seven of his older students to the lower ranks of Yano's class, and the senior Sensei had complimented him on their discipline and knowledge of basic technique. Sensei, teacher; Tegné was beginning to understand the meaning of his position and the pride of fulfillment through his students.

It was toward the end of the one-hour session that the Elder silently entered the Dojo and stood watching from the back of the room. Tegné noticed the Exalted Brother and assumed he had come to oversee his work and would then quietly leave the training hall. But the Elder did not leave; instead he waited patiently while Tegné instructed in the stretching postures of the warming-down exercises, finally bringing the class to attention. After the traditional recital of the Dojo code he dismissed them. Still the Elder remained as Tegné rose from his kneeling sei-za position and walked toward him.

"I trust all is well with you, Tegné? Your work progressing?" the Elder asked.

"It is," Tegné replied.

"Good, good. Because I have a special task for you," the Elder continued. "A young boy, younger than you usually teach, but I feel if he is not taken in hand soon, he will be lost."

"And you wish me to admit him to my class here in the Dojo?" asked Tegné.

"Eventually, yes," said the Elder. "But first I would like you to take him on a one-to-one basis. Your own uchi-deshi."

"And what age is the boy?" inquired Tegné.

"Seven," the Elder replied.

Surprised, Tegné repeated, "Seven?"

"Yes, he is very young. But at the same time, he is very wise in the ways of the world. You see, unlike the other boys here and very like yourself, he did not arrive as an infant. In fact, it was only nine months ago that he was brought into the Temple by one of our wandering Brothers. The reason for their meeting was that this little fellow had managed to remove the Brother's bo as well as his woolen shawl while the Brother was in meditation beneath a tree. When he was finally able to capture the little boy and recover his bo and his wrap, he discovered that the child was homeless, orphaned, and had been living by thievery for nearly two yeons. True to the spirit of compassion which we foster within the monastery, the Brother offered the child food and shelter inside our gates. I am sorry to say that the story deteriorates from there, for there have been a multitude of unexplained thefts and a series of minor disruptions amongst the very young novices. All instigated by our most recent admission," the Elder concluded, opening both hands in a gesture of frustration.

Amused, Tegné nodded his head, looking up to meet the eyes of the Elder. "And I am to show this little one the Way?"

"Yes. That is correct," the Elder answered.

Rin stood dwarfed by the high plaster walls and vaulted, sky-lit ceiling of the Dojo. He studied his reflection in one of the four squared sheets of silvered glass that were mounted on each wall. His new gi was crisp and white, tied tight at the waist by an equally white sash which caused the rather large training suit to billow out at both top and bottom, giving the small boy an unintentionally comic appearance. Rin, however, found nothing humorous in his reflection. He saw only the stark beauty of the clean white cotton and felt only the great satisfaction of owning the new training suit.

He walked closer to the mirror, trying to move in the sure-footed, composed fashion of the older Brothers he had seen walking in similar suits across the small courtyard and into the training complex. He moved to within an arm's reach of his reflection.

I look like a girl, he observed with great annoyance, roughing up his jet black hair so that it stood out at jagged, irregular angles and did not so softly frame the wide, almond-eyed face which ended in a nearly pointed chin; the chin which gave an elfin quality to the otherwise angelic countenance. Then he thrust his hips forward and squared his shoulders. Still not satisfied that his appearance warranted the "special training" with the "great white Sensei" whom he had often seen in passing yet never had the courage to so much as meet eye to eye, Rin slapped his full brown cheeks just to give them a tougher, reddish quality. Finally, the little boy turned and marched stiffly across the floor and into the center of the Dojo.

Tegné waited in the partially open door at the far end of the training hall. He had managed to watch the latter portion of the boy's private performance without breaking into laughter, but barely. And now, as he carried the heavy wooden bucket of water and the two thick rags toward the expectant child he fought to control his urge to smile.

Without a greeting or salutation of any kind, Tegné placed the bucket at Rin's feet. Then he dropped the two rags so the coarse material just covered the tiny brown toes which protruded from the folds of overlapping cloth which formed the bottom of Rin's gi.

"I noticed your interest in the mirror," Tegné began, his voice purposely harsh and ungiving. "This floor is also a mirror. It reflects the work and sweat which the students of this Dojo give in their training. But since you have walked upon it I can no longer see it shine . . ." he continued, trying to give authority to his prearranged speech.

Finally, Tegné turned his head aside. *Do not smile, do not soften,* he told himself, beginning to feel ridiculous for these overbearing tactics, particularly when he was reminded that the recipient of his tirade was a seven-year-old child who stood not much more than three feet in height and wore a gi which would have fitted Tegné himself.

"Do you mean, Sensei, that before I walked upon it I could

have seen my reflection as if I was looking into the silver glass?"

"What I mean, Rin, is that you will scrub and polish this floor until it shines," Tegné ordered.

"But, Sensei," said Rin, lifting his arms to emphasize his bewilderment, "It already shines!"

"Enough talk!" Tegné snapped, shifting his attention to the bucket and rags. "From this moment on, when I ask you to perform a task, you will respond, 'Oss, Sensei,' and nothing more. Do you understand?" Tegné picked up the nearest rag and dropped it into the bucket.

"Oss, Sensei," Rin answered.

"Do not turn away from me when I speak to you," Tegné continued, moving closer to the quaking child.

"Oss, Sensei," Rin shouted in his effort to please this golden-haired tyrant who loomed above him.

"Now lift the rag from the bucket, wring the excess water from it, kneel upon the floor and with a circular motion of your arm, like this . . ."—Tegné demonstrated the clockwise sweep—". . . clean the floor. When you have cleaned a good-size patch, take the dry rag, and with a reverse pattern of your arm, like this . . ." again Tegné demonstrated, ". . . polish the wood until it shines."

"Oss, Sensei," Rin answered, devastated at the dismal reality of what he had anticipated to be his initiation into the mysterious order of the Empty Hand.

Tegné stepped back, away from the bucket, indicating with a motion of his head that Rin should begin. Rin bowed.

"Stop right there," Tegné said. Rin froze, looking quizzically into the Sensei's eyes.

"The bow is the first sign of etiquette, and etiquette is the foundation on which our training is based. We begin with a bow and we finish with a bow. So you may as well learn to bow correctly," Tegné stated.

Etiquette? Rin wondered what the word meant as he straightened more to attention.

"Now, on my command I want you to bend at the waist, keep your hips in, your hands outstretched, fingers straight and down at your sides—and keep your eyes focused on me." Tegné instructed, remembering Tabata's insistence on retaining an awareness of one's training partner even when exchanging courtesies. *Consider your opponent's hands and legs as you would sharp swords. One strike. Finished. And always when you would least expect it.*

"Rei," Tegné said, using the formal command.

Rin stood frozen, unsure of the word and less sure as to the proper execution of the bow.

"Rei." Tegné repeated the word, this time bowing correctly toward the child. "Now you try it . . . Rei."

Rin bent at the waist, his hips going naturally backward, his chin tucking in and causing his eyes to point to the floor. Quickly but lightly, Tegné swiped at the top of the little boy's head with his open hand. Startled, Rin jumped back.

"Hips pushed in, arms and hands straight, eyes forward," Tegné explained, and this time demonstrated as he spoke. Rin copied the movement, never breaking eye contact with Tegné.

"Rei," Tegné repeated for the one hundredth time. And Rin performed the one hundredth bow, properly, even adding, "Oss, Sensei," as he flowed naturally into the forward bend.

"Now you may begin to clean and polish the Dojo floor," Tegné said, satisfied that this first lesson in propriety had taken hold.

> *"They stand like ivory gods at the gates of Heaven*
> *Loving all men. Understanding and open*
> *Bearing yet not possessing*
> *Working yet taking no credit*
> *Leading yet not dominating*
> *They are the sacred circle*
> *The Seven Holy Spirits*
> *They are the primal Virtue*
> *The Seven Protectors."*

The Elder read the words aloud.

"Are they real, Elder? Do such entities actually exist?" Tegné asked, looking up as the aged Brother turned the old, yellowed page.

"As surely and as purposefully as we ourselves exist," the Elder answered. "It is a matter of reaching out for them, recognizing their call, their will," he continued. "Find them through your meditation, beg them to come into your heart. For there may come a point in your life when only these Protectors can show you the clear path."

The Elder stopped speaking and let his gaze rest on the man before him. *Five yeons, he has only five yeons,* he thought as he quietly assessed the clarity of the blue eyes, the discipline of the seated posture and even the unconscious control in Tegné's breathing.

"And have you seen them, touched them?" Tegné asked hesitantly, in no way wishing to offend this master teacher, yet needing to establish whether these spirits existed in a philosophically abstract form or, in fact, were tangible in a physical sense.

"I understand your question, Tegné, and if I may, I will answer it with a question of my own," the Elder suggested.

"Please do, Elder," Tegné urged.

"Have you been successful with your exercises in projected consciousness, successful in entering the astral state?" the Elder asked, referring to the practice of projection in which the practitioner shifted his conscious awareness from his corporeal Earth body to a much finer, less densely vibrating, astral body.

"I have made the separation perhaps half a dozen times," Tegné answered.

"Illusion?" the Elder asked.

"No. A separate reality," Tegné replied.

"And does your projected self 'think'?" the Elder continued.

"Yes, but at a much greater level of detachment than my Earth body," Tegné responded, beginning to follow the Elder's line of reasoning.

"Detachment from the possessive nature of our flesh and blood," the Elder stated.

"Yes," Tegné agreed.

"Well, if you can accept the reality of that first level of projected vibration, that first level beyond our flesh, then try to imagine a level of reality which is seven levels beyond, which has no corporeal lust or need. Which is pure. The 'primal virtue,' " the Elder said.

"I cannot comprehend such purity," Tegné answered.

"Nor can you hear the gentle beating of the silken wings of a single butterfly. Yet the butterfly exists. You see it, so you believe it," the Elder said.

"And you have seen the Protectors?"

"Yes," the Elder replied.

"The Protectors exist?"

"Yes. Synchronous with our Earth plane. To help us, to guide us," the Elder continued. "And on the infinitely rare occasion that an Earth body becomes momentarily connected to this sacred circle, then that Earth body receives knowledge of a divine task or inspiration. And that Earth body must fulfil its mission."

"What kind of Earth soul would be the recipient of such a connection?" Tegné asked.

"One who is pure of heart, free from corruption. A prophet, even a warrior," the Elder stated.

"It would be an awesome experience," Tegné said, then added humbly, "A tremendous burden."

"Yes. Most certainly," agreed the Elder, consciously bringing his spirit in tune with the spirit of the man before him. *I must tell him without words, without betraying the trust, without breaking the pact. Five yeons; he will not be ready*, he worried, then quickly curbed the anxiety which threatened to force a reckless word, an untimely revelation.

"And are you managing to adhere to the teachings of our late Goswami?" the Elder asked, diverting the path of the conversation while at the same time keeping it within its spiritual confines.

"I sit in meditation for one hour in the morning, and at least two hours in the evening," Tegné replied.

"Transcending?" the Elder asked.

"During both sessions," Tegné answered.

"And the projection?" the Elder pressed, sensing a way to lead Tegné closer to the truth.

"In the evening before sleep," said Tegné simply.

"Before we meet again, Tegné, I want you to combine the state of transcendence with your exercises in projection. In other words, I want you to attempt to project your astral spirit up and into the void. Invoke the spiritual aid of your Sensei Tabata; he will guide you. And remember our discussion today," the Elder said, indicating that their conversation was over.

Tegné rose from the mat, leaving the Elder in the seated, half-lotus posture. "I will listen for the silken wings of the single butterfly," he promised.

"And I believe you will hear them," the Elder replied.

VI

THE SEVENTH INCARNATION

She is spewed from the bellows between
Heaven and Earth
Her shape may change but never her form
A woman
A cat
The Beast is born
Darkness
Evil
On Earth she is born.

*(Book of Knowledge, Temple of the
Moon, Lunan Province)*

Yeon 999

Temple of the Moon

Lunan Province

"**And when the** power of the Seven shall diminish, the Great Snake shall rise in the East, blinded by turmoil and uncertainty. It is then that the state of Earth shall be vulnerable and weak, and it is then that the Cat shall join the Snake, guiding him with eyes of avarice, for she shall be the daughter of the Beast, sent to do his bidding on Earth. And she shall cry out for a pure soul with which to make union.

"The yeons shall number 999 when the Golden Son shall walk forth from the House of God: the Sign of the Moon as his ally. And this Golden Son shall endure the Test of the Heart."

The Elder closed the ancient book, turned the iron key and locked the heavy wooden binding. He stood up from the small reading bench, lifting the book as he rose. Still deep in thought, he walked to the far corner of the private temple library and climbed the double-runged ladder. Carefully he placed the volume back amongst the other sacred works, then stepped backward onto the stone floor. Very slowly he raised his open right palm slightly above his bowed head and executed the circular Sign of the Moon.

He felt the rush of spirit as he drew the palm inward, finally placing the open hand against his robed chest, above his heart. He remained like this, his eyes closed; he could feel Tabata close to him now as he recalled the wide, emotional eyes of the Sensei on the occasion of his single visit to this private library. And on that occasion the Elder had permitted Tabata the treasured privilege of reading the Book of Knowledge; a right rigidly withheld from all but the Patriarch of the Order. However, the Elder had judged this an exceptional time, realizing the Book's prophecy would be fulfilled within his charge of the Brotherhood, and knowing with all certainty that Tabata would play a critical role in the outcome of fate. And Tabata had indeed played his part; he had given his life.

Now the Elder remained motionless, feeling once again at one with Tabata's true, brave spirit.

The early summer sun rose just above the large, circular iron disc which was mounted high on the inner courtyard wall. The backlight formed a fine haze, highlighting the golden moon and single silver star which stood out from the black iron.

The Elder looked down from the leaded window, three levels above the courtyard. By the position of the sun behind the Sign of the Moon he judged that the time was nearing the eighth hour. He could hear the echo of bare, hard-soled feet approach from the north gate, and watched Tegné walk onto the smooth stone floor of the large yard, remove the black silk robes of the senior order, fold them carefully, and lay them on the far side of the wall. Now Tegné stood bare-chested, his loose, rough white cotton gi bottoms tied at the waist with a wide black sash, cross-knotted and hanging evenly at each end. Then Tegné began the warming-up exercise.

The Elder noted the spring in the knees as Tegné jumped lightly in place, at first up and down, then shifting from side to side. After a short time he stopped, stretching upward, forward and sideways. He rotated his hips, turning, twisting, pushing. The Elder could see the fine latissimus-dorsal development, giving the back a wide V-shape, tapering into the tight, well-defined abdomen. Tegné's chest was deep, the major pectoralis muscles full at both top and bottom range, creating a square, jutting appearance to the rib cage.

A result of the chikaraisha, the Elder surmised, forming a mental picture of the power stones, each weighing twenty pounds and embedded on the end of a foot-long wooden stick. Each chikaraishi was gripped at the end opposite the weight, enabling any number of straight- or bent-arm strength exercises to be performed with the extended chikaraisha. The Elder could see the thick muscles in the forearms as Tegné snapped three relaxed punches into the air. Even from the height of the window the enlarged and calloused first and second knuckles on the punching fist could be distinguished.

Makiwara, the striking board. Punch the surface five hundred times each morning, both hands. One year and your hands will strike like hammers. Yano's words, and Tegné had followed them faithfully. In fact, Tegné felt most comfortable using his hands in combat, for his strength and reach were both extraordinary for a man of slightly less than six feet in height.

One more session and the trial is finished. I shall be glad of that, the Elder thought as he moved silently down the twisting, narrow passage and emerged in the warm morning light.

Tegné straightened and bowed to the Elder, watching the waist-length single braid of silver hair swing gracefully from side to side across the back of the fine turquoise robes. *He must be nearing a hundred yeons, and still his energy is that of a young man,* he marveled as the Elder walked easily toward him. Tegné smiled, looking into the dark, glowing eyes. The Elder returned the smile as he extended his hands to feel the newly repaired cartilage in Tegné's nose.

"No pain?" the Elder inquired.

"None," smiled Tegné.

"Looks the same. No difference," added the Elder, pleased with his manipulation. For barely three weeks ago, during the third phase of the "Trial of One Hundred," a sharp, upward palm-heel strike had fractured Tegné's nose in three places. The Elder had reset the cartilage while Tegné lay unconscious from the strike. The senior Brother remained concerned for the appearance of the fine, chiselled face, and remembered his momentary distaste for this Trial. Then he recalled the deep-set blue eyes opening, looking up, as Tegné asked, "How many, Elder? How many?"

"Twelve more and it is finished," said the Elder, answering the question of three weeks ago. Skillfully, he examined the mild bruising above Tegné's sternum. "And the knee?" he inquired, remembering the powerful and badly misdirected leg sweep which slammed awkwardly into Tegné's left knee during the last combat.

"The knee is fine, Elder," replied Tegné, grateful for the other's concern as to his well-being. "Thank you very much," he added, straightening himself and turning toward the open North Gate.

Both could hear the muffled footsteps of the hundred participants in this test of body and spirit. Each yeon one senior Brother from the Dojo was chosen for the Trial. This honored Brother would undertake full unarmed combat, excluding death blows, with each of one hundred of his highest-ranked contemporaries. The Trial was halted only when the chosen Brother was injured or unable to continue, then the number of successful, two-minute encounters was tallied and a rest interval granted. At the end of this interval, the Trial was reconvened and continued until the entire hundred Brothers had tested the chosen man.

The Trial of One Hundred had its origins in the ancient Jlon-Ji Temple, and the ritual, strictly adhered to since its inception, was now nearing three hundred yeons old. Yet recently several Brothers on the Council had spoken openly against its continuation, arguing that it was an obsolete and barbaric tradition. The Elder had, in his heart, understood their protests. Yet he realized that for the Brothers whose predilection was the Dojo—the Martial Way of Life—the Trial was invaluable. A test of courage, skill and endurance, it led its participants, both the one and the one hundred, along the path of insight and toward perfection of character.

And if there was ever one who needed strength, it is the one who stands before them now, concluded the Elder as he watched from the shadows of the courtyard. Tegné stood alone, facing the five lines of Brothers, their faces set firm, revealing no emotion.

In unison, the final twelve stepped forward and bowed to the Elder. Then they straightened, turned full face and bowed to Tegné. Tegné returned the courtesy. Etiquette, in this instance, was paramount.

The Elder walked four paces forward. "Perfection," he allowed the word to ring sharp and clear, "Sincerity. Perseverance. Propriety. Control." Each word was a lesson in itself.

After a respectful pause the first Brother ran from the line, halting smartly in front of Tegné.

"Hajime!" The Elder's order to "begin" ricocheted off the far wall . . .

* * *

Rin's right hand shot out, his fingers relaxed, open. Quickly the hand withdrew as he stepped sharply backward, clenching the large, ripe lemon. He stuffed the fruit securely down the front of his loose trousers; the trousers were tied tightly at the ankle for just this purpose.

That makes three—I'll try for one more, she hasn't even turned her head, he thought, studying the back of the short, mountainously fat village woman as she pulled the fruit cart into the Temple's main courtyard. He shuffled close to the side of the cart, head down, his face hidden by the thick, brown cotton hood. He strained his eyes to the right, keeping his head forward.

Bananas, potassium. Yes, potassium for strength, he thought, just as the woman, sensing a presence behind her, turned and looked over her left shoulder. Rin just managed the grab as the cart handle was dropped and the heavy wooden stick careered toward his head.

"Stop, you! Thief, thief! Stop!" the hulk screamed.

God, she moves fast, thought Rin as, trousers bulging with stolen fruit, he evaded his pursuer by crawling beneath a stone ledge and through the damp, narrow crawl space that led into the meditation chambers of the Temple. He paused to catch his breath; he heard her above him, the deep, rasping breaths intertwined with unyielding curses. Then, quietly, Rin removed his double-heeled wooden geta and, barefoot, entered the complex of small stone rooms.

Rin was the lowest order of novice, and he knew the penalty should he be discovered in these chambers. For the tiny vaulted cells were rigidly reserved for only a few of the senior Brothers. Still, his excitement for the adventure and his curiosity at what, in fact, transpired in these rooms drove him forward.

He crept toward the first occupied cell; he could hear the deep, even breathing coming from the tiny, arched stone doorway. He inched forward, timing his own footsteps with the rhythmic breaths. Rin was barely a yard from the entrance when the loud, reverberating blast stopped him dead.

No, it couldn't have been . . . He struggled to control his laughter as he dropped silently to his hands and knees. Again the sound, this time thin, loose, trill. *God, it is! A fart!* Rin bit his lower lip hard, holding back the snorts of laughter. *Control, control . . .* he commanded himself as he moved on. *Who can it be? Brother Randu?* The image of the corpulent astrologer flashed through his mind. *No, no, it has to be Minka, Brother Minka. He is forever lecturing on the value of lentils and other fibrous foods in the diet. "Roughage, Rin, you need more roughage . . ."* Rin visualized Minka's skeletal, sunken-eyed face in front of him.

Varoomp! Another explosive blast cut the air. Now Rin *had* to know. Resolutely, he took hold of the doorframe and pulled. Silently he slid the last few inches along the rough stone floor.

Brother Kao stood on his head before Rin. His long, thick, shining black hair was clumped and pressed hard into the small, square tatami mat, and his legs were bent inward, forming a full lotus. Rin stared in amazement at the naked senior Brother. Kao's eyes were tightly closed; the rhythmic breathing and obvious relaxation of the sphincter indicated a deep meditation. Rin viewed the small, hooded penis and long, hanging, inverted scrotum with naive fascination. The sheer privacy of the vision, the act of viewing a senior Brother in such a personal, vulnerable state, held Rin transfixed. Only the flash of deep blue, to the right and slightly behind Kao, distracted his attention. The robe was neatly folded, beautifully clean, and the pristine silk seemed alive with an inner glow.

Rin could not resist. He held his breath as quietly, stealthily, his small hand crept around the corner of the doorway. Without sound, he lifted Kao's robe, pulling it smoothly from the tiny cell. *It is not for me, anyway,* he rationalized. He could smell the warm aroma of sandalwood as it wafted gently from the fabric. *He will look like a god in this,* Rin concluded, holding the new treasure close to him as he climbed back up the tight passage and into the light.

Randu backed away from the low, slant-surfaced astrological bench. He felt his heart pound as he stood and overlooked the table-size chart. Its complex system of meridians and circles stared back at him.

"No, it cannot be," he muttered to himself, bending to pick up the shining steel astrolabe. Then he climbed again into the ridged, straight-backed chair and placed the instrument in position. Again the steel began to grow warm, vibrate, pulling Randu's hand along the smooth, oiled skin. This time he did not resist. He allowed the unseen force to guide him, to form the chart.

Twenty minutes later, Randu sat back in the bench, sweat dripping from his forehead, as he stared at the conjunction of planets before him. "But the formation receives no major influence from any other house," he said aloud to himself. "It just does not make sense. Totally powerful, yet totally receptive without guidance."

As if in answer, Randu felt his right hand jerk forward, the fingers in spasm, gripping the instrument. *Am I going mad?* he wondered as the steel began to move toward the oilskin. The second ghost chart actually intersected and added to the original, Urak and Neptinis sat perfectly square to the unguided element of the first chart, the conjunction falling in the ninth house; the house of vision.

She will totally dominate him, take his raw, unpolished energy and direct it, Randu thought, then shuddered at the fact that he had given the second rendering a female personality. *Why? What is happening here? What force is using me?* Again he felt the urge in his fingers, but this time he held back, pushing himself up and turning from the bench; he walked from the room.

The Elder moved quickly to the center of the circle. He knelt on one knee above the fallen, choking body. With a single, sure movement, he inserted his thumb and middle finger deep into the larynx and gripped the displaced thyroid cartilage.

The same power that extinguishes life is also able to give life. Tabata's words repeated in Tegné's mind as he heard the desperate, choking breaths become clear, full, and finally at ease.

Thank God, thought Tegné. Still he retained the rigid sei-za position, his back turned in humiliation, staring at the wall, away from the fallen man. His sharp, spinning knife-hand strike had been an accident, a reaction to the powerful leg sweep which was intended to knock him to the ground. The Brother's ashi-bari had, in fact, succeeded only in sweeping Tegné's body in a counterclockwise rotation and, as he moved, vulnerable and out of balance, Tegné had instinctively flailed his left arm. The hand, in knife-hand position, had landed flush on his opponent's throat. Without the Elder's intervention, the strike would have been fatal.

"Refrain at all times from impetuous and violent behavior"—the first rule of the iron-clad Dojo code. To strike without control, to inflict injury with malice, to take life; these were the greatest affronts to the order, and today Tegné may well have walked alone from the Temple gate, forever to wander, a Ronin-monk, a man with no master, no temple. Control was of the essence, and this type of accident was not permitted.

"Continue." The single word jolted Tegné from his thoughts. He stood and turned to see his Temple Brother standing, fully recovered, in front of him. There was no animosity, no blame in his eyes as the man bowed, turned, and ran back to the line.

Now the twelfth and final opponent jumped to his feet, running forward into the circle. He was younger, heavier and taller than Tegné, and he moved easily into the kiba-dachi stance, side-on, bouncing lightly on his toes.

The Elder stepped back and away from the combat. He was strangely nervous as he watched the two fighters close.

Ke-komi . . . Tegné read the stance, noting the rear left leg taking most of the body weight, the right foot inching forward. He anticipated the slide, the lead foot lifting and the foot edge thrusting toward him. He met the technique with a flat double palm-heel block. The augmented palms pushed down, negating the powerful kick as Tegné maintained his forward momentum, lunging with a straight left punch. The heavier man dropped to the ground as the fist snapped into the air where his jaw had been, leaving Tegné momentarily extended. He had no time to recover as the scissor-grip clasped quick and strong against his shins.

For a split second there was only white light as Tegné's head cracked against the courtyard floor. Sheer instinct forced the roll to his left and freed his legs from the closed grip. Tegné continued the roll, regaining his feet as he avoided the axe kick which was intended to finish him.

Now both men stood, facing each other, preparing for the next exchange. Psychologically, the younger man had the advantage, for Tegné was exhausted, his legs heavy, without spring. The two eyed each other, waiting. Then the younger man began his move.

Stop him straight on, Tegné reasoned desperately as he turned his left foot inward, bringing the right leg up and aiming the heel of the back-thrusting kick toward the hard, flat abdomen. The pivot was too slow. The other man continued confidently forward, smothering the technique and hoisting Tegné off his feet and upward in a powerful wrestler's grip, Tegné twisted within the grasp, managing to wrench his arms free. He stared a moment into the cold, determined eyes, feeling his body crushed as it was heaved upward.

Timing . . . timing . . . Now! Tegné grabbed the sweating clump of coarse brown hair, gripped firmly with his left hand and pulled the head sharply back. The movement was enough to break the balance of his opponent. He felt the struggling body buckle as he maintained the pull. As they hit, Tegné remained on top, and before his opponent could twist or roll he applied the tiger-mouth hand. His fingers dug into his opponent's throat at each side of the windpipe. He did not apply pressure.

'Yame! Yame!' the Elder's voice rang out, halting the flow of adrenaline, putting a cold stop to the action.

Tegné maintained zanshin as he disentangled himself from the beaten man. He rose up, backing away, never once breaking eye contact. The twelfth Brother stood up slowly; he and Tegné faced each other and bowed, finally turning and bowing low to the Elder. Tegné could see satisfaction in the Elder's eyes.

The Trial was over, and he began to feel a flush of love and gratitude rise within him. Close to tears, he straightened from the final bow and met the eyes of his Brothers. They stood quietly before him. A state of peace pervaded the courtyard, simple and empty. *Through the art of the warrior, Heaven and Earth become one.*

The sharp, rapid clapping of small hands shattered the moment. Tegné saw the Elder's brow furrow and his eyes become hawklike. The long silver braid swung to the side as he spun toward the north gate, keen to spot the perpetrator of this breach of etiquette.

Rin stood, his eyes fixed on Tegné, clutching Kao's robe close to his body, under his arm, the baggy trousers swollen grotesquely with the stolen fruit. Every eye in the courtyard focused on the child, every ear awaited the Elder's furious tirade.

Randu's sudden, unexpected appearance averted the inevitable. His plump, corseted body, its moonlike head perched on the shoulders with no apparent neck, waddled past the panic-stricken imp. With irksome authority, and a look of desperation, he bowed and walked straight toward the Elder. Rin seized the moment; he ran to Tegné, his small, shuffling steps made awkward by the stuffed trousers.

"Tegné . . ." The thin, high voice trailed off in the face of Tegné's glare.

Tegné's voice was harsh. "What are you doing here? You know this is not an open session. You know that no one applauds after a Trial . . ."

In answer, Rin dug frantically into his trousers, his hand running down inside the leg and rummaging around near the ankle. "I thought you would be thirsty," he sputtered, extending a shining yellow lemon.

Tegné suppressed a smile. *Why am I always so close to forgiving this child?* he wondered. Then his eyes focused on the blue robe. "Rin?" he began.

The child anticipated the question. "Isn't it beautiful?" he said, pushing the robe toward Tegné. "For you. It was made for you."

Tegné did not touch the extended robe. He was, for the moment, at a loss for words. *Five yeons I have known this child, taught him, disciplined him. Five yeons and he is still a thief,* he thought, feeling suddenly angry, frustrated by his own shortcomings. Finally he knelt down, so as to be face-to-face with the boy. He looked deep into Rin's eyes, seeing the unashamed cry for love and acceptance, and placed his hands on the frail shoulders.

"You have not done anything like this for a long time. Why now?"

"Because it is a special day. The last day of your Trial," Rin answered, still holding the robe forward. "I had to bring you a gift."

Tegné nodded slowly. "Well, I appreciate your thought. I am thirsty, and the robe is very fine," he said softly. "But . . . I cannot accept them."

"Why?" said Rin, knowing the answer.

"Why?" Tegné repeated the question.

"Because they are not mine to give you," Rin admitted.

Tegné waited a long moment. "Now I want you to return the fruit . . ."—Rin's face rose up in horror—". . . and go to Brother Kao. That is his robe, is it not?"

"But—" Rin began.

"Do it before you enter the Dojo again. You cannot live as a thief and a liar and expect to learn the true spirit of Empty Hand."

Rin knew there was no reprieve. "Oss, Sensei," he said, then bowed before he turned to leave. Tegné caught him by the shoulder, holding him firm, as he bent close to the top of the small, covered head.

"One more thing—what is that smell? It is coming from beneath your hood."

A faint smile began to transform the elfin face as Tegné lifted the heavy, drab cotton garment, pushing it back to reveal the dry, bleached patch of hair above the child's forehead. Tegné stared in amazement.

"Cow's urine, Sensei. Two more days and my hair will be the same color as yours."

"No. No, you cannot do that," Tegné managed, caught off guard, backing away from the rising fumes. Rin looked mortally wounded. Tegné continued, "God has given you fine black hair, you must not interfere with it." Rin stood on the verge of tears.

"Now go," Tegné added, regaining his command. "Return what you have taken."

The child sniffled, then began his shuffling journey toward the north gate.

"And no more cow's urine!" Tegné called after him. Tegné remained still, watching as the child disappeared through the high arched gate. Only then, as he turned to retrieve his own robes, did Tegné allow himself to laugh. And only then, as he walked from the nearly deserted courtyard, did he notice the Elder and Randu, deep in conversation.

Yeon 999

Walled City of Zendow

Vokane Province

Sixteen Celebres had come and gone. Zato was twenty-eight yeons, and this was the fifth time he had led the Procession. Renagi watched from the ramparts as the group of twelve galloped up the east road toward Zendow. He could hear the great iron-linked chains unwinding, their gigantic cranks being pulled round to lower the massive gate. He moved resolutely down the steep, winding steps, timing his action to coincide with the Warmen's entrance.

The horses moved past him at a walk as each man raised his clenched right fist, the black leather gloves punching straight up in unison; a salute to their Warlord. He watched from the mid-level sentry post which elevated him just above the heads of the mounted Warmen. He felt the surge of power as the Procession passed, yet the power was somehow distant, no longer his own. He studied Zato, his agile muscularity, his attitude, the tension of his thighs as he pressed them inward, controlling the stallion. Renagi saw the thick, plaited hair.

Did I once look that way? So strong, so proud? Renagi wondered as his gaze followed the Warmen until they turned from the main courtyard and proceeded in a single file toward the stables. The Warlord stood, looking after them, locked in thought. The matter of the Ashkelite had become his obsession, deep and private. He recalled Maliseet, her strange dreaming eyes, her silken white hair and soft skin. Many times during the last months he had awakened in the night, to lie alone, trying to conjure the boy's face. Boy? No longer a boy, he would be a man now, two yeons older than Zato. But the face . . . he could not imagine the face.

During these sleepless spells he would grow furious with himself, his weakness of mind, his inability to control this grim fascination. Often he had risen from his bed and, in the single beam of moonlight from the arched window, he would perform the most basic movements of the Morning Form. These simple, external exercises had the effect of solidifying his spirit, holding the demons at bay and winning him three or four hours' sleep before the rising sun. Then, when he awoke, he would brace himself against the day, assuming what had become the façade of Warlord.

He feared the rumors amongst his men, ever since the return of that first war party, sixteen yeons past. Rumors of the Ashkelite's escape and disappearance coupled with reports of the slaughter of his own Warmen had proved a base for all forms of conjecture. Renagi did not hear Zato walk up behind him.

"They are waiting for you. The kumite is set to begin." His son's voice was deep and warm.

Renagi turned, trying to conceal that he had, again, been far away. He placed his hand on Zato's shoulders. "Did you go through Asha-1?" he asked.

The same question, always the same question, Zato thought as he controlled his urge to be abrupt with his father, to cut him off, to tell him pointedly to drop this obsession, to let the past go. Instead, he looked at the bearded face, the distinct silver-streaked hair, and into the strained, questioning eyes.

"Yes, Father. We went through Asha-1. Their production has been high since the Solstice, so there was no need to threaten them," he answered.

"Slaves! Filth!" Renagi blurted. "My skin crawls at the thought of them. Do they still speak of him? Their savior? The impostor!"

Zato stepped back as if the force of the words had pushed physically against him. He answered Renagi with a look of compassion, but there was impatience within the look. Renagi's eyes grew darker.

"Do they?"

"I don't know!" Zato snapped.

Desperately, Renagi's hand shot out, the open thumb and first finger wrapping round Zato's windpipe. The Warlord tightened his grip, momentarily raging, out of control. Then, suddenly aware of the twisted futility of his action, he let the fingers go limp. Zato stepped back and the hand fell from his throat.

'Shall we go to the Great Hall, Father?" His tone was flat, condescending.

Zendow had seen an influx of northern village fighters for the past three months. The young men had come purposely to enter the competition. Their chance to become Warmen far exceeded any opportunity they would find in their tiny, parochial villages. Zendai was, of course, a condition of birth, but the title of Warman could be won in combat. Although the northern style of rough grappling lacked the finesse of the fighting practiced in the southern region, the big, strong northerners compensated for their naive skills with courage and ferocity.

Zato studied Renagi's face as the Warlord sat in the Velchar, overlooking the combat. He watched his father jerk forward, his eyes alight as the huge grappler in the center square smothered a tentatively thrown back kick, and hoisted his opponent in both arms. Savagely, the stout, northern fighter head-butted the taller, slimmer man. Once, twice he butted him, all the while holding the now-unconscious man in his bearlike grip. Then, in a final and unnecessary move, the northern man bit deep into his opponent's throat. Even the hardened, more ardent spectators of the event murmured in protest, as the dying man hung limp in the bulging, veined arms.

Zato was sickened. He turned his head away from the bloodletting only to glimpse his father nodding with vigorous approval.

Finally, they had come to the last combat, and through his pure savagery the northerner had earned his chance to fight for the title of Warman. All eyes turned to his opponent—a lanky, southern fighter. The southerner stood motionless on the outside of the square, his face staring down in horror as the last mutilated body was dragged unceremoniously in front of him and out through the main door. The neck of the corpse was a raw, gaping hole. For a long, unsettled moment the southerner seemed lost, unaware of where he was, what he was expected to do. Then slowly he raised his eyes.

The northerner stood waiting; his only movement was the heaving of his enormous chest. Thick, semi-congealed blood smeared his jowls. Then there began a slight twitching in his hands, just a flicker of the fingers, a faint taunt which seemed to beckon his opponent. The taller, less aggressive man remained frozen, all eyes upon him.

The sound of water broke the stillness, a thin stream hitting the stone floor. Zato looked closely; he could see the yellow stain begin to discolor the front of the cotton fighting costume as the urine dripped from the southerner's calf-length trousers onto the floor. Then the voices began.

"FIGHT! FIGHT!" followed by the unified stomping of cleated heels "FIGHT . . . FIGHT!"

Still the southerner did not move. Renagi seemed twenty yeons younger as he rose from the Velchar, pointing to the guards on the outer perimeter of the combat zone. On his command, they approached from behind the stricken man, each gripping him under one arm, carrying him bodily into the square. It was only in the last few yards that the southerner came to life, squirming, kicking, screaming. But the guards held firm and the chant of "FIGHT!" was now a thunderous roar within the Great Hall. Closer, closer, until he was within an arm's reach of his opponent . . . then the guards dropped him to his feet.

"Fight! Fight!" the northerner joined in the staccato chorus. But the man was beyond renewal, his energy dissipated, his courage lost. Futilely, he began a slow, wide, hooking punch. In sheer contempt, the northerner allowed the fist to land, grazing against his shoulder. Then he stepped forward disdainfully shoving his opponent, watching as the terrified man stumbled and fell to the floor. The southerner refused to rise.

Renagi sprang from the Velchar, both arms raised above his head in a signal for silence. Abruptly, the chant ceased and the hall fell deathly quiet.

"Mark him a coward," the Warlord boomed.

The two guards ran back into the square; they lifted the quivering man to his feet and held him firm. A third guard rushed from the far corner of the room. Drawing his katana as he moved, he brought the shining blade down, slicing the skin of the southerner's chest as the razor edge cut through the drawstring of the stained cotton trousers. Naked, the southerner stood before the jeers of the crowd. Then the guards forced him to bend forward, exposing his buttocks. The two men held him in this position while the third guard, his katana still unsheathed, turned to the northerner and urged him to take the sword.

The northerner hesitated, looking up toward Renagi. The Warlord nodded yes, and the northerner gripped the katana, raising it high above his right shoulder. He swung the blade awkwardly in a horizontal strike, leaving a deep and uneven gash.

The southerner began to scream, as the blade was pulled free, hoisted up and swung again. The two wounds crisscrossed severing his hamstrings and tendons. Finally, the guards released him.

"Get out of my sight," Renagi growled. Slowly, the southerner pulled himself up into a seated position. He could rise no farther without the use of his legs—and he would never use his legs again. Agonizingly, he bent forward, extending his trunk as he braced himself with his hands against the floor and began to pull himself toward the door.

Zato studied his father's face. A strange, cathartic expression washed over it as the Warlord watched the shamed man crawl from the Great Hall and into the night.

* * *

The Feast of Celebre was a loud, raucous affair. It was as though everyone, from Zendai to Warman, sought release from the horror of combat.

Renagi drank heavily, and often his rasping laughter could be heard above the din of the revelers. Toward the end of the evening and the last of the traditional toasts, Renagi was vehement that the entire table should be quiet as Gazan, the newest Warman, stood to deliver his pledge of allegiance.

The resulting speech was fumbling and nearly inarticulate; the only memorable quality being the northerner's overwhelming conviction of his newly acquired self-importance. Still, Renagi led a hesitant and somewhat embarrassed table into a forced response of cheers and clapping that managed to grow, at the Warlord's urging, until the long, heavy dining table virtually shook beneath the pounding fists.

Zato studied his father in continued amazement. He was at once repelled and fascinated. Finally, hours later, when the men had begun their traditional trek to the Willow World, departing in twos and threes, Renagi wrapped a heavy arm around his son.

"Wang's. Madame Wang's . . . ," the Warlord slurred. Zato turned to meet the bloodshot gaze. "Yes, tonight," Renagi continued, turning Zato toward the door.

Thirty minutes later, Zato was supporting the Warlord's lumbering, drunken body as father and son staggered down the dark, unpaved streets and into the old part of the city, en route to the Royal brothel.

Renagi's weight was beginning to bear uncomfortably against Zato's shoulder, and he cursed himself for not summoning the Warlord's carriage for this unexpected journey. It was with great relief that he recognized the long, torchlit string of adjoining, single-storey dwellings that formed the front section of the Willow World.

Zato saw the freshly plastered white face of the brothel and noted that, aside from the plaster, little had changed since he had first seen it on the eve of his thirteenth birthday. These were the "Rites of Manhood," Renagi had assured him on that summer evening nearly sixteen yeons ago. Since then, Zato had been an infrequent visitor to this pretentious building with its gold-framed, curtained windows and enormous polished mahogany double-arched doors.

Zato could detect the dark eyes through the observation lens as he halted in front of the closed doors. For all her sixty yeons, the Madame had changed little over the time Zato had known her. He could see the warm glow of excitement in her face as she focused fully on her Royal patrons. Zato released his grip on Renagi and watched as the Warlord straightened, somehow composing himself in the outspill of light from the doorway. Wang beamed, throwing her arms up in appreciation for her guests.

Everything about the house mother seemed oversize and round. Her face was flat and her dark slanted eyes were huge. The luxuriously long black lashes beat a steady rhythm up and down as she used them to punctuate her frivolous patter.

Her arse always seems to have a life of its own, observed Zato, noting the rippling flesh bouncing in opposing directions beneath the synthetic jewels on her skirt as Wang emptied the thick ruby port from the decanter, then spun back toward her more favored guests. As she turned, her billowing breasts followed her body movement, yet remained one beat behind, so as to make them appear somehow detached from the rest of her torso. It was true that Wang's bosom was legendary, and although it had been fifteen or twenty yeons since any Warman or Zendai had admitted to lying with her, tales were rife as to her ability to use these enormous, pink-fleshed mounds in the performance of startling sexual feats.

Zato noted the oversize green, star-shaped gemstone mounted prominently above the fantastic cleavage. He knew that the stone, like everything else in the brothel, including the port and the crystallike decanter in which it was contained, was a replica. Wang kept her original hoard of treasure locked safely in the stone vaults beneath the Willow World.

Zato could not help but admire the spirit and fortitude that had enabled Wang to control this group of drunken men and often temperamental young women over these many yeons. And now he watched as the fat, short-toed, sandaled feet moved toward him.

"I have something for you. I have kept them apart from the others, waiting. I knew you would visit me again." Wang's tone was always conspiratorial, hushed. "They are very special," she added, then looked from Zato to Renagi. The Warlord's drooping eyelids parted slightly. "Twins, virgins from the north. Former temple dancers." Still not getting the desired response, Wang continued. "They have both taken the vows of chastity. This will be a first . . ."

Zato nodded, believing his father wanted this entertainment. He helped Renagi as they followed Wang beneath the ornate, pillared arches and along the corridor, through the reinforced door and into the steam which blew, heavy and warm, from the bath chambers.

Wang moved quickly ahead of them, surprisingly nimble, as she turned to offer them clean towels and two matching robes. She motioned toward the small changing rooms, where the Royal guests were encouraged to shed their clothing.

Renagi seemed to sober instantly as he settled, naked, into the steaming pool. The baths were, in fact, a natural phenomenon, the waters rising of their own accord from the mineral-rich underground springs beneath the bath chamber. Each bathing pool was cut square into the stone floor and was large enough to accommodate six persons. The frothing water swirled around them.

Wang had been careful to provide the Warlord and his son with the largest, most secluded bath, and now she allowed her guests time to relax as she held the two giggling sisters at bay, preparing for their entrance.

"Stop it! Immediately!" Wang's voice was modulated so as not to disturb the two men. Instantly, the sisters ceased their chatter and stood still as Wang gave them a final inspection. *They are so alike, they could be twins, it is possible,* she concluded as she opened the first girl's kimono, inhaling the delicate orange-scented oil which caused the firm breasts to shine slightly in the torchlight. Wang could recall acquiring these two; she had paid a three-kon premium above the standard five for each of them. She realized then that the two, working as a team, could earn her a fortune. They were indeed virgins, for in the six months that Wang had owned them she had permitted the sisters to be hired only for arousal and oral sex. She had preserved their hymens for a special occasion; an occasion such as this.

The Warlord will reward me handsomely, thought Wang as she parted the second girl's kimono and lightly, with her feather, touched the long brown nipple. The response was excellent; the nipple stood erect, a full fingertip in width and at least three-quarters of an inch in length. *I do think these provincial girls are more responsive . . . it must be the cross-breeding, produces a stronger stock,* mused Wang as she stroked the second nipple and considered having the girl visit her own chamber later in the evening. As a final gesture, Wang ordered each sister to part her legs. Then Wang employed her own hand to rub the full, black pubic hair upward. The result was to give the pubis a high, wide crown, rising to just below the navel. Then, fully aroused herself, Wang closed the kimonos, inhaled a commanding breath and led the girls into the bathing chamber.

Zato saw at once that the two women were not twins. He knew that Wang was actually incapable of speaking the truth. *Probably from thirty yeons of peddling restitched virgins,* he decided, as his eyes caught on the slightly taller of the two girls. Something in her attitude, the almost challenging manner of her walk, interested him.

Wang halted five steps from the pool. With a dramatic lift of both hands, she signalled for the "twins" to halt behind her. There was silence, a dramatic gesture intended to build excitement, to allow the prospective clients to view the skillfully presented merchandise.

In this instance it was effective. Zato felt the first pulse of awareness thud through his penis. The girl of his choice knew she had inflamed him and allowed her kimono to part slightly, revealing a hint of the large, jet black patch of hair and a partial view of the soft, inside curve of her breasts. The other girl appeared less sure of herself, more demure; she kept her kimono closed and her eyes down, staring shyly at the floor.

"Would you like them to bathe you?" Wang asked.

Zato was now gazing straight at the taller girl. She was meeting his gaze and encouraging him with her eyes. He looked at Renagi, hoping his father did not desire the same girl, for, if he did, Zato would be obliged to give way to his father's wishes.

"I do not want a woman." Renagi's words were clear, and without any hint of inebriation.

"If these do not please you, I have more. Perhaps these are too coarse, common?" Wang said, suddenly sneering at the girls, ready to whip them, to drive them from the room if their presence offended the Warlord. "I have many more for you to take as you choose," she added.

"I want no women. None."

"As you wish," Wang replied submissively.

"Hold on," Zato stopped her as she prepared to take her offerings from the room. "That one, I would like that one . . ." he said, pointing to the embarrassed, taller girl, ". . . if my father does not object."

Wang looked quickly at Renagi. "If my son wishes a woman, I have no objection."

Zato held out his hand and Wang extended the robe as he rose from the steam. Wrapping the robe around himself, Zato stepped from the pool. "Will you excuse me, Father?"

"Yes, of course. I would actually prefer to be alone."

"I will not be long," Zato said, observing the sudden lack of expression in Renagi's face. *As if one moment he is charged with fire, the next drained of all life*, he observed.

"Go! Leave me!" Renagi insisted.

Zato stood for a moment, then finally turned, took hold of the tall girl's arm and led her from the room. Wang and the unwanted "twin" followed.

Renagi closed the door to the chamber, locking it from the inside, and sat alone, quietly, in the hot bath. Steam rose from the water, filling the room, making it impossible for him to see more than a few feet in any direction. He was glad to be alone, and finally ready to confront the demons which stalked and tormented him.

I have been no more than a hollow shell, a frightened man, a beaten man. A man unworthy to be called Warlord . . . His insight was scathing, but at last he would no longer turn away. *If what I feel is my own death, stalking, ready to leap, to take me, then I am ready.* Renagi breathed in, took the heavy, salt steam into his nostrils, and breathing out, surrendered to the waters and to the strong, foreboding presence which surrounded him. His mind rolled back the yeons and again he stood outside the gates of Zendow, looking down into the blue eyes of his Ashkelite son, his first-born. It was at that instant the curse had begun. For he knew that this child was more than a breach of the sacred laws, more than a damning transgression, more than a dark secret to be swept away and forgotten. He felt it even as he took the girl named Maliseet, even as he released his seed within her. And now he grew frightened that his lust had been merely a superficial device of destiny, and the creation itself, the child, had been the true purpose of his act. *Fear? A Zendai, a Warlord, bowing in the face of fear?* He could not, he would not.

He was deep in thought when he felt the soft, smooth hand against his thigh; he bristled, straightening his back, looking down through the steam into the water. Was it a reflection, a mirage? She seemed to be part of the water, a transparent form rising from the shallow depths of the pool, caressing and arousing him.

How did she get in? I heard nothing, saw nothing . . . His mind raced as she broke the surface, smiling, reaching out with long, graceful arms. The slender fingers extended toward him. Her eyes were like no eyes he had ever known: green, the color of emerald, the iris not round but a thin diagonal which appeared to glow with a shimmering violet light. They were not the eyes of a woman. Renagi's rational mind searched for the meaning of this hallucination, for surely what he saw was not mortal. Then he heard the low, sensual purr as the full, soft lips pressed against his chest, the warm, rough tongue licking his nipples, lapping upward as the arms entwined around his body, the fingers sending shivers through him as they kneaded the muscles in his shoulders and neck. He brought his own arms and hands upward, fondling the full breasts which waited, warm and velvet-smooth.

Every nerve, every part of him was alive, burning, screaming with the desire to be touched, caressed. He felt the tingling begin where her fingertips pressed gently behind his neck, sending a current down the length of his spine. His body jolted as the first uncontrollable pleasure of orgasm began . . . It was then that she released him, allowing his intensity to subside while her knowing fingers maintained just enough contact to hold him within her spell.

"Master, may I guide you to my chamber?" The low, throaty voice was an extension of the purr, exquisitely female, completely submissive.

Renagi studied her from behind as she stood, walking the three wide, flat steps up and out of the pool. Her hair was a lustrous blanket, falling down her back, across her hips and stopping just above the slender, sure ankles and small, faultless feet. In response to his unspoken wishes she stood still, reached her right hand upward and gripped the thick black hair, pulling it from the left side of her long neck and draped it to the front of her, permitting the Warlord to view the rear of her naked body.

Renagi inhaled with pleasure as his gaze fell upon the long, perfect legs, the calves gently rounded, tapering into the small, graceful knees, then blossoming again as the finely proportioned thighs rushed upward to the hard, round hips. A hint of silken hair showed between the slightly spread thighs as she turned toward him, and Renagi felt the sheer strength which her body exuded. She moved closer to the pool, and in the small movement there was a visible sinew beneath her copper skin. Renagi sat, captivated, as she beckoned him.

He rose from the steaming water. He was fully erect and her warm gaze drew him forward. He wanted to take her, to enter her there, on the steps of the bath, but she moved back and away from him. She controlled him with her eyes, yet he was unaware of her command. Instead he felt the promise, the wetness of her youth, the vitality which he had lost long ago and somewhere forgotten.

She turned, picked up the bathrobe, walked toward him and draped it round his shoulders, guiding him to the heavy door which was still closed and bolted from the inside. Renagi slid the bolt and pulled the door open.

Madame Wang coughed loudly, waving her hands to disperse the steam as it rolled from the room and gathered before her eyes. Zato stood beside her, equally astonished at the sight before him.

"I don't know how she got in, master! I swear I had nothing to do with it!" babbled Wang. Then, before Renagi could speak, Wang moved closer, staring at the girl. "Master, she is not even one of my women! I swear, I swear!"

"We were worried, Father. It has been nearly four hours," Zato said, cutting her off. Zato was controlled, calm, less concerned than Wang as to the origins of the young woman. Renagi did not answer. Instead he reached out and wrapped his robed arm around the woman's naked shoulders, pulling her close to his body. Then, together, they walked past Zato and Wang toward the pleasure chamber.

Wang flew after him. "Yes, now I remember! She is new. I found her just yesterday in anticipation of your visit," she lied. The Warlord closed the carved wooden door in Wang's face.

Valley of Death

Lunan Province

The Elder had departed from the Temple gates at sunrise of the morning following Randu's disclosure. He had done his best to quiet and comfort the confused Temple astrologer, assuring the distraught man that the charts were not proof of possession but were, instead, a transmission from benevolent forces, a warning of impending events. Randu had pressed him for more explanation, but the Elder replied that he was certain of nothing more. And now the Elder sought the answers that only one place could provide.

A journey of seven days on a single burro, no food and only the mountain water to cleanse his physical body. Seven days and seven nights in which his resting moments were spent in deep meditation, in preparation.

And finally, on the morning of the last day, he could see the twin mountain peaks in front of him, looming on the horizon like two gigantic breasts rising from the bosom of the Earth. The Seat of Power lay on the flat plain in the center of these two peaks. It was a perfect, natural granite formation which was as old as the planet itself. A place known only to those who had experienced the height of spiritual evolution, revealed through the vision of the heart.

It was sunset when the Elder tethered his burro to the sapling at the base of the rock face that formed the western side of these sacred mountains. Already he could feel the ancient energy stir within him. He began to chant the "aoum" as he walked toward what appeared to be a sheer wall of rock. The setting sun cast jagged shadows against the uneven mass of stone, and it was into one of these shadows that the Elder walked.

Only at sunset is the opening visible, he noted as he squeezed his body tight against the wall, turning in a counterclockwise direction so that he actually faced away from the mountain, then turned again, clockwise. Now he stood at the base of a clearly delineated footpath, which led to the summit. The Elder inhaled a deep breath, filling his lungs. Then he took the first in the series of nine hundred and ninety-nine steps which led to the Seat of Power.

By nightfall he had traveled three-quarters of the way to his destination. He stopped and rested, continuing his chant, building energy. He started again before dawn and, shortly after sunrise, the Elder completed the journey.

The golden sun awaited him, sitting dead center between the soaring mountain peaks. The cloudless sky was a glorious blue and the fresh, clean air brought the faint fragrance of wild hyacinth. The Elder experienced a weightless clarity as the divine energy began to fill him, making him ready for the impending communication.

He removed his geta and placed them aside before brushing the dust from his robes. Then he turned and bowed reverently toward the crystalline, cylindrically shaped rock formation that rose three feet from the flat stone base. He walked forward and settled his hips into the inwardly curved surface of the Seat of Power.

He felt the gradual interlock between his own swirling energy and the stable, deep-rooted vibration of the ancient stone. Physical life temporarily ceased as the stone drew him into tune with the ageless vibration of the mother planet. His body became a hollow vessel of flesh and bone, his heart suspended in time as his soul was propelled upward, departing the physical shell through the crown of his head, passing quietly through the fourth level of vibration, entering the fifth, then passing up through the sixth plane, outward and beyond.

The Elder's soul hovered a moment above the external subtle vibrations of the planet, still drawn by a slight magnetic attraction. Then it flew free, toward the Light . . .

It was there, within the supreme radiance, that the Protectors awaited him. It was there that their astral souls merged with his own and basked for an endless moment in the mother warmth. Then they began their slow spiral down, down through the single point in space which provided the opening for their life energy to come into the material world. The contact was complete.

The Elder opened his Earth eyes. The Seven formed a half-diamond, facing him, their brilliant auras swirling, encompassing the Seat of Power and bathing the Elder in their warm, green and golden light. The Elder directed his thoughts toward the central figure. The fine, vibrating beams extended outward as the Father Protector received them, allowed them to penetrate him and establish the communication.

I have heeded your warning . . . is it true? Is she now amongst us, on the Earth plane? the Elder questioned.

Father's reply was a solemn nod in the affirmative.

And she is, at this moment, with the Great Warlord?

Yes. The seventh incarnation has taken place. The prophecy will be fulfilled. Now the Cat plays with the Snake, teases him, tempts him, but soon she will command him. Father's thoughts were crystal clear, the communication penetrating, imprinting the Elder's mind-source.

Then it is time? The Elder echoed a sense of reluctance from deep within his Earth nature. Father detected the attachment and concentrated his mind, shattering the Elder's thin shell of possession.

Have you trained him, prepared him? The question was quick, to the point.

We have, Father, we have, the Elder confirmed, once again in perfect tune with his host.

And you did not violate our trust? Father's aura vibrated less brilliantly as the six held close to him, their energies fueling the last moments of their contact.

He knows nothing of his origins, the Elder responded.

Good. Then you will know what to do when his moment comes . . . Now, we shall make ready for him. Father was growing faint, the brilliant colors now a dim flicker as the strain of function on this physical plane taxed the resources of the Seven.

Renagi lay stretched on the canopied bed. The morning sun was just beginning to send its warm beams through the small, star-shaped openings in the vaulted ceiling. The Warlord was at peace, his body sated and his mind relaxed.

She knelt above him and massaged his tired shoulders. Then she bent closer and playfully, gently, licked the small, oval wound on the side of his neck where she had bitten him during the peak of their lovemaking. As her warm, rough tongue made contact with his skin, Renagi closed his eyes and allowed the memory of her purring whispers to wash over him, rekindling his desire. Never had he known such passion, such strength and such fury as she coaxed, urged and finally tore the seed from his loins. Three times she had taken him to the place of Supreme Bliss and now he lay beside her . . . *Reborn, yes, I am reborn* . . . he thought as his lips parted, awaiting the stem of the pipe, its sweet elixir burning in the dark, carved bowl, the tiny red coals sending the pure smoke spiraling like silver ribbons into the air.

"Deeply, draw deeply," she whispered. His eyes remained closed as he drifted, watching the brilliant colors swirl round and round inside his mind. Now the colors began to form, shaping, creating a bright, moving picture . . . He was there, close, absorbed, watching as the blue-white water bubbled and splashed before him. He could see the bundle, carried by the water, rushing toward the cascading fall. It traveled easily, buoyantly, on top of the surface, bouncing happily up and down as, unrestrained, it moved with the current.

Renagi inhaled, intensifying the effect of the elixir as he smiled at the sheer joy of his dream. For although he did not know exactly what he saw, or its meaning, there was an innocence, a wonderfully naive quality to the vision.

Renagi exhaled as the bundle turned over, rolling gracefully, and he began to see more clearly. It was a child, a baby. The skin was pale against the blue of the water. Renagi wanted to touch the infant, to lift it. He raised his arms, and as he did so, the full face flashed before his eyes. But it was not the face of the infant; it was the face of a man. The face he had tried to imagine, the face that had eluded him. Deep, intense blue eyes, wide, full lips, a hard, angular jaw and long golden hair. The eyes seemed to focus, to lock onto Renagi.

"No!" the Warlord screamed, punching wildly at the vision.

Quickly, quietly, her warm hands gripped his shoulders, immediately releasing him from his horror. "My master is upset?" Her voice calmed him, brought him back. He stared at her, speechless. "A matter that was never resolved, a man-child who was never found," she continued as she refilled the long-stemmed pipe.

Renagi stared at her, his eyes desperate. "I have knowledge of this Golden Son, half-Ashkelite, half-Warlord . . ." she went on.

How can she know these things? No one can know these things . . . Renagi's mind raced, his fear growing.

"Yes, I know him. The one they call . . . Tegné." She gave the name a space of its own, a clear, final ring to the last syllable.

"Tegné, Tegné . . . " Renagi repeated.

"He threatens eternal shame upon you, upon your house, upon your family," she said, drawing him closer to her.

So I have not been insane. I have known. Known all these yeons that the child was mine, that he lives, that he will destroy me.

"You must find him," she said, anticipating.

"Where?" Renagi's voice was quiet yet demanding, as he tried, even now, to maintain control.

"To the west. Beyond the Valley."

Renagi reeled backward, his worst suspicions confirmed. "The Valley of Death? My Warmen cannot cross that Valley. There is no water, no shade, no shelter."

"Shhh . . . shhh," she whispered, stroking his shoulders, bringing her naked body close to his, rubbing her breasts against his chest—not to excite, but to calm him.

"And who are you? Why have you come here, how do you know these things?" Renagi bristled, withdrawing from her.

She followed his movement, never allowing their physical contact to be broken. "I am called Neeka, and I have come from beyond the Valley. I have come for you. I am your ally, your strength. This knowledge I have is your knowledge. It is your heart that I read. Trust in me," she continued, pressing close to him, "because I am yours. Yours alone."

Slowly, gently, he cradled her. She picked the pipe up from the soft sheets and blew upon the tiny, smoldering coals inside the bowl, rekindling the elixir. "Take the dreams, they will be our dreams," she said as she held the stem to his lips. Finally, secure in her spell, Renagi drew slowly from the pipe.

"The dreams will guide you," she purred. And as he permitted the thick smoke to enter him, he saw only her eyes before his face and he was lost within them.

VII

THE DOMINATION

If one desires to weaken something,
   he must first strengthen it;
If one desires to destroy something,
   he must first raise it up.
If one desires to take something from others,
   he must first give them something.
This is called the "subtle-but-clear."
   The soft and weak subdue the brittle and strong.

(Lao Tsu)

Yeon 999

Zendow

Vokane Province

It was spring, and the hills surrounding Zendow were alive with the small, bright-red leaves of the tiny hapaver plant. Their appearance seemed to herald the joining of the Great Warlord and the secretive, veiled woman who remained constantly by his side.

The highest Zendai advisers and Warmen quietly resented the intrusion of this new concubine, particularly since her origins seemed untraceable and shrouded in mystery. Yet it was undeniable that she had fully rejuvenated the failing Warlord. It was also true that because of her expertise in the gleaning of the thick, clear sap from the seed pod of the hapaver, a product was created which drew foreign buyers from as far east as Yusun and Miramar. Drew them like a magnet, causing them to trade irrationally with their horses, precious stones and kilo weights of silver and gold.

Questions arose as to how this woman, who had been no more than a creature of the Willow World, could have acquired the skill to extract the bitter sap of the hapaver and transform it into the dark, tender brown squares which were worth ten times their weight in gold. The questions remained unanswered.

Even Madame Wang, as crafty a businesswoman as any brothel in any province had ever known, bartered greedily for the new "elixir." She replaced the old, less-desirable mixture, made from the bark of the myristica tree, in each of her most expensive pleasure chambers. So desperate was Wang to possess a stock of the magic substance that she traded from her jealously guarded underground vaults of rubies and emeralds. *After all,* she told herself, inhaling a long pipeful of the bitter smoke, *if the harvest of hapaver should suddenly fail, I will become the sole supplier of "dreams."* The new elixir was used everywhere, from Wang's Willow World to the finest bedchambers of Zendow.

"As always, I have saved the very essence for you," Neeka said softly, holding up the tiny, sparkling crystal bottle.

Renagi lay naked on the heavy spread of the wide, canopied bed. He remembered the Celebre of their first meeting, yet the memory seemed clouded, distant, long ago. It was as if he had known Neeka always. He studied the fine, aristocratic features of her young face, marveling at how youth could so belie profundity. For he knew she had resurrected him, given him strength when he was weak, courage when his courage had faltered and had, in fact, pulled him from the very brink of obsession and insanity. *Yes, this beautiful creature has been my anchor, my very salvation,* he acknowledged.

"Shall we try just one drop?" she said, teasing, coming close so he could smell the sweetness of her perfume.

Renagi smiled, leaning forward as she slowly drew the thin glass stopper from the neck of the bottle. Then, tilting the bottle, she allowed a single, glistening drop of the fluid to gather on the tip of her first finger. Reinserting the stopper, she moved close to Renagi and slid the fingertip into his mouth, massaging his gums gently with the bittersweet moisture.

Renagi closed his eyes as the warm tingling began in his gums and worked inward, lulling, soothing, yet awakening within him a deep longing. It was more than a physical passion; it was a desire to possess, to envelop.

"Come here," he said, lifting his arms toward her.

She sat beside him, pouring another drop from the shimmering bottle into the palm of her open hand. Then, reaching down, she rubbed the oily warmth into the crown of his semi-engorged penis. The Warlord moaned as his organ came completely to life, growing huge in her small, soft hand.

"We do well together, do we not?" she teased, gripping the circumference of his shaft and beginning a gentle stimulation. He reached for her as, playfully, she pulled away from him.

"Zendow is prospering as never before," Neeka said, then waited, timing her next sentence. "Even Ashkelan is producing twice its usual harvest." She felt the blood cut off sharply inside him at the mention of Ashkelan. Now she moved closer, but allowed the hand which gripped him to relax as her fingers perceived his fear, his vulnerability.

"The older Zendai still talk. Rumors . . . rumors," she repeated, allowing the words to settle. "And now, with Zendow so strong, you must maintain control. For your sake, for the sake of Zato, for the sake of your lineage," Neeka whispered, manipulating his emotions, studying his eyes, watching her words take hold. "Now, of all times, you cannot afford insurrection."

Renagi pulled back, his organ becoming limp. She followed his movement, gently caressing his thigh with her long, flowing hair, licking along the top of the musculature with her warm, rough tongue, bringing him, in spite of his fear, back to life.

"The time is right for you to erase the final doubt," she continued, hesitating before she spoke the name. "Tegné," she whispered.

"Tegné." Involuntarily, Renagi repeated the name, the name he had refused to speak since the eve of their first meeting. "Tegné"; it sounded strange as he rolled it from his tongue. Somehow less threatening. The Warlord was completely hard by the time her lips reached his center. "Yes, now is the time," Renagi agreed.

The war party was five strong, including Gazan, or "Animal," as he had come to be known. At first the men had been reluctant to volunteer, but the promise of promotion plus a full kilo weight of the fine, cured hapaver provided adequate incentive to attempt the crossing. Besides, Renagi had assured them that he had plotted their course and could guarantee water and shelter from the blazing sun, the sun which burned in the Valley for eighteen of its twenty-four-hour cycle.

Neeka was mounted on a huge black stallion; she cantered ahead of Renagi while the Warmen remained only a few paces behind. She led as they traveled along a path that cut through the sheer rock face and down toward the forsaken Valley. Suddenly she brought her horse to a halt. Renagi reined in behind her.

They had arrived at a slight clearing, wide enough to group their horses. Neeka nodded to Renagi.

"This is the place," she said, motioning out over the vast, spreading vista. The Warlord dug deep into his leather saddlebag and produced a metal compass. He handed the instrument to Tabar, the senior Warman.

"Keep to the compass, due west. Do not alter a fraction of a degree. You have water enough in your canteens to travel for five hundred vul."

Renagi turned, looked at Neeka. She nodded her head, confirming his words, her hair blowing like a black banner in the gusting wind. He continued, "At five hundred vul you will find a lake. The water is clear, drinkable. Rest there, the cactus plants surrounding the lake are edible, so cut the leaves, clean them thoroughly and store a supply of them in your saddlebags. Refill your canteens and continue west for another five hundred vul. At this point you should find yourselves at the western rock face. Look upward from the base; you will see two high-peaked mountains. They stand alone; there should be no trouble recognizing them." Again Renagi stopped and looked at Neeka.

"At the center-point of these peaks, at the base of the rock face, there is a small passage," her voice rang out.

"The passage will be wide enough for you to enter and ride in line for approximately a half-voll. You will emerge in the Province of Lunan. Continue to ride west. There are several villages in Lunan, and one monastery. The monastery is called the Temple of the Moon," she concluded.

"Search and . . ." Renagi hesitated, faltering as he looked toward Neeka. She nodded her confirmation. "I want him brought to me alive," he concluded.

Use him as your consummate show of power. Banish all fear, all doubt. Display him openly as an imposter and you will forever silence the dangerous tongues which speak against you. They were Neeka's words and, reluctantly, Renagi had accepted their wisdom.

The candle burned bright on the waist-high wooden plinth in the center of the Dojo.

The line of twenty-four novice Brothers stood in front of the flickering flame, their white cotton gis saturated with sweat. Last in line was Rin.

Tegné had saved the exercise of the candle until the end of the session, leading the novice Brothers first through the basic forms and then through the prearranged five-step sparring. They had been training for over two hours, and Tegné felt they would welcome this variation. He often incorporated Tabata's lessons into his own teaching, and now, after so many yeons, he had gradually come to understand the depth and subtlety contained in his own early training.

"We are going to practice gyaku-zuki," he began, looking from face to face as he demonstrated the flowing counter-punch. "I want you to aim at the candle. Do not hit the flame, stop a half-hand in front of it. Focus your fist and send the flow of energy up from your center, through your striking arm, allowing the air caught between your fist and the candle to push forward and extinguish the flame." Tegné slowly performed the technique.

"Oss, Sensei," the small, excited voices chanted in unison.

"Remember," Tegné continued as the first novice took a low sochin position, "relax your body, relax your mind. Do not 'try' and punch the flame out. Try to perform a perfect gyaku-zuki. The flame will go out naturally."

The first child punched, putting his entire body into the movement.

"Too much tension. Too much concentration on victory. Relax, be natural."

"Once more. Three times each," Tegné said.

One hour later, the novices stood tired and frustrated before the dancing flame. Tegné knew their tiredness was good, for through fatigue of the body the mind and spirit became strong, willing the exhausted muscles through one more movement, less intent on success and more on the mere performance of the technique. It was at this stage that true understanding took place.

"Not once has the flame even wavered," Tegné said, smiling, looking from face to face. "Now I want you to try an exercise with your mind," he continued, singling Rin from the others and placing the boy in line with the candle. "First let us be sure that the position is correct," he said as he helped Rin into the forward stance, making certain that the child's extended fist was the required half-hand from the flame, then guiding the same fist so that it cocked back, drawn in tight to the right hip.

"Now, close your eyes, grip the floor with your feet, your hips turned clockwise, your body relaxed," he said, gently leading Rin through the correct form. "Think of your fist as a weight, a stone on the end of a string. Throw the stone by rotating your hips toward the flame. Relax your arm, throw the stone."

Tegné watched as Rin twisted his hips. The fist moved easily, fluidly.

"Good, good. Now open your eyes." Rin opened his eyes and looked with dismay at the burning flame. Tegné recognized the disappointment in Rin's face.

"The technique was fine. The feeling was perfect. This time you must keep the same feeling, the same flow, except open your eyes and concentrate on the flame. Allow your body to work by itself."

Rin cocked his right arm. The other Brothers watched closely, each sure that Rin was on the verge of mastering the mysterious ki—that energy which flowed up from one's innermost source and made impossible feats such as this possible.

Rin could feel the eyes of his brothers upon him. He knew that the flame was expected to go out, and he realized that his Sensei, Tegné, had chosen him to perform this magic. Rin was determined that he would not fail.

"In your own time," Tegné said calmly.

Rin's arm shot out, the fist pushed hard by muscle alone, the hips and their rotation forgotten in his effort to defeat the flame. Tegné watched as the fist reached its full extension. Then the small hand snapped open and the fingers stretched the final distance and flicked the candle wick. Rin and the falling candle hit the Dojo floor at the same time.

Tegné towered above the child, his eyes concealing none of his dissatisfaction at Rin's attempt at deception. Finally, Tegné stooped and picked up the candle, its flame miraculously still burning. Rin lay where Tegné had swept him.

Ignoring the child, Tegné placed the candle back on its base. As the class watched, he assumed a low, loose sochin-dachi stance.

"Relax, be patient. One time, one chance. Flow like water, then become iron." Tegné spoke softly. He moved easily, gracefully, straightening his back leg as he punched. His fist stopped a full hand in front of the flame. "Whoosh!" With a rush of air the light was extinguished. Then, gently, Tegné turned to the young Brothers.

"It is easy. Every one of you can do it. There is no magic, no trick. It is a matter of finding the gentleness within you; relaxing and allowing the stream to flow."

"Oss, Sensei," the twenty-three students responded, their voices joined.

"Now line up," Tegné said, before turning to the fallen boy. "Line up with the rest of the class. And you, Rin, lead the Dojo code."

"Exert oneself in the perfection of character . . ." Rin's voice was shrill, self-pitying. The class, speaking as one, echoed his words.

"Be faithful and sincere. Cultivate the spirit of perseverance. Respect propriety. Refrain from impetuous and violent behavior. Shomen-nei. Rei."

The class, including Tegné, bowed to the oil portrait of Tabata. "Sensei-nei. Rei." The young Brothers bowed toward Tegné. He returned the bow and dismissed them.

Rin had nearly reached the door of the changing room when he heard Tegné's voice.

"Rin."

The child turned.

"Did you think I would not see what you were doing? Do you think I do not know that trick?" Tegné spoke softly, searching the sheepish eyes. Without waiting for the boy to answer, he continued. "I do not want to see you in the Dojo for seven days. Instead I will arrange with Brother Minka for you to work in the pottery kilns. I believe Brother Minka will put your inventiveness to good use. If, in seven days, he tells me you have worked hard, I will test you myself. We will see if you are ready to return. Do you understand?"

A single teardrop ran down the child's cheek.

"Seven days, Rin," the Sensei said firmly.

* * *

The Warmen traveled carefully, conserving both their horses and the precious supply of water in the canteens. They had used the light, cotton-net tents to shelter from the relentless sun. They had been fourteen days in the Valley.

Groton lay very still, stretched out on his back, the cotton scarf wrapped loosely around his head, flapping down over his eyes, shielding them from the rising sun. He felt the first pangs of hunger gnaw at his empty stomach; he thought instantly of the dried, tasteless meat in his field kit and then remembered Neeka's instructions regarding the cactus plant. He pulled the scarf away from his face, rolled over, and crawled headfirst from the one-man tent.

It had been a hard ride from the east, and now he could hear the heavy snoring coming from the tight cluster of sleeping Warmen. He looked with satisfaction at the glistening water of the lake. So far they had been successful, traveling five hundred vul due west by the compass, and Groton congratulated himself, for he was amongst the first Warmen ever to attempt this crossing.

Quietly, with his short sword in hand, Groton walked from the encampment toward the giant cactus, its armlike leaves outstretched toward him. As he drew close he noticed an elegant cluster of tiny, pearl-shaped mushrooms. They grew in a perfect diamond formation at the base of the plant. There was a strange, sweet aroma surrounding them. He knelt down and sliced the first button from the small stem. He brought the cream-colored mushroom up under his nose, inhaling its scent.

Nectar, like honeysuckle, he thought, as he bit into the button lightly. *No bitterness, no poison*, he reasoned as he began to chew. He waited as the mushroom entered his stomach. There was no nausea, no burning, simply a warm, satisfying feeling.

Then Groton cut the buttons from the remaining mushrooms. There were fourteen of the pearls in his hand by the time he had finished. He ate half of them and carried the remainder to his tent.

His fellow Warmen had remained asleep, and Groton crawled back inside the cotton net. He felt content, at peace with himself, and the warming sun induced a dry euphoria as he replaced the scarf around his head and drifted off.

Groton was just entering the most blissful of dreams when he heard the beautiful, high female voice singing a plaintive song, somewhere far away. The song trapped him, lured him; he could very nearly make out the words.

Singing to me, she is singing to me, he thought, and, lifting the scarf from his eyes, he seemed to float from his tent and into the sunlight, hovering above the crystal-clear water. The sun appeared to reflect at odd angles from the shimmering surface; bright flashes from every quarter, as if there were four suns moving upward to converge as one. And from the rapidly distorting reflection of the water, the convex shape suddenly reminded him of the old, bleached white begging bowls he had so often seen carried by wandering temple monks.

He knelt down; the lovely singing seemed to envelop him. He stared into the shining glass surface. He met his own eyes, and marveled at the clarity of his mirrored image. He bent closer, cupping his hands in the water, bringing the wet coolness to his face, tasting the chill. And as he stood to remove his garments, he was certain he could see his own face smiling as if the image had remained in the water, independent of its source.

Groton felt the water lap gently against his skin, drawing him inside its calm. The singing was now a fine, high-pitched whine as, naked, he dipped below the surface. The lake was deep, and his body submerged slowly into the cooling depths. He breathed in, amazed that he could derive such pure oxygen from the water. And for a moment he was certain he saw an exquisite, ivory-skinned face in front of him. The blue, swirling eyes of the face were part of the lake itself. The eyes knew him.

"Over here! Over here!" Gazan called, motioning for Tabar and the two other Warmen. They ran toward the single tent, the only tent that remained standing on the shore.

Groton lay naked inside the tent, face down, his nose and mouth pushed into the wooden bowl from his field kit. The bowl was full of water. Something was clasped tight in his right hand.

Tabar hauled the dead Warman from the tent and roughly rolled him over. Gazan noted the strange, beatific smile which seemed frozen on Groton's lips.

"In the three yeons I knew him, this is the first time I ever saw him smile," remarked Tabar as he pried open the clenched hand. The seven mushrooms fell from the fingers.

"Let it be a lesson," Tabar continued, matter-of-fact. "Drink the water from the lake, eat the leaves from the cactus, nothing more." Then he saw the tiny golden butterfly. It flew from the tent and alighted gently on the mushrooms as Tabar added, "Leave the mushrooms to the insects." With that he turned to Gazan and motioned toward Groton's carcass. "Bury him, fill the canteens; it is time to move out."

Tegné sat alone in the meditation cell. His back was straight, unsupported, his concentration centered within the eighth chakra. He took in a slow, deep breath, drawing the energy up into his pineal gland. He swallowed to stretch his throat slightly, making a hollow and relaxing the muscles. He continued the breath, feeling the pulse run down and into his heart. He held the count for ten beats.

He became aware of a faint building of tension within his body; he relaxed and felt the tension drift away. As he exhaled, he kept just enough air inside his lungs to maintain the sense of expansion, then he inhaled a second time, drawing a more powerful, surging current inward, through the open passage.

Tegné willed the current to do its work, to unblock the center and allow the dark feelings that had plagued him for these last days to surface, to make themselves known to his conscious mind. He felt a sharp rush of anxiety that hovered below the level of his consciousness.

What is this foreboding? Like a black cloud within me, Tegné thought, deepening his breathing. His body temperature began to climb, and he recognized the warmth as the first sign of the Dragon Zone.

He continued his breaths, pushing against his own rational fear, toward the place where all ki is unblocked and conscious function surrendered. For the Dragon Zone was the supreme state of introspection, and if the mind was in turmoil the Dragon Zone was the supreme hell. Tegné felt the perspiration drip from his body.

You can still stop; regulate your breathing, his conscious mind made a final plea. Tegné ignored the plea and increased his respiration, cutting through the last threads of fear.

The village was called Zacatec. It was the last inhabited region before the final hundred vul west which led to the monastery. The search of the six previous villages had been fruitless, and all but Gazan were satisfied that the simple dirt farmers knew nothing of the Ashkelite.

Zacatec, however, was a different story. There was an assured opulence to the row upon row of adobe houses, their sun-dried bricks forming varied shapes, some octagonal while others were square in structure and painted white. There was definite pride here, pride and purpose.

Tabar was first to note the complex irrigation system, connecting three main wells to six cylindrical water tanks which were attached to each of the visible dwellings by a network of terracotta pipes. *Running water, plumbing* . . . he surmised.

At the far end of the road stood a fine, bleached stone building, perfectly round with a shining domed copper roof. *A chapel? But what form of worship?* Tabar mused, finally acknowledging the three Zacatecan men who had come forward, anxious to be of assistance to these imposing strangers.

"Have you lost the main road?" The voice was gentle, genuinely concerned. Tabar looked down onto the dark-haired, bearded man.

Finally, he spoke. "Listen to me very carefully," Tabar began . . .

Within half an hour every man, woman and child had, as commanded, fallen into formation; opposing lines at the sides of the main, earthen road. Still, the Zacatecans were a nonviolent group, and the Warmen's black-lacquered body armor with its tight, hard leather and distinctive red Sign of the Claw, aroused as much curiosity as fear within them.

This apparent complacency irritated Tabar. He drew himself up, sitting squarely in the saddle.

"We have come from the west, from the Clan of the Great Warlord," he began. "We travel in search of an Ashkelite. A slave.

An impostor. A man who claims to be the son of our Warlord. He is a liar and a fugitive. We intend to arrest him, to take him to Zendow; there he will be punished."

At this point, Tabar paused dramatically, turning in the saddle of his horse, searching the wide, puzzled eyes of the people below him. Gazan and the other Warmen positioned themselves along the two lines, allowing gaps of twenty paces between their horses. Tabar could feel the frustration and tension in the three men. The ride through the Valley had taken every bit of their courage and fortitude. Water had run out, the field rations had been spoiled by the constant heat, and the horses were virtually exhausted by the time they reached the western rock face. That, coupled with the vacant eyes and babbling, nonsensical denials of the inhabitants of the preceding villages, had fostered an explosive atmosphere.

Tabar realized that to keep order amongst his men something concrete, something that would at least validate their journey, was vital. Reflexively, the fingers of his right hand feathered on the hilt of his katana. He eyed the cluster of faces in front of him. Their curiosity had passed and now each Zacatecan lowered his head in submission. Finally, Tabar focused on the last man in the group. The man met his gaze. There was no hint of challenge in the eyes, but perhaps a spark of self-righteousness.

That will do, thought Tabar, maintaining the contact, his nostrils beginning to flare.

"You! Step forward."

The man took two steps toward Tabar. The senior Warman studied the stocky, middle-aged man. He noted the first sign of nervousness as the dark eyes wavered, decidedly less sure than they had been moments before.

"Please! Please, he is a priest," the shrieking voice rose from the crowd as a small elderly woman ran to the man's side.

"I am not a priest, Mother," he said, putting a comforting arm around the woman and looking again at Tabar.

"A priest? From the monastery?" Tabar asked. Then, without waiting for an answer, "Does the name Tegné mean anything to you?"

The man remained silent. Tabar turned, looked toward Gazan and gestured for him, the Animal, to approach.

"My men and I have traveled very long and very far," Tabar

said as Gazan dismounted and walked toward the man. The Warman glowered down at the mother and son.

"It makes no difference to us if we kill all of you, every man, woman and child," he continued, then nodded to Gazan.

Instantly, Gazan hauled the old woman off the ground. She screamed as he suspended her by her long gray hair. Her son reacted quickly, and the short front kick caught Gazan sharply between the legs. The instep snapped loudly off the hard leather groin guard. The kick had no effect other than to enrage the Animal.

Gazan's half-gloved free hand shot forward and the long, powerful fingers gripped the desperate attacker's face in a vice, squeezing so hard that blood ran from his nose.

"Enough! Enough of this! Tell him, Yung, tell him!" an old man urged as he lurched from the line.

"Free them . . . ," Tabar commanded.

Gazan reluctantly released his grip on the man while setting the frail, frightened woman on the ground. The old man stood, staring at Yung, nodding vigorously, pressing him to speak.

The alleged priest turned to the senior Warman; his body trembled and his voice was a jagged monotone. "I know of him."

Every ear tuned to the unsteady voice.

"Sixteen yeons past, I was a novice at the Temple of the Moon. It was during my first term there that the boy was brought into the monastery." Yung's voice had begun to settle, his nerves to quiet, as he continued. "He was unconscious, carried on a litter. They took him to the remedial quarters. I saw little more of him, I never even spoke to him, but I do remember his name. 'Tegné'—an unusual name, 'Tegné.' "

Gazan looked up, hoping that Tabar would be dissatisfied with this information, for nothing would have pleased him more than to slowly wring the neck of this insolent bastard. Tabar kept a steady eye on Yung, allowing the moment to hang ponderously, wanting him to feel the full animosity in the Animal beside him.

"How long did you spend at the monastery?" Tabar asked, finally breaking the silence, as the first sweat broke out on Yung's brow.

"Four yeons, until I withdrew," Yung said. "I did not take the vows."

"And you never spoke to the Ashkelite? Not in four yeons?"

"No, never. He was kept isolated from the other novices, trained in the Dojo, tutored privately by the senior Brothers." Yung spoke quickly, freely, trying hard to satisfy his interrogators.

"Is Tegné at the Temple of the Moon? Is he there now?" Tabar pushed.

"Yes, I believe so," Yung answered, unsure and yet certain that this would be the only answer to protect his mother, himself, and the rest of his people.

"Right!" Tabar snapped, then turned to the waiting Warmen. "Gather every man in this village. Group them and bring them here," he ordered.

Two hours later, every Zacatecan male above the age of puberty lay hog-tied in the far corner of the village. Thick lengths of rope formed tight nooses around their necks, anchoring them firmly to the two rigid stakes which had been driven deep into the ground.

Tabar wiped the sweat from his brow, remounted and looked down on his prisoners. Then he pointed to Yung, who sat bound on Gazan's horse.

"Pray that your 'priest' has spoken the truth," Tabar said, loud and clear, "for he will guide us to the temple. If we find the Ashkelite we will return and free you. If we do not . . ."—Tabar hesitated as he let the fear sink deep into the Zacatecans, ". . . I will instruct my Warman, who will remain as your . . . guest, to indulge himself upon the flesh of these men."

Then, with a final, confirming glance toward the Animal, Tabar reared his horse and galloped from Zacatec. The two mounted Warmen, with Yung firmly in tow, followed.

The quiet of the evening floated on the spring breeze which blew through the stone window, bringing a sense of rebirth to the small, austere bedchamber. Tegné's gold and silver medallion lay on the low oak table in the center of the room, within arm's reach of the single tatami mat and its thinly upholstered cotton mattress.

Tegné sat up on the mattress, his back resting against the white-plastered stone wall. Almost unconsciously, his fingers outlined the claw-shaped mark on his right wrist.

For three days Tegné had been unable to transcend during

meditation and equally unable to continue his exercise in projection. Instead, his mind remained locked on the succession of ever-changing images that had swept through and over him during his ascent to the Dragon Zone. A kaleidoscope of black and red, ominous silhouettes which had nearly formed, nearly crystallized, yet, within this introspective dimension, remained a breath away from his inner vision.

Something black, something red. Something I have seen once and forgotten, or suppressed. Something that unconsciously motivated me, something that will turn the final key, provide the final answer, his thoughts raced and collided, his rational mind arguing the illogicality of a quest for a "final answer." Yet he had come to a most definite impasse and, recently, had begun even to question his role amongst the Brothers, his position within the Order. A teacher of children? A monk? No, something else called to him. The voice was distant but, nevertheless, the call had begun.

And now, more than ever before in his life, Tegné felt the need for spiritual guidance. *The Elder? Surely the Elder will help me*, he thought as he rose from the mat, placed the medallion around his neck and walked toward the closed sliding door.

He stopped as he heard the faint, irregular knock. Again the knock, this time louder. Tegné twisted the round wooden handle of the frame and slid the panel open. Rin stood in the fading light of the corridor.

"I have finished my seven days, Sensei."

Tegné looked into the round face, still dusty from the kiln. He had thought long and hard about Rin since the last episode in the Dojo. *Why is he still given to these outbreaks of misbehavior?* A stolen piece of fruit, a small lie; trivial misconducts but enough to force Tegné to reassess his own worth as a teacher. *Perhaps he is a born thief?* The thought crossed Tegné's mind as he studied Rin's eyes.

Influencing a person's being is not unlike finding the combination of a safe; each advance and retreat is a step toward the final achievement. Perseverance. Tegné maintained an air of detachment from the child forcing Rin to break the silence.

"I have come to ask you to readmit me to the Dojo."

"And Brother Minka is satisfied with your work?" Tegné questioned.

"Yes, very satisfied," Rin confirmed.

Tegné nodded his approval. "Then you will recall that I promised you a test of my own when your seven days had ended," he added.

"Yes, Sensei, I do remember," Rin replied.

"Very good, Rin. Now let us go to the Hall of Light . . . Brother Kao is expecting you."

"Brother Kao!" Rin gasped, the memory of the stolen robe fresh in his mind.

The Hall of Light was a wondrous cavern; a long white stone room with a low, vaulted ceiling and endless rows of chest-high burning candles.

Each newly initiated Brother, having sworn the sacred vows and having been fully accepted into the order, was given a single candle to carry to the Hall of Light. The enormous candle remained lighted, replaced only when the wax had melted and the wick burned down, a symbol of the new Brother's commitment to the Order and of his eternal loyalty to the Temple of the Moon.

Rin's eyes grew wide as he entered through the ancient arch and beheld the sea of light. Brother Kao, upon their approach, struck a firestick, touched it to the wick of a new, conspicuously positioned candle, and stood back as it ignited.

"I see you are ready," Tegné said to Kao.

"I am, Brother Tegné," Kao replied.

Then Tegné turned to Rin, "You should be honored," he said to the astonished boy. "Most novitiates must wait until formal acceptance before they are permitted to enter this hall. You, on the other hand, are not only privileged to be here, but your candle is here also."

Rin stared at the imposing candle; it was very near his equal in height. Then he looked again at Tegné, knowing there was more to come.

"However," Tegné continued, "until your formal initiation, your light must be extinguished."

"Extinguished?" Rin repeated.

"Do you remember our last lesson in the Dojo?" Tegné asked, already beginning to adjust Rin's posture so that his pupil stood in a forward stance in front of the candle.

"I do, Sensei," Rin replied.

"And will you repeat for me the third line of the Dojo code?" Tegné asked, stepping back, away from Rin.

"Cultivate the spirit of perseverance," Rin answered.

"Good. Good. Because if you wish to reenter the Dojo you must learn to live by that code," Tegné stated. "Now; relax your body and . . ."—Tegné hesitated, looking at the smiling Kao—". . . persevere."

"All night if necessary," Rin heard his Sensei's final words as he threw the first punch toward the flame.

Tegné did not need to look back; he knew that the candle still burned as he walked through the arched doorway, up the stone staircase and out into the moonlit courtyard. Tomorrow he would visit the Elder. Tomorrow.

The morning sunlight fell upon the great iron disc which hung above the main courtyard gate. The single silver star and golden quarter moon were radiant in its glow. The powerful emblem seemed to revolve in space as the rising sun warmed the precious metal. The ritualistic morning chant echoed from the Temple, built into a single voice, hung harmoniously in the chilled air and washed over the influx of village people as they entered with their full wooden carts of fruit, grain and raw cotton fiber.

The Elder stood in the center of the courtyard, smiling and welcoming the traders, his silken robes resplendent in the warming sun. Morning, his favorite time of day. Morning, a new beginning.

Suddenly the harsh, loud clang of the huge brass warning gong shattered the tranquillity of his thoughts. The Elder looked up toward the high arched temple roof.

The sentry-monk stood straight, staring out over the trees. "Armed riders approaching the main gate." His voice was sharp, certain. Silently, without question, the courtyard cleared; the traders with their carts, horses and donkeys, along with the few Brothers who had come to exchange finished product for raw material, pulled back beneath the shadows of the slanting roofs.

The Elder hesitated, taking a full breath of air. Then he carefully adjusted his robe as he surveyed the empty courtyard. "Open the gates, admit them," he ordered.

* * *

The leading stallion was huge, black, and the man upon it blacker still. And with each of its slow, measured steps, the Elder fought his own desire to move backward, away from these dark intruders, to lose himself amongst the shadows and the observers. It was a desire inspired not by fear but by a desperate wish to avoid the inevitable. For he knew why they had come.

Still, the Warmen rode forward, looming large and out of place against the austerity of the scrubbed cobblestones and high yellow brick walls.

Tabar was watchful, wary, his eyes flashing with the sharpness of a hawk, assessing the surroundings, searching for potential danger. "Leave the gates open," he commanded, as the two trailing Warmen, their prisoner in tow, followed him through the heavy wooden entrance. The Elder's eyes flickered, a mere hint of recognition as they rested on Yung, then he turned again to meet Tabar's intense gaze.

"We want water, food for ourselves and for our animals," Tabar said slowly.

The Elder bowed, standing only as high as the stirrups on the great black stallion. "You are welcome here and you will be given all that you ask for on condition that you lay down your arms. This is a temple of peace."

"Lay down our arms?" Tabar challenged, "We are Warmen of the Zendai Clan—we will not lay down our arms."

"I know who you are," the Elder answered.

"Then perhaps, old man, you know why we have come," Tabar pressured.

"Perhaps," the Elder responded, willing himself to relax, to accept this confrontation. He turned toward the edge of the courtyard and clapped his hands once. Within seconds, two Brothers, carrying large jugs of water, walked toward the Warmen.

"We have been informed, and, we believe, reliably," Tabar began, dismounting while he looked back at Yung, "that you, or rather, your temple, has given shelter to an Ashkelite, a fugitive from justice."

The Elder appeared puzzled. "We have no fugitive from justice within these walls," he said.

Tabar grabbed the clay water jug and lifted it to his mouth, drinking deeply, allowing the overspill to run down his neck, inside his leather uniform. Then he concentrated again on the fragile old man who stood before him.

"Tegné." Tabar pronounced the name bitterly, distinctly, studying the Elder's eyes, awaiting their reaction.

Kao sat in half-lotus posture at the base and slightly to the right of the enormous candle. Rin lay curled asleep beside him. Above them the flame burned brightly. Kao kicked out with his top foot, and it thudded firmly into the boy's hip. Rin remained still, pretending to be asleep.

"Let your body flow . . . your fist is a stone . . ."—Kao yawned, then continued—". . . on the end of a string."

Rin's lifeless voice completed Kao's line of wisdom, "Throw the stone."

"Come on, Rin, the flame is tired. It has been awake all night," Kao continued.

Rin rose to his feet and looked hopelessly at the candle. The burning flame seemed as large as his fist. He positioned his body before it. He could feel Kao's eyes upon him, suddenly and genuinely curious as to the movement, the balance, and the distribution of weight in the stance.

"What is it called?" Kao finally asked.

"Gyaku-zuki," Rin answered.

"And how long have you practiced?" Kao asked.

Rin pulled his hip back, clockwise, so that he was half-facing toward the flame. "Two yeons in the formal class," he answered, drawing his right, striking fist into position just above his hip.

With Kao attentive to his every move, Rin's concentration was totally absorbed in performing the technique properly. *Seek perfection,* he repeated to himself as he inhaled.

The flame was now merely a focal point, no longer an adversary. Rin exhaled as he executed the reverse punch.

Whoosh! The light extinguished, leaving only the smoking black wick. Rin remained still, staring, hardly believing his accomplishment.

Kao was already on his feet, examining the result of Rin's "perfect" punch.

"I did it, I did it," Rin said, incredulous, looking at Kao, then bowing to the senior Brother. "May I leave now, Brother Kao?"

"You may."

"I will come back one day," Rin vowed as he lowered himself into the sei-za position, touching his forehead to the floor. Then, jumping to his feet, he turned and ran from the Hall of Light, in search of his Sensei.

"Tegné! Tegné!" Rin shouted.

"Tegné! Tegné!" The piercing voice echoed through the silent arches as Rin ran toward the courtyard.

"Someone here is familiar with the Ashkelite," Tabar said, listening to the shouts. Slowly, he drew his katana and rested the razor-edged blade against the Elder's throat.

Rin burst from the last corridor into the bright light of day. He sensed the danger, but it was too late.

"You, boy, come here!" Tabar called. Rin stopped, staring with disbelief at the scene in front of him. "Now! Or this old man dies," Tabar commanded. The boy was about to obey when he heard footsteps behind him.

"Stand with your Brothers, Rin." It was Tegné's voice, calm and sure. He turned to see his Sensei and a dozen or more senior Brothers from the Dojo walking toward him.

Tabar saw the long golden hair, the pale skin, and he knew that at last their journey was over.

"You!" Tabar called, pointing at Tegné. "Come alone."

Tegné held up his right hand, halting his Brothers, and continued by himself toward the Warmen and his beloved Elder.

Tabar was sure he could see the mark on the Ashkelite's wrist. *This bastard* is *tattooed*, he thought as he observed the low, centered walk and compact, solid body of the approaching man.

Tegné studied the three Warmen, making careful mental note of the two swords each of them carried. If he was to be effective, he must first remove the Elder from danger, then disarm the Warmen. His breathing was deep and even, his energy centered low in his seika-tanden. He was twenty paces from the group when his eyes focused on the blood-red Sign of the Claw which was etched into the Warman's black chest shield. Unconsciously, the key began to turn . . . the missing piece began to fit into place. He knew that sign; he had seen it before, on the armor of the Warmen who had murdered Tabata. A rekindled fear hung like a red mist before his eyes, the fear of a child. Then a raw hatred began to fill his man's heart. A sudden heat enveloped him, finally centering in his right wrist, as if a blade of burning steel was being drawn slowly across his flesh, and for a moment his spirit was lost.

Tabar watched the Ashkelite stumble, not more than ten paces from him. *Good, he is frightened,* the Warman thought as he pushed the tip of his katana deeper into the old man's neck; a thin scarlet rivulet ran from the wound.

Tegné drew close, less than a body's length away. *The Sign of the Claw; it is my sign,* his mind reeled, *it is the mark on my wrist.*

"Tegné." Tabar spoke the name, but the Warman no longer needed confirmation.

Tegné stopped in front of him. "You should have no further need for our Elder," he said, barely controlling the tremor in his voice. The Warman ignored his words.

"Get rid of that one, we need the horse," Tabar ordered, turning his eyes toward the mounted prisoner.

The movement was too fast to anticipate, the katana drawn and sheathed, and within that split second had come the horizontal strike. Yung's headless body sat a moment on the horse, as if it were poised, somehow, to escape, to gallop from the gates. Then, twitching, the body fell and lay beside the head, its wide eyes staring up from the dirt. The blood came in spurts, gushing from the headless neck, as if the heart had continued to rail with anger against this injustice.

Tegné felt the pull in his stomach, the urge to move, to act. Still he remained motionless. The two Warmen dismounted and walked cautiously toward him.

"Tie him to the horse," Tabar commanded.

"He is marked," the younger of the two said, noting with surprise the birthmark on Tegné's wrist.

"It is a forgery, bamboo and ink. The man is an imposter, a filthy, Ashkelite impostor!" Tabar stated, then added, with bile, "A bastard who calls himself the son of our Warlord, the son of Renagi."

"He is the son of Renagi," the Elder's unexpected words rang like two swords clashing in the still air, cutting the final cord, the last hope.

"For that you die," Tabar snarled.

Tegné lunged toward him. Too late, for the Warman's blade had already cut deep into the Elder's throat. The Elder slumped to the ground.

He has killed our Elder, killed him . . . The realization exploded in Tegné's mind as his right fist connected with Tabar's nose. Tegné felt the cartilage break on impact; still he pressed the punch inward, driving the broken gristle, like a splintered sheet of glass, up into the Warman's brain. He left no time for retaliation as he pivoted in a continuous, fluid motion, the same right hand forming the haito, and with a wide, spinning movement, hips driving the ridge hand on an up-sloping, forty-five degree angle, Tegné attacked the second Warman's neck. The blow caused an instant blockage of blood to the heart, as the Warman seized in cardiac arrest, Tegné stepped in, grasping the falling head. With a pull of his left hand he snapped the spinal column. Then he turned on the last man.

The Warman unsheathed his katana, more as a warning than as an intended weapon. He raised the sword above his head.

Tegné moved with violent contempt for the blade, sliding, inching closer. Now he could feel the Warman's fear, and the fear drew him on, making him more intent on destruction. Tegné feinted once, noting the downward, defensive move of the katana. Again he feinted, and then, with a roaring ki-ai, he unleashed a powerful, side-thrusting kick. His knife-foot caught the exposed chest beneath the blade; driving inward, focusing directly below the sternum, catching the lower, attached xiphoid cartilage and smashing it up and into the chest cavity, puncturing the Warman's heart and lungs.

The Warman collapsed and Tegné moved on top of him, punching down, over and over, into the unguarded face, the features turning to pulp beneath his fist.

"Tegné! Tegné! Tegné!" Somewhere he could hear his name; he felt strong arms pull him back and away from the face. He heaved a breath, regaining a level of control, his eyes focusing on the carnage around him. In the background he could hear the sobs of the village women, the low wailing of the Brothers. Then all sounds began to merge into a mournful chant.

He saw two monks cover the Elder's lifeless body with a shining black cloak, and finally he met Minka's eyes as Minka stepped toward him, carrying the Elder's bloodstained robes in his hands.

Tegné remained transfixed, locked in the horror, as if he had entered a timeless vacuum where all action was eternal. No words were exchanged. He felt the tears well within him, saw them run down Minka's face. He knew that Rin had watched, had witnessed the killing, had seen his Sensei frenzied, responsible for death. A murderer. A killer.

Unworthy. He withheld his tears, turning the sorrow, shame and self-loathing inward. The hellfires already began to consume his soul as he turned away from the bare faces of his Brothers. He walked alone toward the open gates; the gates which led out and away from the Temple of the Moon.

Awakening,
The lotus flowers
The leaves unfurl
Running red with blood
The beauty is tainted.

VIII

THE SHAPING OF THE BLADE

Weapons are not instruments of
   the superior people
Only when there is no other choice
   will they be used.
Regarding tranquillity and peacefulness
   as the highest good.
In victory, there is no elation.

(Lao Tsu)

The Plane Beyond

Time: Synchronous

The Seven Protectors maintained the vortex through which they had witnessed the predetermined act of violence; the act that forever separated Tegné from the Brothers of the Moon. And in its aftermath they felt the hollow of his heart, felt his rage, his shame. They knew its purpose but could not enlighten him; not yet.

Seven days and seven nights; he had taken no food, sleeping only in fitful spurts, waking to the screams of the Warmen and the sad, knowing eyes of the Elder. Thrashing out with his arms and fists, keeping the demons at bay, yet knowing that the true evil was within him, its malignant stamp etched upon his skin. His robes were torn, dirty; his body unwashed, his long golden hair matted with sweat and filth.

The forest, which as a child had loved and sheltered him, now loomed above like a dense, suffocating cloud. He was a stranger, alone, alien. He could feel it, hear it in the animal cries and the warning calls of the birds. He did not belong, all unity was lost and his soul was splintered.

Tegné stumbled into the clearing, a natural barren patch amid the full forest. He was weak now, and the thought of death calmed him. His only desire was to lie down and forget, to sleep and never wake. His eyes searched for a place to settle.

Facing him he saw the giant, a redwood standing alone on a

solitary patch, somehow defying the cluster and congestion of the lesser, surrounding trees. The long, deep roots and full, magnificent branches extended like strong, protecting arms from the thick, gnarled trunk. The green leaves danced proudly in the fresh breeze of spring.

Tegné stood beneath the tree, looking up, dwarfed in size and spirit. *Yes,* he thought, *I will die, and you will be my opponent, my executioner.* For he knew he could never defeat such power, such perfection. He bowed before the redwood, then lowered himself into the "immovable stance," pulling his tightly clenched fist back to his rotated right hip.

His first ki-ai came from a vast reservoir of self-hate and pity. The hip twisted violently as it threw the arm forward, smashing the fist mercilessly into the waiting bark. He felt his flesh rip and his bones break as he repeated the movement, striking with all his strength. Slowly, his spattered blood began to cover the birthmark.

The Plane Beyond
Time: Synchronous

Time and again the fist slammed into the bark of the tree, seeking to merge, to become whole, yet unconscious of its own intention.

And through the swirling funnel the Seven Protectors watched as the tiny Earth figure drew his energy from the ground source, through the leaves, into the vortex and up through the spiral, allowing their own delicate and ethereal bodies to act as conductors for this violent charge. And as the thudding waves pulsed through them and outward, they concentrated the converted energy upon the block of shining silver which jumped and undulated like liquid mercury before them.

Night was falling, yet time held no meaning. The pain of the broken fist had given way to cold numbness. The blood from the raw, open wound dried and caked on the birthmark.

Over and over again. Tegné punched into the bark, his hips rotating on their axis, driving his swollen hand with a force that had nothing to do with muscle and flesh; for he had become a part of the Earth, drawing his strength from its source, as deeply rooted as the tree which gradually and lovingly surrendered to the man. For the tree was also with purpose; to be the anvil on which this warrior's heart would be forged.

The Plane Beyond

Time: Synchronous

When the block *is carved it becomes useful. When the sage uses it, he becomes the ruler.* (Lao Tsu)

And with each rush of energy from the pounding fist, the shining silver, at first white hot, folded in upon itself, turning red, forming, becoming wide and flat. Finally the metal tapered to a point. Cooling. Hardening.

The moon remained hidden behind dark clouds, and only the steady, incessant thud of the fist against the bark drew Rin's attention; he cautiously entered the clearing.

He had remained ten days in the monastery. Ten days, and his heart could stand no more. Without Tegné, his Sensei, the boy had no light, no guidance. He needed his Sensei and, he believed, Tegné needed him.

As he crouched low, hidden by thick bushes and trees, Rin could make out the silhouette. He stared as, in the darkness of night, both man and tree seemed to move in unison, the man punching, the tree bending, absorbing the blow.

Quietly, Rin moved closer, until he could recognize the figure; it was Tegné, his Sensei, yet the faraway, vacant expression on the face and the empty, flowing motion of the body made Rin unsettled, confused.

Empty mind, empty body . . . empty mind, empty body . . . Tegné could hear the words. It was Tabata's voice, fresh and clear, as if Tabata were standing next to him.

Tegné punched after each command, barely conscious of his body, aware only of the blissful breath of life which filled his lungs and carried him on silken wings, high above the plane of Earth.

You are a wave; become the sea. The words were fulfillment in themselves. *I am a wave; make me the sea . . .* Tegné answered, feeling his spirit soar.

His fist was broken, his wrist splintered, the blood dried and congealed. Rin was close enough to see the damage as he watched through his streaming tears.

The child no longer made an effort to conceal himself; he stood only paces away from his Sensei. Tegné's punches appeared heavy, as if the motion were slowly grinding to a halt. The forest had grown dark beneath the thick layers of cloud, and somehow Rin understood; death was approaching.

The sound began at the base of the redwood, a low groan which came from the roots and rose up through the tree. Tegné ki-aied with every punch, a ki-ai of such intensity that his entire body appeared to vibrate as the rush of air was forced up from his diaphragm and augmented the weight of his blows. Rin listened as the groan from the tree increased with each of Tegné's ki-ais. Soon the combined sound was so great that the child covered his ears with his open palms. Still the ground shook, and Rin's sorrow and compassion were replaced by fear. He stared, the tears dry in his eyes, as the redwood buckled, giving way at the point where the fist impacted against its bark. Slowly, the tree strained backward, bending away from the fist. A deep, splintered indentation was visible in the thick bark.

"Hee-aa!" The ki-ai, like a roar, loud and demanding. Then, in a splendid moment, the clouds parted, and a cascading burst of sunshine shone down upon both man and tree. And in that moment the proud trunk split open in a mighty chasm. Rin shuddered as the earth moved beneath him and the tree began its slow, majestic fall. The thick, heavy body of wood bounced once against the forest floor, coming up, trying to rise, to stand once more before the man, as if, perhaps, its work was not complete. Then, finally, the redwood settled, quiet and still upon the ground.

The Plane Beyond

Time: Synchronous

The sacred blade was finished. A shining, perfect creation. Shaped by the Protectors, forged by the Warrior, waiting for him to grasp it, to give it life. For in its singular beauty was the mirror of Tegné's soul.

Tegné knelt before the broken redwood, bending forward, kissing the earth. Now the rain began, washing him, cleansing him, mingling with his tears. He felt the cool, gentle fingers upon his wounded hand; he was not startled, nor did he move quickly. All quickness, all passion, was momentarily erased. Slowly, Tegné raised his head.

Tabata smiled down upon him, the twinkling brown eyes, the fine, round face, the gray beard.

"Is this death?" Tegné asked.

The old Sensei smiled. "No, this is awakening, the beginning of your journey."

"Journey?"

"The journey of the Warrior; your journey," Tabata replied.

"And my purpose?" Tegné asked.

"To understand the source of dreams, the nature of illusion, and the meaning of reality," Tabata answered.

"Dreams. Illusion. Reality," Tegné repeated. "You speak to me in riddles. Please, Sensei, I am no longer a child."

Tabata held him within his gaze. "Then beware you do not fall prey to the enemies of a child. Anger, passion, fear."

Tegné bowed his head.

"And strive to know inner peace. For inner peace is the true resource of the Warrior. Discipline your human nature, conquer it, use it, become fully awake. It is only then that you will know the path of your heart," Tabata continued, strength bursting from his voice. "Learn to see, to accept, to understand the difference between passion and love, between purpose and desire. For, without purpose, the Warrior is a hollow, wasted man."

"I must go to my father," Tegné stated, as if the decision was without choice, irrevocable.

"Travel east, through the Great Valley," Tabata answered, finally releasing Tegné's hand. Then the Sensei rose and walked toward the forest, turning only once to bow to his student.

The redwood stood full, renewed, above him. Tegné lifted his right hand, examining the fingers, the wrist, the birthmark. The hand was perfect, healed, the birthmark clear and, in its way, beautiful. He breathed the clean morning air as the sun warmed his back through the heavy silken robes.

The barking howl came from close by, jolting him to full consciousness. He turned to see the wolf walking toward him, a familiar twinkle in the flickering animal eyes. There was no fear between the wolf and the man, and Tegné bent forward, intending to stroke the rough fur. As his hand drew near, the wolf looked up, its face shy, expressive.

Tegné hesitated a moment, then touched the coarse fur on top of the hard, bony head. At that instant the sound of light, running footsteps came from behind them. The wolf backed away, suddenly wary. The footsteps came closer.

"Sensei! Sensei!"

The wolf spun quickly and bounded into the forest, disappearing amongst the brush and trees. Tegné stared after the animal for a moment, then turned to face the wide-eyed youngster. Rin carried fruit, robes and several canteens of water.

"I am so glad you are alive. It was a terrible dream! The tree, you were punching the tree!" Still frightened, Rin motioned to the redwood, then dropped his cargo at Tegné's feet, leaning forward to examine his Sensei's hand.

"Yes, yes, it was a dream. Because . . . your hand; you had broken your hand!"

Tegné bent down and looked into the pleading eyes. "Why have you followed me?"

"I am coming with you. You are the son of a Warlord. You will need these things," Rin answered, pointing out the supplies he had brought. "And you will need a servant."

"Thank you, Rin. It is true, I will need the food and water. But, Rin, I cannot take you with me. It is impossible."

"Impossible?"

"Your life is at the monastery, among the Brothers," Tegné explained.

"I have renounced the monastery. I am free, free to serve you," Rin said, firmly.

Tegné nodded "no" as he stood, stone-faced, looking down at the child. "Thank you for the water. Thank you for the fruit, and I thank you deeply, Rin, for your concern. But now we must say goodbye." A forced severity in his tone. Rin's mouth opened in protest, but Tegné stopped him before he could speak.

"I do not need a servant, I do not need a companion . . . I want to go alone."

Rin's eyes filled with tears. Finally he turned and ran from the clearing.

The Warlord and his concubine sat quiet and alone in the small antechamber adjoining their private dining room. At last, Renagi spoke.

"Five weeks and nothing; not a sign, no word," he said, his spirit low, teetering on the edge of defeat.

She looked up at him, her eyes reassuring. "They have found him, he is coming. Trust me," Neeka answered. "I can feel it," she added, remembering that night, nearly three weeks ago, when she had lain restless, unable to sleep. Finally, as Renagi slumbered, drugged and snoring, she had risen from the bed and walked to the arched window. There, in the clear, full moon, she had seen his face, his deep eyes, his long, golden hair. She had experienced a yearning, an exquisite warmth which filled her loins. She had wanted to cry out in ecstasy at what she knew would happen, must happen. For, finally, she would be complete. And that night, as she turned back toward the bed, she understood her loathing for the Warlord; for his corpulent body defiled her bed, their bed—the bed she would share with the Warrior.

Tegné reached the crossroads and looked up, raising his hand to his forehead, protecting his eyes from the sun. The road to the east pointed away from the lush forest and toward a dark column of smoke. The smoke rose in the sky and hung heavy and black, disturbing and out of place. He followed the eastern road, into the heat and toward the smoke.

As he approached the far boundary, less than a single voll from the village, he noticed the sickly-sweet odor that rose with the smoke, thick in the air. An odor that he could not identify.

Tegné stopped in front of the faded road sign, bolted tightly to the high, wooden stake.

"Zacatec," he said, reading the name aloud. He had heard of the village, and was familiar with the fine weaving and woollen rugs which its natives produced.

One hundred paces in front of him he saw a child running forward through the haze. Her long black hair hung loose to her waist, contrasting with her white cotton dress. Her skin was tanned and her bare feet were covered in dry dust from the road. Tegné smiled as he watched her approach.

"Better not come into the village . . ." Her voice was sweet, shy.

"And why is that?" he asked, gently.

"Because there is a man, a giant man, and he will burn you on the fire."

Tegné saw the tears begin to form in her eyes. He placed his hands on her shoulders. "Please, do not be frightened. I have come to help you. Just show me where the giant man is."

The child turned, pointing toward the dark, pungent smoke. Tegné followed the line of her finger as the realization gripped him. *The odor was the smell of burning human flesh.*

"Maona! Maona!" The screams were desperate, shattering. The village woman ran toward them, her arms outstretched. "Please, please do not hurt her!" she continued, sweeping the child up and turning pitifully toward Tegné. "She knows nothing . . . Please!"

"It is all right, I am not going to hurt her," Tegné replied.

"We do not know him, really. We do not know where he is," she carried on.

Tegné reached out and, before the woman could pull away, gripped her firmly by the arm. "You must believe me. You must trust me."

His voice was strong, solid. She recovered, focusing on his face, his eyes, then she saw the medallion hanging from his neck.

"They say he is from the monastery." Her voice was more controlled as she stared at the medallion. "They took one of our men with them."

"To guide them to the temple?" Tegné asked.

"Yes," she confirmed, "But they have not returned with the Ashkelite."

"Ashkelite?" the word took Tegné by surprise.

"The man they seek is an Ashkelite. A slave—who claims to be the Warlord's son. They believe he is hidden at the monastery," she said, her words growing slow as she looked from the medallion into the extraordinarily blue eyes of the stranger. "For a moment I thought you could be the one, the Ashkelite. Your hair, your coloring, but it is not possible."

"Why?" Tegné asked.

"Because of your eyes. Ashkelites have pink eyes, eyes without pigment; they cannot bear the light of day. But you . . ." she hesitated, holding his gaze. "Your eyes have the color of lapis." Suddenly self-conscious, Tegné turned from her.

"And what, exactly, is going on in your village?" he asked, looking toward the smoke.

"A Warman has remained behind. Every day until they return, or until we give up the Ashkelite, he throws one of our men onto the fire. They are burning alive!" she cried.

Tegné moved closer to her. "Come, we will take Maona, leave her safely inside," he said, touching the woman's cheek. "Then I will go and put an end to this killing."

Gazan stood straddle-legged in the center of the rough clearing. He wore a tight black leather hood, concealing his head and giving him an evil, terrifying countenance. In his right, gloved hand he carried a long-handled, double-edged axe.

Tabar and the others had been gone nearly twelve days and, as instructed, the killing had begun. Gazan turned, his breathing like the loud hiss of a snake through the leather mask; he viewed the prisoners. A sudden surge of power ran through him as he saw the fifty men cowering, some crying, before his gaze. They lay, bound, in a heap; humiliated, defeated, their clothing fouled from the twelve days of captivity. He walked amongst them, occasionally rolling one over with his boot, checking the knots of their bindings, making sure they were secure, unable to break free. He said nothing, uttering only low grunts as he kicked out, breaking their spirits as well as their bodies. Gazan enjoyed this work, the feeling of total dominance. In fact, he hoped Tabar would not return for another day or so; by then he would have burned more than a dozen men.

Gazan looked up. He judged the time by the position of the sun in the late-morning sky. He circled the mound of living flesh and stopped in front of the pyre. Bending down, he tossed another dry log onto the blaze, and watched as it caught, the orange flames weaving up into the dark tunnel of smoke.

He knelt and pulled the charred rabbit from the outer edge of the blaze, waving it in the air to cool. Finally he laid it on the ground, chopping the legs and tail free. Then, lifting the small body, Gazan bit greedily into the hot flanks, devouring the animal's unskinned flesh before washing it down with the water from his canteen. Finished, he wiped the grease from his mouth and turned his attention to his prisoners.

"Time to die," he muttered, walking toward them. "Time to die."

Gazan's eyes settled on a tall, thin Zacatecan. *He still has the gall to look at me*, thought Gazan, noting the man's upturned face amidst faces too terrified to do anything but stare at the ground.

"You," he said, standing directly above his captive. "Would you like to burn?" The man did not answer, but neither did he avert his eyes.

"Good," said Gazan, bringing the axe sharply down, slicing cleanly through the rope which connected the prisoner to the others. He hauled the man to his feet, then let him go, delighted as the Zacatecan fell awkwardly, his legs seized from the days of binding.

"Get up," Gazan ordered, and was surprised when, by sheer strength of will, the Zacatecan struggled to his feet and stood before him.

"Move," Gazan commanded, pushing the shuffling man toward the pyre. He saw that the prisoner's wrist bindings were worn, nearly broken, as he walked close behind the Zacatecan toward the flames. He made a mental note to check the wrists of the other prisoners after he had disposed of this one.

They were now close enough to feel the heavy, stifling wall of heat. This was the moment Gazan cherished, the look upon his victim's face at the time of entry. Gazan watched as the man came to a trembling halt before the burning wall.

"Well? Why do you hesitate? Move forward," Gazan snarled, placing his war axe on the ground to ensure his two free hands for the final push.

"ENOUGH!" Tegné's voice boomed.

Gazan turned to see the blonde, barefooted man approach. He knew instantly who it was; the hair, the pale skin, the mark on the wrist. *All the better,* thought the Animal. *I will take him myself; I alone will have the honor of presenting him to the Warlord.* Gazan forgot completely about the Zacatecan as he turned and walked toward Tegné. The bound, beaten village men strained their eyes upward as the two men closed.

Gazan crouched, his fists moving in a slow, circular pattern. *As long as he is alive . . . Alive but crippled . . .* the Animal concluded as he beckoned Tegné to advance. "Come on, little man, come to me."

Tegné studied the Warman, caught for a moment by the sheer aggression in his posture, and the absolute confidence in the dark eyes which glowered through the slits in the black hood. Tegné watched the forward somersaulting roll begin, but did not recognize the movement or its purpose. His slide back and away was a moment too late as the massive, muscled body bunched up and tumbled toward him. Then the rough, cleated boot heel of Gazan's right leg extended, kicking out, catching Tegné's solar plexus. Gazan completed the roll, landing, balanced, on his feet.

Tegné was hunched over, winded; a dreadful nausea filling him as Gazan leapt forward and gripped him, pulling him close. He felt Gazan's hot breath an instant before the sharp incisors broke through the skin of his neck. The Animal's head twisted from side to side, ripping at the yielding flesh. Surprise and indignation buffered the pain, and Tegné heard the echo of his own ki-ai as he brought his right fist upward, the fore-knuckle extended, pounding into the soft temporal bone at the side of the Warman's head. The jaw released its bite, and Tegné gripped the leather of the black hood and again drove the fore-knuckle into the soft target, then once more into the nose beneath the mask.

Gazan staggered backward, surprise flashing in his clouding eyes. Then his vision blurred and he saw five Ashkelites, not one, standing before him. *I will kill him . . . Now, I must kill him.* Tegné waited, timing his movement to Gazan's advance.

Another step and Tegné brought his left foot up sharply, then retracted as his instep made contact with the groin guard. The mae-geri was well timed, perfectly focused, and Tegné felt the leather break inward against Gazan's testicles. The Animal buckled, collapsing on the ground. Tegné watched, alert, as Gazan tried once to rise, then fell heavily, unconscious.

"God in Heaven! Thank you!" The woman's voice rose, high and emotional. Tegné turned to see mother and daughter, tears streaming down both their faces.

"It is over. I promise you, it is over," Tegné said, walking toward them. As he walked, he raised his hand to the bleeding wound on the side of his neck, castigating himself for being taken unawares. He saw the sudden change on Maona's face—without breaking rhythm, he pivoted toward the fallen Warman; Gazan was again standing, staggering forward. Suddenly, the sun flashed on the blade of the axe as it swung down and dug deep into the Warman's shoulder. A dull thump accompanied the impact, and Gazan bent, lurching, falling. Blood poured from both sides of the blade.

The Zacatecan stood defiant behind him; it was the man Gazan had intended for the fire. Again the Warman struggled to his feet, looking first at Tegné, then at his attacker. He hesitated, unsure. Then, with his last failing reserve of strength, he ran for his tethered horse, pulling himself clumsily into the saddle.

Gazan glared down as Tegné came closer. With a pained cry, the Warman tore the axe from his shoulder, waving it murderously.

"Come another step and this blade finds a home in that pile of flesh!" he snarled, looking at the bound Zacatecans as he pulled the leather hood from his bloodied head. Then he turned back, staring at Tegné. His eyes burned like hot coals. "Remember my face, little man, I will not forget yours."

Gazan used the axe to cut the leather strap which held his horse to the post. He galloped from the clearing, up the dirt road and away from the village.

Tegné turned to the Zacatecan. "Thank you," he said. The man acknowledged the thanks with a faint smile as Tegné shifted his attention to the mother and child. He spoke softly to the woman as, gently, he stroked Maona's silken black hair.

"Get a knife, cut their bindings. Bring more of the village

women, massage their arms and legs before they try to walk," he instructed.

"And you will not stay with us?" she asked.

"I cannot. I must go on," Tegné answered.

"It is you—it is true," she said, looking down at the mark on his wrist.

"If any more come, tell them the man they are searching for is traveling east. Tell them I am going to Zendow," he replied. "Goodbye, Maona, take good care of your . . ." He hesitated a moment, looking once more at the child, then again into the woman's eyes. "Take good care of your mother."

Tegné turned and walked from Zacatec.

Renagi sat at the head of the mahogany table. Neeka sat close to him, in the chair to his left. She wore the ninjinka, the traditional Zendai half-mask which veiled her eyes and nose. The ninjinka marked its female wearers as "taken" and, from the moment it was worn, only the Zendai male, in this case Renagi, could lift the veil and lay eyes upon the wearer.

Zato's empty chair was positioned to the right of Renagi. Yanon and Zakov, the highest-ranked military advisers, sat in line with the sixty Zendai men and the three visitors who occupied the rest of the table.

The feast had been a necessity of business, a polite formality to display the opulence of Zendow to the three northern merchants who had come to trade their precious blue lapis lazuli stone for quantities of processed hapaver. The evening had been a long one, and now Renagi discreetly eyed the three merchants. He noticed their slurred speech and awkward movements.

The Warlord was glad the evening would soon be over. For the last hour his mind had been on Zato, hoping that his son would bring news of the original party of Warmen.

After all, Renagi thought, quietly unhooking the buckle of his belt and releasing the pressure on his engorged stomach, *Zendow is already rich beyond measure. It is not riches but purity which I seek. Purity . . .*

He relaxed in the wide, padded, thronelike chair. *Zato, Zato's children . . . Yes, that is my goal, my task. To ensure that the Royal lineage is extended, multiplies. The lineage of the Warlord Renagi, the ruler of Zendow, the most powerful clan in the history of mankind.* Renagi's thoughts were interrupted by the touch of Neeka's hand upon his own.

He looked into her eyes. "You have been far away, my love," she whispered.

Renagi smiled, inhaling the musk of her body oil.

"Your son has returned," Neeka continued.

"What? Zato? I have not seen Zato; he has not been here, I am sure."

"He awaits you in your chamber," Neeka insisted.

Renagi rose abruptly from the table, holding his silver goblet in his hand. Both Zendai and guests quietened instantly, attentive to the Warlord.

"I am sorry to say that a family matter requires my immediate attention. However, the evening is young, and I implore you to relax and enjoy yourselves." Renagi hesitated, looking from man to man, stopping at the coarse, raw-boned faces of the visitors. "Naturally, we have arranged entertainment for you, and we would be delighted if you would avail yourselves of our gifts." With that, Renagi nodded to the guards who attended the arched wooden doors.

The doors were opened to reveal twenty of Wang's finest. Barefoot and giggling, they swept into the room. Behind them, two drummers and a string player launched into a sensual, festive rhythm. The girls moved forward, swaying easily to the beat.

Renagi emptied his goblet, then the Warlord and the Royal concubine walked from the Great Hall.

Zato sat on the hard, high-backed dragon chair beneath the window. He was prepared for a long wait. He knew his father was hosting the northern merchants and he anticipated the evening would stretch into the early hours. He was somewhat startled to hear the two sets of footsteps outside the chamber door, and he stood, his hand on the hilt of his katana, as the brass knob turned.

"Zato, my son . . ." Renagi's voice broke the tension. Neeka followed, keeping a respectful distance behind.

Zato did not like his father's concubine, nor did he trust her. Yet, like the other Zendai, he acknowledged the stability and renewed strength that was apparent in Renagi, and he could only attribute this to the woman.

"Is there any news? Have you found them?" Renagi asked.

"Father, I have ridden as far as the western summit, located the place you described," Zato replied.

"And?" Renagi was anxious.

"And I have been through every Ashkelite village, including Asha-1," Zato continued. Renagi bristled at the mention of Asha-1.

Zato's voice was slow, tentative; "There is no trace of the Warmen, but in Asha-1 I spoke to the people."

"Yes?" Renagi said, backing away.

"Perhaps it is better if we speak alone," Zato responded.

"I have nothing to hide," Renagi snapped. Zato hesitated, then began.

"There is the story within the village that many yeons ago a young Ashkelite woman was kidnapped and brought to Zendow." Zato grew hesitant, then continued, "She returned pregnant. There was a child."

"Yes, yes, the Savior, the legend," Renagi pressed. "But no one has ever seen this man."

"They claim the woman left Asha-1 directly after the birth. She took the infant with her. They say her mother is still alive," Zato answered.

"And did you see the mother?" Renagi asked.

Zato shook his head, as he answered. "She is a recluse, mute." Renagi stood quiet, waiting.

"Father, for yeons I have heard of an imposter, an Ashkelite who claims Royal blood. I have never believed in his existence. But now . . . now?"

"Now you begin to understand my obsession," Renagi stated.

Zato looked directly at his father, a question in his eyes. "There is more to the legend."

Renagi swallowed hard. "Well?"

"The young woman was abducted by the Warlord's personal attendant. Your attendant, Father," Zato finished.

Renagi used every reserve to remain in control, to present an impenetrable front. "They lie, and they will pay for their lie," he said. "Our blood is pure, Zato. You are my heir, my only son. In time you will become Warlord, you will rule Vokane, as will your son, and his."

"Then let me cross the Valley. If an imposter exists, I will rout him out—I will bring him back to Zendow. Then we are free, clear," Zato replied.

"My son," Renagi said, moving close to Zato and placing his hands on the broad shoulders, trying to reason with him. "Not one Warman has yet returned."

"But Zato is your finest, Master." Neeka's voice broke the link between father and son. They turned toward her as she spoke. "It would bring great face to both of you."

"It is true, Father. It is certainly true," Zato said.

Renagi was caught in the middle, every instinct urging him to forbid his son the journey. Yet the combined will of Zato and Neeka prevailed. He looked deep into his son's eyes, considering. Finally he spoke. "Pick four of my best Warmen to go with you." There was a sad resignation in his tone.

Zato's mouth tightened as he nodded in agreement. Then he bowed to his father and walked from the room.

Tegné knelt beside the wide, flowing stream. Patiently he baited the wooden hook, using the earthworms he had soaked overnight in the moss-based mixture of radium, juniper and cedarwood oil.

With a fat, wriggling worm securely in place he sat on the dirt bank, letting his bare feet touch the cool mountain water, and tossed the line into the stream, watching as it sank slightly below the water's surface. The lively current caused the stream to babble gently as the water ran across the jutting rocks and fallen logs. He could just make out his distorted reflection.

"Ashkelite." He said the name as the gold of his hair flashed briefly in the rippling water. From his geographical studies at the temple he had been vaguely aware of this isolated, interbred race of albino slaves. He knew of the stigma attached to them, yet he had never laid eyes on an Ashkelite. *Until now*, he thought, looking at the lightly tanned skin of his arm as he drew back on the fishing line. *So that is my heritage; half-Ashkelite, half-Zendai*, he mused, not quite understanding why the Elder, or indeed his own Sensei, had never told him of his origins.

You will know in time . . . The phrase played over and over again in his mind as he caught the first glimpse of the silver-bellied trout. The fish swam up from darker, deeper water and cautiously approached the baited hook.

Acceptance. Inner peace, he thought as he played gently with the line, pulling the bait toward him, then slackening off, allowing it to drift. The trout followed, nibbling, but not committing itself. *A time for patience, a time for action,* he said as he teased the beautiful fish. Once, twice, Tegné tugged on the line, causing the worm to break the surface, then slide backward. He believed he could see the fish make the final decision an instant before he felt the strong, sharp pull on the line. Tegné responded as quickly, snapping the line back, firmly hooking the catch.

The trout was strong, and struggled tirelessly against the hook. Tegné released more line, allowing the fish a short run, then pulled the line back and drew the trout closer. Again and again he repeated the movement, until, finally, he could feel the fish weaken, growing less active against the line.

Now Tegné squatted on the shore, an arm's reach from the trout.

"Fate is the hunter . . ." He spoke another of Tabata's phrases as he gripped the dorsal ridge of his catch, his fingers holding it firmly beneath the heaving gills. He lifted the struggling body from the stream as he used his free hand to seize the heavy, fist-size rock. He laid the trout down, holding it secure as he raised the killing stone above his head. "Fate," he said again, as he hesitated, then lowered the rock, unwilling to slay the captured fish. Carefully, he disengaged the wooden hook from the open mouth and tossed the gasping trout back into the water.

Tegné stood a moment, watching as the silver giant floated, stunned, beneath the surface. Then, at last, the fish began a gradual, tentative movement, testing its fins, seeming to grow aware that it was still alive. Finally its tail broke the surface in one strong, sharp snap and the trout swam for the depths of the stream.

"Free?" Tegné asked as he watched the fish disappear, somehow knowing that if he threw the baited hook back in the water, he would catch the same trout again.

"Free!" he laughed, then turned and walked toward the eastern trail which led to the Valley.

* * *

By nightfall Tegné had arrived on the high, rocky precipice. The fine white mist obscured his view down into the Valley of Death. The cold mountain air caused him to pull his robes tight as he gathered kindling to begin a fire.

Within an hour the seven logs were placed so that the ends nearest the burning kindling began to smolder as they dried. As the fire grew stronger, Tegné pushed the logs closer together, feeding the blaze with a little tinder, ensuring that it would burn throughout the night and leave a good supply of embers for the morning.

He sat peacefully by the fire, gazing into the dancing flames. He had consumed only the pure mountain water for the past three days and, with the exception of the trout which he had thrown back, he had had no desire for food. *Perhaps that is the proper way to enter the Valley,* he thought, looking out over the moonlit vista. He breathed in, filling his lungs. He felt clear, clearer than at any time in his life, his body strong and part of the Earth, part of its spirit, clean and unafraid. He exhaled the breath and sat quiet, motionless, listening to the dry crackle of the thin branches which burned in the center of the logs. Tomorrow he would survey the precipice, search and find a way down, but now he would sleep.

He stood to unfurl the heavy woollen blanket. It was a small sound, like the yelping of a young puppy . . . it came from the bushes on the perimeter of the clearing. He moved quietly toward the sound, stopping above the short, full shrub . . . Nothing. He pulled the thorny branches back.

The tiny, torn piece of cotton cloth clung to the innermost branch. He pulled the cloth free, examining it, listening. Far away he heard light, running footsteps.

Tegné rose before the sun, warmed himself by the burning embers and performed the six basic asanas, relaxing and stretching his body. He folded his bedding, packing it into a tight roll, slung it across his shoulder and walked along the ridge of the Valley.

The gulf stretched as far as his eyes could see, and the fine, white mist of last evening was nearly transparent in the morning sun. Tegné followed the ridge into a northerly, downward slope and by early afternoon he stood below the mist, overlooking a rocky but negotiable passage. He began the descent, at times having to cling precariously to the jagged masses of stone; yet, slowly, he made his way down.

Midway, and he was aware of the radical change in temperature. The heat seemed to rise in waves from the desert floor. He paused, sipping water sparingly from one of three full canteens. Looking up, he watched the mist as it parted for a moment, allowing the radiant, multi-colored beams of sunlight to break through. His eyes caught briefly on a dark speck moving high above on the rock wall, then the mist covered his view, and the speck was gone.

A burro? A wild dog? he wondered, remembering the running footsteps of last night. He turned and continued his descent into the suffocating, dry heat of the Valley.

Two hours later, Tegné stood on the white, sun-baked earth. He reckoned it to be late in the afternoon, near sunset, and still there was little sign of the sun having shifted position in the dazzling blue sky. He squinted as he looked up, shielding his eyes with his open palm. Even through his closely held fingers, he could bear no more than a second's glance. He realized that protection from the powerful rays was vital if he was to survive. He pulled his robes tight to his body, using his wide silk sash to wrap around his face and up over his head. He took the zori from the sling bag and placed his feet in the tough rope sandals.

Again he looked up, not directly at the sun but to the left of it. He hoped he was correct in speculating the westward movement of the great orange ball, for this was his sole means of direction. Then he turned and walked directly away from the sun.

The heat reflected in relentless waves from the hard, burnt earth. There was absolute stillness, not a sound within the Valley, just the steady clack of his rope soles against the ground. Giant cactus grew in sparse, sporadic patches, their thick, spiked leaves jutting out like ferocious, clawed hands. Yet Tegné knew that the moisture contained in those leaves could sustain him, and their flesh nourish him. And in this empty, lifeless space, the great cactus was indeed his ally.

He walked on, losing all track of minutes and hours, sipping his water sparingly and searching through the ever-rising heat mist for any sign of life. The sun hung in the sky, moving slowly toward the wide horizon.

It was the stillness which was most disconcerting, so still that he could hear his heart beat, so quiet that his thoughts became voices. "*Travel east, through the Valley, the Valley of Death . . .*" Yet it was less than death he felt around him, for death must be preceded by life, and surely there could never have been life here, inside this inferno. *Yes, less than death . . .* He had entered the void.

The Plane Beyond

Time: Synchronous

He was not alone. For they waited for him on the other side, as if the Valley, its heat and rock, were simply a mirror, and he would walk through, travel beyond his own reflection and find his true self, his soul and his purpose. That was the desire of the Seven Protectors, and now, as they watched through the vapor, they prayed his test would be decided in a single moment; yet within their prayers there was doubt. For he was mortal, with a mortal heart, and the task which he was required to perform must transcend mortality.

So they watched, and waited.

No fatigue, no thirst, no hunger . . . The realization gradually dawned on him. *Why? What property does this Valley have that could erase these human needs?* The terrain had not changed, and for one desperate moment he thought that he had not gone forward but had, in fact, been walking in one place . . . but no, that could not be, because finally the sun had set and the moon risen. So time had passed, even though he was unaware of it passing.

Before embarking on this crossing, he had planned to travel by night and during the early morning, resting in the heat of the day. Now everything had changed, he would just keep moving; he had no need of rest. In fact, the more he walked, the greater his energy.

The Plane Beyond
Time: Synchronous

The Seven Protectors formed the sacred circle around him, chanting the "aoum," filling him with prana. They willed him forward, guarding him from the dehydrating heat, viewing him with love and with hope. For although they would never fully understand the complex nature of his Earth soul, the attachment, the possession, they could feel within this man the God-self trying to fulfil.

"Be at one with the dust of the Earth; this is the primal union."

Renagi was fraught with anxiety. Had he been wise in risking his only son? Should he not have waited until he had, at least, some sign from the original Warmen? Neeka responded by soothing him, flattering him, and plying him with hapaver.

And now she felt warm and wonderfully alive as she meticulously mixed the fresh-cut flowers of the primula veris with the familiar red poppy buds, kneading the mixture into a fine, sticky blend. Then, carefully, she placed the resulting paste into the waiting pot of boiling water, allowing the essence of the combined plants to infuse into an aromatic tea. She breathed in the sweet fragrance and her mind began to drift . . .

Tonight . . . yes, tonight. Finally I will touch him, test his Warrior's heart, feel his clean, Earth soul surrender . . . Tonight I will be victorious . . .

The Valley spirit never dies
It is the woman, primal mother
Her gateway is the route of Heaven and Earth
It is like a veil barely seen . . .
Lift the veil.

He was walking, yet he was not walking, the feeling was more of gliding. His consciousness seemed to hover just outside and above his body. *And what is my body?* he asked himself. *A conveyance, a shell, discarded at death, dust to dust . . . And my father? A Warlord; my mother? A slave. How absurd, the human drama. No anger, no shame, simply compassion. Compassion for ignorance, for ignorance is the human condition . . .*

Tegné walked all night and through the day, alone yet not alone. *Yield and overcome. Bend and be straight. Empty and be full. Wear out and become new. Have little and gain. Have much and be confused.* He understood "The Way." Time had dissolved; sunlight, moonlight, all was illusion.

The lake shimmered before his eyes. A mirage? *Heat against earth.* He walked toward the water. Water? *Inside the water is my true self . . . Tegné . . . I have come from the water . . .*

His thoughts collided and merged, and finally the dialogue ceased.

The tea had done its work; lulled the Warlord, pacified him, and sent him into a deep, dreamless sleep.

Neeka lay far away from Renagi in the wide, flat bed. Far enough that she could not feel the touch of his skin nor the heat of his body. She loathed him and she would enjoy the moment of his destruction.

But for now, she lay still, quiet, in the soft sea of silk, alone within herself as she began the projection. She could feel her body grow numb as she became conscious only of the minute jolts of energy that ran like pins and needles through her spine and played delicately inside her womb. She breathed the cool air into her lungs and exhaled, giving no resistance to the short, sharp spasms which began and continued at ever-decreasing intervals. The feeling seemed to originate in her belly, expanding and filling her. She placed her soft, open palms on her navel and felt a subtle warmth which grew rapidly into a fine, encompassing heat. She controlled her urge to moan in the exquisite agony of its embrace.

Neeka became aware that her consciousness was shifting, centering within her abdomen, and finally she relaxed, arching her back, closing her eyes, as the projection was born. Floating easily down the black tunnel and drifting out, over the abyss . . . Flying into the crystal night . . .

Tegné rested on his hands and knees, looking into the glasslike water. Never, in any mirror, had he seen his reflection so clearly. It was as if he was studying the face of someone he was meeting for the first time. The hard, high cheekbones, the deep-set blue eyes, the proud, defined jaw and full wide lips. His golden hair was now nearly white, bleached from the constant sun. His skin, in spite of the scarf wrapped round his face, was tanned, near golden in color. He looked deeper into the face, into the eyes, and as he stared, hypnotized, the eyes began to grow dark, swirling in tight, spiraling circles, until finally they were still. Magnificent eyes, alive and glowing.

He bent closer to the water, watching in amazement as a new face formed. A beautiful, feminine face, yet the shape seemed to materialize from his own reflection. The violet eyes held him as the rich, full mouth smiled up, and the long, jet black hair lay flat on the water's surface.

At first he was confused, his rational mind doubting the validity of his perception. Then, rationality became clouded by sensuality, as if the violet eyes were transmitting desire; it was a warmth that began in his loins and spread through his body. Until, finally, it was a pure physical attraction. Coming in waves, each stronger than the preceding one, enveloping him. It was something for which no Dojo had prepared him. Something that had layed dormant inside him, and was now awakened.

She rose from the water. Tentatively, he accepted her extended hand, and she guided him into the Lake of Dreams.

He was vaguely conscious, on the outer edge of peaceful sleep, his eyes closed He felt the soft, light fingertips trace the outline of his mouth, travel upward over his cheeks and caress his forehead. There was such trust and contentment within the fingers that he relaxed, unaware and unconcerned as to where he was. Finally, almost reluctantly, he opened his eyes.

She sat on the bed, leaning toward him. "Tegné." Her voice was low, purring, velvet.

He smiled as she wrapped her arms around him, pulling her body closer, nestling into him, kissing him softly. He breathed her scent.

The chamber was octagonal, the color of pure, driven snow. The ceiling was high, its sloping sides meeting in an apex. In the center of the hard, white floor lay a flat, smooth stone slab, three feet in height. The six Protectors stood, surrounding the slab, while Father Protector knelt before the small altar at the far end of the chamber. Incense burned, filling the air with the delicate aroma of pine.

The sacred blade lay upon the altar, glowing and powerful, awaiting its master. Father rose from his knees, turned and locked focus with each of the six.

"Ready?" he asked.

All wore flowing white robes with full hoods, exposing only their eyes.

"We are."

Father nodded once and walked toward the solid wall. Without altering his movement he passed through the wall and out of the chamber.

Tegné lay cradled in her arms, completely satiated, soundly asleep. The bright, full moon shone through the leaded glass of the window, the thick red curtain pulled tight and sashed to the side. The door was closed and bolted, completing the sense of security within the bedroom.

She listened to his quiet, even breaths. He had been all that she had hoped for; innocent yet strong, naive but wonderfully physical. She reexperienced the warm, sexual rush as she recalled the moment she had guided him inside her. He had filled her, completed her, and now she had found him she would never release him. They had become one, inseparable, a single soul, and in time he would come to realize that, through her, he would live, grow, rule an empire, produce a son.

She turned slowly, gently, so as not to disturb him. She studied his face, and somewhere in the recesses of her primal memory she remembered the helpless babe, thrown into the river and left to drown. She blinked her eyes and saw him again, this time as the youth, alone and unconscious on the forest floor. She had saved him, guarded him, guided him, held the power of fate over him and now, finally, he had returned.

"Love me. Love me," she whispered. He moaned and cuddled closer to her as she felt the wetness grow between her legs.

* * *

Father entered the room through the oak door, his ethereal form passing noiselessly through the coarse, slow vibration of the wood. He stood above them, next to the bed, then reached out with both arms and gripped her tightly by the shoulders.

She knew this moment must come and she was prepared for it, confident of the Warrior's heart.

"Tegné! Tegné!" she called into his dreaming mind.

He awoke and saw her being dragged, helpless, toward the closed bedroom door.

"They must not do this to me!" she pleaded.

Tegné rose from the bed. To his amazement he was clothed in a soft, white, loose-fitting garment similar to a gi, but without the stiffness or weight. He ran quickly to the door and pulled it open.

He stood in a grand, mirrored corridor. He functioned by instinct alone. Something dear to him, close to him—indeed, a part of his soul—had been stolen, and he would fight to reclaim it.

He ran down the corridor of mirrors and toward the darkness at the end of the hall. Faster and faster, his image becoming diffused as his own reflection converged inward, giving him the feeling of headlong flight. The solid wall was directly in front of him.

"Do not stop; go through, go through . . ." The message entered his mind as surely as if the words had been spoken.

He continued his rush forward and met no resistance. At first the whiteness blinded his eyes, causing him to blink, trying to focus as he came to a halt. The scene before him seemed enclosed in a veil of gauze.

She lay naked on the stone slab, held firmly at the wrists and ankles by the six white-robed and hooded figures. The tall, broad-shouldered man rose from the altar, the shining blade extended in his open palm. His voice was soft and rich.

"We have waited for you. The blade is yours."

Tegné stood still, staring, frozen. His heart and soul lay with the raven-haired girl upon the stone, yet there was something of such trust and purity within this man's turquoise eyes and fine, melodic voice. Something so familiar . . .

Father stepped toward him. Tegné did not move. The blade glowed warm.

"Pierce her heart. It is your purpose. Pierce her heart," Father urged. The chant began; the low, rhythmic "aoum . . ."

Tegné wanted to touch the blade, to hold it; for, as much as he knew that she belonged to him, he also knew that the blade was his. Slowly, decisively, he extended his hand. The chant magnified in volume. He touched the warm metal and a charged flow of energy surged through his body.

He turned toward the raven-girl. The gauzelike veil dissolved before him and he saw the black, demonic shape of a huge creature. A devil? A cat? The image of the Beast locked in his mind. He lifted the blade high above his head, his heart beating in rhythm to the "aoum," his intent true. He would pierce her heart; that was his purpose, pure and simple. He could hear the low, guttural growl as he approached the creature. All else in the blinding whiteness had disappeared. He was alone with the Beast, the silver blade his only salvation. The "aoum" filled him, gave him clarity, gave him power. Then, through the chant, through the vibration, he heard her voice. "Tegné, Tegné . . ." The words were like music.

"Love me, love me." It was the voice of the raven-girl, crying, pleading. He stopped dead, the blade held back by the strength of his arms.

The chant was soft as the veil again fell before his eyes and the raven-girl lay naked on the slab. Father stood behind him, close. Tegné turned and held the blade outward, returning it to Father. A single tear formed in the turquoise eyes as the blade was accepted. Tegné looked away from the eyes, turning, bending, and lifting the light, feminine body from the slab. There was no resistance. The "aoum" ceased abruptly. He placed the raven-girl on her feet and leant toward her waiting lips. As their mouths met, the roar exploded inside the chamber. It knocked him backward, pushing him like a gusting wind against the stone altar. He held up his arms to protect himself from the onslaught. But there was no onslaught, just the black vision of death as the Beast reared on its hind legs. The long, pointed foreclaws lashed savagely before him and the fine white robes dissolved in a rush of blood and flesh.

Tegné sat helpless, staring, as the roar turned into a mocking howl. The Seven lay dead, mutilated, strewn about the chamber.

Now she turned and faced him. Slowly, silently, the Beast approached. He felt the futility of resistance. Closer, closer she came, until he looked into the red, bottomless eyes. He felt the sickness within his soul. Her breath was hot, deathly sweet, as the rough, warm tongue licked his neck, causing the skin to chafe and bleed beneath it.

Then she turned and leapt. He watched the black shape vanish into the white of the apex.

"My son, my son . . ." The voice came from Father.

"There is no blame," Father whispered.

Tegné felt the first rush of emotion as tears gushed from his eyes.

"Take up the blade. You have seen her. You know her heart," Father continued, his words coming through dying lips.

Tegné knelt, cradled the fine ivory head, searched the swirling turquoise eyes, saw the life force ebb. Finally, the body relaxed in his arms, and he lowered Father gently onto the floor.

The blade lay still in the ivory hand. Carefully, Tegné lifted the glowing metal from the long, cold fingers.

"Tegné! Tegné!" The voice was familiar, but far away, like the rolling of waves on some distant shore.

"Tegné! Tegné!" Again his name was called, insistently, urgently. Slowly, he opened his eyes to the burning sun.

Tabata stood in a haze above him. Tegné drew himself to his knees.

"Tegné!" Tabata shouted.

He looked up and saw the smiling face beneath the large parasol. Tabata seemed somehow mischievous in his demeanor. He bent down and rubbed his open hand lightly over the raw chafe mark on Tegné's neck.

"I see you have been with her," the Sensei said.

Tegné was taken aback. "A dream, it was a dream," he answered.

"Yes. You are correct, yet in a way that you do not yet understand. By that, I mean you do not yet understand the nature of dreaming . . . illusion," Tabata said. Then, before Tegné could respond, he continued, "Within us, there exist many planes of vibration," the Sensei said, "each plane is interrelated. The Lake of Dreams is aligned to the vibration of your soul. It reflects both good and evil, both virtue and desire. It is a place of testing, and a place of learning. Experiences within its waters must be used for guidance . . . Now, let us examine your dream."

"I was looking into the lake. This lake," said Tegné, turning and indicating the glasslike water. "She came up from the water."

"And you got on well? She liked you?" Tabata inquired. Tegné turned away, embarrassed.

Surely he cannot know my dreams, he thought.

"A cat is a sensuous creature, am I not correct?" asked Tabata.

"She was beautiful."

"The Cat?" Tabata pushed.

"The raven-girl," Tegné stated.

"And . . . She has taken your purity. Be careful," the Sensei's voice grew more serious.

"Purity? I do not understand what happened to me?" Tegné responded.

"You have looked into the Lake of Dreams," Tabata explained.

"Lake of Dreams?" Tegné repeated.

"You have touched the daughter of the Beast," Tabata stated. "For a moment you saw through her veil of illusion but, finally, she was too strong for you, and too strong for the Protectors."

"The Protectors? They were the Protectors . . ." Tegné sputtered, a feeling of despair overcoming him.

"Theirs is the light within your soul. They are the guardian spirits of this Earth," Tabata answered. "And they have chosen you, just as she has chosen you. And soon, Tegné, you will make the final decision."

"Final decision?"

"To accept the task which the Protectors have given you, to take up their blade, to break through her veil of illusion . . . or to fall prey to the weakness within your own heart, to be seduced by the power that she will offer you. To join with this woman in an unholy union. To father her child, a child that would be the son of Darkness, of human flesh and blood yet possessed with the soul of the Beast."

"Sensei?" There was undisguised fear in his voice.

"This truth has been prophesied for one thousand yeons. The Elder was made aware of its imminence, as I was, before your birth . . . We could not tell you," Tabata said.

"Why?"

"Because the knowledge must come from the Warrior's soul, not his heart or his mind. It must be your single purpose and you must recognize that the superficial drama of your Earthly life is no more than a means to carry you to its end. You must be able to see in the deepest sense of the word, beyond dreams, beyond illusion," Tabata stated.

"And Renagi, my father? Must I not go to him? Face him?" Tegné asked, confused.

"Yes. You must."

"But . . . ," Tegné began.

Tabata reached toward him, touched his arm, calmed him. "Tegné, trust in what I say. All the paths of your life will lead you to only one place." Then Tabata stood, raising the parasol high above his head. "Keep your soul free from the thoughts and emotions of the Beast. Become the sea. Give his daughter no place to grip with her fierce claws."

Tegné rubbed his face as if he was finally waking from a deep, heavy sleep. When he looked again, Tabata stood on the far side of the lake. He stared straight at Tegné, his brown eyes penetrating. His voice seemed close, as if it was displaced from his standing figure.

"Remember, you must not dream her dreams." With these final words Tabata folded the parasol. There was a sharp, cracking sound as both the Sensei and the lake disappeared, leaving Tegné alone, lying on the hot, burnt earth.

He sat up, opened his canteen and gulped the warm water, splashing it recklessly on to his head, rubbing his eyes with the overspill.

Dreams. Illusion. Reality? his mind questioned, but already the memory was less vivid. *The tree, the lake; what is happening to me?* he wondered, then he glimpsed a flash of silver. He turned to see the blade lying next to him; wide, unique in its simplicity, shining, perfect. Tegné reached out, touched the warm metal.

Dreams, illusion, reality . . . the words danced again in his mind as he lifted the knife from the ground. *All paths lead to only one place* . . . He remembered the words.

The blade was his; he knew this beyond doubt. And in some

way this finely honed creation of silver was the last turn of the key; he was complete. He breathed in, attuned to the stillness of the Valley.

The whimpering voice was faint, barely audible, as it drifted up from behind the slight rise, perhaps one hundred paces to the left of Tegné. It was the single sound in a void of quiet. Cautiously, Tegné stood and walked toward the rise.

Rin lay on his side, his skin burnt and dry. He had followed his Sensei, tracked him through the forest, asked after him in Zacatec and finally caught up with him on the ridge of the Valley. He had injured his leg during his descent, scraping it on the rocky wall. Still he followed his master, never losing sight of him as he weathered the heat and sun of the desert floor. But now his canteens were empty and the child could feel the certain fingers of death. His feet were blistered and his legs had given up. He wanted only to lie down. He could feel himself grow light, dizzy, and he knew death was close as his wide, vacant eyes beheld the Angel of Light. The brilliant white, glowing halo came close and the fine blue eyes looked into his soul while the sure, strong hands began to free the spirit from his expired shell.

"Rin! Come on, Rin. Come on!" The angel spoke to him as he bathed his head with the holy water. Then blackness . . .

Rin knew he had sinned in his brief time on Earth. There was the stolen robe, the freshly baked bread from the hearth, the fruit, the books from the library that had gone undiscovered, but he had atoned for all these. Surely he had not transgressed enough to end in hell? But here he was, without light, lost in darkness.

"You are going to be all right. Just hold on," he heard the angel's voice from far away. *Perhaps all is not lost, at least someone is fighting for my soul.* He could feel the strong arms pick him up.

"Rin! Talk to me, talk to me . . ." The angel's voice was somehow familiar and he knew that if he wanted to enter the gates of pearl, now was his last chance.

"I am sorry, God. I will never sin again."

Tegné removed the dark, wet cloth from the child's forehead. The light was blinding. *I am in heaven,* Rin thought as the face of the angel became more clear.

"What are you doing here?" Tegné's voice dragged him back to Earth.

Rin's answer was spontaneous. "I am following my heart." To give credence to the words, he extended his right hand. The knuckles were cut and bruised. "I have punched the tree and found my way."

Tegné lifted the child's body in his arms. His eyes searched for shade, and finally rested on an enormous cactus, less than fifty paces away. Its long arms cast shadows in the setting sun. He carried Rin to the cactus, realizing that he would now have to take the boy with him, at least as far as Shuree.

Zato and his Warmen camped on the ridge overlooking the Valley. They woke early. From far away, the barely discernible sound of a single horse drifted on the parched wind. Zato stood, looking out to the horizon, searching the scorched earth for the origin of the sound.

"Magniscope, medium power," he ordered.

Zato lifted the scope to his eye and began a slow scan of the Valley below. The thin line of magnetized mercury in the viewfinder formed an arrow, indicating a speck to the northwest in the upper corner of the lens. Zato adjusted the scope.

The figure was clear in the lens. The rider was hunched forward in the saddle, the black lacquered body armor dusty and torn. The red Sign of the Claw stood out sharp and certain. The clickety-clack of the trotting hooves came closer and closer.

"Gazan! The Animal!" Zato recognized the hard, uneven face hidden behind a thick stubble of beard. He watched through the lens as Gazan rode directly below him and entered the low passage which cut through the rock face.

Thirty minutes later, Gazan's exhausted stallion climbed the last of the rocky trail to their encampment. Zato ran toward him as the injured, sun-blistered Warman began to dismount, then fell from his saddle. His black hair was streaked with yellow, sunburnt patches, his face was puffy and distorted, and the skin below the socket of each eye was blood-raw from overexposure. White, sticky pus oozed from the torn padded leather of his right shoulder.

Zato knelt beside him and examined the deep, festering wound, then pulled back and stared questioningly into his face. An ugly black bruise ran from his temple, down across his left cheek and broken nose.

"Water . . ." The single word dropped from the split, swollen lips.

Zato grabbed a full, fresh canteen. "Sit . . . sit," he said, using his right arm to support the Animal. "Bring me a blanket," Zato called, then offered the canteen, taking care that Gazan did not guzzle the water and cause his empty stomach to seize.

"What happened?" Zato asked.

Gazan sat motionless, silent. Zato took the blanket and wrapped it round the broad shoulders. Finally Gazan looked up.

"He is coming . . ."

How long have we traveled? Ten days, twenty days? More? Tegné wondered as he began to count his every step, seeing each of them as an individual bead on Yano's abacus, and somehow imagining, as in his early yeons as an uchi-deshi, that when he reached one thousand he would be free.

Time had dissolved, its hours and minutes melting into a burning pool beneath the sun. Still Tegné moved on, the weight of Rin upon his shoulders seeming to double with each new step. Finally, tired and discouraged, he stopped.

"We must find out if you can walk."

"Oss, Sensei, I am ready," the boy replied.

Tegné lifted the small body up and over his head, then brought Rin down, placing him lightly on the ground. Rin stood, uncomfortably.

"I am healed, I feel fine," Rin assured him. He took two tentative steps and landed in a heap.

"It will take at least another two days," Tegné said, bending down and hoisting Rin back onto his shoulders. Then, tired and dry, Tegné continued the slow walk across the hard, unforgiving earth.

He walked on through the heat of the day, away from the setting sun.

Twilight in the Valley was strangely beautiful, a glowing half-light of gold and blue. The hazy incandescence lasted hours, shadowing the barren earth with a peculiar tranquillity. Tegné felt his mood lighten as the walking grew easier now that the sun had set.

Even his constant thirst had abated, making their regimen of one quart of water a day seem nearly tolerable. The cactus buds were a nourishing, if somewhat bitter, food, and Tegné bit into one as he walked, passing another to Rin. He was estimating the amount of ground they had covered when he saw footprints. Quickly, he lifted Rin down.

It cannot be, he thought, as he ran toward the single set of prints. Kneeling beside them, his worst suspicions were confirmed: the footprints were his own.

He looked back at the last strains of daylight. "We have come in a circle." The words carried the weight of utter futility. Slowly, he looked up at the child.

Rin stood very still, his eyes wide, frightened, and staring directly behind Tegné.

She stood not more than fifty paces from them. Tegné's hand went instinctively to the hard, knurled silver grip of the dagger. At this moment he was thankful that the boy was with him, if only to confirm that the enormous black cat was real, and not an hallucination.

His eyes linked with the eyes of the Beast. He felt his heart pound as the blood surged to his temples. All his energy converged at the center point of his forehead. He held back the cry of pain as the first beam of thought penetrated him.

Tegné. His own name flew forward from the red, glowing eyes. Then the second thought formed in his mind; *I have come for you.*

Who are you? he questioned before his lips could form the words.

I am your soul... she answered, and he felt the shadow of darkness cross his heart.... *Come*...

She led them into the night. And when, finally, near daybreak, Tegné and Rin lay down to sleep, she remained close by, watching over them.

Tegné awoke before the child, called from his dreamless sleep by her compelling presence. He turned toward the rising sun.

She stood with her back to the early light. He faced her and walked slowly forward, listening to her deep, low breaths as she watched him approach.

How delicate he is, she thought, studying the lines of his clearly defined abdomen and the strong, lean hips. *His hair is like gold*, she observed, as he came within the last three yards.

Touch me . . . touch me . . . she willed. She sensed no fear as he stood beneath her. She lowered her head and Tegné raised his arm, his open hand extended as he touched her, at first tentatively, then growing more sure. The hand was ecstasy as it stroked her, kneading the sleek muscles of her neck. She bent her head toward him, allowing his fingers to rub deep into her shining black fur.

"Sensei! Sensei! Sensei!" The child's scream ripped the still surface of the morning.

Tegné's movement was sharp, abrupt; she felt his moment of fear, of guilt, as he withdrew from her. Rising to her full height, she towered above him. Her heart blazed and her giant mouth pulled tight back, revealing white fangs.

It was the child who came between us. The child must die! she vowed.

"No!" Tegné's shout was charged, powerful. "No!" Again he cried out. He stood squarely before her, the boy behind him. The sun shone on the drawn silver blade.

It had been their moment, and now their moment was gone. She backed away. There was only her sorrow as she turned and leaped into the sky, leaving the man and the boy staring after her, alone in the Valley. Then, in the wake of her disappearance, Tegné and Rin beheld the fading of the morning mist as the eastern rock face grew clear before them.

The heavy iron-mesh net was spread its full four paces square, hovering above the clearing, supported and partially concealed by the leafy branches of the surrounding trees.

Zato squatted down, hidden behind the tree at the far corner of the net. Gazan, his face wrapped in white cotton bandage and his right arm in a crude sling, knelt beside him. The four other Warmen were in position at opposite corners of the clearing.

The trap had been set for two days, and now, after much faith and patience, the Warmen knew their prey was close. Zato had spotted the man and child through the magniscope, nearly two hours ago. He had watched with fascination as they approached the rock face, finding and entering the passage that led into Shuree. He had strained to pick out the details of the face, the blue eyes, the golden hair. And now, at any moment, their wait would be over.

Tegné inhaled the cool forest air. A rush of memory overcame him, and he stood still for a moment, letting the memories pass. It had been more than half his lifetime since he had breathed this air and felt the soft earth beneath his feet. He watched as Rin moved ahead.

He could feel the deep fatigue within his own body and now he noticed how thin the boy had become. *As soon as we come to a village I will see that Rin is looked after, and then go on alone,* he resolved as he increased his pace, overtaking the youngster. The trail before them was of fine, broken stone and gravel. Tegné saw the deep hoof-marks.

"Rin!" he called. Rin turned and walked back.

"Sit quietly beside me," Tegné said, calm but firm, as he knelt above the prints, breathing in, sensing danger. "I want you to stay behind me. Keep me in your sight, but no closer."

"The men that came for me at the temple—there are others from the same clan. They are close, I can feel it," he told the boy, looking at him closely to make sure he understood. "If we should separate, you must follow the path of the rising sun. Travel east," he continued as he pointed Rin in the right direction. "There are many villages in the east, one will surely take you in." Tegné paused, then stood up. "Now I will go on up the trail, and you follow. But keep a distance between us."

To ensure that the boy would be safe, Tegné took the medallion from his own neck, Tabata's medallion, and placed it carefully around the neck of the child.

"If ever anyone should ask where you have come from, show them the medallion, tell them of the Temple . . . Do you understand?"

"Do you understand?" Tegné repeated.

"Oss, Sensei," Rin replied, his voice quivering.

Tegné smiled at the child, suddenly aware of how it must feel to have a son, an echo of one's own flesh and blood. He leaned forward and touched the small shoulders, drawing Rin close and embracing him. Then he stood, his facial expression hardening as he turned and began his climb up the steep trail.

* * *

The Warlord had awakened before dawn, sensing the strange emptiness in the wide bed. He turned, relieved to see Neeka lying peacefully on her back beside him. Slowly, gently, he reached out to her, letting his fingers rest above her naked shoulder. Then he brought his fingers down upon her ice-cold, waxen flesh.

His heart jolted as he rolled over, coming up on his hands and knees above her closed eyelids. "Neeka! Neeka!" he called. There was no response, nothing except the mask of death.

No, it is not possible! his mind screamed.

"Neeka, Neeka," he cried as, at last losing control, he fell forward, gripping her, cradling her, lifting her to him. His tears spilled into her hair and down upon the silk pillowcase.

"No! No! No!" he sobbed.

She watched from above the bed, her astral form hovering, vibrating, ready to realign with her Earth body. She recognized the irony of the scene below; the old Warlord, weeping with grief over a soulless bit of flesh and bone.

Why do they attach such sentiment to this transient state of physical life? she pondered, listening to his sobs as, finally, he prostrated himself on the bed beside the body. She finished the realignment and began her descent, the finely vibrating astral form entering perfectly into her corporeal shell.

She experienced the uncomfortable numbness in her bloodless limbs as she readjusted to the limited state. Now she could hear him beside her. She listened to his sobs, as gradually she regained the feeling in her hands and feet.

Renagi's back was toward her and slowly, painfully, she inched closer to him, her movements light upon the bed. Finally she was behind him.

"Is something troubling my Warlord?" she asked.

Renagi was instantly still, his heart missing a beat. Then he turned to her, the tears dry in his wide, disbelieving eyes.

It was not the danger of death that whispered to him on the warm breeze. A different sort of tension clung to the thick branches.

An ambush, a trap . . . His mind relayed the message to his body, warning it to prepare. He deepened his state of zanshin, maintaining a slow, steady pace as he walked toward the clearing.

Zato could see him clearly now. *He is not so big, quite strong-looking, but not big,* he noted as he knelt lower, concealing himself behind the trunk of the oak.

Tegné was at the perimeter of the clearing. The breeze came from the southwest, blowing the smell of the iron net away from him. Still, he felt the danger, knew this was the place of ambush, yet his body movements did not alter. *Do not draw the dagger. Give no indication of preparedness . . .*

Two steps. Three steps. Four steps. He heard the snap as the short sword sliced through the rope, releasing the net. The dark shadow descended as he dived forward, tumbling, landing free of the heavy-meshed iron.

"Take him! Take him!" a rough voice commanded. Tegné heard the *whoosh!* of air and ducked beneath the six-foot bo as, pivoting from a crouch, he rose up and grabbed the wooden pole. He twisted away from the Warman as he executed an ashi-bari, sweeping the man's legs from under him and wrenching the bo from his grasp. The Warman attempted to rise, and Tegné thrust the tapered end of the fighting stick into his solar plexus, dropping the man again before pivoting to face his next assailant.

Zato remained at the side of the clearing, studying the Ashkelite as the three Warmen closed. Gazan stood next to him.

"He has been trained with the bo," Zato observed, watching as Tegné warded off the first vicious, horizontal strike of the twin rods which were connected to a short iron chain. The Warman wielding the nunchaku stepped back from Tegné's block and began swinging the weapon in a whistling figure-of-eight pattern. Tegné stepped forward, within range of the weapon.

He will certainly go down, Zato thought as the Warman suddenly changed to a aggressive motion. Tegné studied the hands which gripped the nunchaku, not the weapon itself. His timing was precise. At the moment the nunchaku began the overhead, downward swing, the striking rod no more than a blur before Zato's eyes, Tegné brought the extended end of the bo sharply upward. The hard wood caught the Warman beneath his chin. Tegné stepped into the movement, using the full forward thrust to push the man's head backward. Then, in a circular swing, he attacked the vulnerable muscles that protected the carotid artery. There was a sharp *whack!* as the bo connected with the Warman's neck, sending the man reeling to the ground.

Tegné half-turned as the third Warman slipped his calloused fingers into the iron-pronged tekko. He moved back and away as the metal fists began a double circular motion. Tegné remained just outside of striking range as the Warman moved forward, bouncing easily on the balls of his feet. To gain full advantage of the iron fists, Tegné reckoned that the man would attack using a lunging, driving punch. He positioned the bo straight to his right side, parallel to the earth, guarding against a rush from either the front man or the one behind him. For a long moment there was only stillness, and Tegné concentrated his awareness into slow, even exhalations, allowing his body to react by trained instinct. The tension was broken only by a hissing, sucking sound from his far right; the sound of steel being drawn quickly against hard wood and leather.

"Stop! Enough! Enough!" Zato's voice cut the air. "I said enough!" Zato repeated, and Tegné sensed a break in concentration. Still he maintained zanshin as, finally, the fighter using the tekko backed away. Tegné pivoted slowly.

Zato stepped from behind the oak, his short sword unsheathed and pointed at Rin's throat. Gazan stood next to him, holding the child secure.

"You," Zato said, motioning toward the standing Warman, "tie him to the sled." The Warman pushed Tegné roughly to the flat wooden bed which was attached to Zato's stallion.

"Tie him securely," Zato ordered.

"Blindfold him. Gag him," Zato continued.

The heavy cloth scarf tasted of salt and smelt of sweat as it was drawn tightly across Tegné's mouth and knotted behind his head. Tegné looked up to see Zato above him, and noticed the alarm in the wide eyes as Zato studied the birthmark, now visible on Tegné's bound right wrist.

A tattoo? Surely it is a forgery, but how? Zato wondered, looking furtively at the identical mark on his own wrist. Then his eyes caught the dagger that was buried in the waistband of Tegné's trousers. *I have never seen such a fine blade*, Zato thought as he withdrew the knife, cradling it a moment in his own hand, noting its superb balance. Then, he turned to Gazan.

"Release the child. We have no use for him."

Gazan hesitated, a question in his eyes.

"I said let him go!" Zato repeated.

Reluctantly, the Animal released his grip. Rin remained still for a moment, then slowly began to rotate his head, trying to ease the stiffness and pain caused by the powerful lock. From the corner of his eye he could see Tegné, tied and helpless. He turned toward the sled, his mind racing desperately.

"Go on! Get out of here!" Zato snapped.

I will help, or die trying, Rin promised himself. He sprinted toward the sled.

The boy's sudden movement was all that Gazan needed. Quickly, he stooped and grabbed the pistol-bow from the small pile of field supplies. He pressed the alloy frame against his body, cocking the mechanism while, with his free hand, he engaged the bolt. In a continuous motion he aimed and fired.

The short bolt entered the child's leg, burying itself in the muscle behind his thigh, just below the left hip. Rin sprawled onto the ground. The pain was white-hot, searing.

"No!" Zato screamed, moving angrily toward Gazan as the bandaged Warman began to load a second bolt.

Tegné could see nothing through the dark cloth, yet from the sound of commotion, from the voices, he knew that Rin had been injured. He strained, cutting his wrists on the rope, choking on the gag as he tried to free himself.

"That was not necessary," Zato spat the words at Gazan, snatching the weapon from his hand. "Mount up! Do not make another mistake, or so help me . . ."

Reluctantly, Gazan obeyed his superior.

Zato bent over the child. The bolt was lodged in the thick of his hamstring muscle. It was a clean entry, and the spring-loaded wartip had not opened. Rin lay still on the ground, whimpering softly.

Quickly, with assurance, Zato pressed his open left palm against the injured thigh; he positioned the bolt in the space between his thumb and first finger. Rin held back the scream as Zato gripped the four inches of extended steel and pulled it free.

"Give me some alcohol, rope, bandages," he ordered.

Within five minutes, the wound was clean and bound, the rope used as a tourniquet, tied high up on the thigh to diminish the flow of blood from the heart. Then, gently, Zato lifted the child's body, cradling him in his arms.

"What are we going to do with him?" asked one of the mounted Warmen.

"Take him as far as Asha-1; we will leave him there," Zato replied.

"Asha-1?" came the question.

"Asha-1," Zato confirmed.

The tiny, windowless cottages stood in the baking sun. It was midday, and the Ashkelites had, as usual, returned from the fields to take shelter from the ultra rays.

Zato raised his arm, halting the Warmen. He looked back at the sled; Tegné was cut and bruised from the constant contact with the rough ground, his golden hair filthy, matted. Zato studied him for a moment, willing himself to despise this man who had caused Renagi such pain. Yet the doubt rose again within his heart, and he turned his head away. *Why? Why do I feel such an affinity with this prisoner?* He straightened in his saddle, looking ahead through the north gate of Asha-1. *Perhaps I can answer my question here*, he hoped, riding through the gates, for he knew the welfare of the child was only a small reason for this journey.

Inside the gates the dirt road widened, leading toward the two uniform lines of thatched cottages. The six horses moved at a slow walk only a short distance from the first dwelling.

Not a sound . . . a village of ghosts! Zato observed. Dismounting, he looked at the boy. Rin was seated in front of the nearest Warman. Zato walked closer, stopping to examine the bandaged leg. For the first few hours of the journey they had been forced to a near standstill by the necessity of loosening the tourniquet every fifteen minutes, allowing the blood to flow freely through the child's leg. The blood had finally stopped pumping from the wound and the bandages were changed and fixed more permanently. Now, four days later, the leg was bruised and mildly swollen. *Gangrene?* Zato wondered as he pressed gently on the swelling below the cotton wrapping. Rin winced, but did not cry out.

"Lift him down," Zato ordered.

As Rin was carried past the sled, he stared at Tegné. He saw the bloodied wrists and ankles, the torn, filthy robes and dark bruises which rose from behind his Sensei's shoulders and wound around his neck.

The child turned to Zato. "Why? Why are you doing this?" he pleaded. Zato ignored him, looking instead at the Warmen.

"You men wait here. I will take the boy into the village."

Zato stopped in front of the first cottage, placed Rin on his feet and knocked on the door.

The look of surprise in Rawlin's pink eyes lasted only as long as the eyes took to focus on the red Sign of the Claw. Then the look changed to terror.

Zato watched the thin, barefooted man back away from the incoming sun. The fear remained in his eyes as he stood in the shadows of the hut. Zato supported Rin as he guided the boy inside.

"He is injured. We will leave him with you." Zato spoke as he saw the two pale children and their frightened mother peer round from behind the curtain which divided the single room into eating and sleeping quarters. "I want you to see that his wound heals. Give him food, rest, and in return you may employ him in the fields when he has recovered," Zato said. "Here, take him," he commanded.

"Yes. Of course," Rawlin responded, stepping forward while motioning for his wife to attend to Rin.

"And there is another matter with which you may help me," Zato said, looking sharply at the Ashkelite.

"Yes, Master, anything you ask."

"I suppose you have heard the rumors, which I believe are lies, regarding an Ashkelite sired by the Warlord?" Zato asked.

"Yes, I have. The story is many, many yeons old," answered Rawlin.

"And what was the name of the woman who had this supposed union with . . ."—Zato hesitated—". . . my father?"

The disclosure came as no surprise to Rawlin. He had immediately recognized Zato, for Zato was the leader of the procession.

"Her name, Master, was Maliseet," he answered.

"And am I correct in saying that Maliseet's mother is still alive and living in this village?" Zato pressed.

"You are. But I fear she will be of no assistance. She has not spoken a word for over thirty yeons."

"I want to see her."

"Now?" asked Rawlin.

"I am going to bring someone with me. I would rather we did not draw any attention. It should take no more than a few minutes to bring him here, then you can take us to the woman." Zato stopped, looking into the pink eyes.

"Certainly, Master."

"A few minutes," Zato repeated.

The blood rushed into his hands as the first ropes were cut. Then Tegné was pulled roughly from his reclining, head-downward position on the sled. He breathed a long, deep breath, letting the oxygen revive him. The scarf was ripped from his face.

A blast of sunlight blinded him and he lowered his head, shutting his eyes, and opened them again, squinting as the pupils contracted, adjusting to the light. His first image was the birthmark on the wrist of the man who stood before him.

Brother? The question crossed Tegné's mind as his eyes traced the mark up the bronzed, sinewy arm and looked into Zato's face. He believed, for an instant, that he saw the same question in Zato's deep brown eyes. Then the eyes hardened.

"The boy is all right," Zato said. "And to ensure his safety I advise you to cooperate."

Tegné nodded.

Two Warmen flanked Tegné and pushed him along while the short rope which bound his legs together forced him to shuffle behind Zato. Tegné guessed where they were; he had read of these tiny, enclosed slave villages. And now, looking down the dirt road, the sight of the small but immaculately kept thatched cottages filled him with a strange sadness.

Could it be true? Could I have come from such a place? Tegné wondered. His eyes widened as he saw Rawlin standing, waiting, inside the hut. It was the near-translucence of Rawlin's skin that astounded him; he stared a moment at the fine paths of veins beneath the white epidermis. *Like a leaf, like a pale forest leaf,* he thought.

The Ashkelite stood a full hand below Tegné in height, perhaps five feet six or seven. His face was finely boned, as were his long, narrow hands and feet. His shoulders, visible beneath the cotton tunic, reminded Tegné of the shoulders of a young, fragile woman. There was, somehow, a frail beauty to this man, yet a dignity in the high, wise forehead, and a resigned strength to the square, clean-boned jaw and pale, wide lips. Tegné looked into the liquid pink eyes.

"The boy will be safe. He is with my wife and children," Rawlin said. "We have given him the bed."

"Thank you," Tegné replied. It was as if he and the Ashkelite were alone in the room, so strong was the link between them. Rawlin seemed completely unaware of Tegné's bindings and even of the three Warmen guarding him.

Zato studied the interaction; he was quietly amazed at the ease between the two men.

"Do you recognize him, do you know who he is?" Zato asked, looking hard at Rawlin.

"I see that he is your captive, but no, I do not know him, Master," Rawlin replied.

"He is the one who claims to be the Warlord's son," Zato stated. "He is the Ashkelite."

"Master, I beg your forgiveness, but this man is not Ashkelite. No Ashkelite has such skin or such eyes," Rawlin said, looking straight into Tegné's face.

"Then you will guide us to the house of the woman . . . the woman we spoke of," Zato ordered.

"Of course, Master," replied Rawlin, then turned and took his blankers up from the rough wooden table.

"First get me a large bucket of water," Zato demanded.

Rawlin moved quickly to the stone work-top and grabbed the metal pot containing the family's cooking water.

"Outside," Zato ordered. The entire group, including Rawlin, assembled in the sun outside the cottage. "Now, a cloth, I want a large cloth," Zato said.

"Marin! Bring us a sheet from the bed!" Rawlin called.

"Pour the water on his head," Zato commanded, looking at Rawlin.

"Master?" queried the Ashkelite, unsure of the command.

"On top of his head!" repeated Zato.

Rawlin lifted the huge pot and let the water spill down, soaking Tegné's hair and running down over his body.

"Now clean him with the cloth," Zato ordered.

Rawlin rubbed Tegné's hair vigorously, scrubbed him, removing the dust and dirt from his skin. Tegné's hair grew golden-white as the hot sun completed the process of drying. Finally Rawlin began rubbing Tegné's right wrist. Slowly, the caked dirt dissolved, revealing the birthmark.

God, he is the one, it is true, it is true . . . Rawlin's mind reeled, his heart bursting inside his chest. Still, he revealed nothing as he looked up at Zato.

"Fine. Now let us go to the woman," Zato said, studying Rawlin, searching for his answer.

Raine's cottage was at the far end of Asha-1, one of the last dwellings on the right side along the road. The walk through the village was slow, and several of the thin doors opened slightly as the occupants peered out to see the strange group pass by. Finally they stood in front of the hut.

It was a building not dissimilar to the others, unusual only in that the thatch of the roof was in need of repair and the wooden door was old and dry.

"Raine! Raine!"

It was Rawlin's voice she heard through the door. *But why does he call for me now?*

"Raine, please open the door."

She drew the locking bolt sideways and pulled the door open, standing back to keep the sun from her eyes. Brusquely, the men entered the room. Raine breathed in sharply as she saw the black lacquered leather and the Red Sign of the Claw. Only once before had anyone wearing that sign crossed her threshold. *Now what do they want of me?* she despaired, keeping her face lowered toward the floor.

"Look up!" Zato snapped.

Raine kept her face averted, willing them to go, to leave her alone.

"Is she deaf as well as mute?" Zato asked.

"She is frightened, Master," Rawlin responded, then walked to Raine and touched her gently on the shoulder.

"Raine, it is important that you see the man who stands before you. It is important for all of us in Ashkelan."

Slowly, her eyes closed, Raine raised her head.

A flood of emotion filled Tegné as he looked upon the tiny woman. She was painfully white, and the single, pale layer of skin stretched like a dried membrane across the fragile bones of her tired face. Her colorless hair had grown thin, and hung in fine, single strands from the soft, ashen scalp. There was a drained, beaten look in her eyes as they gradually opened.

The pupils dilated rapidly, causing them to flicker as if they were afloat on a clear pond of water, unanchored. She squinted as she struggled to focus on the vision before her.

Akid, my husband! Have you returned from the fields? Raine wondered, her mind awash, past and present blurred. Through the haze of her vision she could see the golden hair, like a bright aura surrounding the strong, square jaw and high cheekbones. She walked nearer to him, her frail, sticklike arms extended. Involuntarily, Zato moved backward, repelled by this feeble, emaciated slave woman.

Tegné bent to her, allowing her outstretched fingers to trace the lines and structure of his face. He felt his own tears begin, and he steeled himself, preventing the moment from overcoming him.

She could see him now, the deep blue eyes, the lightly bronzed skin. *No, it is not Akid. But I know him. I know him,* she thought as the silent, inviolable wall began to crumble. For, glowing through the blue of the eyes, she recognized the spirit of her beloved Maliseet; she felt her child's soul reach out to her. It was a memory that she had kindled, nurtured with her own silence and finally locked away forever. Now the memory was alive before her.

The word began slowly, as if it was forming for the first time from the lips of an infant. "Ma . . . Mal . . . Maliseet," Raine cried, her body going limp, legs giving way beneath her as a lifetime's sorrow began its warm, cleansing embrace. Tegné knelt beside her, touching her gently with his bound hands.

Zato stared, awkward, uneasy, wanting to avert his eyes. Yet something compelled him to witness this open, unashamed emotion, Something within him was touched, made aware; a deep, closeted yearning. He thought of his own mother, Natiro. He could not remember ever having held her, touched her. *It was not the way of the Zendai,* he told himself as he moved closer to them.

"Cut the bindings on his wrists," he whispered to the Warman.

"But Master, he—"

"Do it," Zato hissed. A fast, downward cut freed Tegné's wrists.

Now Tegné cradled Raine in his arms, rocking her gently, allowing her tears to run onto his cheeks and down his face. Still he held back the waves of his own emotion, yet through the tears of his mother's mother he found peace. Finally he rose, helping Raine to rise with him.

"Your name?" Her voice was a whisper.

"Tegné," he answered.

A faint, proud smile parted her lips. "Tegné," she repeated, reaching up and lightly touching his cheek. He took her hand, held it for a moment, then turned, looking at Zato.

"I am ready," he said simply.

"Cut his ankle binding," Zato ordered the Warman. Raine watched from her hut as Tegné, surrounded by Zato, Rawlin and the Warmen, walked slowly up the dirt road of Asha-1 to the waiting horses. It was late afternoon and the work parties were emerging from the shelter of their cottages.

These are my people, my people . . . The thought filled Tegné's mind as he looked upon the tired, undernourished bodies and into the docile but inquisitive faces, their eyes hidden behind the dark lenses of the blankers.

Was it conclusive? Was an old woman's breaking heart the proof of legitimacy? Is the birthmark real, or some finely crafted counterfeit? And if it is true, if Tegné is indeed my half-brother, the product of an illicit union between my father and an untouchable, what will become of my family? The questions burned in Zato's mind as they rode through the outskirts of Zendow.

They had dispensed with the sled and tied their prisoner to the rear of the youngest Warman's horse. Tegné's wrists were bound in front of him, and his head concealed by a sack cut into a crude hood. Zato looked back quickly.

Gazan rode behind him, his face bandages dark with grime and perspiration. Zato was aware of the Animal's wishes. He let his eyes rest only a moment on Tegné. *Maybe I should let Gazan kill him and be done with it*, he thought. Then Zato recalled his father's orders. *But why? Why keep him alive? Why bring him into Zendow? Why take such an enormous risk?*

"Because it is your duty as Warlord. To yourself, your family. Expose him. Truth is power," Neeka concluded, having had this conversation innumerable times with the Warlord.

Yes, and if only she knew the truth, Renagi thought, looking into the eyes behind the golden openings of the ninjinka. *Or perhaps she does*, he speculated, studying her veiled face. She had been somehow estranged from him since that morning he had supposed her dead. It was a subtle change, a pulling away, and the pulling away only caused him to become more desperate, more grasping of her affection. He sensed her awareness of this, felt her quiet manipulation, yet he was powerless to oppose her. For now, more than ever, he knew he would be lost without Neeka.

They sat in silence at the small chestnut table in the private dining room. The decanter of Miramese claret stood full and untouched between them.

Zato entered Zendow through the small concealed passage, wide enough only to ride the horses in single file. The group emerged from the torchlit tunnel and rode into the rear courtyard beneath the high stone walls of the fortress.

The gate guard recognized the Warmen instantly and issued no challenge. Instead, the iron-slatted door leading to the recesses of Zendow opened before them. They rode beneath the spiked slats and entered a square stone enclosure. In each of the four walls was a large, wooden door.

Zato raised his hand and gave the order to dismount. The sound of feet hitting stone echoed in the high, ceilingless square like a solitary clap of thunder. Only Tegné remained alone on the stallion. Gazan moved toward him.

"I will do it," Zato said, moving quickly between Tegné and

the Animal. Then, turning, he pulled Tegné from the horse, allowing him to land roughly on the hard floor. Zato squatted down and retied the rope binding Tegné's ankles. Then, rising, he looked from face to face.

"I know each one of you," he said, hesitating as he stared into Gazan's dark eyes, "And I am ordering your absolute silence. Should I hear anything regarding our captive, anything at all, I promise that I shall find out which one of you has spoken and I shall have the tongue burned from his mouth. Am I understood?"

Each man nodded a solemn "yes."

"Gazan," Zato said, addressing the Animal.

Gazan straightened. "Oss."

"You and I will take him to the cells . . . and you . . ." he said, turning to the remaining Warmen, addressing them as a single entity, "use the inner tunnel, take the horses to the stables." *I will show no feeling, no concern for this man,* Zato promised himself as, roughly, he shoved Tegné toward the wooden door. *Give away nothing; no fear, no emotion,* he vowed, looking at Gazan and motioning with his head for the Animal to follow. They walked close together as Zato pushed Tegné forward. *Then why can I feel no hatred for him?* he questioned.

"Hold him," Zato ordered as he pounded three times on the steel-reinforced door.

Gazan gripped hard, employing a pinching finger-vice to squeeze the narrow trapezius muscle which joined Tegné's head and shoulders. Gazan found no difficulty in unlocking the vast reserves of hatred for this prisoner as he used every ounce of his strength in trapping the sensitive nerves.

Tegné fought against the pain, prayed the door would open. Again Zato's palm slammed against the wood. One, two, three times. Tegné breathed in as Gazan dug deep into the soft muscle tissue. He could spin, use his leverage and body weight to attack, yet he knew he must not. He knew that a struggle, a violent reaction, could result in his death, and death, now, would be selfish. His purpose lay within these walls.

"Come on, come on!" Zato muttered beneath his breath. Bang! Bang! Bang! His gloved hand beat against the door.

Tegné's eyes began to water and a fine line of perspiration broke on his brow, gathered and ran down his face. The pain was concentrated, intense, like a burning fork driving inward where the Animal's thumb wrapped round and under the muscle fiber. He felt his body give way as the pain began to generalize, filling every limb, every space.

"What are you doing? Get away from him! Away!" Zato's shout broke through the red haze. At last the Animal released him, leaving his right arm and shoulder paralyzed. Zato's strong hands lifted him from behind, guiding him through the open door and into the darkness as Tegné's gasping, hollow breaths caused the material of the hood to fill his mouth, nearly choking him. He smelt the mildew and felt the cold damp as, gradually, he regulated his breathing, and his legs moved, carrying him forward.

He was vaguely aware of the hollow eyes staring from the bars to the left and right of him as he moved awkwardly down the dimly lit passage. A single torch burned on the wall in front.

"Only six in this one, Master," the gaoler's dry laugh accompanied his words and cracked the morbid silence. Tegné heard the jingling of the key ring, then the sound of the single key entering the old, worn lock. An empty, hopeless sickness filled the pit of his stomach as the hands pushed him forward. He stumbled across the hard, bony limbs of a prisoner lying silently in the dark and landed on the wet, thick straw which covered the floor. The cell reeked of urine and excrement. Tegné pulled himself forward, reaching the wall, and in the darkness struck his head on the fixed wooden bench.

"He will be safe in there . . ." The same voice, the same cackling laugh, then the sound of the iron key turning in the lock. Tegné crawled up on to the bench and finally, mercifully, felt the blackness wrap round and protect him.

Zato found his father standing alone, high on top of the eastern ramparts of Zendow. He mounted the steep brick steps quietly, unobserved by Renagi. He remained silent, studying the profile of the Warlord. Renagi's face had fallen with time, and the eyes had become narrow slits beneath the slightly protruding forehead. The nose was long, the bridge straight and close in to the cheekbones. Renagi's lips were tight, and reminded Zato of a desperate, clenched fist as the Warlord stared out, over the treetops and into the distant sky. Zato took two steps forward and Renagi spun, his right hand already beginning to draw the katana. Zato held up his hands in mock surrender.

"Zato, Zato my son! When did you come back?" Renagi's voice was gruff, strained.

"One hour ago," Zato answered.

"And no one alerted me? That is not possible," Renagi protested.

"We came through the eastern tunnel, straight in through the cells," he explained.

"Through the cells?" Renagi was quick to grasp the implication.

"We found him in Shuree. There was no need to enter the Valley," Zato said flatly.

"Tegné? You have Tegné?" Renagi stuttered, fear and relief waging a batle within him.

"Yes. He is below. No one saw us enter and my Warmen are sworn to secrecy," Zato replied.

Renagi grasped his son by both shoulders, hugging him, genuinely moved by his success. Then he stepped away from Zato, holding him firmly at arm's length. His voice became hushed, conspiratorial. "Take me to him."

Zato looked closely at his father, measuring his own silence before he spoke.

"I took him into Asha-1," he said.

The words cut into Renagi, straightening him, moving him backward. "You did what?"

Zato grasped the moment. "Is it true? Is he your son?"

Renagi did not answer. His eyes raged and for a tortured moment Zato believed his father would draw his katana and lash out at him. Then Renagi grew calm and, finally, he spoke.

"Think very hard and carefully, my son. Try not to allow the self-righteousness of youth to destroy us both." His voice had somehow mellowed, and the hardness in his eyes vanished. "Look around you," Renagi continued, using both arms in a grand gesture to encompass all of Zendow. "Now, look out there. Vokane . . . Shuree . . . Ashkelan . . . Miramar, Yusun, the Valley beyond. I am Warlord of all this, and you . . ."—he hesitated, moving closer to Zato—". . . you are my successor."

Zato knew exactly where his father was leading and he well understood the logic. "Is he your son?" he repeated.

Renagi faced him, looking directly into his eyes. "He cannot be my son."

Tegné lay on the hard wooden bench. He had entered the first level of waking sleep, his eyes closed, his mind drifting, yet his consciousness was in control of his deep, even breathing. The presence had been close to him for at least ten minutes, and now he listened as the stealthy, shuffling footsteps drew near. He opened his eyes.

"Go in. Get him out." The deep, grainy voice broke the darkness of the cell. Tegné looked through the iron bars and saw the gaoler searching nervously through the large, jangling ring of keys. Zato stood behind the gaoler, and next to him was another, bull-like man. Finally the gaoler found the key and opened the lock, then shuffled swiftly into the cell.

"Come along, come along," his nervous voice urged. Gnarled hands pushed him through the cell door. It clanged shut behind them.

"Bring him to the interrogation chamber," the deep voice rasped.

The interrogation chamber was a high, square stone room, not large enough to lie down in and barely wide enough for Tegné, Zato and the Warlord to stand. The two faced Tegné, who stood with his back pressed hard against the wall.

"Leave us," Renagi ordered the gaoler, noticing the man lingering curiously outside the iron-grilled doorway. The man spun and hobbled rapidly down the corridor.

Renagi moved close to the hooded figure, staring, silent. He looked hard into the blue eyes, then stepped back as far as the narrow chamber would allow.

"Do you know who I am?" he asked, venomously.

Tegné remained quiet for a space, amazed at the facial resemblance between the two men before him. Finally he replied, "You are Renagi, Warlord of Zendow."

"Yes."

"And . . . you are my father." Tegné barely finished the sentence when he saw the tightening of the Warlord's right shoulder.

The movement began with the sucking *whoosh!* of steel against raw, untreated wood. The blade whipped past his left eye in the downward cut, then continued in a single, flowing motion, and was returned to the scabbard. Tegné stood, the crude hood sliced cleanly in half, his face bare before them.

"Pull the hood from him." Renagi ordered.

Zato reached out and threw the cloth to the floor.

"Now cut the ropes from his wrists."

Zato moved forward with his short sword. "He is marked, I have seen it," he said, severing the thick bindings.

Renagi grabbed at the freed right wrist, pulling it to him, running his rough fingers over it, examining.

The birthmark was deep blue and its shape resembled the front leg and foreclaw of a wild mountain cat, the leg running several inches down the natural line of the wrist. At the lower end, where the mark joined and lay upon the back of the hand, it opened outward, stretching into what appeared to be four jagged claws.

Renagi stared at the mark, rage and fear building inside him. Finally he released the wrist, stepping back against the iron door. Zato studied his father's movement; he saw the moment of indecision as Tegné remained impassive before them.

Truth is power, Renagi thought, looking up into the blue eyes. *And it will be his power, not mine*, he reasoned as his right hand twitched nervously. *Do it now, finish it*, his mind willed as his fingers moved toward the hilt of his katana.

Tegné saw the hand move sideways across the wide belt. His wrists were free, the cell was tiny; he could attack, perhaps kill both Renagi and Zato. Now the hand rested on the hilt of the katana; the filigree of gold and silver sparkled through the braided binding. *Another breath*, Tegné thought, centering himself. *First the Warlord, then his son*, he resolved as he focused on Renagi's middle chest. The hand tightened on the sword.

Now, now! Tegné's instinct for survival screamed, urging him to attack. Yet a stronger, more dominant intelligence held him back.

Kill him, be done with it. Then it will be over, Zato thought, relieved somehow to see the first inch of steel as the blade began its ascent.

"Renagi!" Neeka's scream came from directly behind the Warlord. His hand froze, leaving only the slight glimmer of the exposed blade. "What are you doing?" Her voice punished.

"How did you know we were here?" Renagi growled, never taking his eyes from Tegné.

"Do not be naive, the men are already talking. Soon it will be all over Zendow," she answered.

Renagi swung his gaze toward Zato, who moved away, his back pressed against the wall. "That is impossible, the Warmen were sworn to silence," he said.

"And you actually thought that no one would see you enter Zendow, not one person in all of Vokane would notice your masked prisoner?" Neeka asked.

The voice, the eyes behind the ninjinka, the soft demeanor of the woman—it was as if Tegné was being summoned by the echoes of some forgotten dream. *The blade, the blade . . .* For the first time since his capture he remembered the shining silver. The blade was his connection, and the blade had been taken from him.

"Please, my lord, allow me to speak to you privately," Neeka said, changing her tack, sweetening.

The Warlord looked into the violet eyes, then at Zato. Finally, his face set firm in resignation, he nodded, "Yes."

"Gaoler! Gaoler! Let us out of here!" Zato called through the grille.

Tegné was alone in the tiny interrogation cell. Aside from the faraway flicker of the single wall-torch there was only darkness. He sat in the center of the square stone floor, noting how like a meditation chamber the cell was.

Your true spirit cannot become manifest while you are in a state of turmoil. He remembered Goswami's teaching as he breathed in the dark, cold air, quieting his mind. The bitter, astringent taste of adrenaline still clung to the roof of his mouth as he assumed the full lotus position and began the long, suspended, low abdominal breathing. He listened to the inner sound of his heart and allowed all thoughts which entered his mind to drift gently away without examination. He was mildly aware of the soreness beneath his trapezius muscle, a result of Gazan's thumb, but he did not move or adjust his position. Soon all distraction vanished and he was totally passive.

I am a wave; make me the sea . . . his mind repeated the beginning mantra. Soon he was flying forward above the smooth glasslike surface of his consciousness. Automatically his breathing rate increased, taking his body temperature higher. The perspiration flushed the impurities from him as the electric serpent began its undulation, uncoiling, rising up from his sacrum, taking him into the Dragon Zone.

Red heat, mist . . . a black form rising. Violet eyes . . . Four suns. A mirrored lake. Ivory men. A silver blade. Her face. The raven-girl. "Love me, Love me . . ." The frenzied roar, overpowering, consuming. Flesh. Blood . . . The sounds and images converged. His breathing became shallow, rapid, chugging as the intensity of the vision multiplied, increasing the pressure at the point between his eyebrows until he entered super-consciousness.

Then . . . Crack! The sound of bones breaking, muscle tearing, and he was free. He looked down, saw the sprawling stone fortress below him. The fine, needle-thin, shining silver thread unfurled; his sole connection to the Earth plane. For a moment he floated, then he lifted up and into the spiral.

Tabata sat smiling, basking in the single ray of sun. His skin possessed a golden inner light, his hair spread outward. Swirling colors of yellow, blue and green emanated from each strand. His robes were of the purest, whitest silk and his face had grown young.

Tegné wept at the feet of his master; his tears were the dust of diamonds, shimmering, alive, tiny prisms of supreme color.

"*You know and yet you cannot remember* . . ." Tabata's voice was a song, rhythmic and lyrical. "*You remember and yet you cannot awaken. I call to you, the Protectors call to you, yet she draws you to her, the Beast who hides behind the veil of maya.*"

The voice came from behind him, caressing him, tantalizing. "*Love me . . . love me* . . ." Tegné clung to his vision of Tabata, holding the contact, sure that if he allowed himself to succumb to the gentle, drifting voice he would be lost. "*Dream my dreams. Dream. Dream* . . ." The words washed over him, gentle and soothing. "*We are one,*" she continued, lapping against his consciousness. So easy to listen to, the words like music, so easy to let go, give up all resistance . . .

"She is the daughter of the Beast. The Devil Cat. You are the Warrior. It is your duty to break through this wall of illusion. Tear away the veil!" Tabata's voice resounded.

"I am yours . . . ," the silken voice continued, seemingly aware of Tabata's words and countering their logic. Tegné felt her strong presence. If he turned from Tabata, broke the contact, he knew he would find her waiting. The struggle would be over. The temptation manifested itself in a deep suffering within him. He wanted to turn toward her, if only to see her once more.

He heard the sharp snap as he experienced the tug against his seika-tanden, pulling him down and away. He watched the brown eyes become distant as the face of his Sensei grew smaller.

"Look at me; I am yours . . ." She beckoned, tempting him, torturing him. Still he held back, maintaining his vision of Tabata as his etheric body was drawn down, through the dense slate roof and again into the tiny stone cell of Zendow. He felt the deep, throbbing pain in the center of his Earth heart, and realized his true test was beginning.

Renagi sat on the carved single-seated chair, his back to the room, his eyes gazing out, up into the night. He studied the solitary star that hung in the northern sky above.

Behind him, on the side table, a single candle burned beneath a suspended brass cup. The sweet scent of lemon permeated the air as the aromatic oil warmed above the candle.

Silently, on bare feet, she walked across the room to the Warlord. She watched his naked shoulders rise as he inhaled, then lower as he exhaled a deep, pensive breath. Now she stood above him, dipping the fingers of her right hand into the heavy, warm oil. Lightly she drew her fingers across the line of his shoulders and slowly up to the back of his neck. She repeated the exact movement with her left hand, first anointing the fingers, then barely touching his skin.

Renagi sighed, relaxing beneath her fingers as she increased the pressure and began a deep, penetrating massage. Rhythmically she stroked his neck, repeatedly dipping her fingers into the brass cup and applying the oil. She could feel his anxiety give way beneath her hands and for a long time there was only the stillness of the night and the long, satisfied breathing of the Warlord.

"Now is the time for you to be strong. You must show no fear." Neeka's words came within the rhythm of her fingers.

"I have no fear," Renagi replied.

"Good. Good. That is how you must be," she answered. "And what will you do with your prisoner?"

"Kill him." Renagi's voice was sure, his mind set.

"Yes, yes, naturally he must die. But the true art lies in the nature of the execution," she said.

"And have you a suggestion?" Renagi asked, a mild irritation in his voice. Neeka did not answer immediately; instead she bent close, her mouth behind his neck, her warm, slow breath caressing his skin. "If you allow me time with him, I will have an answer," she whispered.

"What? What are you saying?" Renagi bristled.

"Permit me to visit him in the cell. To take him food," she replied.

"That is out of the question."

"Please, let me finish," Neeka said.

"Right now we know very little about him. His strengths, his weaknesses. I could gain his trust, then . . ." She hesitated, feeling the Warlord weighing her wisdom. "Then we will dispose of him in the most effective fashion."

Renagi sat in silence as Neeka moved slowly to his side, bending to look into his eyes. She sensed his reluctance.

"There is absolutely no way of getting rid of him quietly. It would be your admission of guilt. You must make the matter known and open . . . that is your way to absolute power."

"Fornication with an Ashkelite? For-nic-a-tion . . ." Yanon exaggerated the words, staring drunkenly into Bakov's eyes.

"Atira was in Zato's party at the time of the capture. He saw the mark on his wrist. And his eyes, his eyes are blue." Bakov added, building the case.

Yanon leaned forward, grasping the neck of the decanter, pulling it toward him. He looked at the half-full vessel, studying the thick ruby port, pondering, almost forgetting his intention to refill the two empty goblets. Finally, Bakov hoisted his glass and held it out to Yanon, urging the other to pour.

"Fornication with an untouchable. Punishable by death,"

Bakov said as Yanon lifted the mock crystal and tipped the warm liquid into the extended glass. "And if the Royal family was deposed," he continued, sipping pensively at the port, "Zendow would be governed by a military junta."

"What are you suggesting?" Yanon asked.

Bakov remained silent, eyeing the tight, round face in front of him, judging whether the man would be an ally or an opponent. *It does not really matter. One word of this and I can have him discredited and destroyed,* he thought.

"I am suggesting nothing!" Bakov said, lightening his tone. Then, as quickly, his smile vanished and he looked straight into the eyes of his under-adviser. "But I do think we must pay careful attention to the situation of this . . . Ashkelite. We may be on the cusp of a crisis, and a crisis creates opportunities—do you follow me?"

Follow you? I am not so sure of that. But understand? Yes, most certainly! thought Yanon.

Madame Wang took her ear away from the paper-thin partition separating her from the reception hall where the two men sat drinking. *An Ashkelite son? A military junta? Would I be better or worse for a shift in power within Zendow?* she wondered as she padded her way toward the main room. *What would it be worth to Renagi to know of a potential plot against him?* she pondered as, silently, she reached the end of the long hall. She could hear the muffled giggles cease as she entered the room and pointed authoritatively at two of the newer, fresher girls.

The two had returned only yesterday from a visit to Doctor Ow, the Willow World physician. The process of having the delicate, wafer-thin dorsal membrane of the monkuno fish stitched two fingers deep inside their vaginal passages was not pleasant. Nor was it comfortable when the fine vegetable fiber cross-stitches tore away during sexual entry, but it was lucrative. Usually a working girl could have the procedure performed two or three times during her professional career. The operation took less than one hour and was accomplished under a local anaesthetic. Minimal bleeding, twenty-four hours' recovery, and the "virgin" could earn a year's wages in one evening.

Tonight Wang would supply these new virgins to Bakov and

Yanon. *I will throw in the port and elixir for free*, she decided as she led the girls toward the pleasure rooms.

Yanon and Bakov looked up simultaneously.

"Virgins," Wang stated proudly, stopping and turning to the scantily clad females. Bakov looked first at the girls, than at Wang. His eyes revealed his satisfaction.

"Naturally," he said.

Neeka stood in absolute silence, observing him through the tight iron slats of the tiny window in the interrogation cell.

Tegné sat with his back pressed straight and firm against the stone wall, his eyes closed and his legs folded easily in the relaxed half-lotus.

So singular, so complete . . . she thought as she rested her gaze on his placid, expressionless face. She read the vulnerability in the full, slightly parted lips and the fine bones which formed a proud, angular structure beneath his skin. *A good face, a kind face*, she mused. Yet this face was much more than the simple product of genetic inheritance. *His face bears a distinct countenance, a dignity, an honor; it is a brave face, a warrior's face* . . . she concluded as her gaze shifted to his open hands, his folded legs and bare feet. There was a certain gracefulness to these hands and feet, just a hint of femininity in their proportion when compared to the broad, spreading shoulders and square, muscular chest—as if the musculature had been created as an armor to protect an inherent gentleness. The way he was positioned, with his shoulders drawn back, caused his rib cage to pull upward and gave the defined chest and flat abdomen the look of a hard, protective shield.

A shield to guard his heart, Neeka thought as her eyes fell upon the smooth skin surrounding his nipples. It was pale, yet contained just enough pigment to affect the faint hue of gold. Fine, silken hair surrounded his breasts, while the only other visible body hair was the short, silken strands which adorned the forearms and calves and the darker, reddish trail which led from the navel down over the lower abdomen, widening as it disappeared beneath the band of his torn trousers. It was a sensitive body that had been carefully and faithfully disciplined, giving the final appearance of great strength. A body and face that glowed with the soul within it;

a body she had known, a soul she had coveted. *I will rule with this man, make a child with him*, she vowed.

Tegné had found the place of peace, of tranquillity, inside his heart, a reservoir from which he drank strength and purpose. He rested in its cool waters, his thoughts drifting easily, slowly, in the clear space surrounding him.

"Tegné. Tegné," the voice called to him, as if it were carried on the very air he breathed. Slowly he opened his eyes. In the dim light he could barely see through the window, yet he could detect the beautiful glow of violet and the warm smell of musk. He heard the twisting of the iron key in the rusty lock, watched as the door creaked open and she entered.

She wore the ninjinka, and the violet light came from inside her eyes, the fragrance of musk from her bare shoulders. A sari of rich silk, its blended colors of blue, red and gold, wrapped loosely round her body, while soft, pale leather sandals protected her feet. She carried a tray of food in her hands.

The door closed behind her. She stood a moment, smiling down on him, then, disregarding the filthy floor, she hoisted her robes and sat cross-legged, facing him. The aroma of the steaming rice with its thin, sautéed pieces of marinated sandafish rose up from the bowl.

"Please, eat," she said, smiling as, carefully, expertly, she lifted the small teacup and warmed it above the lighted candle on the edge of her serving tray. As she warmed the fine china she ceremoniously wiped the cup with a white cotton cloth. The almond tea steamed from the ornate, single-handled pot, and at no time did Neeka take her eyes from Tegné.

He sat quietly, enraptured by the grace of her movement and the dexterity of her hands.

"Are you not hungry?" she asked quietly.

"Yes, I am hungry," he replied, still making no move toward the rice. Gently, she placed the warmed cup down beside an identical cup on the wood and brass tray. She lifted the china spoon and dipped it delicately into the rice, bringing a small portion to her own lips. Taking a few grains into her mouth, she nibbled at the rice, then smiled faintly as she swallowed. Now she reached out, extending the spoon to his lips.

"It is delicious," she said softly as Tegné opened his mouth and accepted the offering. Finally, she placed the spoon down beside the bowl, gesturing for him to continue as again she picked up the cup and began to warm and clean the vessel above the flame.

"I understand you come from the Temple of the Moon?" Neeka asked, continuing her work. Tegné nodded, slowly chewing the rice, then taking another spoonful. "And does that mean you are an ordained priest of the Temple?"

"I am not a priest," Tegné answered, lowering his eyes. "And I am no longer a Brother of the Order."

"And that is upsetting you?" she inquired.

"My purpose was never to be a Brother of the Order," he answered, his face placid.

"Your purpose?" she asked.

He looked into the warm violet, somehow believing that he knew the face behind the ninjinka, remembering the Lake of Dreams, and for a moment there was a sense of uncertainty between them. Then, slowly, she reached out to him, touching his wrist so lightly that it seemed her hand merely lay upon the fine golden hairs of his arm. Her warmth soothed him as she smiled. "I understand your purpose."

At that instant his heart was touched and his love for her began to cloud him. She stroked his arm gently, closing her eyes. Finally she whispered, "You must trust me—I am your ally."

Tegné felt the choking of emotion, his Earth heart wanting her, his Earth mind desiring this trust, this union. And yet he felt the wrenching grip of conscience twisting him, holding him back, warning him. She noticed the subtle shift of expression in his eyes, felt him pull away from her.

"You are Renagi's son, are you not?" she asked, removing her hand.

"Yes, I am," Tegné answered.

"And your mother?" Neeka continued.

"My mother was Ashkelite," Tegné stated.

"I need not tell you the consequences for the Warlord if his transgression became public knowledge," she said. "He would be executed and his family discredited."

"That is my intention," Tegné answered.

She remained silent, handing him the full cup of tea.

"Do you hate this man . . . Renagi?" she asked.

He sipped the tea, searching her eyes, then said, "No man has the right to violate another human being, to rape, to kill. I do not know my father, but I do know what he has done."

"And you have never sinned? Never?" she asked.

Tegné lowered his head.

"And there is no dark side to your own nature?" she continued.

Now he looked at her, his eyes clear, concealing nothing. "Why have you come here?"

Neeka met his gaze. "Because I am as you are; hungry, incomplete. Searching for something intangible, something which will make me whole. And uncertain whether to love or fear, to embrace or destroy it," she answered. Then, she stood and walked to the iron door. She pushed it open. "I will see you again," she said. Then, closing the door, Neeka was gone.

The invitation to dine with the Warlord came as only a slight surprise to Bakov. After all, it was nearing the end of the third trading quarter and, no doubt, Renagi wished to discuss the military budget. In fact, Bakov expected the entire staff of advisers to be in attendance as he knocked three times on the outer security door to the dining hall, hesitated and knocked twice more.

Instead, the door was opened by Yanon, who appeared anxious and alone within the windowless room. Seven bottles of Kanton Red stood open in the middle of the mahogany table and fluted crystal glasses sparkled in the warm light of five burning candles. The table was set for three, and the bone-handled, serrated knives indicated that the main course would be a meat dish. There was an ominous quiet to the room.

"We seem to be the only ones invited," Yanon said.

Bakov surveyed the table before he answered. "Apparently," he agreed.

"But why? you don't think . . . ," Yanon began.

Bakov's hand shot out, his index and middle fingers pushing flat and hard against Yanon's lips, halting his speech. "I think that we have been invited to a quiet dinner with our Warlord, that is what I think," he stated.

Both men spun round as the heavy doors parted and Renagi entered the hall. The Warlord walked straight to Bakov, smiling broadly as he embraced him with both arms, then turned and repeated the greeting to Yanon.

"It has been too long, far too long, since we dined together," the Warlord said. "My two senior advisers, my two most trusted advisers," he added, motioning for them to take their seats at the table. "And tonight I must beg your absolute confidence, your loyalty, your support and, above all, your advice, in a most personal and delicate matter." He rubbed his fingers over the embossed red Sign of the Claw, which stood out from the velvet at the very top of the arched back. The red lacquered leather seemed to shine beneath his hand as, satisfied, he sat in the chair, resting his arms on the table before him.

Yanon relaxed, the tension in his body gone.

"But before we talk, I think we should drink, then we will dine, drink some more and then . . . yes, then we will talk," Renagi said.

"Exquisite," said Bakov, nosing the wine, then sipping and rolling the warm liquid on his tongue before closing his eyes and swallowing.

They emptied three of the amber bottles within the hour.

"Food? Hungry? We must be hungry," Renagi said, his voice just beginning to slur as he poured the last drop into Yanon's glass. Without waiting for a reply he leaned back, and pulled the tasseled cord, signaling the servants.

Yanon gasped audibly as, ceremoniously, the double doors opened and the huge rhandoconda was brought in, its entire body skewered, marinated and, now, rotating above a burning bowl of coals. The serpent's head remained intact, the mouth drawn back and a small, stewed plum artistically impaled between the two long, bent fangs. One servant turned the handle of the spit while another pushed the entire wheeled serving tray to the table. Renagi laughed aloud at the horror on Yanon's face, noting at the same time Bakov's strained control.

"A delicacy, I assure you, but so very difficult to prepare that I serve it infrequently. Generally reserved for my immediate family. Tonight is an exception!" Renagi exclaimed. "Difficult to prepare," he repeated, then looked directly at Yanon. "You see, the serpent must be skinned while still alive, then boiled slowly from the neck down. The head must always remain above the water. In that way the venom is excreted through the pores and diluted. The water must be changed at least three times during the process or the flesh is unsuitable for consumption. Here . . . here!" he said, stabbing his fork into a section of the snake and ripping the flesh from the spit. "You must try a little," Renagi insisted, holding the loaded fork toward Yanon. "I promise it will melt on your tongue."

It is a test; everything this man does is a test, damn him, Yanon thought, forcing a smile and intercepting Renagi's fork with his own, lifting the meat from it.

Renagi settled back, watching as Yanon brought the rhandoconda up under his nose, sniffing tentatively.

"Go ahead," the Warlord commanded. Yanon placed the meat on his tongue. His face expressed pleasure as he tasted the fine, spiced sweetness of the flesh.

Rather like chicken but sweeter, fuller, he thought, relieved, as he chewed the first bite and swallowed. Then he turned to his host. "Delicious, absolutely delicious!"

Bakov's explosion of laughter was a mixture of acute nervous relief and genuine humor as he kept his eyes on Yanon, still half-expecting his fellow adviser to fall face forward, dead on the table. After all, the venom of the rhandoconda was legendary, causing its victims an incapacitating muscular paralysis. Tales of men lying in the fields, unable to move, while the carnivorous serpent ate the eyeballs from their sockets or the tongue from their mouths were legendary in Vokane Province. Bakov had been aware that it was possible to eat the meat of the serpent, but the process of cooking was exacting and known only to a few. A single error in the distillation and the first mouthful would be fatal. Still, Yanon seemed perfectly well and, in fact, enjoying the delicacy.

Bakov pulled two of the thick, sinewy ringlets from the skewer as it was passed to him. He purposely avoided the stare of the dead serpent's eyes. Somewhere, in the underlayers of his now clouding mind, the eyes reminded him of the eyes of his Warlord.

The meal progressed easily, and the men were into the last of the heavy wine when Renagi changed the tone of his conversation.

"I do not need to inform you that I am holding an Ashkelite in the cells below Zendow," he said, looking slowly from Bakov to Yanon. Neither man responded. "Come along, come along," Renagi urged, "I am not telling you anything you do not already know."

Bakov cleared his throat, holding Yanon in his gaze, willing the under-adviser to remain calm. Then he turned his eyes to Renagi. "Warlord, of course we have heard of the man's capture. We understand him to be an imposter, subject to trial and death."

Renagi rose slightly from his chair, then settled again. "I want you to be honest with me. Hold nothing back. If I cannot rely on you, then who can I rely on? I want to know what the men are saying, do you understand me?"

"Yes. Yes, of course we understand," answered Bakov, hedging for time, realizing the double edge of the situation. "There are those who claim he bears the Royal mark," he continued.

"I want a list of those men," Renagi ordered.

"But, Master, they are few, and even they believe the mark to be counterfeit. The work of a man skilled in ink and bamboo," Bakov countered.

"And you? What do you believe?" Renagi asked, suddenly shifting his attention to Yanon.

Now was the moment and Bakov saw the flicker of fear in Yanon's eyes. He wondered if Renagi had also seen the involuntary shift of expression.

"Master, I would never question the truth of your words," Yanon answered.

Renagi relaxed. "Good, good. I knew I could rely on your support," he said, then leaned forward, his arms spread wide on the table, as if he intended to take both men within his grasp. His voice grew hushed. "I have a horse carriage and a driver waiting in the courtyard. I would be honored if you would accompany me to the Willow World."

Surely with his new vixen he has no need of the Willow World, Bakov thought.

"I know what you are thinking," said the Warlord, "But occasionally even the owner of a thoroughbred desires the excitement of an unbroken mount . . . even if it is only a cart-horse!"

Wang peered nervously through the convex lens which allowed her a complete view of the winding, cobbled street leading to the brothel. She had expected them for over an hour, and the muscles in her calves had become cramped from the continual raising and lowering as she stood on the tips of her toes to look through the lens.

Nothing! Where can they be? The girls cannot stay like this forever, she grumbled as she stood flat-footed, resting against the locked door. *And if they do not come! God, the business I am losing!* she continued, muttering as she calculated the loss of closing the brothel for an entire evening. It was then that she heard the sharp clatter of hooves and the clickety-clack of the metal carriage wheels. She raised herself to the lens and smiled as she saw the Royal carriage pull up directly outside, the dark curtains drawn to conceal its occupants. She watched the driver open the door and saw the Warlord climb from the seat to the single step and down onto the cobblestones. Bakov and Yanon followed. She noticed the slight nervousness in both men in spite of the intoxication, which was apparent in their unsteady footsteps. Renagi turned and instructed the driver to wait before he guided his guests toward the door.

Wang hesitated another beat, then unbolted the entrance and swung the door open. "Master! I am honored," she exclaimed. Graciously, she stood aside as the Warlord, followed by his two advisers, entered the reception hall of the Royal brothel.

Wang followed them in, excused herself and disappeared momentarily through the curtained entrance to the inner chamber. Yanon nudged Bakov as three girls were led from the adjoining room. They were tall, dark beauties, and Bakov surmised them to be of pure Yusun stock, judging by the richness of their skin and the large, widely spaced ebony-lashed eyes. There was a dignity to the women as each walked slowly forward and offered a soft hand to her predetermined partner for the evening. Wang experienced a brief moment of anxiety as the tallest girl moved cautiously in Renagi's direction.

No, you fool! the Madame thought, then breathed a sigh of relief as Lemar turned at the last and smiled gently at Yanon.

"The first three pleasure chambers on the right have been made ready for you," Wang said, satisfied that each of the girls had made the appropriate choice. "As much hapaver as you like," she added as Bakov made the first move toward the lamp-lit corridor. Yanon followed, turning only once to offer a token bow of gratitude to his Warlord.

Renagi smiled broadly, standing between Wang and the last of the girls. He listened as the doors of the adjacent chamber were closed and bolted, then waited another minute to be certain. Finally, he motioned with his head for the girl to leave them. Silently she obeyed. Now he looked expectantly at Wang.

"This way," she whispered, taking him by the arm and quickly leading him to the narrow passage which ran the entire length of the rear of the chambers. *I wonder how much more this fat old cow has heard through these walls*, he pondered as his ears grew attuned to the sound of heavy breathing and the low moans which filtered through the taut cloth partition.

Several minutes passed, and Renagi looked at Wang. She read the beginning of doubt, mixed with anger, in his hooded eyes. The entire scheme had been her idea, and she had no intention of incurring the Warlord's wrath or, indeed, losing the kilo weight of hapaver, the one hundred golden kons and the immeasurable gain of face that would accompany its successful conclusion.

She had labored for days getting the exact measurements of each of the girls' pleasure passages, moulding the wax, shaping it, fitting and refitting the artificial canals. It had taken twenty kons each and no end of convincing to assure the two that the jagged-edged razors would do them no internal damage. Finally, the razors were inserted into the hardening, rubber-based wax. And now Wang prayed that the men would be sufficiently intoxicated by the hapaver to take no notice of the slight difference in feel as they entered the warm, oiled passages.

Another minute passed, and Wang reached inside her small, jeweled purse and produced the thin brass finger cymbals. Renagi watched as she slid her thumb and middle finger through the leather strap on the back of each cymbal. Then, noiselessly, she walked directly behind the partition of Bakov's room. The two humming rings of the cymbal were nearly inaudible.

Wang listened a moment as the sounds of passion coming from behind the partition seemed to intensify. She smiled sweetly at Renagi and then tiptoed the twenty feet to the back of Yanon's chamber. There was a practiced artistry in her movement, even an air of theatricality as again she raised the hand wearing the cymbal and twice brought the fingers together.

"Zing! Zing!" Yanon was certain he heard the "Bells of Bliss" as he prepared for his ascent to the heavenly plane. He hoped that the hapaver, combined with the red wine, would give him the staying power of youth as he parted the long legs beneath him on the bed. Looking down proudly at his hard, fat penis he prepared to drive the shaft inward, burying it in one explosive thrust. *That should make her scream a bit*, he thought as her light fingers held him gently below the testicles. He clenched his buttocks as he drove forward, penetrating her fully. She gasped, a strange, expectant gasp, and he opened his eyes to gauge the expression on her face.

She stared up at him from the pillow. He withdrew and drove in again. Now there was a look of horror in the eyes below him. It was then that he began to feel the white, searing heat. He looked down to see the blood exploding from between his legs as his mind raced to make sense of the icy numbness that spread from his organ. He pulled away from her just as Bakov's agonized scream reached him from the next chamber.

Renagi listened a moment to the anguish on the other side of the partition. With a single downward cut he sliced the thin cloth which separated him from Yanon's chamber.

Yanon lay writhing on the floor, doubled up, holding himself, sobbing, begging. The girl stood frozen, watching from the corner.

"Out!" the Warlord commanded. She disappeared into the corridor. Renagi hovered above the bleeding man, his katana raised high.

"An Ashkelite son? A military junta!" The Warlord screamed the words as they had been repeated to him by Wang. "A time of opportunity!"

"Bakov . . ." Yanon barely managed to whimper his senior's name.

"Yes, I understand," answered the Warlord. "And for that I will give you the gift of my blade while your 'superior' will die dishonored."

Yanon turned his head to face Renagi, meeting his eyes. The blade seemed to flow in slow motion as it fell toward his neck.

Has it been two days or three that I have been here? Tegné wondered as he stared into the hopeless darkness of the cell. Slowly he unfolded his crossed legs and stood, stretching his arms up, then down, placing the palms of his hands flat against the stone wall and breathing in as the long hamstring muscles relaxed, allowing him to grip his ankles and pull his head down to touch his upper thighs. He held the position, regulating his breathing and letting his mind flow with the surging of blood.

Far away he could hear the awkward, limping gait of the gaoler as the man carried out his rounds, dispensing the watery gruel made from beef bones and stale, soggy bread. Only once since Neeka's visit had Tegné been offered the slopping bowl through the small, diagonal opening at the base of the door. He had attempted to eat the cold, stinking broth, but his belly, unused to animal flesh, reacted with nausea and vomiting.

The footsteps seemed to come closer as he released his grip on his ankles, stretching upward once more and squatting down, pulling his arms tight around his bent legs. Then he lowered his hips to the floor and sat again in the resting half-lotus.

Now Tegné could hear the disgruntled noises which accompanied the uneven footsteps as the gaoler turned the final corner and approached his cell. He expected to hear the sound of tin sliding across stone and see the sickening gruel as it was pushed through the door, but instead he heard the iron key twist in the old lock, and for a moment the thought of escape swept over him.

"You are very lucky, my friend," the gaoler said, looking down on Tegné, his small, pitted eyes as dead as the stone walls which had surrounded him for the thirty yeons he had been in charge of these cells. "She says you are to be moved. A larger cell, a toilet, a bed," he continued. "A cell of your own, no one to trouble you." The gaoler handed Tegné a set of leg irons.

"Put them on," he ordered. Tegné clamped the circular iron restraints, attached by the heavy, foot-long chain, to his ankles. The gaoler nodded as Tegné snapped the last clamp shut. "Good. Good . . . now walk ahead of me."

Tegné walked from the door and turned down the dim corridor. "That's right. That's right, keep moving," the voice behind him said. "Now to the left," he ordered, seeing Tegné hesitate at the point where the corridor ended in a T-junction. Tegné turned left and moved along the bars which enclosed a series of adjoining cells. He could see the sallow, wasted faces, their hopeless, hollow eyes staring at him as he passed. He reached the end of the cells and the passage narrowed, leading him to a staircase. The floor grew damp and cold beneath his feet.

"Go ahead," said the gaoler, urging Tegné upward. He tried to take the first step, but the chain binding his ankle locks would not permit his right foot to reach the plateau.

"Jump!" the gaoler commanded.

Tegné obeyed, clearing the first step and landing with a clank as the chain hit the rock between his bare feet.

"Again. All the way."

Twenty minutes later, Tegné stood in front of a solid wall at the upper end of the staircase. He was drenched in perspiration, his legs leaden and his feet had begun to blister. Behind him the gaoler cursed and wheezed.

"Move aside, move aside," the voice rasped as he squeezed alongside Tegné on the top, wider step. *Whap!* His palm slapped against the indentation in the wall. This time the action was smooth and oiled, and the panel rose without sound.

It took a moment for Tegné's eyes to adjust to the glowing light cast by the moon as it penetrated the star-shaped openings in the high domed ceiling. A bed was positioned in the center of the room, soft and canopied.

"Get out!" Neeka's voice was sharp. Neeka rose from the chair which sat to the left and slightly behind the huge bed. She moved quickly and menacingly toward the gaoler. Before she could reach him he turned and scurried from the landing.

She stood a moment looking after the fleeing man, then turned, smiling, to Tegné. Her eyes rested on him. Then she bent down, kneeling by his feet, running her cool hands down the sides of his calves and resting them a moment on the rusty iron manacles. Again she looked into his eyes, then tugged gently on the lock of the clamp. He felt his left leg grow light as the restraint fell from his ankle to the floor, and she repeated the small, deft movement, running her hands down his right lower leg. Then she stood, rubbing her body softly against his.

"Come. Come," she said, touching his naked shoulder and directing him to the bed. He walked across the moonlit room, the sweat dry upon his body and a strange, comfortable warmth rushing over him. He sat on the edge of the bed.

She sat beside him, a long-stemmed pipe in her hands. He

watched as she struck the firestick and held the thin yellow flame above the silver bowl. The flame was drawn downward as she inhaled, igniting the tiny brick of hapaver. Finally, a winding ribbon of blue-gray smoke floated toward the ceiling.

"Here, it will give you strength," she whispered. He hesitated, looking into the eyes behind the ninjinka. He knew her, he knew what he must do, yet he longed for her, longed for the heat of her body. He ignored the pipe and instead reached for her, his fingers extending toward the ninjinka.

I must see her face, I must be certain, he thought.

"No, no," she said, pulling back, knowing his intention. "The time is not right. Not yet." He withdrew his hands, and she continued, "Please, share the pipe with me. Share my dreams." She moved close again, placing the stem between his parted lips. Tegné inhaled the bittersweet smoke.

"Yes, yes . . . hold it within you . . . close your eyes," she purred, nestling into him, sipping the smoke which escaped through his nostrils and mouth.

The first rush of the elixir sent a warmth flooding through him, extending down his arms and into his fingertips. The sensation was unlike any he had known before.

"Relax, let the smoke take you, guide you . . ." Neeka's words floated to him from far away. He lay back on the bed, his eyes remaining closed as her warm, rough tongue licked the skin around his nipples, tasting the salt from his dried perspiration. The silken-soft lips kissed and caressed the area below his navel where the fine golden hair thickened and spread. He felt her untie the sash which held the rough cotton pants on him and he arched his hips upward as she slid them down, her hands working quietly as her rough tongue and full lips kept contact with his skin. Now the long, fine fingers touched him as lightly as a single feather and she exhaled her warm breath along the sensitive skin of his manhood. The core of him begged to her, pleaded to be held, touched, and at last she gripped him gently with both hands, bringing her mouth down to him. He shuddered as she licked, slowly, circling the head of his penis.

She held him in the grasp of a single hand as she threw off the scented robes that covered her. Naked, she straddled him, pulling him toward her, rubbing his penis against the wetness of her vagina. Tegné opened his eyes, marveling at the sleek sinews of her body, the strong fluidity of her movement. He raised himself up, burying his face in her neck, breathing her, licking her skin, seeking her lips. He felt a power he had never known, a fulfilment, a totality. Yet behind the feeling of his body was a deep, shivering guilt, a knowledge of doom, of betrayal. And the conflict angered him. He listened to her moans as he lifted her up on the arch of his own body, penetrating her, enslaving her.

Their tongues entwined, as his body thrust into hers time and again. Still she seemed to devour him in her heat, and with each thrust his rage increased. Was he loving her or killing her? The thoughts tore at his mind like claws against flesh until, finally, he pulled his lips from hers and looked down into her eyes.

The eyes seemed to mock him, then in an instant they filled with love, pleading with him. He bent his head, inhaling the scent of her body, and kissed her fine skin; then again the anger rose inside him as he felt her urge him on, challenging him with the pumping rhythm of her loins, forcing him to surrender. He opened his mouth and bit down, hard, into the flesh of her neck.

Her animal scream crashed through his senses, ripping through his consciousness like a scorching, single rush of flame. Tegné jumped up, away from the burning bed, his body covered in sweat, his heart thundering in his chest. He took a deep, lower breath, trying to shake the fear from his soul.

He stood alone in the quiet of the room. The leg irons clanked against the wooden floor.

Dreams. Illusion. Reality . . .

He heard the twist of the key in the lock, heard the gaoler clear his throat, watched the inner door open and saw the tired eyes staring at him across the room.

"You are very lucky, my friend. She says you are to be fed," the gaoler said as he carried the steaming bowls of rice, fish and vegetables to the low table beside the bed. Sunlight streamed through the starred dome above him as Tegné sat up, instantly hungry for the food.

The gaoler salivated as he arranged the teapot, cup and saucer on the outer edge of the matte-black table. "You are very, very lucky," he repeated, straightening himself as he prepared to exit.

He looked down for one last time at the fish in the bowl, wiped his mouth with a swipe of his sleeve and walked to the inner door. He halted a moment, locating the correct key on his jangling key ring, then placed the key in the lock and twisted.

Tegné caught only a glimpse of the black-tiled marble floor and the fine, gold-trimmed cornices as the door opened and the gaoler walked from the room.

He devoured the rice, fish and vegetables and was sipping the blended, honeyed tea when Neeka entered through the wooden inner door. She wore the gold ninjinka and her white silk robes.

As she came closer he became aware of the sweet scent that hung delicately in the air surrounding her. It was her perfume that brought the images of seduction rushing back to his mind. He felt his body tighten as she drew near.

"These must be very uncomfortable," she said, kneeling down and running her hand along his left calf and on to the leg iron. He wanted to pull back, escape from her spell, yet he felt the warmth begin to fill his loins. His body shivered as she rose and sat beside him. She placed a calm hand on his neck.

"Why? Why are you troubled?" she asked. "Was the food not to your liking, the tea not satisfying?"

Why does she so unnerve me? he wondered.

"I dreamed of you last night . . . a lovely, lovely dream," she said, smiling as if to one who shared a deep secret.

He remained silent, but now a slight smile played on his own lips as he saw the violet shimmer of her eyes.

"Have you never dreamed of me?" she teased.

"Yes, I have," Tegné answered.

She rested her hand on his upper thigh, savoring the heat of his body, stroking him gently in a slow, circular motion. She watched as he grew hard, his manhood straining against the cloth of his trousers. She knew that she could take him; that his will was as nothing against her own.

Neeka heard the footsteps from far away; the sharp clicking of boot heels against marble. She knew her ears were many times more sensitive than his, and estimated another ten seconds before Tegné would become aware of the approaching men. She bent to lick his neck, his cheek, and finally kissed him full on the lips. She tasted the sweetness of the honeyed tea as her tongue penetrated his mouth and she pressed her palms flat against his ears as he wrapped his arms around her. His awareness was lost in passion.

The key twisted in the lock. She held him a second more, then released him, pushing him away from her. Renagi stood, stunned, in the doorway.

"What is going on in here?!" he bellowed. The gaoler remained at the door, hoping secretly that his Warlord would take the head, not only of the Ashkelite, but of the surly bitch beside him.

"Nothing, Master. Nothing at all," Neeka said, rising, knowing full well that Renagi had witnessed the embrace, for that had been her intention.

"Nothing? Nothing!" Renagi shouted.

"Yes," Neeka said, firmly placing her hand on the Warlord's heaving shoulder. "Nothing."

Tegné watched as Renagi calmed, his breathing becoming relaxed, choosing to believe her lie, even against the proof of his own eyes.

She is in complete control of him, Tegné thought as he began to understand the woman's power.

Finally, Renagi turned and looked down at Tegné. There was the beginning of fear in the Warlord's eyes. "Take him back to the cells," he commanded. "At daybreak put him in the cage."

Tegné looked once at Renagi as the sliding stone panel rose to reveal the torchlit steps leading down. Renagi looked old and bewildered as he stood beside the bed and Tegné felt a wave of compassion before he turned and walked through the arch and into the dark passage.

Neeka had broken the Warlord completely, her last, dramatically timed scene injuring him beyond repair. For a moment silence filled the room. She knew he was open, his inner wounds raw and vulnerable. Finally he turned toward her and she saw the hint of tears in his eyes.

"Sit down beside me, please," Neeka said. He obeyed like a lost, sad child.

"I did what I had to do to find out about him," she began in a plot to ease and erase the pain, whilst keeping him unsettled. He turned to face her fully, wanting to embrace her, to love her, and at the same time to smother and destroy her.

"And what did you discover?" Renagi asked.

"That it is time for him to die," Neeka said flatly, studying his face, watching the hope return to his eyes. "He does intend to discredit you," she continued, watching the Warlord bristle, gaining confidence as each of her words reassured him as to her love and loyalty.

"Tomorrow. I will do it myself. Then it is over, finished," he concluded.

"Why? When you are so close to victory?" Neeka countered.

"Because I am threatened," Renagi answered, the final layers of his psychological armor falling away. "Last night I executed Yanon and Bakov, my two senior advisers. I have a list of half a dozen more. They are plotting against me."

"A list? Half a dozen? So tomorrow you kill the Ashkelite, then what? Go through the list, one by one?" she questioned. Renagi nodded, a vacant commitment in his expression. Neeka continued, "And the result will be more lists, more conspiracy, more executions, until finally Zendow will turn against you. You will have confirmed not only your guilt but your inability to rule," she stated. "What you must do is find people you can trust. Forget the Council of Zendai; they are old, obsolete. Inject new blood into the hierarchy. Replace Yanon and Zakov with military men, men who are loyal, men who would give their lives for you and for Zato," she said.

"Military men in the Council?" Renagi retorted.

"Why not? A great leader is always the one who institutes reforms," Neeka countered.

"But the Council has governed Zendow for two generations, it is a succession of blood," he answered.

"And now that succession has turned against you," Neeka stated.

Renagi stood silent.

"What better way to restore order and loyalty than to implant military men—men who understand the meaning of blood," she continued. "Who are your oldest, most trusted Warmen?"

Renagi remained quiet, his mind working, considering. *There is*

Kein . . . and Miyaz . . . No, no, Kein would not be suitable. A fine Warman, perhaps, and loyal certainly, but illiterate. No, he would command no respect, not in the company of the twelve men who oversaw such fastidious details as the balancing of the trading budgets and the tax paid by Wang's brothel. Kein is definitely out . . . but what of Kase? He has been with me for nearly thirty yeons, risen through the ranks of the Warmen . . . and he is educated . . . Yes. Miyaz and Kase . . .

"Well?" Neeka urged.

"I would trust Miyaz and Kase with my life and the life of my heir," Renagi said slowly.

"Good. Then it is done."

"The Council will resist," Renagi said, still uncertain.

"Not if you move quickly while they are in a state of unrest; they will all be badly shaken when they learn of Yanon and Bakov."

Renagi looked into her eyes, taking strength, before he nodded yes.

"Then, once they are in place and the situation settled, you can convene the trial," Neeka continued.

Renagi drew away. "A trial?"

"Yes, a test of honor," Neeka answered. "Combat. In front of the people of Zendow, in front of your 'revised' Council," she went on, hesitating only long enough to allow the words to sink in. "From what I have learned of the Ashkelite, he has been trained at the temple in the Way of Empty Hand," she said. Then, noting the resistance in Renagi's eyes, she added, "Enough anyway to make a plausible appearance in the arena."

Renagi watched as Neeka rose from the bed, her eyes burning. "Yes, that is the answer. A trial beneath the eyes of God. A trial for all to see. The man who claims to be Zendai pitted against your chosen Warman."

Renagi sat upright, his spine straight, a nervous energy beginning inside his stomach.

"Too much of a risk," he stated flatly.

Neeka threw her arms up, nodding her head in genuine amazement.

"Risk? There is no risk! You have ordered him to the cage at daybreak. You have told me yourself that no man has ever survived more than four days in the cage, let alone emerged to fight in the arena? We will plan it; make the announcement, organize the event, choose the Warmen. It will be perfect, a spectacle, not a denial but an open display of truth!" she said.

"Yes . . . Yes, but they will know he is weak from the torture," Renagi countered.

"No one need see him. Close the inner courtyard—it is rarely used anyway. The gaoler will not speak, particularly if he feels the touch of the heat-prod against his tongue. The hour before the event we will bathe the Ashkelite, clothe him in a fresh combat uniform, drug him. Believe me, it will work. Believe me."

They were the highest walls he had ever seen, ten times the height of the monastery. *I will never get out,* Rin thought, trembling, as he pulled the heavy burlap up around his shoulders and over his head. He limped forward, joining the other beggar children. Each carried a box of sugar candy, chewing molasses, or thin, badly made firesticks, anything that could be sold for a mili-kon or even less inside the walled city of Zendow.

The children formed a narrow, ragged line behind the two hundred or so market traders with their donkey-drawn carts and haggard, worn-out horses. It was a sad, spiritless mass of people who waited each Thursday for sunrise and the gigantic twin armored gates to swing open. Rin stared upward as the mechanical crackle sliced the morning air and the generator cranked energy into the speakers of the voice-enhancer.

"Stand back. Stand back. Wait until the gates are open. Do not crowd the gates. Stand back. Stand back." The voice was thin, cutting and metallic. A hush fell over the milling crowd as again the speakers came to life.

"All grain and carts will proceed to first in line, horses and vinegar kegs will follow. Adults on foot will fall in behind. All below the age of sixteen will enter last." The piercing command was exactly the same in words and phrasing as it had been for as many yeons as any of the older traders could remember, but still there was the inevitable reshuffling in position as the late-arriving carts drew close to the demarcation line.

"Stand clear, stand clear," the voice echoed as the enormous iron-wood and alloy gates began their outward swing, revealing two cast-iron inner gates, which moved simultaneously in the opposite direction, their spiked corners parting like the jaws of a giant beast. Rin took a sharp breath as the city of Zendow opened before him.

He fell last into line, behind a boy of about his own age. The boy carried two small yellow birds in a tiny, crudely crafted wooden cage. Rin noticed the method with which the boy held the cage out in front of him, his arm stiff. Rin imitated the movement with his own small, perforated box. He was not even certain what type of animal he had captured and contained in his box-trap. He had constructed the trap only last night, and felt immeasurably lucky that anything at all had taken the bait of stale cheese that he had stolen from a dozing trader. Now, as he held his arm out straight and walked slowly, in single file, toward the entrance, he could see the pointed brown nose and dark, beady eyes peering angrily at him from one of the holes in the box.

Two armed guards flanked the wide opening. They questioned and checked each person upon entry. They were now beginning the long line of children, and Rin watched nervously as one waif-like girl was turned away, her barter of dried, lifeless flowers deemed unacceptable to gain her access.

Rin watched as the boy ahead of him was summoned to the entry guard. He strained to hear the low, matter-of-fact voice ask about the contents of the box, the type of birds and the proposed value of the trade.

It is a game, just a game, Rin assured himself. Then the guard motioned for him to approach.

He shuffled forward. The guard paused dramatically, suspiciously eyeing the burlap bag which Rin had fashioned into a hooded robe.

"What is in the box?" the guard asked.

"A gotja," Rin replied.

"A what?" the guard said, running his hand across the top of the closed lid.

"A gotja," Rin repeated.

"I do not believe I have ever heard of such an animal," the guard said as he slowly raised the lid and placed his outstretched third finger beneath the nose of the gerbillion.

"What did you call it?" he asked again.

"Got-ja," Rin's answer coincided with the guard's yelp as he shook the sharp, clinging teeth from his finger. He glared furiously at Rin.

"Get out of here!" His words snapped at Rin's heels as the boy ran through the gates, dropping his box and losing himself amongst the crowd.

"What is the meaning of this?" Zato challenged bursting into the private dining room adjacent to the Warlord's chambers.

Renagi stared up from his chair, anger in his eyes, as Zato threw the large white scroll down on the table.

"It is correct. I am holding a selection. Three Warmen," he said.

"Three Warmen for what purpose?" Zato pressed.

"One of the three will kill the Ashkelite in combat," Renagi answered flatly.

"And I suppose that is intended to prove the supremacy of our Royal bloodline?"

"Exactly," Renagi replied.

"And would it not give this event true meaning if I"—Zato hesitated to drive his words into the old man—"your only son, was the Royal champion?"

Involuntarily, the Warlord withdrew, pulling himself backward, tight against the high, padded chair.

"It is out of the question," he said, his voice sharp. "Out of the question," he repeated his words, this time relaxing, allowing his son to feel the warmth and concern within his heart.

"But it is a matter of honor," Zato countered.

The Warlord placed a hand on his son's wrist. "We are alone, you and I, and I will not take a risk with your life."

Does he think I am not equal to Tegné? Zato wondered.

"Now, please, dine with us. Let this matter be forgotten, at least for one evening," Renagi insisted.

As Zato sat in the chair closest to the Warlord, he felt Neeka's gaze upon him. Finally he looked up.

Your father shames you! The thought projected from her eyes. It was as clear, as undeniable, as if she had spoken the words. Zato lowered his head, unable to look at her again.

* * *

Alone, Renagi walked slowly down the winding steps and into the dark corridors of the prison. He would take Tegné to the cage himself; after all, it was the only way to ensure security! Yet there was another, deeper, hidden reason for his insistence. He had never been alone with Tegné, had never fully faced the fear that had obsessed him and driven him for sixteen yeons. And now, if he was to be truly strong, truly able to control the destiny of Zendow, he must conquer the uncertainty and dread that churned and twisted his heart.

He turned the final corner and saw the narrow door of the interrogation cell. He heard the hobbling steps of the gaoler behind him as the man, having seen the Warlord enter the passage, struggled to catch up.

"Shall I open the cell, Master?" The voice came from close behind.

"Just give me the keys," Renagi said.

"Shall I not accompany you to the prisoner?"

"I will see him alone," Renagi answered.

He walked the final distance to the cell. He hesitated only a moment, composing himself, feeling the hard steel of his katana pressing warm against his side. Taking a deep breath he exhaled slowly as he twisted the key and pushed the door inward.

Tegné sat against the far wall; he looked up, making no effort to rise or change his position. Renagi entered the cubicle, standing directly over Tegné. The door clicked shut with an ominous finality and father and son were, for the first time, alone.

There was absolute stillness in the cell. Tegné could feel both fear and indecision in this man who stood glowering down upon him. He studied the dark, hooded eyes, the wide flaring nostrils and the tight, full lips. The black, silver-streaked hair framed a face that had once been strikingly handsome and now still retained a distinct but pained pride. The deeply etched lines descended from the nostrils to the upper edge of the lips and continued beyond, cutting into the bronzed flesh. Renagi's forehead furrowed as he tightened his mouth in a mask of hatred, causing his eyes to sink low within their sockets. Tegné could hear the sound of angered breathing grow more intense as the Warlord glared at him. Yet Tegné felt no fear. Instead he was aware only of the sorrow which welled within him.

Renagi read the compassion in the deep blue eyes, and for one moment he saw his reflection within them.

He spun away, avoiding Tegné's gaze, overcome with shame. Then Renagi hardened himself against the sob he felt rise from his tortured soul. The Warlord stood, head bowed and vulnerable.

"Why?" Tegné's voice was soft, somehow naive, and in its naivety reminded Renagi of the Ashkelite girl, Maliseet.

Why, why? The word repeated in Renagi's mind as he turned again to Tegné.

"It is a matter of survival." Renagi forced the sentence. "Now stand," he ordered, backing away, his hand hovering close to the hilt of the katana.

I will not weaken. I will see this through, Renagi commanded himself as he found his eyes searching the fine, pale face for a resemblance to his own.

The cage stood in the center of the small, enclosed courtyard. At first sight it appeared to be a simple iron barrel, half-buried in the floor of the yard, but as Tegné walked closer, his leg irons clanging noisily against the stone, he saw the full horror of what lay ahead. On top of the hollow barrel was what appeared to be the inside metal frame of a war helmet. Two padlocks held the face shield in place at the front of the helmet. Welded to the top and to each side of the frame, pointing inward, were three sharpened metal spikes.

Tegné hesitated.

"Your first test of strength," Renagi said, his voice low and determined. He pushed Tegné toward the cage.

Tegné looked up and around the courtyard. He could see no escape from the high, barbed compound, and although the morning sun had barely risen above the western wall, the enclosed yard was already uncomfortably warm. Renagi eyed him cautiously as he unlocked the front of the iron barrel, pulling the two heavy metal sides outward and open. Then, with the same key he freed the bottom padlock and lifted the gridded face mask. He turned and faced Tegné.

"I am going to remove your leg restraints and cut the rope binding your wrists. You will climb into the cage. You have my word that if you do this you will be given a fighting chance to live. If, on the other hand," Renagi said, drawing his short sword, "you make a single move against me, or a single motion to escape, I swear to you that I will have your head, here and now."

Tegné's expression did not alter as he bent down to retrieve the key that Renagi threw at his feet. He fitted it into the rusty lock of the leg irons, turned it once and stepped free of the restraints.

Renagi backed a half-step away, his short sword in his left hand and his right ready to draw his katana.

"Get in," he ordered.

Tegné walked forward, his wrists still bound, and awkwardly climbed into the metal barrel. The cage was hollow; it was as if he was stepping into a well. A thin, round metal bar ran across the emptiness below him and his bare feet perched painfully on it.

"Hold your wrists out," Renagi ordered.

Tegné extended his bound arms and Renagi hooked the blade of his short sword beneath the rope and cut it. "There are two iron handles, one on each side of the barrel," Renagi explained. "You will last longer if you hold onto them. If you do not, your body will hang free in the shaft and you will strangle."

The sun-heated metal enveloped Tegné like a suffocating furnace. He breathed a long breath inward, already attempting to control his respiration in an effort to limit his fluid loss.

Renagi pulled down on the face mask and the thick steel locked into position, the spikes pushing close to his head, permitting no movement. A sharpened half-plate closed on the front of his neck and the locks secured the face mask.

Tegné's hands quickly found the twin handles and he shifted his bare feet so the pressure of the lower bar bore evenly beneath his arches. He stared out through the grid of the face mask and his eyes met the hard, fixed gaze of the Warlord.

"If you should survive I will allow you a trial of combat," Renagi said, his voice set and firm.

The great white stallion reared on his hind legs as Renagi dug his boot heels into the bulging flanks and forced the horse forward, up the ramp and on to the platform.

Zato followed, entering the yard at a canter as he rounded the far corner of the north gate. Then he slowed his mount to a walk and smoothly climbed the wooden ramp.

Father and son sat side by side on their horses, high on the raised floor. Renagi remained still, allowing the nervous tension to descend upon the waiting Warmen. He scanned the faces, noting the effort his soldiers made to maintain a perfect, straight posture. For each Warman understood that the test was under way the moment the Warlord's eyes met theirs.

Zato saw Gazan standing last in the back of the four lines. The Animal looked even more forbidding than Zato had remembered, then he noticed his wide, broken nose which had set flat and crooked. Even from this distance Zato read the determination in the dark eyes and he observed the distinct twitch in the ridged muscles behind the jaw.

How on earth did Tegné beat him? Zato wondered, holding his eyes on the massive Warman who stood at least a head taller than any of those around him.

"My finest, most courageous Warmen! You!" Renagi began.

It is a voice that drives, inspires, Zato observed as he watched the chests swell and the eyes harden.

"You all know why you are here. You have all chosen to be here," Renagi continued, looking from man to man. "And from you I will choose three; the finest, the fastest, the strongest." He hesitated, letting the words grip, already able to pinpoint the real contenders by the look in their eyes and the attitudes of their bodies.

"You will bring your Warlord great honor . . ."—he paused again—". . . and you will gain great face . . . heroes of Zendow!" Renagi boomed.

"Oss!" The single word reverberated from the lips of the forty Warmen, the word that meant, *We will push ahead. We will never give up.*

Renagi looked down on them, his eyes glowing, his shoulders drawn back so that he sat perfectly square in the saddle of Kano. He breathed in; a long, slow breath.

"Now, form one line. Facing me!" he ordered.

"Back up. Leave plenty of room before the first man and the wall," Renagi instructed, motioning for the leading Warman to move back, away from the wooden platform. Now the line was formed and the men waited expectantly for the "test" to begin.

Wisely, Gazan had taken a place at the back, preferring to see what form the trial would take, to gauge the difficulty of the test.

He watched as the less experienced, more exuberant participants grabbed positions near the front. He watched as the Warlord rose slightly in his saddle, his head turned to face the west gate. Then Renagi raised his left arm and, with a sharp gesture, signaled an anxious, waiting servant.

The servant walked forward, straining to hold the body-size wicker basket at arm's length. His steps were small and precise, his head pulled back from the top of the basket, which was roped shut.

Whatever is in the basket, he does not want to disturb it, Gazan thought, studying the servant's tentative approach.

Zato craned his head sideways, his curiosity aroused.

"You will like this," Renagi whispered.

The servant and basket were directly below them now, the servant breathing laboriously with his nervous exertion. Zato's horse shied, jerking backward on the platform. Quickly, he tightened his hold on the reins, squeezing his thighs, controlling the stallion. The Warman standing first in line tensed, his eyes riveted on the wicker basket.

Renagi looked directly at the man, holding his gaze, until the Warman looked up.

"First test—speed," Renagi stated. Then he turned to the uneasy servant.

"Now!" he commanded.

The servant tipped the basket away from him, simultaneously pulling the rope attached to the lid. He jumped backward, then turned, dragging the empty basket, and sprinted toward the west gate. The thick, tightly coiled rhandoconda hit the ground with a thud.

The three Warmen at the front of the line gasped as the eight-foot serpent lifted its flat, flaring head. Hissing, the snake bared its long, curved fangs. The sharp black tongue darted in and out of the gaping mouth, a mouth that could easily envelop a man's fist.

The rhandoconda was angry, its body pressed tight to the rough wooden wall of the platform; the fear and nerves of the men standing before it only added to its feeling of capture, of containment

Every Warman was familiar with the large, diamond-shaped, orange and black markings on the shining skin of the monster. They knew the rhandoconda had no natural fear of man and was, in fact, the single member of its species that would aggressively pursue and attack with no provocation.

"Catch the snake!" Renagi bellowed.

"Catch the snake! Now!" Again Renagi shouted, as the rhandoconda closed to within a body length of the Warman. The line of men pulled back, out of range, as the Warman crouched, using the spring of his legs to bounce lightly on the balls of his feet, his right hand cocked and extended, the fingers pressed together while the thumb opened in the tiger's mouth position.

Zato watched as the man moved counterclockwise round the snake. He was impressed with the physical control the young Warman exhibited.

The rhandoconda remained still, the anterior portion of the tube of swollen muscle arched high, the head flared and facing the Warman as he drew closer, his sure, muscular feet gripping the stone and gravel floor. All eyes followed his movement, every stomach tight, waiting, wanting him to snap the hand forward, to grip and break the thick neck, which had begun to sway ever so slightly . . . willing him to succeed in this test, if only to save themselves from an identical fate.

The serpent and the Warman stood eye to eye, the man's low, crouching stance causing them to be adversaries of equal height.

Zato sat stone still. He watched the extended arm as it drew back, readying for the strike. The serpent's head seemed to mirror the movement, drawing slowly away from the hand.

Yes! thought Zato as the hand flew forward, the full weight of the Warman's body behind it. The rhandoconda's head moved only slightly, the mouth appearing to open and snap lazily shut.

Yes, he has him! Zato was convinced, seeing the Warman grasp the long, heavy body with his left hand and attempt to lift the rhandoconda off the ground. His attacking hand remained intertwined with the serpent's head.

"Aaaah-eee-ahhh!" the spasmodic screams began as the Warman released his left-handed grip on the snake's body. He was already beginning to convulse as he pulled back, trying to escape from his enemy.

Zato could now see exactly what had happened, for as the Warman strained backward, his right arm stretched out, the splayed open hand remained in the grip of the huge mouth. The twin fangs pierced and tore at the soft flesh between the thumb and first finger. Gradually the sheer weight of the serpent dragged the paralyzed Warman forward until he dropped, face flat on the ground. Within a single beat, the rhandoconda let go of the hand, reared back, and bit once into the man's exposed neck. Renagi looked at Zato, nodded and grimaced as the venomous serpent held firm, twisting its head from side to side. Finally, the snake released its death bite. Then, as if through some instinctive intelligence the creature was conscious of its task, the rhandoconda rose up, its head once again flared, ready for the next man in line.

IX

THE TEST OF THE SPIRIT

Those whose courage lies in
tenacity are usually killed.
Those whose courage lies in
diffidence usually remain alive.

(Lao Tsu)

The sun hung in the clear sky directly over the enclosed courtyard, beating relentlessly on the iron barrel and the attached steel cage. The metal simmered, sending its baking heat inward.

Tegné maintained an even footing on the lower bar while balancing the bulk of his body weight with his wide-armed grip on the side handles, forcing himself into a straight-backed, crucifix position.

He inspirated through both nostrils with a soft, sobbing sound, then held the breath, counting a full sixty heartbeats before exhaling. His head remained rigid, the sharpened spikes positioned perilously close to his forehead and temples. It would have been possible to let his mind go, allowing himself to drift into superconsciousness, but Tegné understood that to sustain the life of his physical body it was necessary, now, to remain cognizant of its condition. Already there had been a dangerous amount of fluid loss caused by the oven effect of the iron enclosure. Perspiration ran from every pore, a quantity gathering high on his upper chest and running in a thin, single stream down between his pectorals and over his abdomen.

His thoughts drifted with the pulse of his heart. *If you should survive . . . If you should survive . . .* The Warlord's words caught and repeated on the quietening surface of his mind.

I will survive, he resolved, without anger or sentiment. *Thirty days without food, three days without water . . .* He had learned at the temple that these were the maximum periods the deprived human body could sustain life. *But that was in the cool tranquillity of the mountains. How many days here, in the heat? In the cage?* He remembered his first survival fast; he had been barely twenty yeons when he had endured the initial exercise in self-preservation. Ten days alone in the forest, permitted only the juice of the seasonal fruits and vegetables. How clever he had thought himself when he had located a grove with full, rich oranges on the trees. Yes, he could live the entire ten days on oranges alone. For the first two days he felt vital, pure and bursting with energy. Yet, by the evening of the fourth, his urine and feces had taken on a distinct change in color and the corners of his mouth seemed slightly sore and blistered. On the fifth day his stomach grew unsettled, his bowels loose and irregular. Still he had continued, sure that his system was merely purifying itself. On the sixth day he began the first mild cravings for fresh, clear water, anything other than the juice or flesh of the orange.

On the seventh day his mouth was tender to the touch and even the movement of his tongue along his gums was sore and irritating. By the evening of the eighth day he was certain the aroma of oranges exuded from his pores and even his skin seemed a yellow-gold color. After nine days his scalp hurt and the mere action of rubbing his fingers through his hair caused shooting, needlelike pains in the top of his head.

His throat had swollen sufficiently by the tenth day to make the ingestion of the flesh of the fruit impossible. His body had become too weak to search for a source of fresh water and he was certain that he would die. Only then had his senior Brothers emerged from their places of hiding and given him the wonderfully cool, clear water to drink whilst chastising him gently for not paying heed to the warnings of his body. "Better to have taken no food, no liquid, than to have unbalanced the yin and yang reserves of your system."

And yet he remembered thinking that his ordeal had been nearly worth the discomfort if only for the near-ecstasy he experienced as he sipped the sweet, fresh mountain water. So chilled against his swollen throat, so light in his stomach. "Water of life"—it had been his water of life.

Water, water, his mind focused dangerously. *Water, water . . .*

His body cried out for the sweet, wet coolness.

And now the sweat that had initially poured from him had stopped, and a damp, clammy film covered his body. The sun perched high behind his stationary head.

"Get rid of the snake, it is unnecessary," Zato said, making no attempt to disguise his disgust.

Twice the rhandoconda had veered away from the line of men, its own predatory urges overcome by its instinct to escape and survive. Each time Renagi had called a halt to the trial while two terrified servants were summoned to net the fleeing creature and drag it back to its position in the courtyard.

Three Warmen now lay dead before the rhandoconda. Still Renagi held firm, determined that one of those in line would defeat the serpent.

Gazan had stayed well back in line, and now he complimented himself on this foresight as he watched the wiry, bandy-legged Warman move in measured half-steps toward the rhandoconda.

This man seems different, or perhaps the snake is tired, noted Zato.

The flared head was up, swaying rhythmically back and forth. Instead of tensing in preparation for the strike, the Warman grew more relaxed, moving in a steady, even rhythm with the snake. Zato studied the man's cocked right arm, watching as the open hand, thumb and forefinger held wide apart, moved in a graceful, mesmeric motion, forward, then backward. Zato found himself captivated by the grace of the hand and whereas, in the beginning, the mood and motion of the rhandoconda had dictated to the Warmen, now the dominance had shifted; the rhandoconda moved in unison with the man.

Simultaneously with the motion of his hand, the Warman began a soft, high-pitched whistle, a lilting flow of music to which his outstretched hand moved. Gradually, almost imperceptibly, he drew closer to the serpent. The remaining men were silent, and the weight of anxiety that had hung so heavily in the air had vanished; every man watched, fascinated. The large, wide, flattened head was within a fingers breadth of his hand, the swaying motion in both serpent and man had ceased. For a moment Zato imagined the two as fine, beautifully carved statues, perfect, still, yet full with the potential of sudden life. He hardly noticed the toes of the Warman's bare feet as they flexed, securing a firm grip on the dirt and gravel of the floor of the exercise yard. Nor did he notice the man's slow, even inhalation as he readied himself for the final movement.

There was no lunge, no sudden strike. Instead the Warman slowly, smoothly, brought his hand below the serpent's head and easily, almost caressingly, rubbed downward, gripping the narrowest part of the muscular neck.

"Yes!" Renagi shouted triumphantly.

In that instant the snake came alive, jolting as it began to open its mouth. But too late, for the Warman was already wrapping his leg around the massive neck as he pushed the thumb of his gripping hand into the soft white hollow beneath the rhandoconda's lower jaw. The thumb broke through the smooth, vulnerable skin and punctured the creature's windpipe.

The Warman held the serpent strongly, with both hands and one leg. The rhandoconda struggled, then with three desperate, hollow gasps the huge body went limp and lifeless.

The Warman looked up at the platform; Renagi's clenched fist was already high in the air.

"Yes! Yes!" the Warlord shouted again, emphatically, then turned to Zato. "That is what I am looking for," he said.

"What, a snake charmer?" Zato replied, but the sarcasm was directed at the superciliousness of his father, not at the display of nerve and control he had just witnessed.

"Get the two geldings ready. Harnesses only. No saddles," the old stable-master ordered. "Come on, move!" he added, shaking his long-bristled sweeping brush at Rin.

Rin looked along the two parallel lines of stabled horses. *Two geldings? Where are the geldings?* he wondered.

"Geldings! Geldings! Last in the line on the left!" the grating voice shouted, although the tall, wizened man was only an arm's length from the boy.

It had been relatively easy, once inside the walled city, to separate himself from the others and find his way to the working heart of Zendow. There were many boys his own age laboring in menial positions; feeding wood to the giant kilns, stoking the forges, carrying bread and pastry from the stone ovens, and generally attending to the innumerable Zenchefs, smiths and weaponmakers.

Although far more grand and complex in its winding alleyways and multi-storeyed buildings, the nature of Zendow's inner workings reminded Rin of the Temple.

I can easily lose myself in here, he had thought as he found his way to the stables and observed the cluster of boys busily going about their tasks of cleaning, feeding and grooming the horses. He remained in the shadows of the adjacent grain holds while he ascertained the seniority of the workers. Finally he watched as a gaunt old man stepped into the center of the straw-covered enclosure, looked impatiently at the surrounding boys and gestured with his hands.

Immediately the two closest to him snapped to attention, then the larger of the two lifted the pitchfork from the ground and disappeared into the stable while the other ran to fetch a wooden watering pail.

So that is the head man, Rin concluded. It was only when he walked close to the stable boss that Rin noticed the dull, nearly opaque eyes.

Cataract? Yes, that was the word he had heard the temple physicians use to describe this condition of the eyes. *I can use this to my advantage,* Rin thought as he stopped in front of the tall, stooping man.

"Sir? What would you like me to do now?" Rin asked.

"What? What did you say?" the stable boss questioned, bending his head and bringing his ear close to Rin's mouth. "I do not believe I know your voice," he added before Rin could speak again.

Rin took a full step back, tempted for a moment to turn and run.

"No, sir, you do not. I have been sent to you from the kilns; they have no more work for me," he said.

"No more work? What? What?" the stable boss muttered.

"No more work, sir," Rin repeated.

"No more work? No more work?" the stable boss echoed, then considered. "Well, good. I can always use you here."

That had been five days ago. Now Rin was ensconced with the dozen other boys who worked in the stables and spent their few leisure hours talking of recent events in Zendow. All were aware that an impostor parading as the Warlord's son had been captured and confined to the cells, but the current excitement and talk centered exclusively on the imminent trial. A trial of combat in which the impostor would face the Warlord's chosen Warmen. A trial that would establish the supremacy of the Royal blood. A trial that everyone in Zendow was entitled to witness.

"Pssst! Hey!" the hushed voice persisted.

Rin turned to see the filthy face staring at him, the two brown eyes the only bright, sparkling spots amidst the grime.

"Stump?" Rin asked, hardly recognizing his new friend beneath the dirt. Stump hunched against the weight of the heavy bag of manure.

"The geldings," Stump said, his voice low, secretive. "The ones you are going to harness. Do you know what they are for?"

"No," Rin answered, turning in time to catch a whiff of the manure as Stump hoisted the sack down from his shoulder. He held the weight extended for a moment on his disproportionately muscular right arm, then let the burlap strap slide down over his wrist, across the joint where his hand had once been and onto the floor.

Whap! Another dense blast of manure made Rin reel away. Stump laughed, then inhaled deeply. "What's the matter, ruin your appetite?"

Rin glanced at the point on his friend's lower arm where the limb had been chopped and the skin folded. He winced as he thought of how the remaining arm would have been held above the burning coals to seal the wound. Stump claimed to have lost the hand in a savage battle with a pack of timber wolves, but Rin guessed the truth: his friend had been caught poaching and the hand had been axed as punishment. Such was the law in the less-civilized northern provinces and Stump was, in fact, a northerner.

"So? What are they for?" Rin asked, turning his attention back to the geldings.

"Right now, while we speak," Stump said, "they are testing the Warmen."

"Testing?" Rin asked.

"To select the man who will fight the Ashkelite," Stump answered.

"And the geldings?" Rin pressed.

"The geldings are part of the test. I have seen it before, once during the Feast of Celebre. They hitched a man behind the horse, then they whip the horse to drive it forward. The man holds the horse back! I have seen it!"

"Do you think we could watch?" Rin asked, reasoning that a closer proximity might enable him to discover the whereabouts of Tegné.

"Yes, if we can convince old Marble Eyes to let us deliver the geldings to the exercise yard," Stump answered.

The servant stood poised on the platform, the small wooden cage held before him. In front of him stood Zanu, the Zendai swordmaster.

Zanu was the only Zendai participating in the selection. So skilled was he in the use of the katana that the Warlord had insisted upon his presence. His performance was merely a formality.

"Blindfold him," Renagi ordered.

Zanu stood alert, relaxed; the divided, skirtlike trousers of his black, square-shouldered hakama flapped easily in the breeze. A second servant approached from behind and carefully placed the scarf in position, covering Zanu's eyes.

It was his kisagake which differentiated Zanu from the other resident swordmasters; the ability to unsheathe the blade and strike decisively with no pause in the acceleration of the blow, creating a lethal whipping action that was the mark of a true master. To draw, cut and resheathe, leaving no room for escape; that was the essence.

The Warmen stood, relaxed, forming a semi-circle around Zanu as the servant holding the cage readied himself. Renagi studied Zanu, trying to perceive the swordsman's short, shallow breaths.

If I can catch him on the out breath, Renagi thought, reasoning that it would then take an extra beat for the draw. He concentrated, waiting. He detected the slight bulge in the heavy silk of the hakama above Zanu's abdomen. "Pull!" he shouted.

The wooden door of the cage snapped open.

Through the blackness of the scarf, Zanu sensed the subtle change in the vibration of the wind. He pushed from his lower stomach, drawing the blade, increasing its momentum, raising the steel high, slicing down, then crossways and to his left before resheathing. His scabbard was still warm from the friction of the blade's exit. The entire movement had been a blur before Renagi's eyes.

The exercise yard was quiet as the servant removed the scarf. Before him, three hummingbirds lay on the ground, each divided cleanly in half.

The Warlord looked down, nodded, then smiled. "Three. Very good. Very good—you missed only one."

Zanu smiled, extending his clenched left hand, palm upward.

"Number four, Master," he stated, opening his hand to reveal the severed bird.

"*Make yourself dead.*" How many times had Tegné heard those three words during the day-long sessions of meditation? "*Make yourself dead . . .*" Goswami had repeated as he walked amongst the Brothers with his long bamboo stick, smacking mercilessly at any dozing novice.

"*Make yourself dead.*" All awareness of self, of action, of thought, had been dissolved. Somewhere, far away, he heard the mantra *I am a wave. Make me the sea.*

"*Make yourself dead.*" The red, shimmering ball of fire dropped lazily behind the western wall. The cage stood alone in the shade of the courtyard and, finally, the heavy corrugated iron began to cool.

"Wait a minute! Hold on," Rin called, halting Stump on the outer edge of the exercise yard.

"What are you doing that for?" Stump questioned, watching as Rin pulled the wrinkled hood up and over his head, then tied the cloth loosely around and over his mouth, securing the hood in place.

"Sunstroke. I am very susceptible," Rin answered, having already spotted the huge, shirtless Warman in the corner of the yard. "Those eyes . . . I know those eyes," he thought as he became aware of the nagging pain in the back of his thigh where the bolt had entered.

Both he and Stump could see the Warlord and his son mounted high on top of the twelve-foot platform. *Like some great, almighty god,* Rin thought as he took in the full grandeur of the older man;

the gigantic white stallion, the shining black leather of his uniform and the wide, padded shoulders. The boys hesitated.

"Come forward!" Renagi's full voice beckoned. Slowly they approached the platform.

"Fine, fine!" Renagi said. "Take the horses from them," he ordered.

Rin and Stump, empty-handed, stood looking up, attentive to the Warlord.

"Move over to the side. Stand with the servants. You will take the horses back when we are through with them," he said. Obediently the boys ran to the far corner of the platform.

The geldings were pulled so that they stood side by side, facing out from the Warlord. A line was cut into the gravelly dirt a full body's length behind them. The harnesses were extended by the use of leather straps so that they reached back and overlapped the line. A group of a dozen Warmen gathered near the horses, removing their shirts, flexing and loosening the muscles of their torsos.

"First two . . . ," Renagi said, lifting himself in his saddle so he could view the proceedings directly below him. Two Warmen ran from the group, took their positions on the line and allowed the servants to adjust the harnesses and straps, wrapping them round their shoulders and making certain that the wide flat straps lay evenly across the Warmen's shoulders. The two Warmen arched back, away from the horses, digging their boot heels into the soft gravel. The men crouched slightly, bending at the knees and flexing their thighs.

"Now!" shouted Renagi.

Simultaneously, each of the attending servants brought his hair-whip down on the haunch of his assigned gelding. Both men held firm as the horses strained forward. Rin watched their bodies shudder and quiver.

"Again!" Renagi commanded, and again the hair-whips were brought to bear on the muscular horse flanks. Rin heard what sounded like the crack of stone hitting stone, then watched as the Warman nearest him went limp, his body lurching forward as the gelding charged ahead.

"Stop him!" Renagi shouted.

A single Warman caught the harness and brought the runaway horse to a standstill. The contest had lasted only a few seconds, and

Rin watched the loser's body as it was carried from the exercise yard, his back broken.

"You stay," Renagi ordered the victor, then looked at the dwindling group of challengers. Gazan stepped forward. Rin could not take his eyes from the mountainous man; never had he seen such muscularity, the thick arms with their ropelike veins twisting down to the gnarled wrists and huge-knuckled hands. Gazan turned to the gelding, challenging the horse with his eyes, his face set and committed. The servant aided him with the harness and strap.

Rin stood off to the side, behind Gazan. From his vantage point the Warman's back seemed to billow outward from the tight waist until the latissimus muscles spread the entire width of his massive shoulders. As Rin watched, the Warman competing against Gazan glanced over, a look of defeat already in the deep, shadowed eyes. They were both ready, and sank into their crouch, toes tight on the line.

"Now!" Renagi shouted, and the sound of hair-whips cut the tense air. For a long, effortful moment, both men held the line. "Again!" Renagi ordered.

Snap! The whips came down on the hard horseflesh. "Whoa! Whoa!" Gazan shouted, seemingly on the verge of losing his footing. Then in a slow, bending motion, as if the gelding was pulling him forward, Gazan leaned across the line, bent at the waist.

Rin expected to see the huge Warman toss the harness straps up and over his shoulders, freeing himself from the contest and escaping injury. Instead, Gazan slid his hands along the flat leather straps on each side of him. Then, screaming through clenched teeth, he straightened, pulling on the straps, heaving upward and back. Rin was certain the coursing blood would explode through the veins of his pumping biceps.

"Yaaaa!" Gazan yelled, rising to a standing position and straining to pull back more.

"Yes! Yes!" It was Zato's voice that cried out, moved by the display of sheer brawn, urging the Warman on. Now the gelding was beginning to give way, losing ground, its legs buckling. Still Gazan pulled, breaking the gelding's spirit as the hindquarters lowered to the ground, the rear legs relaxing, giving up, and the horse was dragged backward to the line.

"Enough! Enough!" Renagi boomed, just as Gazan's competitor lost his footing and toppled headlong, his body beginning a dangerous skid across the gravel. Renagi turned his head in time to see the sprawling man rise to his knees as with a lightning reflex he pushed the harness and strap from behind his shoulders, throwing them away from his body while the gelding continued its charge, dragging the empty rigging behind.

"Are there any other challengers amongst you?" The Warlord called out.

"For any of these three?" he continued, looking down on the snake charmer, the swordmaster and the Animal.

"Then I say, these shall be my chosen Warmen!"

"Oss! Oss! Oss!" the cheer echoed, unifying the ranks as the clenched right fists punched skyward.

"Well? Are you satisfied that we will be properly represented?" Renagi asked Zato.

"That is not the point, Father," Zato responded. "They are not of Royal blood, and with the exception of Zanu they are not even Zendai."

"They will carry the Sign of the Claw," Renagi snapped, then he turned, heeled his white stallion and clattered down the wooden ramp.

Zato followed, catching his father at the base of the platform directly in front of Stump and Rin. The boys stood quiet, unobtrusive, waiting for the servants to bring them the two geldings.

"And what, after all this, if Tegné defeats our chosen Warmen?" Zato asked bitterly.

"Never!" Renagi replied, confident. "There will be no chance after the Ashkelite has spent three days in the cage!" he added, letting his secret slip in bitter retaliation for Zato's persistence.

"The cage!" shouted Zato angrily.

Renagi turned in his saddle and looked hard at Zato.

"Yes, the cage," he said flatly. Then he galloped toward the gates, leaving Zato to stare after him.

"*The cage* . . . ," Rin whispered to himself. *Where is the cage?* he wondered.

Night, and time drifted on a smooth, cool sea, midway between sleep and wakefulness, as if Tegné's open-armed body sailed through a black void while images formed in his mind like the converging shapes inside a kaleidoscope. The symmetrical figures created faces then, breaking up, they swept past in the whirling tide of consciousness.

For a second, Tabata's face hovered in space. The image evoked instant emotion; love, trust, and a filial loyalty to uphold all that was pure and honorable. Tegné felt the clarity that the image produced, a clarity that he struggled to maintain as Tabata's face fragmented against the blackness, the composite pieces splintering before, gradually, drawing back together.

This time it was the raven-girl who smiled from the ether, and this time the rush of emotion was centered in his heart, a longing, a yearning, a promise of what could be if he would put aside his purpose and become merely a man of flesh and blood, a husband, a father. As rapidly as this thought passed through him her image split apart, replaced by the face of the Elder and the feelings of guilt. *Guilt? Why am I not freed from this guilt? Everything in my past . . . is it not part of the divine plan, the divine purpose? Surely that was the point of my instruction, my meditation. Self-knowledge. Or is my meditation a trick of consciousness, a figment of my imagination? Self-deception . . . Perhaps there is no divine purpose, no leap of faith. The Warrior . . . I am the Warrior. Or is that some façade behind which I justify my existence?*

His mind raced back, creating distorted images of his childhood; *Abandoned, chased, hunted . . . Alone . . . alone . . . An outsider at the Temple, a destroyer of life. All paths lead to one place—here. Imprisoned, trapped like an animal, sentenced to death. My existence is a crime against nature, the result of an atrocity committed by my own father. A father who denied me. Indulgence, self-pity; the enemies of a warrior . . . But am I really a warrior? Am I not simply a tired, dying man?* A lifetime of training had made him strong but now his strength gave way. His tears were dry; he had no body fluid left with which to cry, but they were none the less sobs of sorrow. *Why? Why am I entangled in this nightmare? I have done nothing. I am a victim, violated, humiliated. I do not hate anyone, why am I so hated? Why can I not die?*

Finally, mercifully, sleep took him in its grasp and the suffering blurred, then dissolved into darkness.

He awakened as the warm, rough tongue touched him through

the iron slats, moving across his forehead, down over his cheek and against his dry, cracked lips. He kept his eyes locked shut as the tongue probed farther, penetrating his mouth, licking his sore gums, transfusing him with a sweet nectar. He sucked, taking the tongue and its liquid down inside him. The tongue dissolved into a full stream of water as it slid along his throat and into his stomach. Then he felt the tongue on his face again, massaging his tightly closed eyes, adding blackness to blackness. Finally it retracted, and a warm, full breath dried the moisture from his skin. The breath cooled and became a rush of chilled air, blowing along his body, reviving him and giving him strength. Then the breath was gone.

He opened his eyes. The moon above was three-quarters full and the stars hung close. He looked straight ahead through the slats of the cage.

She stood only a few yards away, her enormous black body resting back on her sleek haunches. He knew her from the lake, from the desert, from his heart. She had always been with him, and now her gaze soothed his anguish.

She remained until the first light of day. Then, as his eyes adjusted, he could no longer see her.

Awake. Asleep. *Dreams. Illusion. Reality.*

Zato stood alone, staring down from the open window. The cage was directly below him, solitary in the midday sun as the heat baked the ground of the courtyard.

Zato studied the device with a morbid curiosity. He felt the compulsion to move closer, to watch, to observe. *Why do I attribute such nobility to this suffering? Would I trade places with the man in that cage?* he wondered as he backed away from the window. *If I need to see Tegné, surely then I could walk down the steps, out into the yard, and face him?* he thought. He turned and began the climb down, slowing his pace as he reached the bottom of the staircase. Finally, he stood before the bolted door leading to the courtyard.

He braced himself. It was hate he must feel, pure and unadulterated. The Ashkelite would destroy him; he had said as much. An exercise in hate.

He unbolted the door and stepped out into the sunshine.

He could hear the labored breathing, he could see the pale flesh and golden hair through the slats. The blue eyes stared straight through him. Still Zato did not stop. Something demanded that he get closer.

The corrugated iron barrel reached the height of Zato's middle chest. He was so close that he had only to reach out his hand and he would touch the metal. Instead he stood motionless, staring at the face, listening to the broken breaths.

"Can you hear me?" Nothing. No answer.

"You have brought this upon yourself! Do you understand that? It is your doing!" he went on, nearly shouting the words. The blue eyes flickered slightly, seeming to focus a moment on him, then withdrew into another space. Zato backed one step away.

"Listen to me!" he demanded, willing himself through his guilt. "It is a matter of honor. There is nothing that can be done."

"Zato!" The voice caught him off guard, and for a moment he thought it came from the cage.

"Zato!" Again his name was called, but this time he recognized the low, gruff tone. Renagi stood in the open doorway. Zato took a last look at the cage then turned and walked purposefully toward Renagi.

There was a mixture of puzzlement and anger in the bearded, brooding face. "What are you doing out here?"

Zato hardened himself, preparing for the confrontation. "You have declared a feast, a combat. Is that not true?" he asked.

"I have."

"Well, I do not believe your prisoner will last until this blessed event. He is dying. Or is that what you want? A corpse to stand in battle against your Warmen?"

"He will not die," Renagi stated.

"Are you going to forbid him that privilege?" Zato asked.

Renagi made no attempt at rebuttal. Father and son stood in silence, the wedge between them driven deeper. Then Renagi turned from Zato and walked through the door and up the winding stone staircase.

PUBLIC TRIAL:

FOR HIGH TREASON AGAINST THE ROYAL FAMILY

AND THE STATE OF ZENDOW

PLACE OF TRIAL:
THE GREAT HALL, CASTLE OF RENAGI
ZENDOW, VOKANE PROVINCE

TIME AND DATE:
THE 22ND HOUR OF THE 22ND DAY OF JULIN, YEON 1000

METHOD OF TRIAL:
COMBAT

TRIAL TO BE WITNESSED BY ALL CITIZENS
AND INHABITANTS OF THE CITY OF ZENDOW

Rin stood amidst the cluster of boys looking up at the announcement.

"What does it say?" a bewildered voice asked.

"It says we are gonna see if'n Ashkelite really has piss fer blood," was the sharp, quick answer. The voice came from behind Rin and he spun round, searching the faces.

The lanky, smirking adolescent was close to his left. Rin eyed the boy, noting the newly sprouted muscles of the biceps, hanging exposed from the ripped, sleeveless work shirt.

"Are you lookin' at me?" came the same arrogant voice. Rin snapped to attention, meeting the close-set eyes.

After all, he does not know Tegné. To him—to all these people—Tegné is a criminal, a slave, Rin reasoned. "Sorry," he said aloud, averting his eyes.

"Sorry?" the boy said, mimicking Rin's high voice and moving toward him as the other boys stepped quickly aside. He was directly in front of Rin, a good head taller and substantially broader.

"Didn't anyone teach ya any manners? Ya don' stare at people roun' here. Not less'n you wan' this . . . ," the boy threatened, his fist clenched and held under Rin's nose.

Rin smelled the caked manure that darkened the ridges between the knuckles. "I said I was sorry," Rin repeated.

Stump stepped forward from the closing circle of boys.

"It's all right," Rin said, halting Stump.

"Got not to do with ya. It's 'tween me an' him," the boy added, eyeing Stump, then turned back to Rin.

"Now ya. Get down on ya knees. Say ya sorry one more time. From ya knees," he repeated.

"No," Rin answered, remembering the temple, the Dojo and his Sensei, Tegné.

"Then I'll bend ya to ya knees," the boy said, gripping Rin's open robe, forcing him downward.

The reaction was instantaneous. Grabbing hold of his attacker's hand with his own left, Rin twisted the hand away from him, turning the palm upward while with his right hand he applied a sharp and sudden pressure to the bent wrist. The larger boy yelped, bending with Rin's grip while his free fist cocked back and flew in a wide, hooking punch aimed at Rin's head.

Rin watched the fist travel toward him. He was accustomed to the fast, linear thrusts of the Dojo and somehow this entire sequence seemed slow and out of time. He released the wrist lock and used the same left arm in a rising block. The block connected soundly with his antagonist's punching arm. Then, with his forward momentum, Rin employed a right leg sweep to dislodge the other's supporting foot. The boy fell awkwardly to the ground.

Always follow a sweep with a finishing blow, Rin remembered as he moved in on the fallen body. But his initial spontaneity was gone and the counterattack seemed slow and mechanical; his opponent was already on his hands and knees and beginning to rise. The larger boy caught Rin by the ankles, wrenching his legs out from under him.

Rin looked up as the first fist crashed into his jaw . . . then another. Now Stump fought his way through the excited circle of onlookers. With his left hand he grabbed hold of the attacker's hair, wrenching him backward, away from Rin.

Stump and Rin walked quickly to the far end of the stable. "You did good," Stump said.

"Good? I lost!" Rin answered, but inwardly he was satisfied that his limited moves had been effective.

"Where did you learn that?" Stump asked as he did a crude imitation of an ashi-bari.

"The temple. I was an apprentice Brother at the Temple of the Moon," Rin replied, holding Tegné's medallion outward on its thong.

"Temple of the Moon?" Stump repeated, adding a respectful mystery to the words as he rubbed his finger over the medallion.

But Rin was already far away in thought. The announcement had set Julin 22nd as the day of combat.

"How many days can a man last in the cage?" Rin asked.

"Two, maybe three," Stump answered, his eyes fixed on the medallion.

Two, maybe three . . . Rin considered. To the best of his knowledge, Tegné had already been in the cage two days, and the combat was still two days away.

Renagi stood in the center of the Great Hall as the laborers, servants and builders worked tirelessly around him. He watched as the giant sheets of silvered glass were wheeled into the room on the low, flat trolleys, then hoisted by pulleys attached to scaffolding until the entire northern wall was covered with the reflection of the working multitude.

"Good! Exactly what I want!" Renagi shouted.

Soon the entire hall would be encased in the shining mirrors, causing the already vast space to appear infinite in size and to multiply the ten thousand expected onlookers by a hundredfold.

Flat wooden seats were being constructed to take care of the lower orders of Zendow inhabitants while the high, more elaborate stone seats would be padded with velveteen cushions to accommodate the Zendai. Renagi, of course, would occupy the Velchar, Neeka would sit to his left and Zato on his right. Miyaz would occupy the seat closest to Zato and Kase next to Neeka.

The appointment of these two Warmen had met with far less resistance than Renagi had anticipated. Again, Neeka had been astute in her judgment, the Council of Zendai were far too unnerved by the demise of Yanon and Bakov to offer more than token objections against two "commoners" assuming seats of power.

And Miyaz and Kase had rewarded Renagi's faith by instilling a loyal practicality into the Council. *Yes, everything is working according to plan,* thought Renagi. He could see it now. Feel the power build inside him as he looked at his mirrored image against the northern wall. He straightened, adjusting the line of his loosely belted, knee-length jacket, the red embroidered Claw distinctly visible against the matte blue of the silk.

Neeka was right; she has always been right. This will be my moment of absolute power; a purging, a process of purification. I will banish all doubt, all fear. I will stand almighty, Neeka by my side, Zato as my successor. I will bask in the glow of Zendow, solid and sure . . .

Again he looked into the wall-length mirror. He would be sixty-eight yeons this year, yet still had the stature and bearing of a soldier. His right hand shot to the hilt of his katana, drawing the blade enough from its scabbard to see the flash of steel in reflection.

"Very good, very good. Why bother with the Warmen?" The voice was warm, if sarcastic.

He watched in the mirror as she glided across the floor, her low-centered movement still in comparison to the hauling, hammering and building which took place all around them. Her shoulders appeared to remain in one line as she walked; there was none of the ordinary up-and-down movement to her steps.

Neeka was dressed in white, the finest of the Yusun-spun cotton, and her long, tight-waisted skirt was so thin that Renagi could make out the hint of her undergarments. They stood together in reflection; her head reached only to the level of his broad, padded shoulders, yet her total demeanor was so radiant, so vital, that it was as if, by standing next to her, Renagi became merely a shadow.

He turned from the reflection. "Magnificent," he said, opening his arms expansively.

She did not respond.

"Is there a problem?" Renagi queried.

"There will be a great problem if, after all this extravagant preparation, you are left with only the corpse of the Ashkelite with which to prove your honor."

"It will go as I have planned," Renagi countered.

"Then, perhaps, you should take a closer look at your prisoner. I have just come from the courtyard and I can tell you that he will not last until the combat. He is barely breathing," Neeka said.

The two glared at each other in silence, and for a moment Renagi thought he glimpsed a spark of hatred in her violet eyes.

No, no, it is only her anger that I see, he reassured himself, recoiling and softening in one involuntary exhalation. "I cannot take any risks with him," he offered.

"It is no risk to have him bathed and properly clothed. Remember, he was a Brother in a Martial Order. Give him the outward appearance and his training and sense of propriety will guarantee us a good, albeit hollow, performance. But let him enter this arena ragged and filthy and you diminish everything this trial stands for."

Renagi did not answer. "Leave him in the cage tonight, even through the heat of tomorrow, but please allow me to have him bathed and dressed when he walks from the cells to the combat," she continued. "I will give him the hapaver tea. That will fortify him temporarily. Anything to make him appear equal to your Warmen. That is the only way this will be effective."

Renagi weighed her words. She had never failed him; indeed, he had come this far because of her strength, her guidance. *Yes, Neeka is right; she has always been right.* He looked again into her eyes, seeing only love and devotion.

"Tegné does not come out of that cage until midday before the combat. Then you may bathe him, clothe him, give him enough hapaver to enter the arena. But no more . . . nothing more," he stated.

Neeka bowed demurely to the Warlord, turned and walked away. Renagi watched, admiring her once again, before he looked up, noting the placement of the second wall-size mirror. Then the Warlord reviewed his reflection from a new, angle.

"I do not want to go back," Tegné said.

"I am sorry, but you must. Your work is not finished," answered Tabata.

"I would prefer to begin again," Tegné insisted.

"You cannot begin again until you complete the circle in its entirety. Then it will be decided if you shall begin again," Tabata continued, his voice rising and falling in soothing waves.

Tegné turned from his Sensei and searched the other bright, glowing faces which surrounded him. There was sympathy and compassion in all of them.

The white robes of the Seven Protectors shimmered in the golden light. Their faces smiled and the swirling turquoise of their eyes reached out to him, forgiving.

The Elder stood directly before him, his face peaceful, He nodded slowly as he reached out his hand and touched Tegné's naked shoulder, urging him to look to his left.

There, beside his Sensei, stood a beautiful young woman. Her white skin was flawless, exquisite. Her large, wide eyes were amber, accentuated by long white lashes and a fine, curved brow. Her lips were pink, like a delicate, full-petalled rose, her face framed by flaxen hair. It was the face his heart had yearned for, the face of his mother.

"Maliseet . . ." He spoke her name. She opened her arms to him, the soft, weightless fabric of her robes brushing his skin. He closed his eyes, and he could hear the beating of the silken wings of a single butterfly.

"Tegné . . ." She said his name and the syllables trickled like spring water, dissolving into a fountain of light. "Tegné, you must turn from me. You must see, you must know," she said. He felt the warmth behind him even before he obeyed her.

The Being of Light stood before him, a spirit different from the others yet loving and familiar. The Being of Light had no face, no discernible features.

Look . . . look at me . . . The command was gentle, nonverbal. Tegné looked into the light.

He watched the images form, the pictures vivid, colorful, rolling before his eyes. He recognized himself; the baby plunging over the falls, rescued by Tabata, chased by the Warmen, saved by the Beast, taken by the Protectors, sheltered in the temple . . . hunted by the Clan, wandering alone. He revisited the Lake of Dreams, saw his naivety, his own seduction. Watched himself as he accepted the blade from the Protectors. He viewed his capture, saw the look of recognition in Zato's eyes as the birthmark was revealed. He saw Neeka's face, waiting behind the ninjinka; always waiting. He saw his own body, unconscious inside the cage, hanging limp in the iron barrel . . .

He understood the absurdity of this death. No . . . he could not die. His Earth life must have meaning, resolve—death, now, was futile. He would not die.

Now Tabata stood before him. "Breathe the breath of life," Tabata ordered, inhaling, filling his own lungs, then with a cool, whistling sound he exhaled.

Tegné took the air into his own body; once, twice, three times.

"Breathe the breath of life . . ." He could still hear Tabata's words as he felt the rough hands lift him from the inferno. Then muffled voices reached him; "Is he dead?" "Maybe." "No, I think he is breathing."

They carried him up, up the winding stairs, along a corridor, their feet clacking against the wooden boards. Finally, they laid him down; a cool, dry hand rested on his forehead, then peace . . . blackness . . .

"Tegné . . . Tegné . . ." It was Neeka's voice that woke him.

The room was large, square, and the late afternoon sun streamed in through the open window.

"You have slept nearly eight hours. I have been worried," she said as she carried the steaming pot of tea across the room to him.

Tegné pushed himself up against the pillow. He was naked beneath the summer quilt. He used his eyes and his hands to take stock of his condition and was amazed to find his body clean, his hair washed and combed, and his face smoothly shaven.

"How do you feel?" Neeka asked.

He thought before answering. Somehow the memory of the torture seemed distant. He remembered the heat, the never-ending heat, sucking the moisture from him drop by drop until his skin felt like a thin layer of parched paper. He had tried to control the dehydration using long, suspended breathing, reducing the beat of his heart, staying close to consciousness. Initially his discipline had kept him alive, for two, perhaps three days. But finally his body would stand no more and at the point of his greatest distress, in the early morning of the fourth day, he had begun to hear a loud, uncomfortable buzz, as if a giant wasp had somehow entered his skull. The buzzing continued, building in volume until the level was intolerable. Simultaneously he felt himself moving rapidly down a long, dark tunnel, and finally he was outside the cage, yet able to see his Earth body within it. He had recognized this as a state of projection, yet the detachment from his Earth form was so distinct, so clear, that he knew he had entered the first stage of physical death. Then he had seen the light and heard Tabata call his name.

"Alive," he said simply.

Neeka was already in the process of warming the cup in preparation for serving the tea.

"I have brewed this especially for you. It will restore you, give you strength," she said.

"Why?" Tegné asked.

"Because tonight, in the arena, I want you to be victorious," she said.

"Tonight?" Tegné reacted. "I will never be able to fight . . ."

"You will, I shall see to it. Believe me. Now sip the tea. Do not swallow it immediately, hold it in your mouth."

The bittersweet aroma reached his nose before he sipped. He held the tea without swallowing, circulating it beneath his tongue and around his gums. He marveled at how the mixture numbed the inside of his mouth.

"Now swallow," she coaxed, studying the pupils of his eyes for the first dilations.

Tegné swallowed, and the coolness entered him, settling only a moment in his stomach before spreading its calm, sure fingers into his extremities. He felt the new, fiery strength rekindle the sleeping muscle fibers of his arms and legs.

She watched, satisfied, as the pores of his skin began to tighten and a visible energy entered his face.

"Better, much better," she said, offering him the cup again. "This time, drink the tea rapidly, empty the cup."

He took the cup from her hand, lifted it, tentative at first.

"Do it," she urged.

He tilted the cup, allowing the liquid to spill into his open mouth. There was absolutely no sensation of heat.

"Drink it! Quickly!"

Tegné downed the tea in one continuous, open-throated swallow. He handed her the empty cup, a half-smile on his face. His eyes questioned her.

It happened all at once; the powerful rush made the first sensation of the tea seem mild, insignificant. His skin positively tingled, every nerve ending alive and vibrating, his muscles virtually exploding, begging to be used, exploited. All doubt, all fear, was erased from his mind. He stared into Neeka's eyes. He felt a sudden wildness, an unfamiliar violence. He wanted to take her.

He reached up and gripped her arm, drawing her toward him as he pulled the cover from him, exposing his aroused nakedness, wanting her to see him. Unashamed, unafraid.

"Yes. Yes. You will do well," she said. Then she reached out with her right hand and placed the cool, open palm on his forehead. He closed his eyes.

I have waited for you. You know me. We are one. Her thoughts entered him, and with them came the vision of darkness, the Black Cat.

He knew the Cat was his ally, his strength, restless, stirring inside him. He drew her closer, looking up, imagining the face hidden behind the ninjinka.

"When the time is right you shall know me. Completely," she said. And for a moment he was certain she bore the eyes of the Cat.

"I want you to turn over, on to your stomach. It is important that you do as I ask," she insisted. And, as if the removal of the hand caused the electricity to subside, Tegné became instantly calm, his mind lucid and the overpowering sexual energy that had dominated him vanished, replaced by a heightened sense of physical awareness.

Her fingers traced the vertebrae of his spine, working, kneading, liberating the vast reservoir of coiled energy at the base of his spine. He recognized the tingling pulses as the serpent began its rise. But this was different; she was controlling the energy, holding it longer in the lower chakras, allowing the nerve centers to open fully, activate totally. Gradually he felt his heart and lungs respond.

He hovered on the edge of the Dragon Zone. She held him back, and finally his mind entered a slow, drifting pattern where all thoughts were one thought.

"Tonight, Tegné, you enter the arena," she began, yet the sound of her voice was far away, coming from the other side of the dream. "You will fight with the quickness of a panther, your claws like razors. One strike. You will not be touched, you will not be harmed, for you are protected. You will look into your adversary's eyes and he will see only blackness, only death. One strike and you will take his heart . . . Tegné, there is death in your fingers. One strike. One strike . . ." The words echoed, trailed off, floating toward infinity.

Rin stood among the milling crowd. It was well into the twentieth hour and still the doors of the Great Hall remained locked. His shoulders were stooped, his eyes downcast, his heart heavy with sorrow and guilt. Too late he had learned the location of the cage, and only then on hearsay from another stable-boy. Then he had filled a bucket with water and dragged it, slopping, through linking courtyards and finally to the supposed location.

There he stood below the high, impenetrable stone wall. He had placed the bucket on the ground and searched until sunset for a way past the thick gray stone. Finally kneeling down on the sharp gravel and using his bare hands to dig, trying to reach under the foundation until, exhausted, his hands cut and bruised, he sat, and sobbed.

"What's the matter with you? You look like you are going to cry," Stump said.

"Nothing . . . nothing. I am just tired of waiting and I hate crowds," Rin answered.

"It will not be long now. They will bring him through, then we can go in," Stump replied.

"Bring him through?" Rin repeated, questioning.

"The Ashkelite. He will be paraded before the crowd. It is all part of the trial," Stump confirmed.

"How do you know?"

"I have seen one other trial like this, two yeons ago; a military adviser, accused of plotting against the state. They executed him publicly. Not here—it was not this grand, but they let everyone see him first. Part of the humiliation."

"But this is not an execution, it is a trial by combat," Rin countered.

"Trial by combat. Execution. Believe me, they mean the same thing. The Ashkelite will not stand a chance. You have seen Renagi's Warmen," Stump said.

As Rin stood, meeting his friend's eyes, the image of Gazan, with veins bursting through his massive, bare chest, filled his mind.

Tegné woke at the twenty-first hour. The sun had fallen like a red, fiery ball, below the horizon, and the after-light cast shadows into the room. Death seemed a long way away.

The black silk hakama with its heavy, shining sash, sat beautifully clean and perfectly folded on the table beside him. A thin, black leather half-glove lay next to it. The air was still, peaceful, no breeze, no moisture within it.

Tegné rose from the bed, stretching his joined hands upward, breathing in, then exhaling as the fingers parted and his arms stretched wide to each side and downward in a circular motion. Three times he repeated the movement, each time expelling all thoughts and doubts from his mind. Then he walked to the steps in the far corner of the room, mounted them and entered the bath-chamber.

Squatting above the sewage hole in the corner of the room, he evacuated his bowels and bladder. He felt the tight-coiled muscle in his thighs as he rose from the position.

Finally he entered the bath, letting the icy water surround him. He took the pumice stone from the marble surround and rubbed the skin of his face and neck, working down across his shoulders and chest until his entire body felt alive and clean.

He threw his head back, submerging himself, running his fingers through his hair, pulling it to his head. When he surfaced he held the hair, rolling and plaiting it so that it hung behind him.

He walked, wet and naked, into the main room and sat down on the wooden floor, bathing in the last glow of sunlight from the window.

Death seems a long way away . . . That was the illusion of life. Death was close, always. In the warmth of the sun, in a breath of air. Sitting beside him now on the wooden floor. Death was his discipline, his teacher.

Tegné opened both arms, breathing in his death, accepting. For a moment he imagined the Warmen. Black, ominous. He saw them move, their huge padded bodies dancing in silhouette before his closed eyes, their fists and swords cutting toward him. He imagined the thudding fists against his skin, their steel weapons burning his flesh. He opened his arms, breathing in, absorbing the pain. Then he breathed out, pushing the pain from him. Separating. His mind was calm.

Every lesson he had learned, every fighting form: the candle, the wolf, the Trial of One Hundred, internalized, assimilated, giving birth to spontaneity. He floated comfortably, empty, without obstruction. Free of desire, of attachment. One strike. His intent was pure, true. All his being centered. His only course was action. He had borne his moment of doubt and weakness, and banished it.

He stood up. His body was dry, his hair clean and smooth. He took the hakama from the table, placing his left leg into the corresponding side of the divided skirt, then his right, pulling the hakama upward. Drawing the heavy, quilted top to his body, he tucked the waist down inside the belt, pulling the ties tight and securing them.

Finally the shining sash. He wrapped it around him, beginning on his left side and doubling the heavy material so it sat in two layers at the back of the hakama, never letting the silk touch the floor. Finally, he lifted the half-glove from the table. He inserted his hand into the smooth leather and pulled it over his knuckles. The glove was cut perfectly, allowing him complete freedom, his fingers bare while the birthmark was covered.

He hesitated, looking at the glove. *Renagi is taking no chances . . .* he thought. A moment later he heard the soft gliding footsteps.

"Water. Clear water," Neeka said, offering him the cup.

"Oss," Tegné responded, turning toward her, his voice curt, distant. He walked the five steps between them, took the cup and drained it. He returned the empty vessel to her hand and watched as she turned and exited.

The door had not quite closed when the four Warmen entered.

"Are you ready to . . ." The sarcastic tone died in midsentence as the Warman's eyes focused on Tegné. Something in his presence, his demeanor, demanded respect. A hush fell as the four gathered round, keeping a measured distance from him. They walked from the chamber.

Boom-bom . . . Boom-bom . . . Boom-bom . . .

At first it sounded like the beating of a heart, the reverberation causing the wood to vibrate as the sound rolled from the double-arched doors of the Great Hall.

Boom-bom . . . Boom-bom . . . Boom-bom . . . The crowd quietened.

"Shhh," Stump said. "It is time, they are bringing him now."

Boom-bom . . . Boom-bom . . . Boom-bom . . . The beat was joined, doubled, increasing in intensity.

The crowd seemed to turn as one unit. The muffled footsteps, walking in counter-time to the rhythm, echoed from the north yard.

"Make way!" Rin could not see them yet; he fought forward as the crowd split, falling naturally into two halves, the walkway between them.

Part of the trial . . . Humiliation. He remembered Stump's words and expected to hear jeering.

But there was no jeering, just the heartbeat of the drums and the sound of the approaching footsteps. Rin strained forward, looking to the right, down the tunnel of people. He could see the leading Warman.

The man was tall, and his high lacquered boots seemed to reflect the gaping faces of the crowd as he marched, his knees drawn high before smacking his feet down into the stone and gravel. His head was enclosed in an alloy war helmet, its leaden face shield pulled down, permitting vision only through the single diagonal opening at the level of his eyes. On the top and to each side of his helmet were the twin tusks of a wild boar. Like a machine, void of all human quality, the Warman advanced. To his left and right two identically clad men moved in perfect synchronization. They were close, not more than fifteen paces from Rin, and now he could see Tegné.

Rin stared, expecting to find his Sensei worn and bedraggled, chained and gagged. He had dreaded this moment, doubting his own self-control, afraid that he would not be equal to the sight of his friend being led like an animal to the arena. Over and over again he had imagined himself as a grown man, faced with an identical situation, and over and over again he had found himself shuddering in fear. But now the time was at hand, and Tegné was walking toward him. Rin gasped, for Tegné was neither chained nor cowed. Instead he appeared the embodiment of self-reliance, courage and dignity. His golden hair falling onto the radiant fabric of his hakama. His face clean and angular, his blue eyes clear and intent, focused straight ahead.

It is as though I never truly saw him, never understood him, never knew what he was, Rin thought. And suddenly Rin straightened, his inner trembling quelled by a sense of duty and belonging. For in one revelation, Rin understood what he was seeing. *It is the final acceptance of death,* he realized, *and it is that acceptance which causes the human spirit to shine, to triumph.* He felt tears come to his eyes, but they were not the tears of fear or pity, they were tears of humility.

Now the Warmen were level with Rin and he could almost

touch Tegné. The boy's move was without premeditation, he lifted the medallion from his own neck, bunching the leather thong against the gold and silver disc in the palm of his hand.

With the hand extended he lurched forward, his unexpected action catching the left-flanking Warman unaware. For an instant his hand touched Tegné's; Tegné turned, his eyes showing no recognition, yet he accepted the medallion, snapping it cleanly from Rin's extended hand.

Tegné concealed the medallion in his clenched fist, continuing his walk with no break in rhythm. The great doors swung open as he and the Warmen mounted the steps; the heartbeat of the demon drums spilling out of the hall and into the night.

Be still while moving, like the moon beneath the ever-rolling waves . . . this is clarity. Tegné was met by the enormous bank of mirrored walls, the myriad of reflected faces and the echoing voices of the eight thousand preseated spectators. One hundred paces straight ahead of him he could see Renagi standing in front of the Velchar.

Even from this distance Tegné could detect the shimmer from the pleated crimson ceremonial robes. Beside Renagi, in a lighter, radiant shade of red, stood Neeka, the gold of her ninjinka sparkling in the reflected light of one thousand torches. Zato, his long black hair running down the back of his white hakama, remained seated to his father's right.

Tegné was bombarded with this collision of sound and vision, yet now a lifetime of preparation held him like a safety net. His mind was calm, empty, and the staring faces and excited voices passed through him like wind through the leaves of a tree. He walked forward.

The twelve drummers formed a single line at the base of the wooden benches to the left side of the hall. Two men for every one of the huge zelkova drums, each hollowed from a single log and weighing close to six hundred pounds. Each pair of drummers crouched in a low, forward stance at opposite ends of the double-headed drum. The player to the right of the drum beat the simple, basic rhythm while the player to the left improvised freely, hitting the taut cowhide with ever-increasing intensity until all twelve players locked into a throbbing synchronization, at one with the sound and the rhythm.

Tegné saw the drummers in the periphery of his vision, their oiled, sweating, naked torsos moving in flowing, mechanical motion. He kept his eyes forward, allowing no distraction. Behind him the crowd from the courtyard entered the open doors and were directed to the lower wooden benches. Within minutes the Great Hall was full, every seat occupied, the anxious excitement building with the crescendo of sound from the incessant drums.

Tegné stood directly below the Warlord, gazing up. He saw the commitment in the snake-lidded eyes and tasted the first bitterness in his own dry mouth.

Renagi raised both arms before him, palms open, fingers tight together. Instantly, as though the entire mass of people were attuned to this solitary gesture, the Great Hall stood silent. And, as surely as if the throngs had vanished behind this curtain of silence, Tegné and Renagi faced each other, alone.

"Tegné," The name rang clear through the hall. "You have come forward to shame my house. You. You who claim to be my son," Renagi began, the words focused on Tegné yet resounding through the hall.

"Tegné, you are not my son. Your blood is not my blood. You are an Ashkelite, a product of an inferior race. A slave," Renagi continued, the passion building in his voice. "Your trial will serve as an example to all who would attempt treason and insurrection against the State of Zendow and the family of Renagi. You stand accused, a liar and an impostor," the Warlord stated, building toward the climax. "Let the people of Zendow and the Powers in Heaven witness your hour of reckoning. And if there is truth in your heart, may that truth give you the strength to survive."

Tegné stood silently absorbing the Warlord's glare. "I am your son," he said finally.

Rin watched from the far corner of the hall, squashed next to Stump on the crude wooden bench. His eyes scanned the room and stopped on the door. Slowly it opened.

Gazan stood framed in the gray stone opening. Then the massive Warman began his walk up the narrow passage and into the cordoned square. He wore only the black, heavy cotton trousers of his combat suit, his chest bare, and the mighty swelling pectoralis muscles seemed to roll in rhythm with his walk, their striations visible in the overhead light. His head was shaved, and his hard, close-set eyes spat hatred.

Renagi's was the first fist to rise as Gazan set foot inside the combat square. "Hei!" The Warlord's cry erupted, sending shivers down Rin's spine.

"Hei!" Kase rose from his seat at Neeka's side, augmenting Renagi's war-cry. "Hei! Hei!" the Warmen, Zendai and spectators joined in, standing, punching their right, clenched fists into the air.

"Hei! Hei! Hei!" the war chant began, boot heels colliding with the cement of the floor; the huge drums pounded until there was only one thundering staccato beat.

Just when it seemed the Great Hall would explode and the mirrors shatter on the walls, the Warlord lowered his fist and raised his open hands. As if by magic, the hall was suddenly and absolutely silent.

"Begin!" Renagi bellowed the command.

Gazan moved forward immediately, his thick feet gripping the stone and pulling him toward his prey. Tegné did not move backward; instead he met his attacker in a relaxed half-facing stance, staying light on the balls of his feet.

Gazan had been informed that his opponent would be weak. He was therefore to make a show of it, demoralize, humiliate, kill.

He studied the blue eyes in front of him. He remembered Zacatec and vowed not to misread this little man again.

How to despatch him effectively yet dramatically, he wondered as he crouched, feinting with his hands and moving closer, gauging his own kicking range. Then it dawned on him.

A reverse spinning roundhouse kick . . . A big, impressive technique which would easily break the Ashkelite's neck yet leave Gazan enough time to claw-hand his throat and rip the larynx free in a final, spiteful gesture. He would have to get close for the claw-hand, but, by then, the Ashkelite would be dead on his feet. Gazan began clapping both hands in a sharp, percussive snap, intending the noise to disturb and provoke his opponent. Yet Tegné would not be provoked, and Gazan thought he discerned a strange lifelessness inside the blue eyes. *The specter of death; his own death*, Gazan told himself.

Tegné sensed the split second of tension, knowing the waza was coming and read the nearly imperceptible twitch in the hammerlike big toe of Gazan's leading foot. He exhaled as the giant began his spin, moving close and into the big man's wide-arcing leg. Tegné continued forward, timing his movement down and under the kick, rising inside the technique and, for a single moment, stood balanced before the Warman's bare, unprotected chest.

Tegné's ki-ai utilized the last of his contracted breath to drive his straight, rigid fingers into the soft, cartilaginous area to the low center of the Warman's chest. There was a sharp snap as the cartilage gave way, pushing up before his spear-hand; the pointed, broken gristle puncturing the soft, muscular tissue of his heart. Tegné held the spear-hand in place, momentarily buried in the heaving chest. Then he curled his extended fingers, pulling down slightly and gripped the third of the upper ribs.

He held Gazan suspended, watching as the life drained from his surprised, frightened eyes. Finally, Tegné withdrew his attacking hand, stepping back and away, retaining zanshin as the limp, muscle-bound body fell to the stone floor. Thin rivulets of blood began to trickle from Gazan's ears, nose and mouth.

Tegné turned and met Renagi's cold, stunned gaze. The crowd remained still, shocked, afraid.

"Move! Do something!" Neeka whispered urgently.

Renagi rose from the Velchar.

"This proves nothing!" he shouted. "It is not over!" Tegné stared dispassionately as Renagi looked out over the crowd. Then, remarkably, the Warlord recovered his bearing.

"Get him out of here!" he ordered, pointing with disgust at the bleeding corpse on the floor.

Two guards rushed into the square. Each gripped one ankle of the twenty-stone carcass and dragged Gazan across the floor, up the narrow passage to the open door. A wide smear of blood trailed their path.

One chance, one strike . . . The words floated in Tegné's consciousness as he deepened his state of zanshin, empty, allowing neither thought nor emotion to separate his mind from his physical movement.

Zanu looked down on Gazan's corpse as it was dragged past him into the antechamber leading to the rear exit of the Great Hall.

"Bad luck," he said, looking up, half-smiling into the assured, fixed eyes of the snake charmer. "Ready?" Zanu asked.

The snake charmer nodded yes, and Zanu led as both men walked from the small room, through the door and toward the bright light of the arena.

Renagi's spirits lifted as he watched Zanu, the Zendai, step lightly into the combat square, his orange robes gathered tight at his waist where the sheathed, three-foot katana was thrust, cutting edge upward, through the red, thickly knotted obi. Renagi saw the wiry Warman enter behind Zanu and remembered the lightning quickness of the calloused hand that had choked the life from the vicious rhandoconda. *Yes. He had prepared for a situation like this. An accident, a mistake. One chance in a million,* Renagi told himself.

Zato sat rigid, his face tight and his lips pressed hard together. Renagi rose from the Velchar and looked down into the combat square, satisfied that his men were in position.

"Hajime!" he yelled.

In an instant, Zanu unsheathed the katana, raising the sword in both hands, elbows bent, above and behind his right shoulder. Tegné held Zanu in his sight, allowing the smaller, unarmed man to circle round and take up a position to his rear.

This is going to end quickly, thought Renagi, watching Zanu shift forward. The Warlord leaned out of the Velchar, his hands gripping the ledge in front of him, his stomach knotted with anticipation.

Zanu and the snake charmer advanced with a distinct yet broken rhythm, one moving forward while the other shifted laterally to the rear. They seemed of one mind as they drew within striking range of the man in the center.

He is too straight, too much target. Why is he standing so straight? Rin thought, staring at Tegné.

Tegné studied the slight flutter of the swordsman's robe, observing the shallow, lower abdominal breathing. Concentrating, waiting for any subtle change in the pattern of the breaths.

Behind him the snake charmer crouched, preparing to launch his tight right fist in a focused, unobstructed thrust. *It will at least paralyze him,* he surmised. *Then Zanu can take the head.*

Tegné saw the swordsman's minute break in breathing. His reaction was to straighten even more, maintaining only a slight bend in the knees, presenting a full target. Then the flicker of light from the katana's blade . . .

Renagi lurched forward as the snake charmer unleashed his strike, the fist relaxed yet ready in an instant to become a deadly battering-ram. Zanu exhaled, loving this moment of freedom, his mind, his body and his sword locked in one cosmic pulse.

Enlightenment. Zanu felt the slice, the cut, saw the gush of red. His katana was nearly back in its scabbard before he became aware of the burning pain in his groin where the snake charmer's fist had entered him. He fell forward, his stomach seizing as the other's severed head skidded across the floor to his front.

Then, from the corner of his eye, Zanu glimpsed Tegné rise from a sideward roll. An instant later the hard sole of a foot came down once upon his face before Tegné's second, more accurate stomp crushed the swordmaster's head against the stone floor.

The silence of the crowd broke with a mighty roar. "Tegné! Tegné! Tegné!" the screaming chant erupted from the lower benches, from the working class of the city. "Tegné! Tegné!"

Tegné turned toward them, a look of astonishment and disbelief in his face. Rin watched through eyes awash with tears. Now he could see the shining silver and gold medallion hanging high on his Sensei's chest.

"Tegné! Tegné!" Rin's voice rose, joining the chant. Several of the spectators on ground level rushed forward, arms outstretched, toward Tegné. Rin moved with the surging crowd.

Suddenly a score of black-clad guards swept from the midlevel seats, assuming a wide formation, spreading out, pushing, shoving the people back. Rin was caught in one huge gloved hand, hoisted from his feet and thrown.

Tegné spun round, searching the faces, finding the Warlord. "Tell them to stop!" he shouted above the mayhem.

"Enough!" screamed Renagi. "Enough!" His voice boomed louder and more clear than the disorganized din below. "This is not over," he continued, climbing down from the Velchar, moving clumsily through the mixture of spectators, some standing, some sitting. The crowd quietened, falling back of its own accord as Renagi and Tegné stood, facing each other, in the combat square.

"If this is how it must end, then so be it," Renagi vowed, loosening his robe. "I am prepared to die for my name, for the name of my only son, and for Zendow."

Tegné backed away, his open palms held up in a gesture of peace. "I want no part of your empire, no land, no name of Warlord. I ask you only to stop the persecution that is taking place in my name, to make amends for the slaughter, to free the Ashkelites."

"You make demands of me?" Renagi asked incredulously. "You will *not* make demands of me. I am Warlord of Zendow."

Tegné stood his ground, watching as the old man closed the distance, wary of a sudden rush. Another step and Zato's hand came from behind, gripping Renagi's shoulder and halting him. Then Zato walked forward and faced Tegné.

"No. You will not kill my father, but so help me, you will fight his son," Zato said, resigned, staring into his half-brother's face. "One son. One heir. One Warlord. That is the law and that is how it must be," he finished.

Tegné weighed Zato's words, then turned to Renagi. The Warlord's face was frozen with apprehension.

"That is how it must be . . ." The soft, penetrating voice came from the Velchar. Neeka stood above them, in front of the throne, confident, poised, her shoulders arched high as she gripped the stone railing. Renagi looked up, past the anxious faces of Miyaz and Kase, and met the cold violet behind the mask.

"Hei! Hei! Hei!" The chant began to build as the smack of metal heels against stone filled the hall. "Hei! Hei! Hei!"

Ten thousand voices, twenty thousand stamping feet. The demon drums. The collective will. Tegné was unprepared, his mind and his body no longer at war.

Zato came forward and Tegné could read the desperation in his brown eyes. Tegné shifted back and away, doing what was necessary to avoid an attack. He studied the midlevel of Zato's hakama, saw the broken, anxious breathing, the low, open hands and the unguarded face.

"Fight! Fight! Kill him!" Tegné heard the voice. It occupied a space of its own within his mind. "Kill him!" It was Neeka's voice, rising above the roar of the crowd. "Kill him! Kill him!" Distinct, penetrating, commanding. And for a moment her face flashed in his thoughts and he knew, more certainly than ever, that it was she who was the architect of this tragic scene, the dreamer of this dream, the creator of this illusion.

I will end it, I will walk away. The thought entered him as Zato began a tentative advance. *I must find the power to break her will,* he commanded himself.

He stopped his backward slide, standing in the low, immovable stance as Zato crept forward. At last they were eye to eye.

"Brother, it is over," Tegné said, quietly so that only Zato could hear him. Then, slowly, Tegné relaxed his guard. He watched the tears begin to well in Zato's eyes; tears of sorrow, frustration, indecision. The tears of a warring conscience. And for a moment Zato also relaxed, his shoulders dropping, the tension falling away.

"It is over," Tegné repeated.

"No!" Tegné heard the scream an instant before his brother's fist pounded into the mastoid region of his neck, then dizziness and what seemed the crashing sound of an enormous stone wall, disintegrating inside his skull.

"No!" Again Zato's scream and again the thudding fist.

Kase and Miyaz rushed from their seats, down to the floor, joining Renagi at the side of the combat square. Tegné doubled over stumbling backward. The Warlord could feel the crowd turn, their excitement building. He straightened, squaring his shoulders.

Renagi. Warlord of Zendow. Zato, my only son, my heir. Yes, this is how it should be. My testimony.

"Finish him!" He shrieked the command at Zato, then, drawing his katana, he stepped forward into the square. Miyaz moved to stop him, but Kase intervened, catching the other man by the shoulder.

Zato stood a full two paces from Tegné, hesitating as Tegné heaved, reeling from the last blow.

"Take it," Renagi hissed, pushing the hilt of the katana toward Zato. "Take it," he repeated, pressing the cold grip into his son's hand.

Tegné looked up as Zato raised the ancient, balanced sword.

Zato breathed in, focused his mind, holding the weapon.

"Yaaaah!" he screamed, rushing forward, already beginning the flowing, horizontal cut.

Sheer instinct saved him as Tegné dropped beneath the blur of steel, feeling the rush of air in the weapon's wake. He hit the floor and, as Zato began the downward cut, Tegné rolled away from the arc of the sword. Simultaneously, he scissored his legs against Zato's shins, using the power of his roll to break his brother's balance. Zato's head slammed against the floor as the katana slid from his grasp.

"Kill him! Kill him!" Neeka's voice rose free from the mounting din. Tegné sprang to his feet, moving behind Zato, gripping his head in a tight, wrapping lock.

"Kill him!" Again the voice, unmistakable, dominating. Tegné began to pull the jaw with his left hand while pushing the head in sequence with his right, listening, listening for the crack of the vertebrae.

Suddenly, breaking the spell, Tegné felt strong hands grip his shoulders. He heard the deep, pleading voice.

"Please. Please, I beg you. Stop. Please!" The voice became a full-throated sob.

Tegné halted the breaking technique just as Renagi dropped to the floor, weeping openly on his bended knees. Tegné stepped away from Zato and turned to face his father. A confusion of hatred and compassion flooded his heart.

Slowly he removed the black half-glove. He raised his right fist; the birthmark was visible to everyone. The Great Hall quietened.

"I am your son," he said simply, softly.

Renagi stared up, helpless, then slowly he stood. He removed the fine, pleated crimson robes; his torso was soft, fleshy, the patch of hair between his breasts coarse and gray.

"Never," he whispered. Then, defeated, he dropped the robes at Tegné's feet, the crimson falling like blood against stone. Only Kase and Miyaz stepped forward to assist him. Then, bending, Renagi lifted Zato's unconscious body from the cold floor. Carrying his son, cradling him against his bare chest, Renagi walked through the parting throngs of people.

Neeka pushed forward. She stopped in front of Tegné, stooping to gather the crimson robes. She draped the pleated silk around his shoulders.

The chant began, throbbing, beginning low and building louder and louder, "Tegné, Warlord of Zendow."

"Tegné. Warlord of Zendow," she repeated, fixing him with the soft violet of her eyes. The drums lifted and the gathering Zendai walked toward him. Rin joined the surging crowd, converging on the golden-haired, crimson-clad figure in the center of the square . . .

"Tegné, Warlord of Zendow!" the voices continued, growing, in unison.

Tegné turned from the swarm of faces. He could see Renagi still carrying Zato in his arms, walking through the wide door at the far end of the hall. He felt Neeka's hand take his own and begin to raise it above his head.

"Warlord of Zendow," she repeated the three fated words.

"No!" Tegné shouted, his anger finally erupting as he threw the robes from his shoulders.

Rin struggled through the crowd, running, stumbling, finally overtaking him, reaching up, touching him, calling, "Sensei! Sensei!" At last Tegné stopped, turned and looked down at the boy.

Rin stood motionless as he saw the pain etched in his teacher's face, distorting his features, causing his Sensei to appear worn, beaten. And within Tegné's eyes Rin discerned a silent plea, as if the eyes belonged to a wounded bird, caught lame and unable to fly.

"Rin." Tegné spoke the name softly. "Thank you," he said, touching the medallion which hung from his neck. Then his blue eyes hardened as he turned and walked quickly from the boy, out of the Great Hall.

It must not end this way. There can be nothing gained from violence. My father . . . My father must understand. He must accept what has been done. I will convince him . . . His thoughts reeled as he entered the long passageway. His father and brother had vanished.

X

THE TEST OF THE HEART

One should cleanse his motley thoughts
and eliminate wanton considerations from the reflections of his mind
But can he be without imperfection?

(Lao Tsu)

Renagi knelt before the raised altar, the symbol of his Zendai Clan carved into the polished walnut. Breathing in, he studied the carving, finding peace within the intricate swirls of the wood.

Miyaz and Kase guarded the locked door of the chamber. Zato had recovered and now he stood, absolutely still, to the right of his father. Both knew what was required; there was no alternative. The shining tanto lay before Renagi on the altar, its snakeskin hilt ornamented with the graceful, painted figures of swallows in flight.

Slowly, carefully, Renagi took the sharp, pointed dagger from the altar, cradling it in his open palms. Then, gripping the hilt with both hands, he turned the blade inward.

"Why are you running?" Neeka's voice followed him along the passageway. "Tegné, can you hear them? They are calling for you. They want you. Everything. It is yours. Take it," she continued, walking toward him, smiling, her arms extended. As she reached him he took her extended hands. Gripping them, he pulled her closer.

"My father, where is my father?" he asked.

"Come, I will lead you to his room."

The door to Renagi's chamber opened on smooth, silent hinges. Inside, the moon hung centered in the arched window, shining its light on the blue embroidered quilt that covered the canopied bed. There was a faint aroma of hapaver in the air.

Two ornate Miramese chairs, a tall mahogany chest and a single bedside table stood upon a red, silk-threaded rug. The room was simple yet elegant. Rich in memories.

Neeka turned to face him, aware that the backlight from the window framed the outline of her body.

Tegné turned away, averting his eyes, yet already he could feel the force of her will, touching him where he was most vulnerable, his heart.

"Why? Why do you turn from me?" she asked softly. "You have defeated the Warlord. You have earned your right to rule the people of Zendow. Think, Tegné, think." She reached and rested her hand upon his shoulder, transmitting her energy into him, weaving her web of illusion. "I have been your ally. I have given you life when you sought death. I have loved you when you could no longer love yourself. I love you now, Tegné, more than life."

He met her eyes and saw only truth. Her truth. Clouding his conscience. She moved closer, nearly touching his body with her own, subtle in her seduction, sensitive to the motions of his mind.

"Renagi, my father? What is to become of my father?" He asked.

She could hear the weakness in his voice; he had been drained by his ordeal, and she sensed the hole in his spirit. She entered.

"Renagi was an evil man. He is gone, dust in the wind. You, Tegné, you and I, are now. Our son is the future."

He lifted his eyes and she felt him drink in the swell of her breasts, the curve of her hips and the darkness of her mound. She felt his desire as he walked forward, and before he could speak she wrapped her arms around him, pressing the thin silk of her crotch against his groin. His body began to respond, his penis growing hard as she rose up on her toes and placed his hardness closer to her opening.

"Take off the ninjinka; it is your right," she whispered.

He lifted the golden mask, pulling it out and away from her face; the face from the Lake of Dreams.

"It is you," he said.

"Yes. I have waited. You are the one." Then she pulled away, just enough to slide her warm right hand inside the front of his hakama while loosening the ties with her left. She ran her fingers down between his legs, gently cupping his tightening testicles, then released them and stroked up, along the skin of his penis, finding the single drop of moisture, gently gripping the throbbing head while she used the soft, cushioned surface of her thumb to rub the slippery fluid into the throbbing crown.

Slowly, she stepped back, releasing him. "Would you like to see my body?" She let her robes fall away, standing before him wearing only the high rope sandals and the pale silk thong.

Her nipples were dark and erect, jutting forward from the full breasts. Yet it was her abdomen and pelvis that fascinated him. Even in the semi-darkness of the room he could see the clearly defined muscles beneath the fine, bronzed skin. The waist so clean, tight, tiny, and the navel perfectly round and deep. A thin line of jet-black hair ran beneath it, widening into a full diamond pattern which remained visible beneath the sheer silk covering her crotch.

He reached out and touched her through the silk. She was wet, and the ebony hair was as thick and soft as velvet fur. He knelt before her, gripping the tight, round buttocks and licked, high up against the smooth inside skin of her thighs. He tasted her sweetness.

She guided him to the bed, sitting down as he unlaced the sandals, taking them from her feet. She lay back onto the blue quilt, then arched upward as he pulled the silk thong down and over her thighs, taking the garment from her.

He inhaled the natural musk of her body, falling deeper beneath her hypnotic spell. She reached up for him as he dropped his hakama, kicking it free as he bent toward her, climbing upon the bed. He straddled her for a moment as she parted her legs, opening herself wide to him. His penis found her with no guidance, rubbing between the soft, hot lips, entering the smooth, wonderful passage and penetrating deep, pressing against her womb.

Renagi did not gasp or cry out, and no sign of the white, searing heat told upon his face as he pushed the pointed steel of the dagger into the left side of his belly. Slowly, he drew the tanto across in the long cut. He kept his eyes concentrated in front of him, focused on the carved wooden Claw. Yet it was not the carving that he saw, not the sign of his Clan nor the spiraling swirls of the polished wood; it was the clear amber eyes of the Ashkelite girl, Maliseet. And within her eyes there was peace and forgiving.

Blood and muscle spilled from the widening wound, seeping down and soaking the front of his undergarment. Zato watched, his face set, his heart aching, his katana raised over his right shoulder, the razor edge of the blade high above his head and aimed downward. It was almost time.

"Hei!" Renagi screamed. It was the last ki-ai of a dying warrior as, with his final rush of strength, he ripped the tanto in a sideways motion. His entrails flooded from the gaping wound.

"Yaaaa!" Zato yelled, pulling the whistling blade downward, surprised for an instant that the katana met no resistance as it entered the sheet of muscle at the base of Renagi's neck; the sword severed the third cervical vertebra, cutting the head clean from its shoulders. For a moment the headless body remained kneeling, twitching, as the blood came in synchronous spurts, timed to the final beats of Renagi's heart. Then the body pitched forward, landing beside the head on the bloodstained carpet, the eyes fixed and open, the mouth forming a sad half-smile.

Zato stood still, maintaining a two-handed grip on the katana, as if preparing to use the weapon for a second strike. Then gradually, he relaxed, shaking the blade as he lightly tapped the base of its hilt with his right palm. Renagi's blood fell from the polished steel, like warm rain upon the floor. Finally, Zato drew the blade upward between his thumb and index finger, cleaning the metal thoroughly before guiding the sword back into its scabbard. He turned to Miyaz and Kase; they stood solemn-faced at the door, studying him, waiting for a reaction. He could feel the terrible sadness trying to escape from inside him. He held it in check, tightening the muscles of his abdomen so hard that it affected the set of his jaw and the thin line of his lips.

A display of grief now would bring the ultimate loss of face, a dishonor to my father. I will show no grief. I will show only pride for his final act of courage, Zato vowed as he walked from the chamber.

His mind raced as he continued through the long passageway toward the seclusion of his father's room. He had watched Neeka during the initial combat; he had seen the satisfaction in her eyes, heard her scream against him. It was as he had always suspected. He had never trusted her and in the end his instinct had been confirmed. But what was her purpose? As he drew closer to the room a sense of doom settled upon him. Now, more than any other time in his life he needed to be alone. To mourn. To heal. To think.

"Be still, be still," Neeka whispered, wrapping her long legs around Tegné's waist, maintaining a counter-rhythm to his slow, deep thrusts, gradually controlling his body.

"Yes . . . yes . . . Just let me feel you inside me," she continued, settling the roundness of her curved hips into the warm palm of his open right hand, bringing him down, deeper still, into her. "Kiss me," she moaned, and as he did she began the strong, undulating contractions against his hot, smooth shaft, sucking on his tongue, matching the rhythm of her vaginal muscles with the rhythm of her tongue and lips. She stretched back on the bed, opening her eyes, watching him in the glow of the moon.

"This is our beginning," she purred.

Now she could hear the footsteps coming slowly along the hallway. She recognized Zato's steps; she had expected him. The door was not locked.

Tegné wanted to raise his hips and thrust into her, but the strong legs wrapped around him would not permit his movement.

"Yes, my love, yes," Neeka whispered, sensing his urgency, holding him tighter, her right arm pulling him closer to her breasts as her left hand moved silently to her side, beneath the pillow, finding the knurled hilt of the silver blade. Her contractions increased, gripping him, running in spasm along the sides of his phallus.

She pulled the blade from beneath the pillow, turning the point downward as she lifted it above his bare shoulders. The metal was already beginning to burn her flesh; still she held on, withstanding the pain, absorbing it as the first hot rush of his semen began to fill her.

"It is done," she said softly.

Zato stood outside the thick oak door, his right hand frozen on the brass handle. From beyond the door he could hear the unmistakable sounds of lovemaking. Slowly he drew the katana, then he turned the handle and pushed against the heavy wood.

The moon through the arched window bathed the room in light. His eyes focused quickly, centering on the two bodies that lay upon his father's bed. He recognized the long blanket of raven hair as it fanned out on to the blue quilt. Neeka's legs extended toward him, her knees raised, her feet flat on the bed. Tegné lay nestled into her breasts, secure in the aftermath of his passion.

The scene sent a shudder of revulsion through Zato. Neeka was already meeting the cold steel of his eyes as Tegné turned toward him. Zato raised the katana, holding the flat surface forward.

"This sword bore the blood of my father. Dead. Because of you. You," he spat the words, "you who defile his name."

Tegné felt the strangely familiar heat of the metal as Neeka pressed the silver blade into his hand. Zato turned the katana, raising the cutting edge in the two-handed grip, moonlight glinting off the curvature of the steel.

First the bastard son, then the betrayer, he vowed, lowering his stance, centering, inching forward.

Tegné rolled from Neeka's relaxed embrace, finding the floor, standing naked before Zato. In his right hand he brandished the silver blade. Zato lifted his katana higher.

One strike, one chance, Tegné knew as he crouched, resting lightly on the balls of his feet, waiting for Zato's rush, preparing to counter with a straight thrust. *One strike, one chance . . .* Tabata's voice spoke the words as surely as if his Sensei stood beside him. And suddenly he could see Tabata's face shining in the reflection of Zato's eyes. And the face was heavy with sorrow.

This man I am facing now is my brother, my own flesh and blood. Yet there is murder in my heart, and murder in the very blade which binds me to virtue. The realization fell upon him, and it was then that he felt the medallion, which hung from the narrow strip of leather around his neck.

The spell was broken; the dream shattered. Tegné dropped the blade to the floor, the metal ringing with the clarity of a temple bell. He stood defenseless against Zato, knowing that in the end, in the final test, he had failed, fallen prey to the lust and greed of his own desires.

He watched the katana rise, ready to begin its sweeping, downward cut. *Now it is over,* he thought, meeting his brother's gaze.

"Forgive me," Tegné said, quiet and soft, surrendering. Zato hesitated, and for a moment there was stillness in the room; then the sound of panting and a low, guttural growl. Tegné watched as his brother spun toward the sounds.

The bed seemed bathed in a subdued yellow light and a white secretion of saliva and perspiration covered the black, ragged fur of the four-legged creature. This was not the beautiful Cat from the desert, nor the Cat from the Lake of Dreams. This was pure evil.

Zato held the katana in the high, ready position as he retreated from the Beast, his body losing its fluidity, tightening with fear. The creature strained forward, its oozing, fanged mouth gaping in a deafening howl. It seemed to be laboring against some invisible chain, the stinking sweat of its body flying in thick globs from its raging, shaking muscles. Yet there was a power to the creature, a captivating power.

Tegné stared, seeing finally, clearly, completely. For it was this power that had called out to him, touched the darkness within his own heart, planted the seed of avarice, weaving inside him a web of illusion. For this Beast was the manifestation of evil, and Neeka was its child, its projection of flesh and blood.

"Take your eyes from it! Turn away!" Tegné shouted, bending down to grasp the blade. But Zato was lost, his eyes locked on the creature which rampaged before him, devouring his seeping energy.

The sound was like the explosion of shattering glass as the creature leapt from the bed, spreading its taloned feet, knocking Zato helplessly against the wall.

"No! No!" Tegné screamed, running forward, throwing himself on the mauling Beast, wrapping his left arm around the grizzled neck, pulling back on the head and driving the blade into the hard surface of the slippery hide.

The blade slid sideways, unable to penetrate. He raised it again, high above his head.

"He-ai!" Again he brought the blade down, focusing his spirit, yet again it glanced off the horny flesh and the Beast rose beneath him.

Tegné rolled, regaining his feet, the blade gripped desperately in his right hand. *The heart, pierce the heart* . . . It was the voice of the Father Protector which came to him as he stood before the creature. *One chance, one strike* . . .

Tegné sank low, his hips pushed forward, his right arm cocked back, the blade held tight in his grip, his left, open hand guarding to the front. The Beast stalked toward him, yet Tegné would not retreat. He felt the hot, burning breath.

The black, shining, animal lips stretched back, revealing long, glistening fangs. Yet there was no attack. He looked deep into the wild fire of the eyes and saw the shimmering trace of violet. A sudden, overwhelming sadness consumed him.

"Neeka! Neeka!" He called her name. "Neeka! Neeka!"

A shroud of blackness fell before his eyes. Then, gradually, the blackness lifted and he was bathed in the cool light of the moon.

"Why? Why are you doing this? We have everything, you and I. We are one, One mind. One heart . . ." Neeka's voice floated on the still air. She stood before him. "Love me. Love me." She walked toward him, unafraid. It was just as her fingers touched the skin of his shoulder that he drove the silver blade inward, burying the metal in the soft, warm flesh below her left breast.

Neeka did not scream, nor did she resist as he forced the blade into her heart, twisting. She half-smiled as he looked into the fading violet of her eyes. Then her body grew limp, falling before him. Still he held the blade firm, lowering himself on top of her, watching the fading violet give way to the gray, dead stone beneath. Finally her eyelids closed and there was only the feeling of emptiness below him. His tears fell against her quiet flesh. Earth tears.

At last he rose, leaving the blade buried in her heart. Suddenly cold and conscious of his nakedness, he lifted the blue quilt from his father's bed and wrapped it around him.

Zato sat with his back pressed against the wall, his body bruised and the jagged, open wound seeping blood through the torn fabric of his jacket. "Is it over?" he asked, staring at Neeka's body, his words disarmingly direct, simple.

Tegné looked once more at the body, then again at Zato. Zato saw the fathomless sorrow in the blue eyes. Then came the growl, distant yet distinct.

The flesh had begun to undulate like a cocoon of molten wax. Rising, distorting; the growl came from within it. Tegné lurched forward, attempting to grip the blade once more, Too late; the waxen cocoon split open and the blade fell, embedding itself in the wood of the floor. Zato trembled as he saw the dark vapor rise from the chasm in the broken, melting shell. Slowly the vapor took shape, form, and for a terrible moment the looming shadow of the Beast hovered above them. Then the vapor grew thin as it dispersed, drifting toward the open window.

Out. Out into the night sky.

"Now it is over," Tegné answered, his voice firm, his passion dissolved. He reached down with his right hand, the birthmark strikingly visible in the light of the moon.

Zato accepted the hand and by the time he had risen to his feet, Neeka's waxen shell had disappeared.

Only the silver blade remained.

Renagi's head looked large, as if it had expanded in death. The ashen skin was drained of blood and the open eyes resembled flat, clouded glass. The mouth had frozen with rigor mortis, and the strange half-smile gave an eerie, distant quality to the overall demeanor of the face.

There was no gore and, in fact, the flesh that had once attached the short, thick neck to its torso was cut in a perfectly clean line, as if the incision had been made with some finely crafted surgical instrument. In all there was no horror, simply a conclusive dignity as the Warlord's head was held respectfully in Kase's gloved hands.

Kase stood in front of the Velchar. Renagi's body lay below him, wrapped in the great black and red banner of his Clan and placed in an open, carved coffin. Miyaz stood to the right side of the coffin.

A cloak of silence hung over the crowd, broken only by an occasional muffled cry of anguish. Finally, Kase spoke.

"In the yeon one thousand, on the twenty-second day of Julin, at the twenty-fourth hour, Renagi, son of Volkar, and past Warlord of Zendow, committed the act of Seppuka. His death was courageous and honorable, attended and seconded by his son, Zato."

Then, Kase raised the head high, holding it still, with outstretched arms, above the people.

"May Renagi's soul be purged and his spirit made pure. And may he rest in peace . . . Long live Zendow!" His voice rose, deepening; "Long live Zendow!" Kase repeated, virtually shouting the three words.

"Hei! Hei! Hei!" The voices of the people responded as one, and a multitude of clenched fists punched into the air. And for a moment, the spirit and strength that had been Zendow lifted the Great Hall, and courage returned to the people. Then the head was lowered, wrapped carefully in a cloth of scarlet silk, and laid gently beside the body. And, as quickly, a hush fell again upon the hall.

Rin could feel the anxiety beneath the quiet. For Zendow was without a leader, a gigantic ship adrift without its captain. And through this trial of blood the line of succession had been broken.

Will anyone step forward to assume control? And if someone dares, shall I stop him? What is my position now? wondered Miyaz, as he gazed into the throng of faces. Still, the people remained quiet, yet the lull was filled with an expectant energy.

Should I say something more? Kase pondered, growing anxious, self-conscious in the combined gaze of the people of Zendow. It was an eerie, awesome silence.

Waiting, we are waiting . . . Rin realized.

The sound of the wooden door scraping against the stone walkway traveled amongst those gathered like a charge of electricity. Rin turned toward the door.

There, silhouetted against the backlight from the hallway, his figure ghostlike in the white hakama, stood Zato.

Rin stared, wide-eyed, as Zato determinedly scanned the faces closest to him. Then, resolutely, the Warlord's son walked forward.

The great wall of silence finally broke and shrill, excited voices cut the air.

Where is Tegné? What has happened? Rin despaired, watching as Zato turned to the steps that led up to the Velchar. Then he saw the ripped cloth of the jacket, exposing the ugly, open wound which began at Zato's right shoulder and ran down the torn front of his padded chest.

Could there have been more violence, another fight? Could Tegné be . . .

"Rin." The familiar voice halted the desperate speculation. The boy turned to see Tegné walking toward him from the door. "Sensei!" Rin cried, rushing to meet the wide open arms.

Zato was already on the first landing, midway to the Velchar.

He stopped, turned, and looked out over the people, finding Tegné, beckoning for him to follow.

But now, after all that has happened, will the people accept him as their leader? Tegné wondered, listening to the building voices increase in volume with each of his brother's steps. He felt a sudden concern as he watched Miyaz and Kase close ranks, apparently guarding the stately chair. Still Zato continued to climb, again turning to wave Tegné forward.

"Stand to the side, Rin. Use the door if the crowd becomes violent," Tegné instructed, walking towards the steps.

"Oss, Sensei," Rin replied.

Tegné increased his pace, trying to overtake Zato, to protect him if necessary. It was as Tegné mounted above the level of the onlookers that the pitch of the voices grew and the tension finally broke within the hall.

By now Zato was exchanging words with Kase and Miyaz, who stood directly in front of the Velchar; Renagi's body lay unguarded in the open casket at their feet. Tegné was close, and he studied their hands, wary of the fingers which hovered above the hilts of their katanas.

A moment of indecision . . . Tegné began to sprint. Suddenly the Warmen stepped aside, leaving the Velchar open, unprotected. Zato stood before the cushioned seat, his face creased into a wide, welcoming smile. Tegné ran forward.

"Turn, look," Zato said, gripping his brother's shoulder, urging him to look out, over the ten thousand people.

Tegné turned. The vast collage of faces gazed back at him, their eyes meeting his. Zato punched his fist skyward, as his cleated heel slammed against the stone floor.

"Hei! Hei! Hei!" the massed voices seemed to explode as the huge drums resumed their beat. Behind the faces of the people of Zendow, Tegné could see his own reflection. A mirrored image, his golden hair streaming onto the black silk of his robe, his shoulders set, squared. He felt an overwhelming power, his heart pounding inside his chest, building with the strength of the drums.

Somehow Rin had maneuvered himself to the front of the crowd. Tegné could see him clearly and, as he listened, he was sure he could distinguish Rin's voice from those around him.

Zato raised his arms. The chanting ceased and the drums became quiet. Then Zato took a long, deep breath.

"My flesh and blood!" he began, and in that moment his voice was the voice of Renagi. "My brother, Tegné!" He called the name, loud, clear.

"Warlord of Zendow!" Zato's words rang, and with them the faces of Tabata, the Elder and the Protectors filled Tegné's mind. A strange, disquieting feeling entered him. A warning? Then the faces faded, like haze against the sun, and Neeka was there, smiling. But only for a moment, as, at last, his mind cleared, and he stared out on to the sea of people.

"Warlord of Zendow!"

EPILOGUE

Better to stop short than fill to the brim. Oversharpen the blade, and the edge will soon blunt. Amass a store of gold and jade, and no one can protect it.
Claim wealth and titles, and disaster will follow.
Retire when the work is done. This is the way of heaven.

(Lao Tsu)

GLOSSARY

Ajna The seventh chakra, also known as the third eye, located in the center of the forehead, equidistant from the physical eyes

Anahata The fifth chakra, the center of the heart

Asana Any of a number of basic yoga postures that are designed to stimulate the chakras and control the flow of vital energy

Ashi-bari "Leg-sweeping technique"—used to unbalance or throw the opponent

Avatar Descent of a deity to Earth in incarnate form

Bo "Staff," "stave" or "stick," approximately six feet long. One of five weapons systemized by the early Okinawan practitioners

Body length A measure of approximately six feet

Chakra Centers of energy. The eight principal chakras are along the axis of the spine, each associated with a different group of bodily functions and a different level of consciousness

Chikaraishi "Power stone"—a wooden stick of approximately one foot embedded in a round stone weighing about ten pounds. Used to develop strength in the upper body

Chudan Middle level of the body, often used to designate a target area for techniques

Dojo "The place of the Way"—a training hall in which martial arts are practiced

Empi-uchi "Elbow strikes"—chiefly used in close-quarter combat

Finger A measure of approximately 8/10 of an inch

Foot Lineal measure of approximately three hands

Gajiin Foreigner or outsider

Gedan "Lower or lower level"—the lower trunk area of the human body

Geta "Clogs"—Japanese wooden shoes

Gi "Uniform" or "suit"—traditional costume worn while training

Gyaku-zuki "Reserve punch"—a punch executed by the hand opposite the forward leg

Haito "Ridge hand," thumb-edge of hand

Hajime A command, "begin"

Hakama "Divided skirt"—traditional garb of the Samurai class

Hand Lineal measure of approximately four inches or five finger widths

Hiraken "Flat fist"—a technique in which the fist is semi-clenched, using the second knuckles of the four fingers as the striking surface

Jion-ji A famous Buddhist temple, from which many of the "classical fighting forms" are thought to have originated

Jodan "Upward level"—face and head level of the body

Karma Actions that determine the soul's progress. The law of karma is that we reap what we sow, that everyone must suffer the consequences of every action and every thought, though the effects may not be immediate

Kata "Formal exercise"—a series of prearranged maneuvers executed against one or more imaginary attacking opponents. The forms through which traditional martial arts are passed from generation to generation

Katana "Sword"—a Japanese sword with a curved, single-edged blade, two or three feet in length

Ke-komi A thrusting kick

Ki Mental and spiritual energy that can be applied to accomplish physical feats, the "animating force of life"

Ki-ai "Spiritual meeting"—expulsion of air from the diaphragm; it reinforces the strength of a striking or blocking technique, both physically and mentally. "Pushes the spirit forward"—usually a loud yell or shout

Kiba-dachi "Horse-stance," "straddle-stance" in which feet are parallel and extended approximately twice the width of the shoulders

Kime "Focus"—the act of concentrating complete mental and physical force into the split second at the completion of a technique

Kisagake A whipping action of the sword as it is removed from the scabbard in an attack

Kizami-zuki Short, jabbing punch

Kumite "Sparring" (*Jiyu-kumite*—a free exchange of blows, blocks and counter-attacks)

Kundalini Latent power at base of spine, often depicted by a coiled, sleeping serpent. Most asanas of hatha yoga are intended to "awaken the serpent" and guide it upward through the chakras, with the ultimate result of super-consciousness

Lotus position "Place each foot on the opposite thigh." The classic yoga posture for meditation

Mae-geri Front kick

Makiwara "Straw-padded striking post"—designed for toughening various striking points. Usually made from a piece of timber seven or eight feet long, three feet of which are buried and cemented in the ground, the top four feet bevelled so that the very top is only half an inch thick. The top foot is wrapped in straw rope and provides the striking surface

Mantra Sacred symbolic sounds, the repetition of which leads to transcendence of normal consciousness. The sound "auom" is the supreme mantra

Maya The physical world, sometimes translated as "illusion"

Nanchuku A fighting weapon comprising two wood or metal rods separated and attached by a twelve-inch chain

Nihon-nukite "Two-finger spear-hand"

Obi "Belt"—knotted sash through which scabbard of katana is carried

Oi-zuki Lunge punch

Pace A distance of approximately eight hands

Prana The life force, the cosmic energy, that which gives life to all things

Rei "To bow"—a command

Seika-tanden "Lower abdomen"—seat of the soul and center of ki

Sei-za "Correct sitting," a full kneeling position, hips resting on the heels of the feet

Sensei "Teacher"

Seppuka Formal word for ritual suicide practiced with short sword. An honorable death (*Hara-kiri*—"belly cut")

Shizen-tai Natural stance

Shihan "Master teacher"

Shuto "Knife hand," "sword hand"—the edge of the hand

Sochin-dachi "Diagonal straddle-leg stance"

Super-consciousness Simultaneous knowledge of all things—state of supreme "oneness"

Tai-sabaki "Body movement"—turning, evasive action of the body

Tanto Japanese dagger with a blade of eight to sixteen inches

Tatami "Straw mat"—usually measuring three feet by six feet and three inches thick

Tekko Iron-pronged fists, similar to modern "brass knuckles"

Transcend To rise above all egocentric thoughts and emotions

Uchi-deshi "Special student"—selected for individual training

Ushiro-mawashi-geri "Reverse roundhouse kick"

Vakos The "supreme state of inner vision," a complete subjectivity, often entering the realms of the unconscious mind

Voll A distance of approximately one mile

Vul Plural of voll

Wakan A spontaneous merging of souls, the deepest rapport

Waza A single technique

Yeon A period of 380 days

Zanshin "Perfect posture"—a state of perfect mental awareness

Zenkutsu-dachi Forward stance

Zori Rope sandals

ABOUT THE AUTHOR

Richard La Plante was born in Pennsylvania in 1948. He has traveled extensively throughout the United States and Mexico, at one time living alone for nine months in the Mexican Sonora desert. In 1976 he moved to London, and in 1978 founded the American rock band *Revenge.* He has studied with Masters Keino-suke Enoeda and Teriyuki Okazaki and is ranked Sandan—Black belt, third degree—by the Japanese Karate Association.